"You know it's suicide. . . ." Sisay's voice came in the tube.

"What's suicide?"

"A head-on assault against twenty dragon engines."

"Yeah," Gerrard shot back, "suicide for them." He glanced over his shoulder and sent her a smile. It was not the careless grin he used to give. Something had died in his eyes. Not something but someone. "Is the mighty Captain Sisay afraid of death?"

"Not afraid of it, but neither am I eager for it."

"It's time somebody brought death to account," Gerrard said, as he faced forward. "I'm that somebody."

Experience the Magic

PLANESHIFT

INVASION CYCLE • BOOK 2

J. Robert King

Planeshift
Invasion Cycle
©2000 Wizards of the Coast, Inc.

Distributed in the United States by St. Martin's Press. Distributed in Canada by Fenn Ltd.

Distributed to the hobby, toy, and comic trade in the United States and Canada by regional distributors.

Distributed worldwide by Wizards of the Coast, Inc. and regional distributors.

Front cover art by Brom
Back cover art by Donato Giancola
Internal art by: Brian "Chippy" Dugan, Dana Knutson, Todd Lockwood, Anson Maddocks, r.k. Post, Mark Tedin, and Anthony Waters
First Printing: February 2000
Library of Congress Catalog Card Number:

9 8 7 6 5 4 3 2 1

UK ISBN: 0-7869-2030-0
US ISBN: 0-7869-1802-0
TSR21802-620

U.S., CANADA,
ASIA, PACIFIC, & LATIN AMERICA
Wizards of the Coast, Inc.
P.O. Box 707
Renton, WA 98057-0707
+1-800-324-6496

EUROPEAN HEADQUARTERS
Wizards of the Coast, Belgium
P.B. 2031
2600 Berchem
Belgium
+32-70-23-32-77

Visit our web site at **www.wizards.com**

Dedication

To Scott McGough,
for his valor against filthy rutting lich lord bastards

Acknowledgments

As Yawgmoth will let you know, Dominaria is no easy world to invade. I couldn't have laid waste to every continent and killed every hero without the help of many colleagues and friends.

Thanks go especially to Jess Lebow, Scott McGough, Daneen McDermott, Tyler Bielman, and Bill Rose. I'd also like to thank Mary Kirchoff and Peter Archer, who made sure the Phyrexian payroll arrived in time to keep the monsters fighting. And of course, I want to thank the fans, every last one of whom is now a subject of the dread lord Yawgmoth. It's been nice conquering you.

(I know some of you hope Urza and Gerrard can pull this thing off in the next book, but don't count on it. Yawgmoth and I go *way* back.)

CHAPTER 1
Every Claw, Every Fang

Multani traced the damage done by the ray cannon blast. The bolt had struck *Weatherlight*'s hull where the figurehead should have been. It had torn a wide gash through seven inches of solid magnigoth wood and had vaporized the first forecastle rib. In the hold beyond, the energies had hit an ensign's pack and burned it and its contents away to nothing. If not for that pack, the bolt might have ripped on through a bulkhead and into the crew's berths. Even so, the damage was severe.

Multani did not peer at the hull breach as would a mere man but felt it from the inside, for he was a nature spirit. He had no true body outside of plant life. He took his form from wood

1

grain. Cellulose fibers were his muscles, heartwood his bones, sap his blood. His true home was the forest of Yavimaya, where he lived in the endless magnigoth trees. That homeland had won its battles, so Multani had taken up residence in the living hull of *Weatherlight*. Her battles were only beginning.

Multani moved through the wood. The laceration seemed a wound in his own flesh. It brought pain, of course, but it also empowered him to heal the ship.

Charcoal sloughed from the edges of the breach. Sap oozed out in golden beads. Dead wood grew green. New fibers extended into the emptiness. New rings appeared where old ones had been burned away. The growth of centuries replenished itself in minutes. Soon, the first forecastle rib was solid again, and the seven inches of magnigoth gunwale above it had filled in. The rent was healed.

Multani continued his work. What was a ship without a figurehead? Wood flowed with waxlike ease, seeming to pour itself into an invisible mold. A torso took shape, feminine and muscular. A pair of powerful arms swept dramatically backward. Wood formed a long mantle of hair that twined vinelike about strong shoulders. A face—beautiful, mysterious, and clear eyed—appeared within those rampant locks. Any crew member who gazed on that face would have thought the features belonged to Hanna, former navigator of *Weatherlight*. Certainly, Multani had used Hanna as a mental model. The woman he sought to represent had Hanna's strength and courage and could borrow Hanna's face, for she did not have a face of her own. The woman was a goddess so had no face and all faces.

Residing in every vital impulse of the living grain, Multani shaped the likeness. He was sculptor and sculpture both. In mere moments, the masterpiece was complete. He did not need to step back to examine his work. He inhabited it and knew its perfection.

It was just as well. He could not have seen the figurehead anyway. Beyond the bow of *Weatherlight* was only desert darkness.

The ship rested on her landing spines in the midst of sandy Koilos. All around her spread a slumbering army. The festival lanterns had been extinguished. The torch stakes had long since burned out. Not a fire smoldered among the coalition forces. Soldiers—Metathran, human, and elf—slept in their tents. Dragons slumbered beneath the canopy of stars. They slept like the dead, though these were, in fact, the survivors. These mortals had stood against hundreds of thousands of Phyrexian monsters, only later to be laid low by a three-day victory celebration. Wine and revelry. Mortals must be allowed their excesses.

Multani was no mortal. While elves sang, Multani had mended a shattered keel. While humans danced, Multani had grown longer, stronger spars. While Metathran slept, he had fashioned a glorious figurehead, which, in desperate straits, could be a brutal ram for the ship.

Hanna, is it? came a voice in his mind. The words rumbled like a distant waterfall. It was Karn, peering from the ship's forward lanterns. As Multani lived in every wooden part of the great ship, Karn lived in every metallic one. A golem fashioned of silver, he was the ship's engineer and, in some ways, the ship's engine. *The face is certainly Hanna's, but the hair. . . ?*

Yes, replied Multani. Smooth, hard magnigoth bark thickened across the figure. *It is Hanna, and it is not.*

Who then? asked Karn.

It is Gaea, the world soul, Multani responded reverently. *This is her war. It is she who is squared off against Yawgmoth.*

There was silence for a time. Karn was as much an immortal as Multani, and together the two had been reshaping *Weatherlight*. Through intuition and inspiration, they transformed her toward her final configuration. She was to be the ultimate weapon in this ultimate war.

It is a good change, Multani.

Thank you. No sooner were these words formed than something shifted in the gloaming darkness beyond the ship, something massive. *Did you sense that?* Multani asked.

3

Yes, was all Karn said. There was no time for more. Already he was drawing back from the main engine core. Metal conduits slid free from the neural nexuses of his hands. He broke mental contact with the engine. Massive and slow, the silver man rocked back on his heels. He rose, a bit unsteadily, and turned to climb to the deck.

Multani was faster. He withdrew from the figurehead and coursed up through planks to rise on the forecastle deck. He assembled a body for himself out of a splintered rail and the living hemp of a frayed rope. Fashioned of plant life, Multani stood at *Weatherlight*'s prow. With knothole eyes, he stared out across the desert of Koilos.

Around the ship in every direction spread dark tents and drowsing soldiers. They numbered fifty thousand. Their empty wine jacks and strewn armor told of the recent revels. Beyond the encamped armies stood the nine metal giants that had helped the army win the Battle of Koilos. These titan engines seemed gods of old, poised at the rim of the world. As huge as ships, as deadly as armies, the titans had left their gargantuan footprints across this barren wastes. Imbedded in those footprints were carapace and bone, all that remained of the creatures that had opposed them. Now the titan engines stood empty, staring darkly at the camp they guarded.

The sudden, massive shift had not occurred within the sleeping camp nor among the titan engines. It had happened beyond them, on the sere rills of Koilos. Though morning was still hours away, an otherworldly red light gleamed on the distant horizon. It lit the eastern hills, and the north, the west, and the south. The full compass of the desert glowed with that horrible light.

A word came to Multani, a word he had sensed in the dying mind of a Phyrexian invader: Rath. It was more than a word. It was a world. It was a twisted other-world built of flowstone, forever expanding, forever mutating into a perfect match of Dominaria. The Lord of Phyrexia had made Rath and filled it with machines of war and demon armies. But why?

Karn strode up behind Multani. Weird light glinted from the silver golem's burly shoulders. Eyes like fat washers peered out at the feverish hills.

Karn rumbled, "It's the planeshift. It's the overlay."

"The overlay?" Multani echoed hollowly.

"The Rathi overlay. A world of monsters is fusing with our world. Rath is overlaying on top of Dominaria," Karn replied quietly. "We have no time."

Karn cupped thickset hands around his mouth. His jaw dropped open. From the cold hollows of his chest came a terrible sound. It seemed the toll of a gigantic bell.

"Awake, Dominaria! Dread is upon you!"

The sound tore out above the sleeping army. It riffled the tents like a cyclone. Elves clutched their ears. Humans lurched up from bedrolls. Metathran staggered into the light of the unnatural morning. The roar crossed the camp and echoed from the circle of titan engines, awaking lights in their skulls. It bore onward over empty sands and into the glowing hills. There it met another roar, more horrible, more inhuman.

No one who had survived the Battle of Koilos would ever forget that sound—a Phyrexian battle cry. When last they had heard it, the noise had risen from hundreds of thousands of fiendish mouths. This morning, it rose from millions.

That second roar woke any whom Karn had not. Every last soldier yanked on clothes and armor, belted on swords and fetched up pikes. Trumpets sounded to-arms. Fighters scrambled to their divisions. Metathran warriors formed up on Commander Agnate. Elves flocked to the banner of Eladamri. Humans and Benalish irregulars streamed toward *Weatherlight* herself. The once-still camp boiled in confusion, but one fact was clear. They would all be at war again in mere moments.

From the chaotic camp rose a singular figure: Urza Planeswalker. He soared into the air. His lightning-bright robe trailed magnificently away beneath him. Under a mantle of ash-blond hair, Urza's eyes beamed like twin stars. In one hand, he clutched a gnarled war staff set with glimmering gems. His other hand cradled a sphere of shimmering blue power. That enchanted orb drew him up above even the heads of the titan engines. It also sent his voice out to the armies forming up below.

"Behold, Dominaria. The foe!"

The words were like a thunder stroke. The coalition forces turned to see.

Beyond the shifting legs of the titan engines, Phyrexians took shape. They resolved out of the red haze. In the front ranks came shiny-shelled beasts that seemed gigantic horseshoe crabs. Behind them charged biomechanical centaurs with four arms and glinting pikes. Next came enormous fists of muscle that galloped hungrily forward, floating beasts the size of clouds and the configuration of jellyfish, ambling artifact engines that bristled with blades, and every other imaginable death. All of them approached at a heady charge. They would reach the encamped armies in moments.

Urza's voice rang from above. "Koilos is ours. We have won it. We have destroyed the portal from Phyrexia. That victory can never be taken from us. Koilos and Yavimaya and Llanowar are ours. We have broken Yawgmoth's hold. His world cannot overlay completely on ours. These are our strongholds. Koilos. Yavimaya. Llanowar. From these we will win back the rest of the world—for indeed, the rest of the world is lost. Even now, the plane of Rath overlays it. Even now, the denizens of Phyrexia are as plentiful as the denizens of Dominaria. Every native claw, every native fang must fight, or die. . . ."

A savage shout rose from the fifty thousand coalition forces there—not a war cry but the half-shriek of a trapped animal. As Urza continued his harangue, the troops rallied as best they could.

The Metathran—who were forty of the fifty thousand there—formed a wall of powerstone pikes and glinting armor. Commander Agnate stood in the vanguard. His pike was set and his jaw as well. The tattoos that marked his forehead and cheeks were drawn in tight drums. He had lost his blood brother in the Battle of Koilos, and now, staring down the converging armies, he knew he would lose himself.

The Steel Leaf elves of Staprion gathered around Commander Eladamri. He was Agnate's equal in battle prowess and strategy. Square jawed and sharp eyed, Eladamri and his lieutenant Liin Sivi had fought their way out of Rath once. Now Rath had come back to them. They beheld old terrors. The savage-shorn elves around them had never before seen the red and tortured world. They nocked arrows to long bows and braced for the charge. Through slitted goggles, the Steel Leaf elves gazed at their coming doom.

The dragons had been slower to rise than their warm-blooded allies. As they roused, the old antagonism between the disparate nations had slowed them too. Only the ancient Shivan fire dragon Rhammidarigaaz could unite them. He stood in their midst, his wise eyes drawing them. The staff he held shone with a crimson power that warmed the cold-blooded beasts. The magic talismans around his neck sparked with possibility. Rhammidarigaaz need not speak a word. He only spread wide his wings and heaved himself up into the air. A surge of leathery skin, and another, and he lifted away from the ground. Like a startled flock, the dragon nations took to the air. They circled the camp, preparing for the all-out onslaught.

The Benalish irregulars meanwhile had crowded about *Weatherlight*. Most of them were human warriors, rescued from the military brig during the initial attack on Benalia. Many others were military prisoners of various configurations, goblin and ogre, dwarf and reptile, porcine and bovine. Lastly were Tolarian helionauts and the pilots of Benalia's ravaged air defenses. These troops lacked the precision of the Metathran and elf forces, but they knew how to fight with their backs to a wall, and they believed in this ship and its commander: Gerrard.

Black bearded and bold, Gerrard stood now on the forecastle deck beside Multani and Karn. He lifted his sword, drawing a shout from the gathered throng. They were ready to fight. They were ready to die.

"Do not fear," Urza continued. "You will not die here today. You will live to fight across this globe. This is the new war, the true war. I knew this day was coming, and I have prepared. Now go, fight for Dominaria!"

The shout that answered was at last unified, at last fierce and warlike. The coalition forces braced to receive the charge. Their war cry was drowned out by the omnipresent shriek of their foes.

Beyond the ring of titan engines, a million Phyrexians crested the hills. Like swarming roaches, they filled the land. Barbed legs bore black-armored bodies over the rills. Skull-white faces appeared above, with blood-red mouths and grave-black eyes. They were undead, many of them. The rest were Death personified. Claws like sickles, fangs like daggers, horns and proboscises, venom sacs and sagittal crests—there would be no defeating them. No mortal can defeat Death.

There were more than mortals at Koilos.

The first wave of Phyrexians swept down the hillside as fast as horses at a gallop. Dust rose in thick clouds from their feet. They charged Agnate and his Metathran vanguard.

The defenders braced their pikes and—disappeared. Forty thousand warriors, rank on rank, they disappeared. The five titan engines that had guarded them were gone as well. Where they had been was only trampled ground and sagging tents.

Blinking in disbelief, Multani whispered, "What's happening?"

Phyrexians rushed in a tidal wave across the open ground.

Gerrard blurted, "The elves will be cut down from behind!" He spun toward them.

The elves too vanished. Eladamri and his Steel Leaf warriors were gone in an eye blink, along with two more of the titan engines.

"What's happening?" Karn echoed, glaring at the empty field where they had been.

It was not empty for long. In a black tide, Phyrexians closed the gap.

"Drop the gangplanks!" Gerrard ordered. He raced along the rail of *Weatherlight*, hurling lines overboard. "Everyone, climb on. We fight from the skies!"

As quick as rats, the Benalish irregulars climbed. They had all ridden to this battle aboard *Weatherlight*, and their numbers had been greatly reduced in the fights. Even so, they were too slow.

Karn dropped overboard, grabbed armfuls of warriors, and hurled them to the decks.

Multani made brilliant use of his woven hemp hands to pull others up.

As he hauled the desperate soldiers aboard, Multani said calmly to Gerrard, "It is Urza who is doing this. See—he charges up his titan engine. He remains to fight along with us."

Gerrard yanked a young woman up over the rail and shook his head ruefully. "He's got to be out of his mind."

"A common theory."

"At least he left us the dragons—" A sudden intuition sent Gerrard's glance skyward, where the dragons had been. There was only the preternatural dawn. The eighth titan engine was gone too, leaving only *Weatherlight*, her Benalish irregulars, the ragged fleet of airships, and Urza's lone titan engine. "Damn him." Gerrard nodded sarcastically, growling under his breath, "This seems about right for Urza. A couple hundred against a couple million. Did I tell you I hated him?"

"You even told *him*," Multani pointed out as he pulled the last of the stragglers onto the deck.

One by one, Tolarian helionauts and Metathran jump-ships buzzed into the air around *Weatherlight*. Soldiers lifted her gang planks.

Phyrexians closed on the ship.

Gerrard shouted to Karn, "Get up here, bucket head! Get us out of here!"

The silver golem solemnly clambered up the gunwale. His feet had no sooner left the sand than a surge of Phyrexians crashed against *Weatherlight*'s hull. Horns and claws tore into the wood.

"I'm needed," Multani said simply, slumping into the deck. He fled from splinters and hemp, leaving them empty. His spirit surged down through the planks to fortify the hull.

Gerrard hardly acknowledged the departure of the nature spirit. He was too busy running along the rail to chop away the lines before Phyrexians could climb them. He knocked aside Benalish warriors who blocked the forecastle stairs and stabbed a climbing Phyrexian in its fangy mouth. It fell back atop its comrades, but two more monsters rose in its place.

There were too many. They were too quick. Claws fastened around the stanchions and seized the rail.

Gerrard hacked viciously at the beasts. His sword clove the horned shoulder of a Phyrexian trooper. He skewered the scabrous mouth of a bloodstock. He split the skull shield of a scuta.

"How about a little help!" he shouted over his shoulder.

Red energy burst into being before him. Sudden flames mantled hackles and poured down throats. Plasma shattered thoraxes and flashed flesh to ash. Where once there had been hundreds of Phyrexians, now there was only fire. Bones and armor dropped in a grisly hail.

Gerrard reeled back from the rail and blinked the red spots from his eyes. His sword had melted beyond the hilt. Tossing the thing overboard, he glared to the forecastle deck and the smoking gun.

Behind the starboard ray cannon, a familiar minotaur hunched in the gunnery traces.

Tahngarth shrugged. "You needed a hand."

Gerrard flashed him a smile and climbed toward the portside gun.

As he went, the ship's engines suddenly surged. The deck pitched. *Weatherlight* lurched from the ground. Most of the warriors went to their knees on the planks, but Gerrard kept his feet. He'd ridden this ship to Rath and back, and he had his sky legs.

On his way up the forecastle stairs, he decked a Phyrexian in the jaw. The bone shattered, and dagger teeth drove into the beast's pallet. Its eyes went dark, and it slumped on the rail. Gerrard shoved it off and crossed to his gun. He charged up the cannon even as he strapped himself into the gunnery harness.

"Grab a gun or get below," he shouted to the Benalish irregulars still crowding the deck.

Gerrard spit on the plasma manifold. The saliva boiled away instantly. With a grim smile, he pivoted the gun about to shoot along the hull. Rays struck the air and turned it plasmatic. Crimson energy spattered across the beasts that still hung there. It ripped them loose and dissolved them on their way to ground.

On the starboard side, Tahngarth's cannon blasted. The fireball plunged to impact Phyrexians. Where it rolled, the sphere of energy obliterated monsters. The blaze spent itself eating through the invading troops.

"They're everywhere," Tahngarth snorted. "How do we defend Koilos against this?"

Gerrard hissed, "Kill Phyrexians."

A charge shrieked from his cannon. It arced down toward the moiling army. The energy column twisted like a cyclone. It touched ground and hurled blackened bodies in its wake.

"There's got to be more to it than that," Tahngarth replied even as his cannon spoke again.

"Not for me there isn't," Gerrard said, firing. "Not after what they did to Hanna."

Beyond *Weatherlight*, Urza's titan engine strode patiently across the crowded battlefield. Each footfall crushed hundreds of Phyrexians. Fireball spells from the pilot bulb paved his way. Rockets sprang from the suit's wrists and punched into monsters, exploding on impact. Lightning blasts jagged from an energy fork above and lanced Phyrexians. Monsters struggled to cling to the metallic legs of the titan, but periodic surges of magical energy fried them where they climbed. Flocks of falcon engines launched in silvery waves from the back of the battle suit. Urza killed with grim dispatch.

"There isn't more to it for Urza either," Gerrard muttered. "Not after what they did to Barrin."

New fire woke from the edges of the world. Phyrexian cannons sent scarlet rays stabbing across the sky. The beams sought *Weatherlight*.

"They're bringing up their mana bombards!" Gerrard shouted into the speaking tube beside him. "Stay sharp, Sisay."

Through the tube came the captain's reply. "I'm never dull."

Sisay spun the ship aside, just in time. Raw power ripped the air along her stern.

"How about some help back there, Squee?" Gerrard called.

The tail gun came to life. Its goblin gunner shrieked over the roar of the weapon. Plasma belched from the end. Like a claw, it ripped the rest of the enemy flack from the sky.

Worse was coming. A ball of black mana hurtled over the hills. It welled up behind the massive head of Urza's titan engine. The goo struck, spattering across the metal. It hissed, seeking to crack through seams.

Pausing in midstride, Urza flung off the clinging stuff. It fell across Phyrexians below and ate them away. Urza's engine took another step, and more black-mana shots filled the sky.

"We're not going to last long up here!" Sisay called through the speaking tube.

Gerrard answered with his gun. A pulse of plasma smashed aside another black-mana bomb heading for the ship. "Take us to Urza! See if he's got any great ideas."

Weatherlight banked and surged toward the titan engine. Rays darted out on all sides of the ship. Beams crisscrossed in a deadly net. As the warship neared Urza, Gerrard stood in the traces.

He saw too late. Scores of Phyrexian cannons had drawn a bead on them. The energy that surged suddenly through the dark sky was inescapable.

"Damn him," Gerrard cursed.

CHAPTER 2
The Urborgan Beachhead

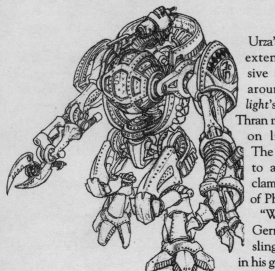

Urza's titan engine extended a massive metallic arm around *Weatherlight*'s amidships. Thran metal clamped on living wood. The ship lurched to a halt above clambering armies of Phyrexians.

"What the—!" Gerrard growled, slinging sideways in his gunnery traces. He slammed against the red-hot chassis of the gun. Gritting his teeth, he managed to squeeze off two more rounds. The rays stabbed from the cannon barrel and turned the air into a pair of red fists. They soared down in a one-two punch that sizzled Phyrexians to nothing and cratered the sand into glass bowls.

New power surged. Along every rivet and seam of Urza's titan engine, blue energy glowed. It swelled out to envelop the titan,

14

the skyship, and its fleet. Through a glass dome, Urza was just visible in his pilot's harness. His form shimmered—the start of a planeswalk. Rings of disturbance spread out rapidly from him. The piloting mechanisms dissolved into fuzz. The armor shell went next.

Weatherlight's hull glowed too. Even Gerrard at his gun, even Tahngarth, turned insubstantial.

The mad world folded up around *Weatherlight,* her scrappy fleet, and Urza's titan engine. Koilos and its cockroach armies slid away into sudden creases in reality. The false dawn faded. The false world disintegrated.

In their place swirled the Blind Eternities. It was a cloudy chaos, a space of shapeless energies and potentialities.

Gerrard gripped the fire controls of his cannon and gritted his teeth. He had soared through this nowhere place before, in *Weatherlight's* own planeshifts, but he'd never been *dragged* through.

Urza Planeswalker and his creations hung for a moment in the void. Then chaos took form. Potentiality became actuality.

True dawn broke over the ship. For a moment, all seemed blue—the robin's-egg sky above and the sloshing sea below. The scene was marred by one black knot of swamp and moss and tree. It was an island, a rather small island, though growing larger all the while.

Weatherlight and her titan stowaway were plunging down toward it.

Gerrard growled. Into the prow speaking tube, he shouted, "Sisay, evasive!"

Her voice echoed back, "Hang on!"

Weatherlight's engines flared. She yawed suddenly, jiggling the titan's arm. With angry insistence, the ship rolled. Sea replaced sky.

Urza half-flipped. Nerveless, his metallic arm lost hold of the ship.

Weatherlight's airfoils slapped together. Fire flared behind. Like a cork from a bottle, *Weatherlight* shot from Urza's grasp. The ship surged up into azure heavens.

Urza's titan engine meanwhile plunged toward azure seas.

Gerrard peered over the rail and watched Urza fall, open-mouthed and panicky in his pilot's capsule. The planeswalker's shock could not have been more profound. He tumbled to splash magnificently just beyond the island's shelf. His impact sent a plume of white water five hundred feet into the air. Limbs sank in sand and muck. The pilot bulb glared like an angry eye as it went under.

Gerrard whooped. Standing in the traces, he shouted over the rail, "How do *you* like getting shoved around, planeswalker?"

From black churning waters, the titan engine's crown emerged. Foam draped the proud dome, and liquid streamed from power conduits. Urza doggedly marched toward the shore of the island.

Gerrard shook his head. "Why did the old bastard bring us here?" He glanced toward the island, and his breath caught in his throat.

Weatherlight had been here before, perhaps a year ago. This isle had once been the home of Crovax.

"Sisay, take us low over the isle."

"Aye."

When last *Weatherlight* was here, the woods were overrun by Phyrexians and the plantation house was destroyed by fire. Crovax lost his home and his family on that day. He lost even more than that. He lost his angel Selenia too. It had been that loss that had turned him to evil.

Now, more than ever, Gerrard understood such loss.

Weatherlight plummeted from the skies, followed by her fleet. She shot low over the waves. Her keel tore past the toiling titan engine. She mounted up to soar above the palms.

Gazing down between the tossing heads of the trees, Gerrard saw an all-too-familiar scene.

Phyrexians filled the island. They slew men and beasts and feasted on them. They gnawed trees and burned thorn brakes. They piled ash into swamps and built redoubts. They set ray cannons and mana bombards in their embrasures. By the end of the day, this island would be a Phyrexian stronghold from which they could control the seas and the outer isles of Urborg.

"Not if I can help it," Gerrard said beneath his breath. "Battle stations!" he called through the tube. "Signal the fleet. We're taking back the island."

Tahngarth stood in the gunnery traces and peered down at the swamps rattling past below. "We'd better take out their artillery before it gets running—"

His words were cut short by a black stream of energy that erupted through the cypresses. It vaulted up toward *Weatherlight*, growing all the while.

"Evasive!" Gerrard called.

Weatherlight folded her airfoils and knifed down laterally above the trees. The black-mana bolt slid away to one side. *Weatherlight*'s wings spread to grab the air, and her engines blazed. Her serrated keel sliced the uppermost boughs as she shot out above the island.

"Too late!" Tahngarth growled. "They've got their guns."

"And we've got ours," Gerrard replied through gritted teeth. His cannon howled as it unleashed its round. The charge whirled a moment among white boles and crashed into a black-mana bombard. Plasma laved the gun chassis. It penetrated the energy stores. The bombard burst. It dissolved into a swelling sphere of fire. Energy pulverized the Phyrexian gunners. It destroyed trees nearby and cracked the very air.

"That's the way!" Gerrard whooped. "Keep us low and fast, Sisay—at the treetops. They won't know where we are until we're on top of them."

Sisay didn't answer except by steering the ship along a low ridge above the swamps.

Atop the ridge, Phyrexian cannons turned a bead on *Weatherlight*.

Tahngarth's gun cackled. The shot struck the first cannon. It melted like a candle. Red metal spattered Phyrexian crews and destroyed the second gun. The third got off a shot. Crimson force rose from the steaming barrel.

Growling, Tahngarth swept the air with answering fire. It caught the other blast like a net catching fish.

Weatherlight roared out over the gun.

Tahngarth pivoted to bring his cannon to bear, but the target slid to stern. Another bolt rose after the ship.

"Look sharp, Squee!" Tahngarth shouted into the speaking tube.

His voice spilled out beside the aft gun. There, a much smaller figure clutched the fire controls. Squee was an unlikely tail gunner—green and warty, with long, pointed ears, a crooked-toothed grin, and a reputation for cowardice. Still, he had downed Volrath's own gunship and had assisted in countless cruiser kills during the opening war. At the tail gun, Squee fought with fury.

This occasion was no exception. Squee loosed a triple blast. The first shot smashed aside the Phyrexian beam. The second ripped a clear way through the treetops. The third soared down the enemy barrel and peeled it back as if it were a banana.

"Nice shooting, Squee!" yelled Gerrard. "That's four guns down! How many do you think they've got?"

As if in answer, a wall of scarlet energy jutted skyward ahead of them. Helionauts and jump ships hurtled away to either side of the red wall. *Weatherlight* was too big for such quick maneuvers. She soared toward destruction.

Sisay dragged the helm hard to port. *Weatherlight* banked sharply away from the raking fire. Her keel cut a deep groove through the air. She rose on angry engines.

The Phyrexian cannons followed her with fire.

Sisay braced her legs and hauled hard on the wheel. The ship climbed almost straight up. Engines belched blue flame. *Weatherlight* rocketed heavenward, enwrapped in killing rays. She rose up past the curtain of fire and skipped away among shielding clouds. The light rays dissipated among drops of water.

"It'd be nice to have a little help!" Sisay shouted.

"I've given up expecting it," Gerrard answered. "At least we've got our fleet. Take us back down to them, Captain."

"Aye, Commander," Sisay said.

Weatherlight dived through the clouds. Vapor rolled from her gunwales.

The isle appeared below. Phyrexian cannon fire clawed the treetops away. One blast snatched a helionaut from the air. Another grazed a jump ship. Though outgunned, the smaller craft sent exploding quarrels down into the Phyrexian armies. It would not be enough. Phyrexians swarmed the land.

"Get the helionauts out of there," Gerrard ordered. "Signal them to hover high and watch for airships. They're no good against ground troops."

"Aye, Commander," came the voice of the communications ensign.

"So, that leaves just us and the jump ships?" Sisay asked.

"Not just us," Gerrard reported, jabbing a finger toward the rapidly approaching shoreline. "Urza's made landfall."

Taller than the treetops, Urza's titan engine marched into the swamp. The hulking mechanism still streamed water and seaweed but looked all the more sinister for it. Rockets jumped away from his wrists and corkscrewed through deadwood forests. They plowed through earthwork trenches and exploded in the bunkers beyond. Hunks of bug flesh rained outward.

Gerrard shook his head in grudging amazement. He lifted a captain's glass to his eye to watch the carnage.

Urza's titan engine strode onward. A huge fireball formed before the planeswalker and swooped down to drive Phyrexians into a shallow marsh. Lightning leaped from the fork above the pilot bulb and jagged through the water. Monsters thrashed and sizzled. Urza strode atop them, paying no heed. He drove straight across the ground, making toward some goal only he knew.

Weatherlight reached the shore and roared out over the treetops.

"There's another titan engine," Tahngarth shouted.

"Another what?" Gerrard asked in amazement.

"Another titan engine—three more!"

Gerrard paused in his attacks to stare at the spectacle. Above the mossy treetops on the far sides of the isle moved gleaming pilot domes. These engines had fought at Koilos and now had come here.

"And ground troops!" Tahngarth called, "Metathran ground troops."

Between the flashing boles of trees, Gerrard saw them. Agnate and his Metathran army of forty thousand had been brought here, too. They swept across the land in a purging blue tide, destroying the Phyrexians in their path.

"Watch your fire, friends," Sisay advised. "Our own troops are down there."

"Yeah," Gerrard confirmed, nodding blankly. "It looks like the old man brought help after all." He folded the captain's glass. "We're useless back here. We can't fire with our own forces on the ground. Sisay, take us to the center of the Phyrexian encampment."

"Where would that be?" she asked

"Where Urza is heading," Gerrard said.

"Aye, Commander."

Weatherlight slid into the wake of destruction behind Urza.

Below, Metathran troops ran. Their battle axes glinted. Their war cry rose above even the thunder of *Weatherlight*'s engines.

She soared out directly above Urza.

Falcon engines launched from his shoulders. They gleamed beside *Weatherlight*'s bow. The silvery birds shrieked as they stooped on their prey—Phyrexians.

Just ahead, a fresh wave of the beasts charged into battle. Some had once been human, their figures stretched on metallic frameworks, their muscles augmented with machines. Others were not remotely human. They had been grown in vats of glistening-oil, sculpted by priests of Phyrexia. Massive legs,

Planeshift

crested heads, dagger fangs, scimitar claws—they were creatures created to kill.

Whatever their origins, the beasts of Phyrexia met Urza's deadly machines. Silver falcons shrieked down upon them. Razor-sharp beaks rammed Phyrexian bellies. Shredding mechanisms tore them apart. The front lines crumbled and bled even as *Weatherlight* hurtled by overhead.

"Stay the course," called Gerrard.

He and Tahngarth unleashed a fresh volley of fire. The bolts disintegrated lichens, stripped trees to their heartwood, and boiled marshes. Fire flooded mana bombards. It melted armor and burned fiend flesh from bone. Fore, aft, and amidships, *Weatherlight's* cannons blazed.

Urza and his three planeswalker comrades meanwhile marched their titan engines inward. They cut converging lines through Phyrexian troops. Wave upon wave of Metathran mopped up behind. The blue-skinned warriors had taken Koilos. Now they would take Urborg.

But why? Gerrard wondered. Why is this fight so important?

On a low hill ahead lay the core of Phyrexian command—Crovax's noble estate. It was in ruins. Smoke blackened everything. Domes lay cracked like eggshells. Columns pointed accusing fingers at the sky. Phyrexian armies were marshaled across the fields. Once the angel Selenia had kept evil from this place. That was before Crovax stole her away. Now, the angel, the plantation, and Crovax himself belonged to Yawgmoth. The plantation had become a Phyrexian staging ground.

"Target the guns first!" Gerrard ordered, folding his captain's glass and bringing his cannon to bear, "then the ammunitions depot, then the command center, then the individual soldiers."

"Aye," answered Tahngarth and the other gunners.

"Sisay, bring us in at the treetops, fast and low. Strafe the damned bugs."

"I think you enjoy this too much," Sisay replied, adding a belated, "Commander."

Weatherlight flew down a marshy hollow. Fronds slapped the belly of the ship. *Weatherlight*'s roar bounced from water and wood.

"Even with bats' ears and flies' eyes, they won't be able to tell where we are," Gerrard assured himself.

His hands were sweaty on the fire controls. Fear prickled the hairs on the back of his neck. There was something not right about this. He'd made a miscalculation—was thinking too much like a human, not a monster. Gerrard flicked a glance over one shoulder to Tahngarth. The bull-man returned his gaze, eyes rimmed with uncertainty. He sensed it too.

Clenching his jaw, Gerrard faced forward. "All right, just watch for the guns. Take out the guns, and we'll be fine."

Weatherlight flew from the wetlands and up the rising fields where Crovax's family had once planted their crops. A darker crop rose now—countless Phyrexians encamped for war. They were arrayed in orderly file, toy soldiers on a brown carpet. In the center of the army, a column of beasts marched—not toward battle but toward the plantation house.

"Hold your fire!" Gerrard called. "Watch for the guns!"

Though *Weatherlight* roared above the Phyrexians, none looked upward.

The ship topped the long rise and reached the broad tablelands where the ruins rested. Rampant vines draped palm and cypress—plenty of cover to hide bombards. No guns fired, though. In the central lane leading to the plantation house, Phyrexians marched in an orderly column.

"What is this?" Tahngarth asked.

Gerrard only shook his head.

At last the ship flew over the shattered mansion itself. Every room lay open to the sky. The ghosts of past grandeur lingered among burned beams and ruined furnishings. The Phyrexian parade entered the plantation house and snaked its way to a specific room—a small room. It was untouched by the ravages that had destroyed the rest, or it had been reconstructed—the room of a young man. There, in that doorway, Phyrexians one by one bowed to the floor in homage.

There was no time to see more. *Weatherlight* shot past the roofless home. Gerrard and the other gunners still watched for ground-to-air fire, but none rose.

In dread realization, Gerrard murmured, "It's not a command center. It's a holy place, a temple to the boy who grew up there. It's a temple to Crovax." A drop of sweat rolled chillingly down Gerrard's spine.

How high had Crovax risen in the Phyrexian hierarchy?

"That's why we're in Urborg," Gerrard said to himself. "Crovax is here." Into the speaking tube, he said, "Bring us around, Sisay. Let's go in with guns blazing. It'll be like shooting fish in a barrel. We'll kill every last bug. We'll capture this isle. It'll become our beachhead for rousting the Phyrexians from all of Urborg."

Even as he spoke, Sisay brought the ship around in a tight arc. All along the rails, cannons hummed hotly, ready for annihilation. The jitters were gone from gunners' hands. There was only the grim set of jaws and the lightless eyes of men who knew they were about to commit slaughter.

Gerrard's gun spoke first. It lashed out a red hand that burned away a whole platoon of Phyrexians. Tahngarth's cannon ripped through fifty more. Death stabbed down on the bowed heads and shuffling claws. Phyrexians died like roaches.

Above the roar of his gun, Tahngarth shouted, "Why don't they even run?"

Gerrard shook his head. "They cannot run. Crovax has commanded their worship."

CHAPTER 3
He Has Commanded Their Worship

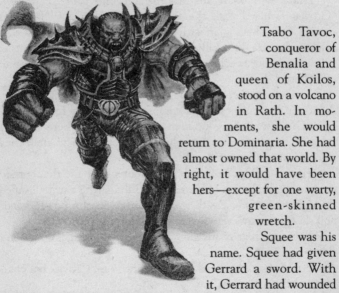

Tsabo Tavoc, conqueror of Benalia and queen of Koilos, stood on a volcano in Rath. In moments, she would return to Dominaria. She had almost owned that world. By right, it would have been hers—except for one warty, green-skinned wretch.

Squee was his name. Squee had given Gerrard a sword. With it, Gerrard had wounded Tsabo Tavoc and destroyed the portal at Koilos and escaped. Her prize had escaped, and Tsabo Tavoc had limped back to Phyrexia.

It had been a long road back, a road paved with torment and humiliation.

First, Tsabo Tavoc had gone to the fourth sphere of Phyrexia for the none-too-tender ministrations of the vat priests. They stitched closed the laceration in her gut. She commanded them to use silk, but they used leather thongs instead. Even vat priests could ignore her orders.

Sewn together like an old sack, Tsabo Tavoc went to the second sphere. There Phyrexian cogwrights replaced the five legs ripped from her thorax. The replacements were crude things, rusty and inelegant. As to the injuries to her spider abdomen, the cogwrights merely sawed away the infected half and welded a steel plate over it. Even cogwrights had dominion over her.

Yawgmoth was displeased.

Next, Tsabo Tavoc received an ominous assignment: Report to Envincar Crovax in the Stronghold, and give account of your failings.

On grating legs, Tsabo Tavoc ambled across the sooty wastes of the second sphere. She reached a portal to Rath. The gate guards—a pair of mogg goblins—dared to mock her shorn abdomen. One of her good legs thrust into the mouth of the first mogg, impaling him from tooth to tail. The other beast leaped on her—a miscalculation. With human hands, she gripped his neck and drove her nails through skin and muscle and windpipe until the flesh seemed only wet rope.

She was still Tsabo Tavoc. She would not be mocked by weevils. This was only a setback. Tsabo Tavoc would report to Crovax, would bear his wrath, and would rise again, one day to kill him.

She was still Tsabo Tavoc.

Painted in mogg blood, Tsabo Tavoc had passed through the portal to a volcanic hillside on Rath.

The ground beneath her feet was red and rolling. It was not lava but flowstone. Each speck of it was a minute machine clinging to those around it. As a whole, flowstone responded to the mental suggestions of the Evincar of Rath—Crovax. He shaped the world. The hills and plains around her bore the mad geography of his mind. They changed always, sometimes slowly, sometimes violently, but always Rath changed—until now.

Even as she stood there, Rath overlaid itself on Dominaria. The flowstone world phased into being atop the real one. It brought with it the races of Rath, the Phyrexian armies arrayed across its surface, and even Tsabo Tavoc herself. She arrived on Dominaria by riding the Rathi overlay, freight on a barge.

Tsabo Tavoc breathed the air of Urborg. It stank of death—not clean, metallic death but the fetor of decaying bodies.

"Of course Crovax brought his Stronghold here," she told herself. "Necrophile." She shuddered with distaste. How much more fun it was to torture the living than to play with the dead.

Nearby on the volcano's side lay a violent crack. Brimstone steam wafted from that space. Dominarians would have thought this a passage into hell. They would have been right. Crovax and his Stronghold lay in the heart of the dormant volcano.

Tsabo Tavoc ambled to the rough crack and climbed within. Through slanting shafts and narrow corners she went. The tortuous route would have killed a lesser creature, but Tsabo Tavoc had the grace of all arachnids. Even light abandoned her, but she could see in absolute dark. The spider woman clambered for miles into deep rock. At last, a new, red glow began ahead. It lit the sulfuric crack, and hot winds rolled up around Tsabo Tavoc.

She emerged in an enormous hollow, perhaps a dozen miles in diameter. When this volcano had been active, the cavern would have been filled with a mountain of lava. Now the vast subterranean chamber held only the Stronghold.

Despite herself, Tsabo Tavoc paused to stare in awe.

The Stronghold was massive—a mile tall and three miles in diameter. It floated in the center of the volcanic cavern and seemed the elaborate pelvis of some titanic predatory beast. It had been grown more than built. Walls and windows and floors all were formed of flowstone, which aped the properties of countless materials. In the superstructure of the city, the flowstone had the consistency of bone. Ivory buttresses and arches connected processes and concavities. Horns jutted from each tower and rail. Slender ribs extended in walkways. Within the complex, the flowstone took the form of metal. Stacked tiers of balconies and inner chambers rose into the high vault above the city. Armored mechanisms dangled beneath.

For all its size and elaboration, the Stronghold performed one simple function: converting volcanic and planar energy into flowstone. The Stronghold had created flowstone and channeled it out the side of the volcano, creating Rath. Now that the plane was complete, the ancient flow of power was stilled. The Stronghold awaited its ultimate task.

Tsabo Tavoc nimbly picked her way around the interior of the cavern. There was only one bridge onto the Stronghold, and even a spider woman could not spin another way across. To reach the bridge, Tsabo Tavoc had to climb atop the mogg goblin warrens that lined the inner walls of the cavern. It was yet another indignity. The beasts emptied their slops out the windows of their warrens, leaving long slick trails.

They would pay, these goblins—they and everyone else.

Tsabo Tavoc crawled from stony sills down onto the main bridge. Her metallic legs chimed quietly on the rocky expanse. More moggs lined the structure. Brutish and mindless, they stood at what amounted to attention for a hunchbacked species. Tsabo Tavoc strode down the gauntlet of them. Her legs itched to knock them over the rail to their deaths. The beasts let her be. They could smell the blood of comrades on her.

Besides, Tsabo Tavoc was expected.

She reached the main gate, called simply Portcullis. It had once borne the stylized emblem of Volrath's face. Crovax hadn't removed his predecessor's likeness. He only added to it a set of grinning shark's teeth. At Tsabo Tavoc's approach, the great gears began to roll, and the gargantuan gate swung slowly upward. This was more like the reception she had expected.

She knew the way to the evincar's throne room. Tsabo Tavoc had memorized the route, intending to ascend to the throne. Through corridors that seemed vesicles in a giant's heart, Tsabo Tavoc wound inward. Windows gave views into the hydroponics gardens beyond. Pits dropped to laboratories and dungeons. *Il*-Vec and *il*-Dal humans moved through the passages. Some were guards in scale mail. Others were slaves in leather coveralls. None sought to impede the march of the spider woman.

She arrived. The throne room was huge. Once it had been the convocation hall in the center of the structure, but Volrath had claimed the site for himself. Crovax had then added his own distinct flavor.

The columns that lined either wall had been twisted by Crovax's mind. Above, the vault dripped stalactites, some of which held impaled bodies. Tsabo Tavoc pursed her lips, calculating how much muscle it would take to hurl a body that high. A few were relatively fresh, sending down a pattering red rain. Around these gory puddles crowded dogs the size of ponies. Hackled and muscled, the vampire hounds lapped blood past enormous fangs. They kept the slate-black floor clean and protected the huge throne, which was fashioned of obsidian, its back carved with blindly staring faces and motifs of death.

All about the room, *il*-Vec guards stood like hypertrophied statues. Among them was the court mage, Ertai. Spine-implanted and metal-trussed, the man had become a whipping boy. Constant desperation rimmed his red eyes. He stood there, statue still, even though his master was nowhere to be seen.

Tsabo Tavoc paused, expecting to be announced. The guards paid her no heed. Even Ertai averted his eyes. This was the most galling of all. Tsabo Tavoc strode toward the nearest guard, intent on slaying him. She was stopped short by a sound from behind the throne—words and laughter.

"—nice to know you have finally noticed, Father," came a mellifluous voice.

Another speaker replied, "No, indeed, Son. It is nice of you to forgive our long ignorance of your greatness."

"Don't even start to apologize, Father. I would not expect imperfect creatures such as you and Mother to understand perfection."

A shrill, false laugh answered, the mocking sound of a man pretending to be a woman. "Well said, Son! We should have made your room a shrine much sooner."

"Yes, you should have." More laughing shrieks. "You've seen how popular it is. Tens of thousands of troops line up to do homage."

Tsabo Tavoc edged out around the throne. Beyond, on a small dais, sat a dainty table spread with a white-lace tablecloth. A silver kettle sent tea-scented steam into the air. Three cups and saucers sat decorously before three chairs of carved ebony. Two of those chairs held human skeletons, crudely wired together. The bones were smoke blackened, some half-burned away, some missing altogether. The skulls were the most obvious absentees.

They rested on the hands of the man who sat in the third chair—Crovax.

The Evincar of Rath had once been a small man. That was before Yawgmoth had transformed him. Now Crovax had a powerful chest and a torso like a bull's. Under black scale armor, huge arms flexed, easily able to hurl a man fifty feet upward to die on a stalactite. His legs were equally broad, like coiled springs. Crovax's head jutted, round and close cropped, from a metallic collar. The worst change of all to him, though, were his teeth—row on row of triangular, jag-edged teeth. Crovax's jaws could distend, allowing him to remove heads with those teeth. He had eyes to match, the soulless eyes of a shark.

Evincar Crovax did not seem to notice Tsabo Tavoc's arrival. Instead, he continued his conversation with the skull puppets he held on his hands. Gravely serious, he stared at his tea guests.

"When I was growing up, I thought you'd never understand me. If I'd known all it took was your murder and immolation, I would have done it much sooner."

His father's skull boomed a belly laugh. His mother shrieked her merriment.

Tsabo Tavoc interrupted. "Evincar Crovax, the Ineffable has sent me to give report."

Blinking, Crovax looked up at Tsabo Tavoc. He did not seem to see her. "And you are?"

Red anger showed on her face. "I am Tsabo Tavoc."

With a nod, Crovax seemed to recall. "Oh, yes. One of the field commanders—"

"I am your second-in-command," Tsabo Tavoc corrected.

Crovax shook his head, a little jiggling motion. "That cannot be. I do not have a second-in-command." Setting down the skulls, he stood. "My second-in-command was destroyed at Koilos."

"Those rumors are false," Tsabo Tavoc hissed. She was not accustomed to dealing with superiors and hadn't even now convinced herself she dealt with one. "I am Tsabo Tavoc. I survived Koilos."

"That cannot be," he repeated. "Ten thousand scuta, twenty thousand bloodstocks, thirty thousand troopers did not survive—"

"But I did."

"One hundred ten dragon engines, six witch engines, forty gargantua, twenty trench worms—"

Tsabo Tavoc loomed up before him. "But I did."

"One hundred heavy ordnance, two hundred field ordnance, five hundred slashers—"

"But I did!" she raged, lunging for him.

Her legs would not move. The floor was not black slate but flowstone. Crovax controlled it. It had latched onto her legs. She could not rip them free.

Crovax continued as though she hadn't interrupted. "All those troops lost, all those machines . . . gone. Worse still, the permanent portal, which had joined Phyrexia and Dominaria for nine thousand years—it was lost too. And Gerrard Capashen, whom you were charged to gain for Yawgmoth? All this lost, and yet you survive?"

A shudder of fear moved through Tsabo Tavoc. She was used to fear, to feeling it in others, but it had been decades since she had felt it for herself.

Crovax walked up to stand before her. His head did not even rise to meet her thorax. Despite all the doubt that rumpled his brow, Crovax grinned.

"Still, I can't deny what my eyes tell me. Here you are. Second-in-command Tsabo Tavoc."

"Yes," she replied tersely.

"You are not as grand as tales have said. I heard silken skin." He gestured at the leather thongs that held together her belly wound. "This looks more like burlap. It's crude work. We'll have to fix that."

He reached up, grasped the wound in a powerful grip, and ripped it out—thongs, laceration, skin, and muscle. His fingers clutched the hunk of flesh. Glistening-oil dribbled onto the floor. Vampire hounds loped up to lick it away.

Shrieking in pain and rage, Tsabo Tavoc struggled to pull her legs free. She would kill this bastard. . . . In a rage, she lunged down to grab Crovax with her human arms.

Crovax casually lifted his bloodied fist and backhanded her face.

The force of the blow was incredible. Tsabo Tavoc would have tumbled across the floor if her legs hadn't been rooted. She reeled. Glistening-oil coursed down her head.

Crovax meanwhile delicately balanced the meaty gobbet on the nose of one of his vampire hounds. The huge canine dutifully waited, oil sliding into its nostrils, until Crovax nodded. Fangy jaws snapped, and the flesh was gone down the beast's throat.

Petting the creature, Crovax turned his attention back to the dizzy spider woman. He gazed gravely at her thorax.

"And shoddy workmanship, these legs. We'll have to fix that as well."

He gripped the first of her new legs and hauled against the joint. Metal cracked. Wires snapped. Sparks flew. A ball sucked free from a fleshy socket. The leg fell to ground.

Tsabo Tavoc tried to grab him again.

Crovax merely caught her arms and ripped them off.

The pain was exquisite. She had forgotten what her own agony felt like.

One by one, he broke her other legs free, all eight of them. With a crash, she fell to the floor. She writhed amid her own limbs. Oil covered her.

Vampire hounds converged. Their eager tongues lapped at her.

"So that's it then?" she screamed. "You'll feed me to your dogs?"

Crovax called off the hounds, speaking a single command in a violent language. They ducked their heads and licked their jowls before loping away.

Stepping across the mess of legs, Crovax towered above her. "No. I will not feed you to them. Despite all your failures, you were a great warrior. It would be foolish of me to let a hound gain the courage of your heart, or the knowledge of your brain, or the wisdom of your liver. Those are delicacies suited for conquerors. And, whatever you once were, my dear, I am now your conqueror."

He set his boot on her throat and stepped down, crushing windpipe and spine.

* * * * *

Crovax retired late that evening, after a perfectly prepared meal. The organ meats were, of course, the main treat, but there were also some fine steaks—sirloin, flank, shank, and chuck. The ribs would make a good lunch tomorrow, and he would have roast brisket for dinner. The rest was being stewed for later.

Crovax felt full and satisfied but not yet good. There was only one thing that made him feel good these days.

Retiring to his private chambers, Crovax dismissed the servants and locked the doors. He strode to center of the room and fell to his knees on the slate-black floor. Hands that had torn apart the spider woman now clenched in prayer.

"Great Yawgmoth, I have served you today. Tsabo Tavoc has been disciplined. My troops have locked down the central island. The battles in Keld and Hurloon progress perfectly. Ertai and Greven stand ready to destroy *Weatherlight* and bring her commander to me. Preparations for the final implementation are underway. I am paving your return to Dominaria, Lord."

He paused, breath hissing in his teeth.

"I beg one favor, only, and you know what it is." He stared up into the dark vault of his room. "You have her. She is yours. I wish only to see her a moment."

Shark eyes studied the emptiness above. Seeing nothing, Crovax bowed his face to the floor.

"Please, Lord Yawgmoth. Please, send her to me."

He lay there, not daring to look up, not daring to see the creature who descended, lest his eyes drive her away again. He did not need to see. In his mind's eye, he knew how she looked— broad-swept wings and willowy arms, slender form and graceful legs, alabaster skin, wan face, sad eyes . . . Oh, it was always her eyes that destroyed him. Those eyes that had pleaded to be released, that had torn at him when she was stolen away by Yawgmoth, her true master, that had stared hatred at Crovax when he had slain her. Those sad, angel eyes.

She belonged to Yawgmoth now. She always had but especially now, when she was no more than a ghost.

Crovax felt her gentle hand upon his shoulder. It was warm. It had weight. It was real.

He lifted his head and opened his eyes. Through jagged teeth, he breathed a simple, sweet sound. "Selenia."

CHAPTER 4
The Uniter of Keld

As the overlay began, Eladamri and Liin Sivi stood at the head of a small but fierce host of Steel Leaf elves. In front, pikes tilted and swords jutted. In back, longbows were lifted, trained on the skies. The dust of Koilos slid across the goggles of the elves and settled in their savage shocks of hair. More dust rose ahead of them, flung into the sky by hundreds of thousands of Phyrexian feet.

Eladamri stared at the oncoming foes. His eyes were steely, the same color as his armor and hair. He should shout something, some battle cry. This was the moment of death. Elves always shouted defiance in the face of death. He could think of nothing. His tongue was a thick lump in his mouth.

Beside him stood Liin Sivi—no elf, but a Vec. Her eyes too were the color of her hair—black. They gazed with an altogether different emotion. Liin Sivi was not ready to die. Humans never

34

were. She was ready to kill. Her wicked-bladed toten-vec was eager to swing out on its chain and harvest heads.

Bowstrings thrummed behind them. Arrows flocked into the sky. They shrieked over the elves and out past the two titan engines. One, a green machine composed in part of living wood, held the planeswalker Freyalise. She was a god to these elves. Glimpsing her engine amid the hailing arrows brought the war cry to Eladamri's lips.

"Freyalise!"

The Steel Leaf elves took up the cry. It roared out among the Phyrexian horde even as the arrows pelted into them. Shafts cracked carapace and lodged in eye orbits and sank into the folds of throats.

"Freyalise!" Eladamri called again. This time Liin Sivi shouted it too, as did all the elves.

The third shout of that name seemed an invocation. Power swelled out from the insectoid engine. It blossomed from each line of armor, each spiracle and gun port. Like an opening flower, Freyalise's might spread to cover them all. In moments, Eladamri, Liin Sivi, the Steel Leaf elves, and even the other titan engine were subsumed into the body of Freyalise.

Koilos disintegrated around them, a sand painting on the wind.

Planeshift, Eladamri realized. She is taking us away from certain death.

The contingent hung unmoving in emptiness. It was not as if the ground had dissolved beneath their feet but as if the air itself had become solid. Within the planeswalker's envelop, all was still. Beyond it, all was chaos. This was the world between worlds.

Soon rampant energies spiraled into patterns and they into solids.

Trees took shape—tall, spiny, and ice choked. Ground formed. The rocky soil was carpeted with snow. The stinging heat of Koilos gave way to the stinging cold of a northern clime under frozen skies.

Eladamri breathed the air. It was wickedly cold. It jabbed chill fingers beneath his armor and tricked away the last of Koilos's heat. He sheathed his sword and wrapped his arms around himself.

Liin Sivi did likewise. "Where are we?" Her breath ghosted in the air.

Casting a glance around, Eladamri saw that the Steel Leaf elves had arrived in this algid wood as well. The two titan engines stood just ahead of him.

"I don't know, but I know who does."

"Freyalise," supplied Liin Sivi.

In silent accord, Eladamri and Liin Sivi strode up the snowy ridge toward the titan engines. Uncertain what else to do, his warriors followed.

Eladamri shoved his way through the prickly pines, alien and harsh to his fingers. He unwittingly triggered an avalanche of snow from the boughs. The white stuff slumped atop him and slipped into his collar. Growling, he shrugged it off. Behind him came snickers, which turned to snorts beneath more frosty assaults.

Jangled, the heroes of Koilos reached the ridge where the titan engines stood.

Eladamri set hands on his hips and looked up at the strange machines.

The titans' feet deeply compacted the snow. Wind moaned in their massive armor. Frost formed geometric designs on observation ports. The dome where Freyalise resided was silhouetted black against the aching blue of the sky.

Cupping hands to his mouth, Eladamri shouted, "Great Freyalise, Lady of Llanowar, where have you brought us?"

In answer, the titan lifted a massive arm and pointed to the forest that spread out below.

Eladamri turned to look. His eyes opened wide, and his jaw dropped.

Intermingled among the aggressive evergreens were tall, twisted trees from another world. The Skyshroud Forest. It was not there in entirety, but large portions mixed with the native foliage. Among pointed peaks of fir, the vast gray boles of cerema trees stood. Wintry sun dappled the waters that stood among their roots. Boreal winds moved veils of moss.

"The overlay," Eladamri realized. "It has brought the Skyshroud Forest here."

Squinting against the snow glare, Eladamri made out walkways curving along prodigious trunks, and aerial bridges joining tree to tree, and knobby dwellings in the hollows of boughs. Worse yet, he made out figures moving. . . .

"The overlay has brought my people here. It has brought our nation to this frigid death."

Without a thought to the Steel Leaf elves in his command, Eladamri ran down the ice-choked slope. His leather boots, excellent for battles in treetops and sand, were treacherous on the snow. He slipped and fell. In a cascade of rock and ice, he rolled to the base of the incline. Scratched and bruised, Eladamri climbed to his feet and ran through a brake of pine.

Beyond, the Skyshroud Forest began. Eladamri staggered to a stop, his feet on warm soil. The forest had arrived here only moments ago, with the rest of the overlay, and it still held the heat of Rath, the smells of home. Eladamri breathed the air. Already it was cold, but the scents of humus and moss filled it. Tendrils of steam rose from the watery sea beneath the trees. A flash of scales shone where a merfolk fled from his gaze.

With sudden realization, Eladamri stooped, putting his hands on his knees. The water would freeze in this climate. The merfolk would die, so would the cerema trees, and every vine, every food crop, every elf. . . .

Eladamri was moving again. He knew this terrain, these very trees. He leaped from the embankment and grabbed a dangling vine. Pulling his legs up beneath him, he swung above a palisade of huge thorns. Landing on the platform of vines beyond, he rushed to an ancient cerema tree. A walkway spiraled up the huge bole. He climbed. Generations of elves had climbed this very tree. Their feet had worn dark wells in the flesh of the vine. Eladamri's own feet had helped carve out these steps.

Oh, he had hoped one day to return home to the Skyshroud but not this way, not on its last day. By evening, the forest would be dead, the sea beneath it frozen.

Eladamri reached the spreading crown of the trees. Pathways led out along the boughs and into numerous bulb dwellings. Eladamri knew the families who lived there—the sons of Dalwryri, the royal line of Gemath, the storytelling clan of Dalepoc. He could hear them in their homes, adult voices fearful and querulous, children complaining of the cold, infants crying. He would go to them, yes. He must go to them but not yet.

He ran across a vine-work bridge that led to a nexus of other paths. Elves filled the trails, some of them struggling toward their homes and families, others standing and staring at the clear, cold blue overhead. A few recognized Eladamri, their long-lost Uniter, and they called out to him. He passed them in a blur. There would be time for them. He would be the Korvecdal again in moments, but just now he was a grieving man.

Another set of paths led to the most familiar tree of all. Its shape was etched on his mind. The green ivy that clung to the bark, the bulb houses clustered to one side of the main stalk, the arching canopy above. His steps slowed, and his hands trembled as he grabbed the walkway rail. The hammering of his heart seemed to shake the bridge.

He entered. The dwelling was exactly as he remembered it the day he left to attack the Stronghold. No one had ventured here. Wooden cups yet sat upon the table. The covers across his pallet were drawn up and ready for him to sleep. The battle plans he had made for the assault still lay in coils of bark on his desk.

"Home," Eladamri said.

Somehow it had not been real until now. This displaced forest, dying under daggers of cold, might have been some weird apparition, someone else's nightmare. Seeing his own home and all the things he alone knew made the nightmare real.

Eladamri sucked a breath. He staggered from the hollow out into the broad lap of the tree. He meant to catch his breath, but then his gaze slid across the cruelest sight of all.

His daughter's bulb opened just before him. The wind muscled through the door and rifled her clothes, hanging on pegs along one wall. Frosted leaves tumbled through the window and onto her bed. She had been abducted from that very spot. An agent of Volrath's had abducted her, and Volrath himself had made her a monster. The Phyrexians had abducted Avila and killed her, and now they had abducted the whole of the Skyshroud and killed it.

Going to his knees on the foot-worn bark, Eladamri clutched his face. "Why did you bring me here, Freyalise? Why do you torment me?"

Footsteps came along the vine bridge. "Great Lord Eladamri, you have returned to us! We knew you would come. We knew that, in our moment of greatest catastrophe, you would come."

Eladamri lifted teary eyes to see who spoke to him. "Allisor." He breathed raggedly, unable to say more.

"We thought you were dead," the young lieutenant said. The skin was drawn tight across his jutting chin and prominent cheekbones, an expression that mix terror and elation. He knelt beside Eladamri and bowed his head. "That is, the others thought you were dead. No one who was trapped in the Strong-hold made it out alive. But I didn't think you were dead. I knew you would survive, somehow."

More soldiers approached across the bridge. They whooped in excitement and called out to their comrades.

"He is here. The Uniter has returned!" The warriors of the Skyshroud converged on that single, ancient tree and the man who once had called it home.

Lieutenant Allisor lifted his head. His breath had condensed on his leaf-scale breastplate, and it began to freeze. "We will follow wherever you lead. We will obey your every command. Only tell us, Eladamri—what shall we do now?"

J. Robert King

The Uniter kept his head bowed. What could they do? Move the forest, tree by tree, to some warmer place? Carry the sea in buckets down beneath the sun? He was a Uniter, not a god.

He was not a god, but he was the scion of a goddess.

Eladamri stood in the midst of the throng. Already, the aerial bridges groaned under the weight of arriving warriors. Clear eyed at last, he gazed out at the gathering might of his nation.

"Skyshroud elves, I have returned to you, yes, in our most desperate hour. I have been called the Korvecdal, the Uniter of peoples. I shall need now to become the Uniter of worlds.

"Rath is gone. Our world—the only world we've known for a thousand years—has now melded with this world. Our home is now this icy wasteland. I do not know where lie the ranges of the Kor and the Vec. I do not know where burn the forges of the Dal. I do not know if they will survive this invasion of world on world. But I know that we will survive."

Lifting his hands to the heavens and flinging back his head, Eladamri called out in a loud, clear voice, "Freyalise, Lady of Llanowar, Matron of the Steel Leaf elves, I summon thee—I, who became savior of Llanowar, I, who am called Scion of Freyalise."

She did not so much arrive but appear. First her wide, beautiful, capricious eyes hovered in the midst of the bowed multitude. Then her lips took form, smiling wryly. Flesh filled in the rest of her face and rolled down her slender neck and out into shoulders. Graceful arms formed from those shoulders and a slim torso in foliage armor. Even when her legs took shape, she did not touch ground but floated inches above the wood.

Eladamri had glimpsed her during the revels at Koilos, but now, to face her here in his dying homeland, he could not stand. He sank to his knees and bowed his head. His folk did likewise.

Freyalise drifted over to him. Her hand reached gently outward and stroked his braided hair.

"You have summoned me, Elfchild?"

Lifting his face, Eladamri stared at her glimmering eyes. "Yes, my lady. I have called you to collect on a debt you owe me."

A flash of pique lit the planeswalker's eyes. She seemed both angered and amused.

"What debt could I possibly owe you?"

"You needed a savior for your people of Llanowar, and you made me that savior. You made me what I was not—your scion—that your people might be saved. As you have made me your son, I claim you as my mother. As you have used me to save your people, I claim the right to use you to save mine."

"Use me?" she echoed.

He could not tell if his statement flattered or infuriated her. "Or perhaps you haven't the power. . . ."

"Haven't the power?" she repeated irritably. "Do you know that once I cast a spell to turn back the eternal ice? Once I freed the whole world from the grip of winter?"

Eladamri smiled, knowing he had her. "Then it would be a simple thing for you to cast the same protection over this single forest."

All the amusement was gone from her features. "You presume too much, Elfchild. You are wrong to think that I would be indebted to you or to anyone. You are wrong to believe that you could use me. You are wrong to suppose that being my scion was a duty rather than a privilege."

His head bowed, Eladamri said, "Forgive me. . . ."

She waved away the apology. "It is the eternal burden of mothers to forgive—or so I have heard. I forgive you, Elfchild, and I will grant your request."

The air was suddenly hot and wet. The frost on armor melted and ran. Ghosts of steam settled back into the water below. The furnacelike winds of Rath moved once again among the cerema trees.

"You have saved us. You have saved us all," Eladamri said.

"I have not saved you," Freyalise said, "only protected you from the ravages of this place. Those ravages include the native warriors here—Keldon warlords. The Skyshroud Forest will be forever warded against them. But that is all I can do. You still must save yourselves. If the elves of Rath have arrived here, the Phyrexian armies have arrived as well."

"Could you ward them from the forest?" Eladamri asked.

"I cannot. They made Rath. It was their world. If you would save the Skyshroud from them, you must do it yourselves—or better yet, ally with the Keldons and do it together. After all, Eladamri, you are the Uniter." She smiled at him.

Returning the look, Eladamri asked cheekily, "Why ally with Keldons when I am the friend of a planeswalker in a mechanical combat suit?"

"Because I must return to the engine," Freyalise replied. Already, she was fading from view. "I'll remain as long as I can, but Kristina and I go for a worse fight." All that remained now were her eyes and lips. "You have quite a fight before you."

CHAPTER 5
Of Metathran and Merfolk

Sea winds hurled back Agnate's silvery hair. Waves parted around his feet and rolled in dual wakes out behind him. In one blue-skinned hand, he held his power-stone pike. In the other, he clutched a long pair of reins, woven from kelp. The reins extended taut down into the turbid sea and attached to a pair of harnesses. The greater dolphins that wore the harnesses swam in precise synchrony beneath the glinting tides. Agnate stood upon their backs. All around him, his Metathran army rode the glorious beasts. They and Gerrard's Benalish irregulars and Voda merfolk surged toward the main isle of Urborg.

It felt great to be in battle again.

The fight for the outer isle had not been a battle but a slaughter. The Phyrexians had stood as if in a trance as Agnate and his Metathran army clove their heads. No adversary should die that

43

way, but Agnate had been ordered to take the isle. With the help of *Weatherlight* and the titan engines, he had. It had been a military necessity to win an Urborgan beachhead from which the true battle could be launched.

"Prepare for landing!" Agnate shouted. He lifted high his powerstone pike. Corded muscles rippled beneath his shoulder tattoos.

Behind him, forty thousand other weapons rose—battle axes, swords, maces, tridents. As metal filled the air, so did a battle cry. It was a deep and pure sound from countless throats, queer like the drone of war pipes. It echoed from the shimmering sea and mixed with roaring billows.

Another call answered beneath the waves. Leviathan songs bellowed through the deeps. Grampuses and cachalots twined their mournful howls. Humpbacks and rorquals added angry shrieks. Porpoise whistles and dolphin clicks, sea cow moans and otter growls—every denizen of the deep came in company of their rulers, the Vodalian merfolk.

Not only did sea creatures bear forward the amphibious assault, but they also prepared the shore. Any Phyrexian who strayed too near the sea was dragged below by tentacles and ripped apart by fangs. In saltwater marshes lurked lightning eels. In freshwater streams flashed schools of piranha. Swordfish and hammerheads and rays made certain Agnate and his troops could come to ground at a run and drive far inland. In their wake would rise the conch-armored Vodalian warriors, who would hold the beaches.

While the music of the deep played beneath Metathran feet, another song swelled the skies. *Weatherlight* was the chorus master. From extreme distance, she sang among the clouds. Her fluted figurehead piped shrilly. Her ray cannons moaned. All around her, lesser craft made their own music. Helionaut rotors drummed the heavens. Jump-ships coursed on keening wings.

The whole world rushed to purge Urborg of Phyrexians.

Agnate raised a cheer as *Weatherlight* roared by low overhead. Cyclones churned the water in her wake. Her gunwales blazed. Energy melted Phyrexians in their trenches. It ripped out gun embankments even before they could hurl flack. *Weatherlight* shot over the shore and strafed the swamps. Her aerial armada flanked her. Helionauts peppered the woods with exploding quarrels. Jump-ships wove among trees and flushed monsters from hiding.

"Charge!" Agnate shouted.

The Metathran's turn had come. On dolphin back, they surged to shore. Sand churned in the water as grampuses and cachalots beached themselves. Blue warriors leaped from their backs and ran up the berm. No Phyrexians stood on the beach, slain already by sea monsters or the aerial assault. In the swampy wood beyond, though, they were thick.

Powerstone pike before him, Agnate charged through a curtain of moss. In the darkness, something leaped toward him. His pike smashed into it. The blade chewed its way through flesh. Agnate had only a moment to glimpse the creature—a scab-skinned warrior with horns protruding from shoulders and skull—before the dead thing fell against him. He let go of his pike—it would eat its way through the shuddering corpse—and drew the battle axe from his belt.

One sloshing step deeper into the wood, and the axe cleft through the head of another monster. It had been a goat-skulled thing. Now it was only a warm mass in the swamp. In the follow-through of his swing, Agnate stooped to snatch up his powerstone pike. He glimpsed a huge and leathery fist falling on him. He set his pike in the muck.

The fist descended like a hammer. Agnate sank down away from it. His pike rammed between scaly knuckles. It ate through the flesh stretched there and burrowed upward. With a shriek, the monster hauled its bloodied hand away. Only then did Agnate see what it was.

The gargantua reared up between the trees. It was a meaty beast, twice the height of a mammoth and eight times the bulk.

J. Robert King

On two hulking talons it stood, its belly scales drawn tight in a shriek of agony. It clutched its wounded fist and bellowed through fangs.

The gargantua was a mountainous monster, and mountains were meant for climbing.

Agnate swung his axe like a pick, chunking a foothold in the monster's leg. He stepped onto the broad blade and flung himself upward. One hand grasped the leathery wattle beneath the beast's throat. The other yanked the axe from the creature's leg.

With its healthy claw, the gargantua reached up and grabbed the Metathran commander. Its fingers flexed around him. In moments, his macerated flesh would spew out between those claws. . . .

Agnate clutched his axe beside him. The blade bit through the gargantua's scale and muscle, down to tendons. They snapped like cables under pressure. Hot oil gushed over Agnate. The beast's claws went slack. Agnate slipped downward.

The gargantua wasn't through with him. Between its injured hands, it caught him. Though claws dangled limply from its palms, the pressure of those arms was inescapable. The gargantua lifted its captive to its fangy mouth.

Agnate struggled to yank his axe free, but it was pinned at his side. Noxious breath billowed over him. He kicked furiously, trying to escape. It was no use.

The gargantua's jaws dropped open. It shoved its prey within. Fangs shuddered. Blood gushed hot up the beast's throat and out across Agnate. It was not his blood but the Phyrexian's.

Suddenly free, Agnate hurled himself from the beast's jaws. He fell toward the swamp, not even trying to get his feet beneath him. As he plunged, he saw a gaping hole in the beast's chest, and he knew what had happened. The powerstone pike had eaten its way down the arm of the beast and out the elbow. It had jutted out only to pierce the monster's chest. In moments, the pike had chewed into the gigantic heart of the thing. It died where it stood, its own oil-blood gushing up its neck.

Planeshift

Agnate landed on his back in the swamp. Gripping his
axe, he got his feet beneath him and lunged away—only just
in time.

The gargantua fell like a tree. Wind rushed up around it,
escaping the enormous bulk. It struck the swamp with a huge
splash and sank into the deep muck. A gassy sound came as
it settled.

Struggling out of the mud, Agnate fetched up against a tree.
All around him, Metathran ran onward through the swamp.
They fought and felled Phyrexians.

A rattling sound came from the back of the gargantua. The
powerstone pike that had killed it dug its way out the spine.

Agnate shoved away from the tree, hung his axe from his belt,
and strode to the fallen beast. He climbed onto the island of its
hunched back and grabbed his pike.

Through torn curtains of moss, Agnate glimpsed merfolk warriors on the sand. Seawater streamed from their chitinous armor.
They walked on fins transformed into legs. In their hands, they
held wickedly barbed tridents. Some had killed Phyrexians
already and hurled their bodies to the sharks.

"Good," Agnate huffed as he strode down the length of the
gargantua. There was no point advancing unless the rear was
secure. Flinging mud and blood from his arms, he loped forward
through the marsh.

The initial fury of the charge was gone. Now all that
remained was grim-jawed killing.

A Phyrexian scuta, seeming a giant horseshoe crab, scuttled
through the marsh toward him. Water churned off its black skull
shield. A once-human face stretched absurdly over that contorted bone. Two long, barbed legs lashed out. One grasped
Agnate's thigh. It yanked, intent on pulling him beneath its
shell. No man dragged there would ever emerge.

With a single swipe of his axe, Agnate severed the first limb
and leaped over the other. A mud-slick boot caught on the
brow ridge of the beast. Agnate vaulted to the creature's back.

He heaved the axe down overhead. It cracked the shell and bit shallowly into the brain. Agnate hauled sideways on the haft and cracked the wound wider.

The scuta bucked, struggling to throw him off.

Agnate yanked his axe free, hauled it high, and buried its head in the same wound. The cut went deep this time, severing a critical nerve nexus. The scuta slumped in the swamp.

Agnate leaped from its back. His powerstone pike was tucked under one arm, and his axe swung overhead. He ran onward. Mud sucked at his boots but couldn't slow him. No foes moved among the trees ahead. Glistening-oil gleamed in rainbows atop the swamp water, and Phyrexian corpses littered the ground. There were plenty of blue-skinned corpses there too, but the Metathran had won this swamp.

With a high-pitched whistle, Agnate signaled the merfolk to advance and hold the terrain. Meanwhile, he and his troops charged onward.

The ground rose. The dead trees fell away. Reeds crowded the banks of the wetlands. Agnate labored through them into a true jungle. Though other Metathran had gone before him, hacking at the man-sized leaves and thick green stalks, the brake was still a visual wall. The shouts and screams ahead told of a fierce battle in the wood.

At a full run, Agnate chopped away a thorn vine that barred his path. He plunged from the relative cool of the swamp into the steam heat of the jungle. His second stride flushed a swarm of mosquitoes from the undergrowth. In moments, they covered every inch of his exposed flesh. Only the mud saved him. He rubbed his face. His hand came away slick with his own blood.

Just ahead, the line of charge had stalled. The Phyrexians were making a stand—a suicidal stand against this many Metathran. They wanted to channel the advance, but why?

Whistling a complex signal to the Metathran with him, Agnate hung his battle axe on his belt and slung the powerstone pike over his shoulder. Then he took to the trees. He climbed. It was the unenviable limitation of most warriors to think only in two dimensions. Agnate and his brethren had been trained to battle in three. Like a troop of arboreal primates, they clambered up the green stalks all around.

Quickly, the roar of battle dropped away below them. The vines provided natural ropes, reaching to the first canopy. Tree to tree, the Metathran advanced. It was another world up there, a battlefield the Phyrexians had ignored. Unopposed and unnoticed, Agnate and a scant dozen others picked their way over the battle lines.

Below them, the fight was ferocious. To one side crowded the scaly and scabrous hordes of Phyrexia—to the other the blue muscles of the Metathran. Where the two sides met, blade and claw tore flesh from limbs. Bodies mounded. Already the dead lay in a broad U shape, with more and more Metathran flooding into the center.

Agnate hurled himself across empty air to a tree beyond the battle line. Scaling to its upper crotch, he ran out along a thick bough and leaped to an adjacent tree. Ahead the boles dwindled into a swamp—broader, deeper, more horrid than the first. Not even dead trees stood in the black water. Nothing wholesome could live in this slough. Nothing lived—but much had died. The air was rank with the gases of decay. Giant flies swarmed above bubbling pockets. Skeletal figures lay in the brackish water.

"Channeling us toward a swamp?" Agnate wondered to himself. Then he saw why.

In the center of that putrid swamp circled three grotesque figures. They had once been Metathran and still walked upright, but there the similarity ended. In place of feet they stood on scabby stumps. In place of hands they had vicious claws. Their heads had been flayed of skin and jutted forward on long, grotesque necks. Where the necks joined their shoulders, a great mass of pulsing matter sprouted. The stuff was barely contained within a sac of veins and membranes. Agnate had been trained to know what those globular spores were and what these creatures were bred to do.

"Plague spreaders," he hissed.

These poor souls had been turned into living colonies of contagion. Their brain stems were infected with a strain of plague that formed an unwholesome pocket of spores. Blood vessels and support structures grew to nourish the pestilence. When fully ripened, the membranes would split. Wind would carry the contagion out to slay any Metathran for miles around.

That's why Agnate's army was being channeled to this swamp—so that it could be decimated in one stroke. In moments the Metathran would break through the wall of Phyrexians and rush to their doom.

It was a clever trap, but Agnate was a clever mouse. Signaling to his troops to remain where they were, Agnate climbed down the tree. The stench of the swamp grew more potent as he descended. At ground level it was nearly unbearable. He crept to the bank of the marsh and knelt. From his belt, he produced flint and steel. They were the only weapons he needed.

Leaning above the fetid waters, he struck the metal against the stone. A single spark leaped away. It twisted in a bright spiral down toward the water. The spark grew. It ignited the thick swamp gas. Blue fire swelled outward. In a moment, the whole swamp went up. From where Agnate stood to the far shore, it all erupted in azure flame. The heat flashed away his silver hair. The roar hurled him back against a tree. He struck it and fell, but as he did, he saw the three plague spreaders riling in agony. One of the amazing properties of glistening-oil was that, when heated to a sufficient degree, it became extremely volatile.

Three blinding flashes burst into being in the center of that blue flame. In the afterimage burned into Agnate's mind, he saw the plague spreaders' skeletons still standing, all blood, all flesh, all plague burned away.

Agnate rolled to his knees, catching his breath. His folk would break through any moment. He would need to be ready to lead them on. Standing, he drew his battle axe and whistled his warriors to him.

CHAPTER 6
The Dragons Primeval

As the overlay began, Rhammidarigaaz, lord of the dragon nations, roared a warning into the charnel skies of Koilos. Phyrexians were coming. His wings spread upon the hot winds. Powerful legs hurled him aloft. Muscles surged. The great serpent rose patiently skyward. Leathery skin caught the broiling air and flung it down in twin cyclones.

The rest of the dragon nations followed. The dragons of Shiv, Darigaaz's own volcanic breed, were first to launch themselves in the wake of their lord. After them leaped the dragons of ancient Argive, alabaster creatures that were more at home among clouds than sand. Like predators after prey, the swamp dragons followed. Their black scales glimmered in the storm of dust, and their eyes gleamed blacker still. The serpents of the forest lunged upward next and spread their cobra cowls out to catch the wind. Last of all, the sea dragons, who languished in this desert heat, vaulted toward hints of blue.

It was an awesome spectacle. These thousand dragons were the greatest warriors of the wide-flung dragon nations. They spiraled into the sky above human and Metathran and elf allies, above Phyrexian foes.

On the horizon, Phyrexian dragon engines approached. They were merely glints of metal now but in moments would tear apart their fleshly kin.

Darigaaz and his folk would fight fiercely but would die today.

It is a shameful thing you have done, Rhammidarigaaz, said a voice that coiled through his head, *shameful to bring the dragon nations to the desert to be slain.*

Even as he labored higher, Darigaaz glimpsed who it was that spoke—a god among dragons. Tevash Szat. He lingered below in his jet-black titan suit. Of the nine engines, his was the most draconic, with a fangy head, scaly armor, and barbed tail. Urza had designed the suit especially for the reptilian planeswalker, but the longer Szat inhabited the machine, the more he mutated it.

Darigaaz returned the thought. *You too have come here, Tevash Szat, to die in the desert.*

I never go anywhere to die.

Neither did we, Darigaaz replied. *We came to fight for our world.*

Szat was snide. *Your world? You do not fight for your world. You fight for a mortal world, a world of humans and elves and dwarfs and minotaurs.* A sadness entered the planeswalker's thoughts. *Dominaria has not been our world for ages of ages.*

I haven't time for wordplay, Darigaaz thought as he reached the peak of his climb. *I have a war to win.*

I agree. Let us be done with word games and begin our war.

Bolts of black power emanated from the titan engine and ripped the air all about Darigaaz and his flying folk. The energy literally tore the sky open. Through rents in reality, an unreal world of chaos shapes and hissing forms appeared. The tears grew wider. They joined. Holes opened in the sky. Serpents banked to escape the shredding reality, but the disintegration was too rapid. The beasts flew into chaos.

Just before the last tatter of sky disappeared, Tevash Szat in his ebony engine leaped in among them.

Darigaaz knew this place. The Blind Eternities was Urza's name for it. To Darigaaz it always had seemed the formless albumen of an egg, the seeming nothing out of which scale and claw, heart and brain would take shape.

I know your thoughts, Darigaaz, that these folk are your folk. I know your heart, Darigaaz, better than you know it yourself.

Why do you take us from battle?

I take you to a truer battle, to one you must win.

Suddenly, the Blind Eternities congealed into a coastal range of volcanic mountains. Lava pumped from dozens of cones. Steam and sulfur jetted into yellow clouds. Basalt channeled molten rock into the sea. Ash made false ground above boiling calderas. Obsidian glinted like glassy jewels in black hillsides.

The place had all the sights and smells of Darigaaz's homeland, Shiv, but nowhere in Shiv were there sheer cliffs beside the sea. Nowhere did the ocean cut so long and perfect an arc into the land. It was as though a gigantic spoon had scooped out a precise hunk of land, letting the sea flow into the space.

The dragon nations circled in confusion above the strange spot.

Here is where you must begin your true war, Darigaaz. Battle for your home.

This is not my home, Darigaaz replied.

Look again. This is what is left of your home, of Shiv, after Teferi took what he wished.

Teferi, yes. Knowing of the coming invasion, the planeswalker Teferi had phased out most of the lands of Shiv—the mana rig, the tribal territories of the Ghitu, and even many of the dragon kingdoms. This was all that remained. Down there, among those sea-shorn mountains, was Darigaaz's own aerie. This place *was* his home.

Teferi was wise, came the mind of Tevash Szat. His titan engine floated effortlessly in the midst of the circling beasts. *A hundred thousand Phyrexians just now are shark food. Their portion of Rath overlaid not on land but in sea. But there are tens of thousands of others that ravage your homelands, Rhammidarigaaz. Will you let them destroy it, or will you fight for dragons as you have fought for mortals?*

Only then did Darigaaz truly see. Figures marched across shoulders of pumice. They trooped like ants over crater rims and swarmed the boulder piles where goblins dwelt. They climbed cave walls to kill Viashino mystics. They marched up lava tubes to slaughter the dragon enclaves within.

Roaring again in command, Darigaaz led his folk in a long dive toward the land. The Shivan dragons soared with alacrity behind him. The others—this was not their home—hesitated. A glare from Szat sent them after their brethren.

Darigaaz angled down toward a column of Phyrexians. They marched across a narrow isthmus between two boiling seas of magma. At the far end of the land bridge lay a Viashino village. There Phyrexians slew lizard men with impunity. But not for long.

Darigaaz dived. His wings rattled with the searing wind. The pendants at his neck sparked scarlet energy. He gathered spells for the coming assault. In the elder dragon's wake, a score more of his folk sliced the air. Wind whistled from their scales. Their mouths gaped in exertion. Between spiky teeth glowed the fires they stoked in their bellies.

The Phyrexian column turned to look upward. They saw. Some stood their ground. Others stumbled back and fell from the sides of the isthmus. They plunged into the magma seas and their blood ignited immediately. Blue flames lined the land bridge. The rest of the column bolted for the Viashino village.

They wouldn't reach it.

Rhammidarigaaz swept low over their heads. From his mouth poured killing fire. It mantled the fleeing monsters. One by one, like corn popping, they burst into flame. More ignited in a chain of azure. Black shells split to gush white innards.

Nearing the domed huts of the Viashino village, Darigaaz spoke an incantation. Power coalesced in the pendants around his neck. It shot out to the cuffs of his wrists and into clawed fingertips. Crimson beams stabbed downward. With utter precision, they found their targets. A Phyrexian trooper was torn in half while the lizard man beside him was spared. A mogg goblin turned to ash that sifted harmlessly onto two Viashino hatchlings. A slasher engine melted, its scythe arm unable to catch a fleeing elder.

Darigaaz came to ground at a run. He folded his wings and clutched up a scuta in each hand. They seemed only pill bugs, and then not even that. He flung the crumpled bodies away and thundered forward to where monsters ripped apart the village elders.

Lizard blood and hunks of skin bounded through the air. The Phyrexians snapped up what they could in greedy jaws, but most of the meat draped the stony dwellings. The monsters turned to find new victims.

Instead they found Darigaaz. He crushed two with his pounding feet and two more with his gory hands and another dozen with a powerful swipe of his tail.

Other Shivan dragons set to ground in the village and fought murderously. The rest of the dragon nations soared onward to defend a goblin village nearby.

Rhammidarigaaz had killed ten more Phyrexians before he heard Szat's voice again in his mind. *Don't waste your fire on such lowly beasts. Your own folk languish.*

Darigaaz lifted his head above the stone domes. Szat stood at the base of a distant volcano, beside a huge lava tube. A quick glance around the Viashino village told Darigaaz that most of the Phyrexians were dead. Those that remained could be dispatched by the lizard men. He roared once, summoning his folk, and leaped skyward.

Their wings cast huge shadows on the village as they ascended. Leathery skin barked in the air and then took hold. Darigaaz and seven other Shivan dragons shot above rumpled ground and glided down toward the lava tube where Tevash Szat waited.

This is no dragon nest, Darigaaz thought. *There are no signs of claw marks, no wards against entry. Why do you bring us here? What is within?*

Everything is within. I will lead the way. The titan engine turned toward the lava tube and climbed within. The cave was so huge that his horn-mantled head did not even scrape the ceiling.

Darigaaz landed on the cooled flow beneath the tube and ascended behind Szat. Seven other fire dragons followed.

Already, Szat fought. Rockets shot from the wrists of the suit and hissed into the dark. Spiraling trails of smoke followed them. One by one, they impacted the floor of the tube. Light flared, and bodies tumbled. The sudden glare reflected from countless scaly backs.

Phyrexians swarmed ahead. They seemed roaches clambering away.

Fireballs rolled from the titan engine. They ignited some beasts and baked others in their shells, but there were too many. Those that roasted fell away, revealing more monsters beneath.

Why are they so thick here? Darigaaz wondered.

You will see. Szat overtook the Phyrexians, trampling them down.

Those that escaped his claws remained for Darigaaz and the others. With flaming breath and stomping talons and crushing claws they massacred the beasts. The air reeked with the smell of burning flesh.

Szat reached the large chamber at the top of the tube. There a broad cavern opened. Within it, Szat unleashed his whole arsenal of destruction. Falcon engines shrieked from coops in his back and impacted and shredded Phyrexians. Ray cannons blasted from his wrists and scored the floors and walls of the chamber. Lightning spells leaped from the observation portals that served the engine as eyes. Hands hurled beasts against the walls, feet stomped them to the floor, tail swept them away.

When Darigaaz and his folk reached the chamber, they joined in the killing frenzy. In moments all the Phyrexians were dead. Smoke curled to the black vault. Bodies littered the filthy floor. The stench of burnt flesh was everywhere.

The fire dragons stood panting in the darkness. Only Szat moved. His titan engine shifted, settling on its joints. Suddenly, one more dragon appeared in the cave—Szat in his favored form.

He was a huge black beast, his skull crested with a forest of horns. At his neck those horns gave way to quills, which bristled down shoulders and wings and spine. On all fours, he paced. His nostrils billowed soot, and his claws raked furrows in the stone.

"Too late," hissed the ebony serpent. "Too late."

Darigaaz spoke for all of them. "Too late for what?"

Szat's eyes blazed. His pupils were vertical slits. "Too late to raise the Primeval." He flung a wing back behind him, drawing it away like a curtain from a stage.

There, upon one wall of the chamber hung a relief carving of a Shivan dragon. The figure was flattened unaesthetically, its details rudely rendered. To these original faults, the Phyrexians had added some of their own. Their claw marks covered the figure. Drills had riddled its head and breast with holes.

Darigaaz walked reverently toward the desecrated frieze. He gently touched it. "Why did they destroy it?"

Szat's nostrils flared. "Before mortals had ruled the world, there had been the time of the immortals, of dragons. Dominaria was ours, divided equally among five great beasts. These rulers were the Primevals. Though separately powerful, in company their strength multiplied upon itself. Together the five Primevals were omnipotent, and their nations ruled the world.

"But the youngest of the Primevals—this very beast trapped here in the lava wall—thought to befriend mortal creatures. He was lured into an alliance with a human ruler, King Themeus. Themeus pretended at friendship, though he really meant only to destroy dragonkind. With his fire mages, Themeus tricked the Primeval to this spot and awakened the volcano to engulf him in stone."

Staring at the figure entombed in the wall, Darigaaz murmured, "It is real? It is a trapped dragon?"

"Yes. After King Themeus imprisoned this beast, he sought and trapped the other four Primevals one by one. Each conquest weakened the remaining beasts. When all five had been trapped, Themeus roused his coalition of mortals—humans and dwarfs, Viashino and elves, goblins and minotaurs. They hunted our people and slew us and shattered our eggs. We fought back, yes, but these creatures were everywhere, just like the crawling vermin here. Without the five Primevals, the dragon nations splintered and dwindled. Mortals drove us into hiding. They stole the world from us.

"But the Primevals were not truly killed. If ever the dragon nations of Dominaria could be brought again into alliance, they could reawaken the Primevals. Should all five Primevals awaken, nothing—not Phyrexian or human or elf or dwarf—could stand against them. The time of the immortals would be upon us again."

Darigaaz's heart thundered in his ears. "Why have I never heard these tales?"

Szat sneered. "No dragon nation that is friendly to humans has heard these tales. The defiant ones were killed off. You did not know these stories, but clearly the Phyrexians did." He gestured to the holes bored through the beast's brain and heart and belly. "They knew that if these Primevals were to rise, the

Phyrexian invasion would be doomed. Already the monsters have destroyed the first Primeval. They will seek to destroy the others as well." The black dragon's eyes glinted in the dark. "You must stop them."

"We can never guard four tombs—" began Darigaaz, but he realized the implication even before Szat spoke it.

"You will not guard the Primevals. You will awaken them."

CHAPTER 7

In Hateful Skies

Bold eyed, the Gaea figurehead peered from the prow of *Weatherlight* down toward Urborg.

As pestilential as the swamps had been before the battle, they were worse now. Mosquitoes and vipers were better than Phyrexians and trench worms. Bloodstocks churned ancient marshes. Gargantuas ripped through thorn brakes. Glistening-oil burned atop every pool.

The Phyrexians weren't Urborg's only ravagers. Vodalian warriors undermined the coastal marshes, joining them to the sea. Metathran mounded dead bodies on the beaches. Serran angels ripped out the bellies of Phyrexian fliers. Helionauts and hoppers sent exploding quarrels into swarms of dragon engines.

Weatherlight was the greatest despoiler of all. She tore through clouds and outran sound. Ray fire ripped from her gunwales. The heavens belonged to *Weatherlight*, and she jealously attacked any creature that dared disagree.

Ahead were the latest offenders. A flight of dragon engines shot from a vent in the volcanic hillside. They seemed lava, so hungrily they ascended. Twenty pairs of wings raked out. The serpents coiled in a broad ribbon and drove toward *Weatherlight*.

"Big mistake," Gerrard growled. Gripping the fire controls of his cannon, he leaned in the gunnery traces and shouted into the speaking tube. "Take us in at full throttle, Karn. Gunners, cut them from the air. Sisay, be ready for a ram attack and keel slam. Multani, prepare for hull burns. Orim, lock down your wounded and get ready for more." The orders emerged like cannon shot, fast and final.

The response came just as quickly. Heat flared beneath the soles of Gerrard's boots—Multani surging through the forecastle planks to reach and strengthen the Gaea ram and the keel. The ship's engines roared. The motion hurled all the gunners about, bringing their weapons to bear on the flock of dragon engines dead ahead.

"You know it's suicide. . . ." Sisay's voice came in the tube.

"What's suicide?"

"A head-on assault against twenty dragon engines."

"Yeah," Gerrard shot back, "suicide for them." He glanced over his shoulder and sent her a smile. It was not the careless grin he used to give. Something had died in his eyes. Not something but someone. "Is the mighty Captain Sisay afraid of death?"

"Not afraid of it, but neither am I eager for it."

"It's time somebody brought death to account," Gerrard said, as he faced forward. "I'm that somebody."

The distant figures swelled. Wings of leather tore the air. Living metal flashed amid clouds. Eyes glowed lanternlike. Mouths gaped with fang and fire.

Gerrard brought the crosshairs to the tongue of one beast and squeezed off a shot. Energy rushed from the nozzle. It crossed the reeling distances between ship and dragon and found its mark. The bolt splashed against that steely tongue and rammed down the beast's throat. The dragon's neck dissolved. Its head hung for a moment on the beam before melting in a metallic rain. The body lasted only a heartbeat longer. It exploded.

Tahngarth's shot was not as precise but twice as deadly. It swept through two dragon engines. The first was cross-sectioned, its chest and belly neatly sliced away from its back and wings. Sparks leaped across the severed vitals of the beast. Both hunks plunged. The second dragon dived aside to avoid the fate of its comrade. Instead of ripping through its torso, the bolt vaporized one wing. The dragon fell twisting from the sky.

That was three beasts out of twenty. The seventeen others closed on *Weatherlight*.

"Fold the airfoils!" Gerrard shouted.

With a snap, Karn complied. *Weatherlight* no longer soared on the air but rocketed through it.

Gerrard managed one more shot. It bounded free of the cannon, dead on for a dragon engine. Before it struck, though, the beast's own incendiary weapon vaulted out. Black mana met red plasma. The opposing energies ate each other away.

More black mana belched in a killing cloud before the dragons. Tahngarth and Gerrard unloaded their cannons into the deadly stuff. A thin corridor opened.

At the helm, Sisay steered into the slim passage. The Gaea figurehead plunged through clear sky. Whips of black power scourged the keel and hull. It ate the wood away in moments.

Multani surged to the affected sites and awoke new life in them.

One tendril slipped past the rail and slapped Tahngarth's arm. His white fur melted immediately. Corruption ate into skin and muscle. With a roar the minotaur flung the stuff away.

"Orim! Get up here!" Gerrard ordered.

Weatherlight punched through the black mantle and was suddenly among the roaring throng of dragons.

Gaea destroyed the first beast herself. Her hardwood brow smashed into the horned head of a dragon. Normally the titanium crest of the serpent would have shattered wood, but

Multani was in the figurehead. He bore the braining blow as an attack on his own being. He held the wood together, diamond hard.

The dragon's skull buckled over its biomechanical brain. Shards of metal cut wires and optic fibers. The dragon went limp in flight.

Even the corpse of the thing was deadly. It folded up before the surging ship and struck it like a hammer.

Gerrard and Tahngarth unleashed twin beams that vaporized much of the body. The rest grated away beneath the compromised keel.

Intent on preventing the keel from giving way, Multani drained from the figurehead down along the line of damage. Green wood swelled out where he went. He did not merely replace what had been destroyed but made it stronger, sharper. He grew a knife-edged spine directly before the keel. It proved its worth a moment later, lancing through a dragon engine and splitting it in half. The segments tumbled to either side of the keel.

"Good work, Multani!" shouted Gerrard. "Sisay, make good use of that spike."

"Way ahead of you, Commander," Sisay replied.

The prow rose suddenly, slicing the blade through the neck of a dragon engine. Its head flung over the bow rail and impacted the forecastle. Its severed neck followed, spitting sparks as it whipped past Gerrard. Head and neck bounded away. Its body meanwhile slumped brokenly off the racing hull. Three more shuddering thumps announced the deaths of three more dragon engines, chopped as if by a cleaver.

Weatherlight shot out beyond the pack of beasts. Sisay brought her hard about. Air spilled over the rail as she turned. The dragons were turning too, the eleven that remained. *Weatherlight* leaped eagerly toward the swarm.

Gerrard sprayed the heavens with ray cannon blasts. A beam struck a nearby dragon and burst over its metallic scales. Energy sank within and melted through flesh. The dragon held together one moment more before the blast dismantled it. Only wings and legs, head and tail remained to find their separate ways to ground.

Another bolt pierced a great black machine. The dragon's core went critical. Seams of white fire opened across its frame, turning it to shrapnel. The pieces tore outward to strip the scales from serpents nearby. Three more beasts spun crazily, tumbling for the ground.

"Think you're death incarnate, aye?" growled Gerrard over the roar of the falling beasts. "Well, Death, you've met your match."

He swung his cannon down and shot away the black mana breath of another beast. Energies ate each other. Gerrard followed up the shot with another. It scoured a dragon's head down to the metallic skull. Another beast lost its wings in a flare of cannon heat.

"You see that one?" Gerrard shouted over his shoulder to Tahngarth.

The minotaur stood with hooves spread on the deck, one arm deftly wielding the ray cannon and the other extended for Orim to bandage. Almost casually, he triggered a bolt of energy. It swatted a dragon engine from the air.

Weatherlight listed suddenly toward port, as if dragged down by a huge weight. The jolt swung Gerrard around. Just before him, gripping the forecastle rail, were a pair of huge metal talons. The wingless creature clutched the hull of *Weatherlight*. There was no way to blast those talons without damaging the ship herself.

Cursing, Gerrard pulled free of the gunnery traces. He raked out his sword and strode toward the spot. He would hew the conduits buried beneath those claws. . . .

The dragon lifted its head above the rail. It reeked, this metallic beast. Its enormous fangs gaped wide, and it lunged toward Gerrard. Black, tarry mana flooded up the neck to spew out.

Roaring, Gerrard rammed his blade at the scaly jaw of the beast. The sword drove through flesh and tongue and up into the creature's ribbed pallet. It pinned the mouth closed. Black mana oozed between its teeth. Ducking beneath the gush, Gerrard jammed the sword higher, into the neural core of the beast.

It pulled back. Gerrard went with it, still gripping his sword. His boots left the deck. The dragon engine arched its head, intent on hurling him away.

Gerrard swung out into the reeling sky. He held on tightly. Clouds tore around him and the impaled serpent. Below, Urborg rattled past in black quagmires. The only thing that kept Gerrard from falling was the monster he was trying to kill.

"Let's do it!" he shouted, releasing his sword and clawing his way up the dragon engine's horn-studded muzzle. He rammed his fist in its eye. Glass lenses shattered. Knuckles smudged blood across mirror arrays. "Let's go down together!"

The beast's struggles grew frantic. It pitched its head back and forth, struggling to shake off its tormentor.

"I've got a friend I want to see," Gerrard yelled as his fingers slid into the housing of the beast's other eye. "I've got things to sort out." He yanked the whole orb from its socket. Its demon glow faded to darkness. Into the dragon engine's ear, Gerrard shouted, "You could broker the deal!"

Beneath his feet, cables went slack. Scales slumped. Will left the beast. Its claws slid from the scarred rail. With an irresistible motion, the monster dropped out of the bright sky toward the blackness below.

Gerrard felt the beast pull away beneath him. He held on tight. Dead trees and stagnant waters flashed in his wide eyes. "Let's do this."

Something struck his shoulder, something that burned like cold iron in his back and burst in a bloody rose out his front. Barbs spread, gripping flesh and muscle and bone. Gerrard roared, his hands releasing the dragon engine and gripping the end of the impaling thing. It yanked brutally on him. He rose, away from the plunging carcass.

The dragon fell to the treetops. A cypress speared the body. It broke free and rolled, flinging water. Limbs, head, and tail were all uniformly crushed around it.

Gerrard saw no more. The weapon that had torn through his shoulder was attached to one of *Weatherlight's* lines. Gerrard had been hooked like a fish. Winds shoved him up beneath the ship's hull, near her saw-toothed keel. It didn't matter. He was prepared to die. He was eager to appear before whatever lord ruled the dead and join his love, his Hanna.

The rope dragged him fore. Someone had other plans for him.

Thumping against the gunwales, Gerrard left crimson spots on the boards. His hands hung limply at his sides. The rope tugged. He slid up alongside the massive figurehead of Gaea. Hair mantled her shoulders and her ancient face. Her body was both maidenly and matronly. Out of hardwood eyes gazed a sad and familiar countenance.

The figurehead spoke, "What are you trying to do, Gerrard?"

"Multani," the man gasped through gritted teeth. Once this nature spirit had instructed him in maro-sorcery.

"Are you trying to kill yourself?" the voice asked.

The rope yanked him higher. Gerrard's back arched in agony, and his shoulder traced a bloody line across Gaea's face.

"No," he managed. "I'm defying death. I'm cheating it. I'm beating it. I'm showing it I am a forced to be reckoned with."

"Why?"

"Because if I can beat it, I can win Hanna back."

The conversation ended with a rough tug of the line. Gerrard surged up over the rail and landed on his side on the forecastle planks.

Above him towered Tahngarth, who was wrapped in rope like a living capstan. Even with one arm injured, he'd had the strength to hurl a harpoon, hold its line, and draw Gerrard in by winding the rope about himself.

Orim was there too. The healer knelt above him. The coins in her hair flashed above worried eyes.

"You boys and your rescues," she said. Expert fingers worked the harpoon head from its shaft. With one mercifully fast motion, she pulled the head through the gouge. "One of these days, I'll not be able to patch you back up." Her hands settled on the wound, and silver fire awoke.

Tahngarth shrugged out of his rope wrappings, his own arm bandaged beneath. He lifted an eloquent eyebrow.

"If I remember, Commander, you saved me in much the same way from Tsabo Tavoc." He reached up to his own shoulder and tapped a star-shaped scar. "We're blood brothers now. Whatever happens to you happens to me."

Gerrard wore a grim expression. "You've gotten the worse end of that deal, I fear."

CHAPTER 8

In Company of Titans

The others were supposed to be here. The instructions had been simple: Deliver the armies where they were to go—Urborg, Keld, Shiv—and then report to Tolaria. Still, Urza, in his titan engine, was the only one who had arrived.

On a smooth ridge of stone, the engine stood like a dejected boy. Its three-toed feet fidgeted. Hydraulic muscles moaned. Metallic hands, with their ray cannons and flame throwers, hung limp beside massive hip joints. The thousand weapons that bristled across the torso of the titan suit were still and silent. Even the engine's shoulders—large enough to hoist a hillside—slumped. The command pod was darkest of all. In it, Urza sat. He stared at his ruined home.

Tolaria had once been beautiful. In his mind's eye, Urza could still see it. Blue-tiled roofs blended with the sky. Domed observatories stood above K'rrik's rift. Crowded dormitories spread out beneath a canopy of leaves. Laboratories and lecture halls, archives and artifact museums—it had been quite a place.

Now all of it was gone. Urza had melted down the old engines, had burned the old plans, had shipped away all the students and scholars he could. He had given the place over to the Phyrexians. It was a diversion to keep them busy while he won the war elsewhere.

Mage Master Barrin had not given it over. Barrin, who for a thousand years had been Urza's associate and only true friend, had always been sentimental. Tolaria held the grave of his wife, Rayne, and his daughter, Hanna. It was hallowed ground, worth defending to the death. Tolaria had became his grave as well.

He had destroyed it all. He had cast a spell to shatter plague engines and kill every Phyrexian on the isle. The sorcery also had leveled forests and razed buildings and melted mountains. It had destroyed the elaborate network of time rifts and covered the whole of the island in a molten cap. Barrin had used himself to power that spell. He who had spent his life humanizing the planeswalker died in a spell that mimicked Urza's atrocity at Argoth.

"Oh, Barrin," Urza said. His breath wisped out within the pilot bulb of his titan engine. He did not have to breathe. His body was only a locus of his mind, a convenience that anchored his spirit, but mention of that name, Barrin, cut all anchors on Urza's soul.

He was outside his titan suit without having consciously willed it. Urza sat on the foot of the engine. The salt air was hot in his lungs. Without trees or hills to stop it, ocean winds tore across the isle. They rifled through Urza's war robes and tossed his ash-blond hair.

"Barrin."

Suddenly another titan engine stood before him. It was a green and riotous thing, designed in part by Multani and further modified by its occupant. She had made it a veritable garden, planting countless living components within its metallic structure. The asymmetric machine held an asymmetric soul.

"Hello, Urza," said Freyalise, materializing beside him.

She wore her usual getup, savage-shorn blonde hair, a half-goggle over one eye, a floral tattoo over the other, and a shift of twining vines. Her slender legs hovered just above the ground, which was how she preferred it. Freyalise and Urza were utter opposites. The Ice Age begun by Urza's sylex blast was ended by Freyalise's World-Spell—just as catastrophically. These two planeswalkers were so opposite, they were nearly the same.

Eschewing both her floating stance and her longtime antagonism toward Urza, Freyalise seated herself beside her brooding comrade.

"Nice place you've got here, Planeswalker."

"Has Eladamri rejoined his Skyshroud elves?"

She nodded, a lock of blonde hair raking across her eyes. "I even saved the forest from icy Keld." She examined her nails and rubbed them on her shift. "He's one lucky elfchild."

Urza nodded absently. "What of the Keldons?"

She shrugged. "They made a couple assaults on the forest and figured out it was warded. They called for parley with 'the King of Elves.' Parley for Keldons means a fight. You know their motto—'prove it.'"

"Yes. Barrin had had quite a time winning their trust—especially after kicking them out of Jamuraa." He shook his head, smiling bleakly at the memory.

Freyalise stared levelly at Urza. "So that's what this mood is all about?"

"How did Eladamri fare?" Urza said, changing the subject.

Lifting her eyebrows, Freyalise said, "Eladamri acquitted himself well. Of course it helped when I showed up in my titan engine. The Keldons have a big thing for titans. It's part of their Twilight mythology."

Before Urza could form a response, another titan engine appeared.

This one seemed a dignified statue in white. Tall, stately, and decorous, the Thran-metal frame of the engine was covered in smooth shields. They could deflect gouts of mana, plague winds, and plasma blasts. Within those shields lurked subtle deadliness—ray cannon slots and rocket launchers. The control dome had a white sheen as well, like a cataractous eye, and the figure within the shell shuddered in irritation as he released his straps. Steam shushed from air brakes, and the engine settled angrily.

The planeswalker pilot emerged—Commodore Guff. He wore a crimson waistcoat and slim knickers above creamy stockings. His hair and beard were a red that perfectly matched the clothes he wore, and a foggy monocle was clutched in one eye. He stared at a book—Urza's instruction manual for his titan engine.

"Where's the blasted exhaust system for the pilot capsule?" He paged through the book. "I'm fogged in! Give me a touch of the wind, and I'd damn well be doomed!"

"Page sixteen-B," Urza replied.

"Is that the entry for wind or for exhaust?" Freyalise asked.

"What's the difference?" Urza muttered.

"And what's this sixteen-B, sixteen-C business?" huffed Commodore Guff. His monocle dropped from his eye and swayed on its chain. The condensation on the lens wiped on his waistcoat. "You know, I have ten hundred trillion histories in my personal collection, and not a one of them has a sixteen-B?"

"I'm an artificer, not a writer," Urza said wearily. "Ten hundred trillion? Haven't you ever had to number them with As and Bs?"

Commodore Guff spluttered. "No need to number them." He jabbed a finger to his rumpled temple. "Encyclopedic, my lad. Encyclopedic." He blinked, seeming to realize that his monocle was gone. He patted the pockets of his waistcoat and began swearing violently. "Must've fallen out in damned Urborg. Filthy rutting lich lord bastards."

"Rutting lich lord bastards?" echoed Freyalise.

Commodore Guff found the monocle dangling before his knickers and lifted it to his eye. "Has Bo Levar arrived yet?"

"My Lady," Bo Levar said, appearing out of nowhere to bow before Freyalise. He was a sandy-haired young pirate with a mustache and goatee and a dangerous twinkle in his eyes. Clenched in white teeth was a fine cigar, emitting a thin blue coil of smoke. He managed to smile around it. "Gents?" Instead of bowing to Urza and Commodore Guff, he tapped the breast pocket of his tunic where a few more smokes waited.

Urza waved away the invitation.

Commodore Guff quickly skimmed the instructions for exhausting the pilot capsule and nodded. "Thank you very much, indeed."

Flipping a cigar to the commodore, Bo Levar said, "It's the only thing that cut the stink of Urborg." He waved over his shoulder to his titan engine. Swamp muck coated the mechanism's legs. The blue torso of the machine was spattered in mud, and its articulated joints were jammed with strange weeds.

Urza gaped. "What did you do with it?"

Bo Levar smiled. "There was a field of wild tobacco—"

"Oh, you didn't—"

"Look who's here!" Bo Levar said. "It's Kristina and Taysir. I didn't think they were still an item."

"They aren't," Freyalise replied. "Daria is with them."

The three new arrivals seemed a family—Taysir the patriarch in white beard and multicolored robes, Kristina the wise and mysterious mother, and Daria the wide-eyed and sassy young woman. Their titan engines were similarly tailored to their personalities. Taysir's seemed an ancient and solemn statue, Kristina's a powerful machine built to bear oppressive burdens, and Daria's an engine so lithe it could dance untouched among lightning bolts.

Dark haired and grinning, Daria bounded toward Freyalise. "Heard you had to go to Keld. Ugh. Still, it's better than Urborg. Leeches and liches."

"Rutting lich lord bastards," Freyalise said, hugging her young protégé.

"I wish I could've gone with you," Daria said.

Freyalise nodded. "Soon enough we'll all be heading to a place worse than Urborg or Keld."

Daria rolled her eyes. "I know. Phyrexia. Ought to be a blast."

"Exactly," Urza said. "With the mana bombs you have and the implosion devices we will take from the fourth level, it'll be a blast."

The final two planeswalkers arrived.

The first had long been a resident of much-maligned Urborg, though he was no swamp-water snake. The panther warrior Lord Windgrace had lived on that isle when it had been a jungle mountaintop—before Argoth had sunk it. Though his land had died, Windgrace had remained. Though undead arose, Windgrace fought for the living. He remembered what Urborg had been and hoped to return it to its former state. On feline pads, he stalked into the midst of the company. At times, Windgrace took a humanlike form, or an amalgam between panther and man, but this day he went on all fours. His tawny titan engine was similarly equipped to stalk or stand, according to the will of its master.

Last of all was the black dragon Szat. His horn-headed engine appeared among the others, and his sinewy bulk paced impatiently.

"When do we start, Planeswalker?"

Without standing, Urza sighed. "Momentarily. You all know the objectives. You all know your engines. Stay within them. The caustic environs of Phyrexia can dissolve even us. Now, suit up, and we fight."

Next moment, he alone sat at the foot of his titan engine. Then even Urza was gone.

He materialized within the piloting harness of his titan suit. It was formfitted—with motor gauntlets for hands, battle boots for feet, and a sensor helm for his head. Every fiber of the suit responded to each impulse of his body. Urza felt the machine awakening around him. His senses extended into what had once been numb metal. All around, the other titans powered up.

In addition to mechanical armaments, each of the nine titans also wielded magic and the arsenals of planeswalkers. Perhaps they should have been called dreadnoughts, for they had nothing to fear.

Pivoting into formation with the other machines, Urza signaled them. As one, they 'walked.

The glassy ground of Tolaria vanished. There was no time spent in the Blind Eternities. Planeswalkers could step from world to world as children step stone to stone. Besides, they had plenty of work to do.

Tolaria was gone. A new, verdant land opened before them. Primeval forests spread thickly to glimmering lakes. Rugged mountains crouched on the horizon beneath a sunless sky. Gray clouds, pregnant with rain, streaked the red heavens. In gleaming waters waded dragon engines. Not scabrous fighting machines, these were living beasts—wild and free.

It was a beautiful, bountiful world. Urza staggered a bit to look at it. How could Yawgmoth rule such loveliness? Urza had fought in the inner spheres—nightmare landscapes—but he had never stopped to admire the first sphere. It was a dream. His brother had come here and told of its glories. . . .

Mishra. He had always been the dreamer, the man who loved tales around the campfire. If Urza had seen this place too, had been with Mishra that day, maybe there would never have been a war. Maybe Mishra would live on.

Mishra . . . Barrin . . . Xantcha . . .

Hey, Urza, take a breath, there, came the voice of Bo Levar in his mind. *Are we going to do this or not?*

Within his titan suit, Urza blinked. He breathed. His thoughts slowly cleared. *Yes, of course. Beyond that brake of forest is the city of Gamalgoth, first metropolis of Phyrexia. In it lie conduits that reach throughout the first sphere. There, we begin.*

The joints of his titan engine felt stiff as he stepped toward the city. His foot struck the world like a mallet on a drum. Dust rolled up in clouds from that impact. In the dust were bits of metal. It was the ubiquitous component of this world. Metal in the soil, metal in the water, metal in the air. Another step and Urza began to run.

The other nine engines thundered after him.

Five more enormous strides brought Urza to the trees. Powerstone arrays imbedded in his helm optically enhanced the leaves, showing them to be living metal—veins like inlay and flesh like foil. That realization made the world only more beautiful. It was the dream of artificers to build a machine that lived. It was the dream of bioengineers to grow a creature out of metal. Here, on the first sphere of his world, Yawgmoth had again and again fulfilled the dream of ages. To destroy this world would be like burning a library. Urza ached to stop and stare and study.

This damned blasted exhaust system! It's filling my suit with oil stench! complained Commodore Guff.

Light up, friend, Bo Levar suggested. *It'll clear the stench and remind you of Dominaria and all the things we fight for.*

Urza clutched that thought to himself. Yes. Once the stench of Phyrexian blood made him ill. Now, he had not even noticed it. Urza had even gotten to like the smell. He wished he had one of Bo Levar's smokes.

Ancient trees snapped like twigs before Urza's titan engine. He cracked his way through the brake and stared down at Gamalgoth.

The city spread across the whole of a vast plateau. Gray mountains hemmed it in on one side and a forested rift on the other. Between them shone a gleaming city in bone-white stone. The tight-packed buildings seemed enormous fungi—irregular domes, hanging plazas, conic buttresses, weird roof lines, mounded stories, citadels growing up out of the larger city. It was a grown city, an ancient city, perfectly suited to this primeval world.

Urza would not pause. He would not show weakness. He must lead the nine down to that glorious city and tear it up and set bombs and activate them. . . .

Roaring a sound of deep dread, Urza ran toward Gamalgoth.

Rockets shot in spiraling paths from his wrists. Falcons shrieked in manifold fury from his back. Lightning leaped from his brow.

Smoke billowed in explosion across the walls of the city. Rock vaulted outward, leaving large breaches. Urza ran toward the gaps. Above the city, falcon engines dropped like silver meteors. They sought oil-blood and the organs that pumped it. With ramrod heads and razor beaks, they punched into the abdominal cavities of countless beasts. Whirling blades sliced the organs to ribbons.

The rockets and the falcons and lightning only softened the outer defenses. At full stride, Urza reached the city. His titanic foot crashed down atop a gatehouse and smashed it flat. A second stride, and a phalanx of Phyrexian troopers died. The buildings seemed as fragile as a wasps' nest. The beasts within burned as easily, buzzed as angrily, stung as impotently.

Bo Levar surged up alongside Urza. A blue wave of energy fanned out from him, macerating Phyrexians.

Szat poured magical fire across the swarming monsters. Their heads flared like jackstraws.

Commodore Guff knelt and clawed within a shattered building as though he sought his monocle.

Freyalise planted rampant growth with each footfall. Vines jagged out to strangle the city.

Even Daria and Taysir and Windgrace cast spells with sanguine glee.

Only Urza killed with numb hands and a numb heart.

CHAPTER 9
Among the Dead, Friends

For five days, Agnate and his Metathran legions had driven inward across fens and bogs. Beneath the blazing sun, they ground forward. Beneath the Glimmer Moon, they camped on whatever terrain they had gained and defended it against an endless assault of nocturnal beasts.

No human would have survived the campaign. Humans were born for other things—for laughing and falling in love and bearing young. They had to give up such things to fight a war. Metathran were different, bioengineered and therefore asexual. There was no falling in love and no bearing young, and the only laughing they did came with victory.

Metathran ate while they fought. Their teeth clenched rock-solid biscuits that contained all the nutrients they needed. They drank while they fought. Enzymes in their throats purified even rank swamp water. Like oxen in the traces, they bulled

78

forward over new ground. They could battle in their sleep. For Metathran, fighting was as breathing, as dreaming.

It had been a glorious five days for Agnate. This was not trench warfare like Koilos, with suicide charges across empty ground. This was guerrilla warfare. Secrecy and cunning and courage were key. Tactics and wilderness skills meant life. Here Phyrexians in their mindless hordes could not combat Metathran in their mindful legions. It was a vindication of the creature that Agnate was. It was also revenge for Thaddeus.

Agnate could still see his counterpart dissected alive— every tissue flayed away, his body dismantled bone by bone to his ribcage, even a stone laid against his diaphragm to help him breathe. Phyrexians had torn him apart to learn how Metathran fought.

This is how we fight, Agnate thought as his battle-axe cracked the skull of a Phyrexian trooper. It clove through the neck and into the beast's sternum. This is how we fight.

"Advance!" shouted Agnate to his troops.

Agnate lifted his axe. The cleft monster came up with it. He brought the Phyrexian down on one of its compatriots. The horn-studded trooper made a weighty mace. Spikes drove through the second monster's torso. Internal organs showed in their slimy complexity as the two beasts fell.

Careful not to slip in the mess, Agnate set his powerstone pike to receive the next charge. A monster obliged. Its face was little more than gray skin stretched over a human skull. Its torso was a bundle of tormented muscle over twisted bone. It fell on the pike, which tore its way inward. Still the creature fought.

Holding his pike with one hand, Agnate dislodge the axe with the other. He swung it. The blade sliced through one of the beast's arms, clove the ribs laterally, and emerged from the torso. The top half of the creature toppled from its legs. Agnate shoved the rest of the polearm through the monster. He picked up the weapon and strode onward.

Shoulder to shoulder with him ran a tight pack of Metathran. They were bloodied from that last charge but unbowed. The shouts of warriors and screams of beasts resounded on the flanks of the advance. Agnate and his corps had punched through the center.

They charged up a slimy bank, past arms of forest, and out onto a wide, sandy plain. Beyond the sand flats stood a scattered army of Phyrexians. They drew back, uncertain, as Agnate and his forces appeared.

Agnate halted. All around him, Metathran formed up on their commander. More of the blue-skinned fighters arrived every moment. One hundred troops. Two hundred troops. Five hundred troops.

The Phyrexians beyond the sand flats began an all-out retreat.

"Charge!" Agnate shouted, his axe lifted high.

His voice was joined by five hundred others. Battle cries shook the air. A thousand boots shook the ground. In ten steps, the Metathran reached the speed of hunting hounds, in twenty, that of hunting cats. It felt good to be running full-out after battling for inches.

The ground suddenly stole his feet. Agnate plunged waist deep into quicksand. All around him, his folk did the same. There was no stopping the charge. They bore forward and were swallowed by the deceptive world.

He had led his forces into a trap. The Phyrexians had gotten him just as they had gotten Thaddeus—lured into a fatal charge. There was no time for shame, not on a battlefield, and this shifting, sinking stuff was the current battlefield.

Metathran were too brawny to float. It wouldn't work to lie flat upon the sand and hope to be buoyed up. Even with lungs full of air, Metathran sank like stones. Already the wet sand lapped at Agnate's ribs. It was preternaturally cold and slick like rot. A current dragged him downward and to the right.

Others warriors sank more quickly than he. A line of them were already submerged to their shoulders. Their necks craned above the sand. They must have been situated over a crevice in the basin.

Whatever underground river fed the quicksand, the water drained there. The current dragged them down. Those warriors were doomed. Sand made little wells in their ears. They would never escape. The current would drag them down and through the crevice and tumble their dead bodies in underworld rivers. Soon the whole army would bump through the arteries of Dominaria.

There was only one hope—to sink to the bottom and walk themselves out.

"Submerge," Agnate commanded, "and stride for shore!"

For some, it was too late. Their heads were covered.

Agnate drew his last breath, closed his eyes, and drove himself into the sucking ground. Hands sculled against the thick grains. His feet plunged deeper. Cold and slick, the sands closed over him. Black ground gripped him and pulled him down.

Any moment now there would be solid rock, or mud thick enough to shove against, or something other than this cold, entombing stuff.

Any moment.

Agnate sank in silence and chill. He wondered if this was what it felt like to die. Most mortals believed their souls rose to some airy otherworld, but Metathran had no souls. Their bodies were their all, and their bodies sank. Perhaps this was what Thaddeus had felt in the moment of death. Perhaps Agnate even now was dying.

The air in his chest was hot. It swelled in his lungs as though they would burst.

Agnate's foot caught on something hard. It seemed a stick, or club—long and slippery. Kicking, Agnate felt more of them— not sticks but bones.

This quicksand had eaten armies before, countless times. Agnate and his troops were only the latest additions to a warrior's graveyard.

Agnate caught a foothold and pushed. The bones shifted. He slipped. His other boot drove against a skull. It was no good. The sand was too thick, the current too strong.

Agnate felt shame for having led his people here to die. Shame meant he had given up.

A hand grasped his leg. There was no flesh on that grip, only bone—powerful, implacable bone.

This was some lich lord's bone yard, his recruiting ground for an undead army. Agnate had not only slain his fellow warriors but had enlisted them to fight for evil.

Another hand grasped his leg, and another. They were all around him, these skeletal creatures. He struggled to break free, but bone and sand were allied. They clutched his arms, his sides, his neck, his skull. Agnate was dead. There was no point struggling. Death had won. Its literal hands would drag him down.

Agnate released the hot breath he had held. It slid away in blind bubbles through the thick sand. Yes. He was dead.

Except that the skeletal hands lifted him through the flood. They bore him upward in the wake of his own fleeing breath. Sand streamed away. In moments, he broke the boiling surface.

Through lips limned in his own blood, Agnate raked in a grateful breath.

Everywhere his army emerged, lifted on undead hands. Some Metathran were borne aloft by skeletal warriors. Others were clutched in the grip of ghouls. Still more were lifted by empty-eyed zombies, or insubstantial specters, or shambling mounds of rotting flesh. These strange benefactors shoved Metathran heads above the sand and bore blue warriors toward the far shore.

Agnate was numb. He had already given up life. He should have been dead. Normally a Metathran would shrink from the corrupting touch of these monsters, but who shrinks from the touch of salvation?

Metathran and undead, the army surged toward shore. There, the Phyrexians waited.

"Prepare for battle!" Agnate croaked hoarsely.

He had lost his powerstone pike in the struggle, but he still carried his battle-axe. Lifting it from the quicksand, he hefted it overhead. His command had been purposely ambiguous. Agnate himself was uncertain whether to use his axe on undead or Phyrexians.

Sand fell in wet clumps from Agnate. It clung a moment longer within the ribs and pelvises of the skeletons. Bony feet splashed through ankle-deep quicksand.

With a roar, Agnate twisted out of their grip. Cold bones slid from hot flesh. Landing on his feet, the Metathran commander flung a pair of skeletons away. They lost hold of his sodden armor and fell sideways. He swung his axe high to drive them back.

He needn't have. The skeletons had not paused in their clattering march. They ran out of the quicksand and leaped with savage fury on the Phyrexians. Finger bones gouged out compound eyes. Rusted swords cracked against sagittal crests. The warriors of old fought fiercely in defense of their island, of their world.

Agnate could only stare after them in stupefied amazement. All around, his soldiers stood in the shallows and watched as zombies ripped apart Phyrexians. Blinking sand from his eyes, Agnate swallowed hard.

This strange circumstance smelled of Urza. Who else would ally the living with the dead?

Lifting his battle-axe, Agnate shouted, "Charge!" On leaden legs, he drove himself forward, to the defense of his undead saviors.

Metathran warriors were nothing if not obedient. They joined the charge.

Straight before Agnate, a zombie clambered atop a Phyrexian trooper, lashing it with powerful but sloppy blows of putrid flesh. The Phyrexian's horns pierced rotting muscle. Chunks of meat hung on the spikes. Keeping its head down, the Phyrexian ripped the gut out of its attacker.

Agnate's axe sang in the air. Steel chopped through the Phyrexian's subcutaneous armor, through its chest, through its heart. Sliced nearly in two, the monster went down. It dragged the zombie with it. Side by side, they struck the sand.

A zombie can fight without its viscera. It pulled itself from the impaling horns and greedily dragged the severed corpse back toward the quicksand. It hurled the body into the deeps. The current dragged it down. In days, perhaps hours, the dead Phyrexian would rise from the sand too, a new member of the shambling army.

Agnate laughed. It was not the victorious laugh that he had voiced so often in battle. It was a more human sound—a recognition of absurdity.

An angry grin spread across his face. He whirled to slay another Phyrexian. His axe hewed as if through firewood. It was fascinating to watch the way they came to pieces. Each chop sent power up the haft of his axe and into his arms. It was as though he harvested the souls of his victims.

Suddenly, there were no more Phyrexians to kill. In a fever fight, Agnate, his troops, and their undead allies had slain them all. Even now, ghouls dutifully dragged dead Phyrexians into the sandy slough.

Setting the head of his axe on the oily ground, Agnate leaned on it and laughed. He could feel the eyes of his warriors on him, but he didn't care. Their shock made it only funnier. Agnate wiped gritty tears from his eyes.

Shaking his head, he muttered, "What has happened to me?"

"You have gained a new ally," answered an ancient and craggy voice.

Agnate raised his eyes to see a tall, strong figure in ornate robes. Within sleeves of embroidered silk, the man's powerful arms spread in a regal, welcoming gesture. Above an upturned collar rose a stout neck and a rugged face. The smile on the man's lips seemed almost boyish, and a fragile light shone in his deep-set eyes. Gray hair stood in an unkempt halo around his temples. So friendly, so familiar was that visage that Agnate at first did not realize the man's flesh was mummified.

"I am Lord Dralnu," he said, bowing deeply. "I command these folk who have saved you. I invite you and your men to celebrate our new alliance in the halls of my palace."

In stunned respect, Agnate bowing his head. A lich lord? He was allied now to a lich lord?

Worst of all, Lord Dralnu looked like Thaddeus, back from the dead.

CHAPTER 10
Elves of Skyshroud, Elves of Keld

Eladamri and Liin Sivi rode great mountain yaks up a long, rocky ascent. Colos, these beasts were called— huge, shaggy rams. They were powerful mounts and utterly surefooted. Eladamri was glad. He and his Skyshroud commanders climbed a cliff face beside a gigantic glacier.

They did not ride alone. The leaders of Keld rode with them. As strange as the colos were, the Keldons were even stranger. Massive and gray skinned, the average warlord towered an easy foot above Eladamri. Savage helms and breastplates in rust red covered tattooed flesh that was tougher still. Scars crisscrossed their flesh. Among the Keldons, a missing ear and a split lip were beauty marks.

Indeed, when these warriors had first encountered Eladamri, they couldn't believed so short, slight, and unscarred a man—so un*Keldon* a man—could be a warrior. They were wrong. Eladamri had fought through the Stronghold and the Caves of Koilos. The Keldon scouts issued a two-word challenge, clear even in their barbaric tongue: "Prove it!" With Freyalise's help, Eladamri did. He killed the first rival, so ferocious was the attack. The second limped away sorely wounded, only to fetch more.

Ten warriors returned, accompanying their field commander. This young man was different—leanly muscular. His eyes shone with bright intellect within his scarred face. He studied the dead scout. With a long sweep of his eyes, he took in the strange, green forest laid down in the icy fastness of his lands. The sights sparked something in him, something he'd heard or read. These elves were no mere invaders. They were emissaries from another world and from the black future.

The young commander jabbed a thumb toward his chest and barked a single word, "Astor."

Astor proved an uncommon Keldon, equally versed in war and lore. He knew many Dominarian languages and took pains to teach Eladamri the rudiments of Common Keld. His rulers, Doyen Olvresk and Doyenne Tajamin, arrived within the week. The former immediately ambushed Eladamri with his crescent-bladed scythe. The weapon opened a long wound from the elf's right temple to his jaw. Without pause, Eladamri responded with a slash of his sword. He struck an identical wound on the doyen's face. Their bloodied blades met between them and locked. Neither man could throw back the other. In moments, the duel was done. Without words, they had achieved détente.

Even now, as the colos climbed the ragged mountainside, Eladamri was still proving himself to Doyenne Tajamin. She rode to his right and poured out a long narrative in Common Keld. She spoke of the end of the world, of Twilight. Most Keldons believed Eladamri and his forest home to be harbingers of this end time. As Keeper of the Book of Keld, Doyenne Tajamin was harder to convince.

Her colos leaped, surging to a narrow shelf of basalt. Snow fell in easy cascades beside the beast's hooves. Aback it, Doyenne Tajamin looked down with fiery eyes.

"True, the books of Twilight speak of allies from another world, but also they speak of invaders. You claim you are allies—perhaps—but you are undoubtedly invaders."

Eladamri smiled winningly, the expression rumpling the stitched scar across his face.

In Common Keld, he replied, "The Twilight legends are yours, Doyenne, not mine. You are more eager than I to make me fit." Eladamri's steed leaped up beside hers.

Tajamin smiled as well, a predatory leer. She lifted an ancient war cudgel. The age-blackened wood was carved deep with runes.

"This weapon will decide. Some folk believe the sword cuts to the truth. We believe a cudgel divines more surely. Only those who can stand beneath its blow are true." Tajamin flipped her arm.

Eladamri braced for another attack. Instead, Tajamin rode her mount up to a higher ledge.

"So, once we are out on the battlefield, I should expect you to club me?" Eladamri asked.

"A true warrior is ready for anything," she responded.

Two more bounds of her mount brought her to the top of the cliff. Glacial light broke over her face, showing up each scar that crossed it. Her wry and dangerous look melted away, replaced by a solemn joy.

Digging his heels into the shaggy sides of his colos, Eladamri surged up over the ridge. He too saw.

A vast glacier extended from the hooves of his mount out to distant black mountains. The ice shone white beneath silvery rafts of cloud. It was a veritable sea of snow, held aloft by an ancient range of volcanic peaks. Numerous lateral glaciers descended from higher valleys to join together in this one enormous ice sheet.

From two of the lateral glaciers marched divisions of the Keldon army. They had taken a slower but less treacherous approach. In their midst rolled massive war engines—trebuchets, catapults, and greater ballistae. Larger than even these machines of war were Keldon long ships on huge runners. At full sail, their bladed bows could rip through enemy lines and their vast rams could smash a twenty-foot-thick wall. Hoardings lined the rails of the warships. Through their loopholes, archers could pour quarrels on troops and battlements alike. Among these enormous machines rode twenty-five thousand heavy colos cavalry. Seventy-five thousand Keldons filled out the warhost.

Eladamri was glad to see his ten thousand elven troops marching among the arrayed might of Keld.

These were grand sights, true, but they were not what lit the face of the doyenne. The grandest vision of all stood to one side of the glacier.

On a conic peak among craggy mountains perched a tall, black city. The base of the structure was crowded with countless dwellings. Their steep roofs dumped incessant snows. Lights shown minutely in their windows. Farther up, the buildings grew dark. In the midst of the dwellings rose a tall pyramid of stone, open on two ends. It seemed almost a hangar for an airship, but the space could have held a vessel five times the size of *Weatherlight*. At the pyramid's pinnacle resided a lofty citadel. It lurked among the raveling clouds.

Eladamri stared so intently at the vision that he was startled to realize the proud doyens and doyennes beside him had dropped from their colos to kneel on the ice. Even Liin Sivi bowed low. Swinging his leg from the saddle, Eladamri knelt among them.

A chant came from the leaders. "Kradak and Jezal, doyen and doyenne, fire and hearth, till Twilight we await your return."

Eladamri kept his head bowed until the chant was done. The clang of armor told that his allies rose. He climbed to his feet with the others and remounted. Only then did he dare speak.

"What is this glorious vision?"

Doyenne Tajamin drove her mount forward across the ice. She spoke reverently. "This is the Necropolis, the resting place for our honored dead. All warriors who die in righteous warfare are entombed there. From the Necropolis, they will rise in the day of Twilight to defend Keld from the armies of evil."

"There are lights lit there," Eladamri said, pacing her.

"The caretakers dwell forever among the honored dead. It is the highest honor granted a warlord to guard the Necropolis. To die while serving in the Necropolis is to be assured a place there."

Nodding in understanding, Eladamri shielded his eyes from the glare. As the war party moved out across the ice, he glimpsed a flash of gold within the open pyramid.

"What rests there, at the center of the citadel?"

"The *Golden Argosy*, ship of titans. It was stolen from the lords of Parma by Kradak, first doyen of our people. In it, he sailed all the world and claimed it for Keld. This was before the other races spilled out across the land, stealing it. Since that time, we have journeyed afar to regain the lands that are ours."

Eladamri smiled in appreciation. "Those other races are certainly larcenous, but how can you conquer the world while the *Golden Argosy* resides in the Necropolis?"

"When Kradak died, the *Argosy* became his tomb. Only when Kradak arises again in Twilight will the *Argosy* sail once more. Then the world will once again be ours."

"Then the world truly would end," Eladamri replied ambiguously.

Tajamin responded with a smile. "Now you have begun to believe."

Shrugging, Eladamri said, "If the Necropolis has its own guardians, why do you bring this army of a hundred thousand?"

She gazed levelly at him. "So, you didn't notice the army of invaders beyond?" She jabbed her finger toward a high and distant hollow. There, a wide river tumbled over a bed of shattered obsidian.

"What army?"

Tajamin wore a sly look. "We often see only what we want to see—allies or invaders."

Shielding his eyes, Eladamri stared.

It was not a river that flowed down that high valley. It was a legion. What had seemed shattered hunks of obsidian were in truth the battle armor of a huge Phyrexian contingent. Mere days ago they had been arrayed on the hillsides of Rath. Now they marched toward the most sacred site to the people of Keld.

His voice was a hoarse whisper. "How many are there?"

"Scouts have reported two hundred thousand in the main army," Tajamin said flatly.

Eladamri tightly clutched the reins of his colos. "And what is your strategy?"

"Reach the Necropolis before the Phyrexians do."

Nearby, Doyen Olvresk stood in the saddle and lifted high his curve-bladed scythe.

"Full gallop to the troops!" he shouted. He brought his arm forward. His colos bounded out across the ice. Hooves cracked solid footholds and sent crystals cracking away.

Doyenne Tajamin drove heels into her mount's flanks. The colos leaped anxiously. It shouldered past Eladamri's beast, which reared back. The beast charged across the glacier. In moments, doyen and doyenne rode neck and neck. Each of their steeds struggled to gain the lead. The other doyen swarmed in their wake.

"Hearth and fire, they are incomplete without each other," came a familiar voice at Eladamri's shoulder. The elf turned to see the young warlord Astor, astride his colos. The warrior's face was utterly grave, but laughter played in his eyes. "Olvresk and Tajamin each can see only his or her own perspective. Since they both trained me, I can see both."

Eladamri smiled wanly. "Your perspective has saved many lives. What do you suggest we do?"

Lifting heavy eyebrows, Astor simply said, "Follow."

As one, Eladamri, Liin Sivi, and Astor drove their mounts forward across the ice. The hooves of the colos made a brittle rumble as they bore along. Behind them galloped the rest of the Skyshroud commanders. They were eager to be reunited with their troops and to return the colos to their Keldon handlers.

Just ahead, a series of deep crevasses opened in the glacier. The ice sheet had stretched over a rocky ridge, and the surface had cracked. Ice dropped away through blue shadows and into blackness. It was an easy thirty feet across the first crevasse, and only a ten-foot wedge of ice stood between it and the next. It seemed an impassable barrier, but the Keldons did not slow the charge of their steeds.

Side by side in the lead, Doyen Olvresk and Doyenne Tajamin drove their mounts to the crevasse. Fore-hooves cracked on the ice cliff. The colos gathered their bulk. Hind-hooves smashed on the edge of the crevasse. As one, the great mountain yaks bounded. Though ponderous on the ground, they leaped weightlessly through the air. Doyen and doyenne stood high in the saddle and fixed their gazes on the far wedge. Their mounts soared down. Fore-hooves, hind-hooves, they surged off the ice over the next crevasse.

Unflinching, the other Keldon commanders leaped their mounts over.

Eyes wide, Eladamri stared at approaching doom. He shouted to Warlord Astor, "What do we do?"

Astor repeated simply. "Follow!" Then he too hurtled across the crack.

Liin Sivi and Eladamri traded looks. There was no time to stop.

Leaning against the neck of his mount, Eladamri held his breath. The final four hoofbeats sounded like explosions in his ears. Then came a deathly silence.

Ice chips floated in tangled winds above the crevasse. Colos hooves pawed the emptiness. Eladamri stared down into unseeable depths. The glacier's heart was as black as death. His own heart hung in the gap. There came not a sound except wind in colos hair.

Hooves struck the ice on the far side. The colos gathered its muscles and bounded again.

Something had changed. Perhaps he knew his mount could make it. Perhaps he had already stared once into death and cheated it. This time, Eladamri sat up in the saddle. He peered with interest rather than fear into this new crevasse. His heart pounded excitedly. The dark rip in the white world was beautiful.

By the time he crossed the third crevasse, Eladamri was laughing aloud. It hurt the stitches in his face, but in every other way, it felt good. He was becoming Keldon, he realized. His people would not merely dwell in this land. They would be reshaped by it until they were Keldon people too.

Eladamri followed his allies as they closed the distance to their troops. With a whoop, Eladamri rode up before the lines of his Skyshroud elves. In their thick thistledown cloaks, they hardly looked like elves. Even their eyes showed the beginnings of transformation.

Eladamri reined in his colos, and the beast reared up. Its hooves spun in the air as he shouted, "Follow me, Elves of the Skyshroud, Elves of Keld! Follow me to defend our land!"

CHAPTER 11
Metal With Memory

Angels and spirits, helionauts and hoppers were no match for Phyrexian cruisers. Five of the enormous black ships now filled the sky. Their mana bombards heaped death on defenders. Their horn-studded rams chased *Weatherlight* across the heavens.

"I thought we'd gotten rid of these bastards!" Gerrard shouted to no one in particular. He couldn't bring his cannon to bear on the pursuing cruiser, but he found a target anyway. His gun hurled a corridor of flack abeam. The red blaze dissolved a dragon engine into claws and teeth. Energy bounded on and melted the stern of a Phyrexian dagger-boat. Deprived of its engine, the ship bobbed drunkenly and plummeted.

On the other side of the forecastle, Tahngarth's cannon shouted. It tore away a gout of black mana that surged toward *Weatherlight*.

"Perhaps these are the cruisers from Benalia."

Gerrard gritted his teeth. "Oh, you had to say that." His cannon barked. Crimson bolts shrieked from the muzzle. The first shot struck a Phyrexian ram and pocked the metal. The second and third shots cored the ship as if it were an apple.

The pursuing cruiser sent fire in a deadly tunnel up around *Weatherlight*.

"How 'bout some rear defenses, Squee?" Gerrard shouted into the speaking tube.

Before his words were even finished, an angry protest answered. "You think dis easy, yeah? You think just 'cause Squee save your butt hundred thousand million times before, he save you now?"

A glob of black mana struck the port airfoil and ripped a rattling hole through it.

"Yes, Squee! Exactly!" Gerrard growled. "The tail gunner's job is to save our butts."

The rapid shots of the tail gun fused into a single, constant, furious discharge. Squee leaped within the traces, spraying beams across their wake. Defensive fire rose from the cruiser but could not anticipate the random blasts. Squee's shots smacked the fuselage, tore holes through conduits, ripped into inner corridors, and clove engine modules. Smoke belched up, and after smoke came fire. The cruiser jolted, dropped backward, and heeled slowly away.

"Nice shooting, Squee," Gerrard called.

"Dat's another two hundred butts you owe Squee."

Tahngarth interrupted the goblin tail gunner. "What's Agnate doing down there?" The minotaur stood and gaped over *Weatherlight*'s rail.

Gerrard peered through his captain's glass, but even with it, he could not make out the figures in the forest.

A metallic voice spoke for all of them—Karn, who could see through the running lamps of the ship. "He marches. He marches with a company of the dead."

"What?" Gerrard asked, reeling. "Agnate has turned traitor?"

Karn's voice rumbled like distant thunder. "No. They march together against Phyrexians. Agnate allies with evil against evil."

Staring over the rail, Gerrard murmured bleakly, "Desperate times . . ."

"Desperate, indeed," Karn replied. "There's a cruiser dead ahead."

Gerrard turned and looked fore. The cruiser seemed only a small black cloud on the horizon, though it swelled outward with alarming speed.

"Evasive!"

"Keep your pants on, Commander," Sisay replied lightly. *Weatherlight* banked to starboard. Her engines thrummed. She rose on thundering winds.

The cruiser shifted into an intercept course. It grew even bigger, eclipsing half of the sky. Its ram, a stout block ending in hornlike protrusions, reached for *Weatherlight*.

"She's trying to ram us!" Gerrard called.

"Yes! Yes!" Sisay replied.

Weatherlight pitched toward port and climbed again.

The cruiser shifted its attitude. It loomed, inescapable, before *Weatherlight*.

"I can't break free!" Sisay called. "She'd drawing us in!"

"She's going to ram us!" Gerrard warned.

"No," Sisay shouted back. "We're going to ram her!"

"What!"

Weatherlight plunged like a cleaver toward the massive ship. Multani coursed into the Gaea figurehead, the stabbing spine beneath, and the serrated keel. It struck first.

Wood as hard as diamond plowed through the armor of the cruiser's upper deck and ripped into its fuselage. The spike struck next. It punctured a gun nest and gored the monster at the machine. The beast was wiped away as *Weatherlight* plunged deeper into the cruiser. Metal parted in black waves before her.

It was as if more than her own momentum drove her forward, as if something in the cruiser's heart dragged at her.

At last, the Gaea figurehead itself breasted the metal wave. Her brow dug in, and *Weatherlight* ground to a halt.

"Reverse engines!" Gerrard called. "Pull us out of here!"

Weatherlight's engines flared but seemed to wedge the ship only more tightly.

"*Reverse* engines, Karn!"

The ship's power core went silent. The hatch to the engine room flung back. Steam billowed out above the deck. From that hissing cloud emerged the silver mass of Karn. He climbed laboriously from the hatch and strode with heavy intent toward the forecastle.

"Karn! What's happening?"

"The power cores," he said, leaping from amidships to the forecastle. His legs drummed the deck. "They're drawing each other together like a pair of magnets. Every time we fire up our engine, it pulls us deeper. The only way to get out is to shut down their engine."

Eyes wide, Gerrard said, "And how do we do that?

Karn gestured toward the prow. Thick metal curled away from the ship's hull. "Give me a door."

Wordlessly, Gerrard nodded. He swung his cannon toward the armor of the Phyrexian ship and squeezed off two shots. Red rays melted air and then metal. It dripped through the breach, revealing the cross section of a corridor.

Dipping his head, Karn vaulted over the prow rail and in through the red-hot hole. His feet struck a floor of metal grate. The sound echoed both ways down the long corridor and was answered by more feet—Phyrexian feet. Gibbering hungrily, monsters scampered down the passage toward the intruder. They loped on all fours like wolves, though their bodies were scaly and their mouths could have swallowed a wolf whole. The monsters converged on Karn and leaped, howling.

Rearing his fist back, Karn hurled a roundhouse at the first beast. Silvery knuckles cracked through rows of teeth. Enamel tumbled in the creature's mouth. Karn's hand rammed down the monster's throat. It closed its bite on him, hoping to sever his arm.

Karn whirled, bashing the second attacker down with the writhing body of the first. He withdrew his arm from the creature's throat, bringing with it a handful of innards. A third hound died beneath a stomping foot, and a fourth with a broken back. The last beast leaped on Karn and bit his head, trying to take it off. Sliding hands into the chewing jaws, Karn opened them wider than they ever should have opened.

He took a moment to make sure all the beasts lay destroyed and then shouted toward *Weatherlight*, "A door for me is a door for them. Defend this breach until I return."

Gerrard's sardonic face shone above the smoking barrel of his cannon. "Aye aye, Engineer!"

Karn looked down, considering the dead. At one time, he would not fight, would not harm a soul. Now, Karn had just torn five creatures apart. Perhaps these were mere beasts, but smarter foes would lurk ahead. They would realize what he was trying to do and would fight—and would die.

"Better them than my friends," Karn thought aloud.

Without another word, he headed down the passage toward the ship's power core. He could sense its emanations. There was an uncanny kinship between Karn's body and the cruiser. Even the runes carved in the ships inner halls resembled the characters scribed on Karn's chest. Living metal surrounded him, half designed, half grown. The dark corridor had an organic logic, more like a vein than a hallway. Each footfall seemed a heartbeat.

For a moment, the passage dissolved, replaced by another from long ago. It was a white hallway. He walked beside a young man, a boy really, though a genius. Beneath his bald forehead lurked impish eyes and a slightly cruel smile. It was no Gerrard. His skin was too dark. It was another friend, Karn's first friend. He struggled to remember a name. Ladlepate? Arty Shovelhead? No, those weren't names for the boy, but for Karn. The boy's name was . . . Teferi?

Karn surfaced from his waking dream in the midst of a fierce fight. Phyrexian shock troops—more machine than creature—swarmed him. Their human heads and torsos were deeply ensconced within a framework of artifact mechanisms. On draconic legs, they ran. With scythelike arms, they fought. Their horns could impale three men abreast, but they could not impale Karn.

Karn patiently grabbed their arms and ripped them loose. It was the treatment he had given Tsabo Tavoc and now to her children.

The beasts fought on. They couldn't destroy him, but they could halt his advance until more troops arrived. That would be enough to doom everyone aboard *Weatherlight*.

Growling, Karn knocked down a trooper blocking his path. It landed on its back. Karn stomped on the thing's chest. Metal failed. Flesh oozed out like paste from a tube. This was worse than killing the hounds. These creatures had once been human.

Karn finished the wretched work. Glistening-oil coated him from feet to hips. It poured in a regular rain through the grating. Trying to shut the sound out of his mind, Karn strode deeper. The engine core called him.

Again, the tunnel closed to a single point. It opened in another place and time, but the circumstances were the same. He was killing Phyrexians to defend a friend.

This was a true friend, not like Teferi. This was Karn's first true friend. Her name came ringing back through his body like the toll of a bell. Jhoira. She had saved him from loneliness, and he had failed to save her from Phyrexians. She lay, bloodstained and broken, on the floor of her cell there at the academy (the academy?), and Karn fought in rage against the negator that had slain her. He was not really defending Jhoira, for she was already dead. He was avenging her, bloodily, with a sense of righteous rage.

The killing strokes of that bygone day—how long ago?—elided with the killing strokes Karn would swing in mere moments.

He had reached the engine room—a huge arched chamber. At its center was an enormous engine, ten times the size of *Weatherlight*'s. Buttresses of Thran metal braced a sloping manifold in foot-thick steel. Within that framework surged energies that glowed red-hot. Power coursed from the main engine into countless arteries. Auxiliary powerhouses crouched on the floor around the mother machine. The air throbbed with noise. The engineers were utterly unaware of Karn's approach.

They were almost human—tall, thin, with weighty brains and narrow digits. Their bodies bore slender metal implants. No doubt these were compleated Phyrexians, but they had not been much modified from the human stock whence they had been drawn.

Without pause, Karn strode to them. They died like birds in his grip. How could he do this? Karn, who had stood by while Tahngarth was tortured in the Stronghold? Karn, who had allowed Vuel to make off with Gerrard's Legacy? Karn, who had failed Jhoira in her hour of greatest need?

No, he had not failed. In fact, he had turned back the hour, had turned back even the day. He'd gone back in a time machine—strange memories!—to kill her killer, to save her and the whole academy of Tolaria.

Tolaria! But Tolaria was a myth, less real even than its master Urza.

If Tolaria was a myth, why did Karn remember its destruction? To save the academy—no, to save Jhoira—he had pushed the time machine to its limits and destroyed it all.

To save his one true friend . . .

The Phyrexian engineers were dead. Gerrard and the others would be dead too unless Karn shut down the engine. There were countless ways, but as Karn read the configuration of power cells, he knew the main core would always restart itself. There was only one way to shut it down permanently.

Striding along the oil-stained flank of the engine, Karn shoved levers upward. Power mounted. One cell began to whine and then the next. Mana superfluids boiled violently. The rumble crescendoed to an angry wail, then a deafening shriek.

It was enough. Karn turned. He ran back the way he had descended. It was an easy trail, marked with bodies. Seventeen engineers beside the power core, twelve shock troops in the passageway, and there, ahead, where clear sky shown through a hull breach, five vampire hounds.

Behind Karn, the core went critical. White-hot fire engulfed the engine room. It burst the walls outward. It flung the doors from their hinges. Pure energy bounded up the corridor behind Karn.

He ran. His feet clanged on the grating. From heat alone, the vampire hound bodies burst into flame. Their glistening-oil blood made a wall of fire before him. White power behind and red flame before, Karn hurled himself through the hull breech. He roared. His bloodied hands burned as he hurtled through the air.

Perhaps, in destroying it all—even himself—he had saved his only true friends.

Then, like a memory solidifying, Karn felt something in his hands. He held on and was drawn away from the incendiary cloud. Black metal retreated beneath his dangling feet. Urborg appeared below.

Karn clung to the forecastle rail of *Weatherlight*. Fires snapped and burned around his hands and feet, but he held on.

Above the rail, eyes worried within a shock of black hair. Gerrard smiled.

"Karn, you did it. You made it back. I don't know what I would've done without you."

CHAPTER 12
The Dragon of Yavimaya

Throughout their flight across the ocean, Rhammidarigaaz had wondered how he would find the second Primeval. Now, as his dragon nations circled above tumbled Yavimaya, he knew.

The Primeval drew him. She lay imprisoned below. Elves had entombed her in the heart of a great tree. For ages of ages, the ancient forest serpent had been a captive to the wood. Magnigoth sap had pasted down her scales. It had permeated her flesh and coursed into her blood and leeched every rebellious impulse from her mind. This dragon, who had breathed forests into being and had flown in a world where mortals were caged birds, this beast was a prisoner of the trees.

But not forever.

Bending his fangy mouth down toward the forest canopy, Darigaaz began a long, spiraling dive. His people followed.

The wet heat of Yavimaya streamed across his leathery wings. Beneath the sun and above the treetops, Darigaaz soared. In this time of war and dark revelations, there was too little quiet and beauty. He watched his own lithe shadow as it surged over the canopy. Tree to tree, the image leaped. In its wake came the shadows of the dragon nations. They seemed fish schooling above a reef. Down to Yavimaya they plunged.

She was here, just here, in the massive magnigoth around which they circled. It was a mountain of a tree, three thousand feet tall. Its crown could hold aloft an elven city. Large white blooms spread across the peak and showered gleaming pollen through the air. Gigantic Kavu basked among its branches, letting the sun warm their reptilian blood. Below, foliage spread in four more levels down the huge trunk. Each had its own climate, its own fauna and flora. The base of the tree was a swollen knob of wood that bristled with spikes.

Even glimmering pollen and acrid sap could not cover the sweet, sharp scent of dragon flesh. The magnigoth was powerful and ancient, yes, but less so than its captive.

Darigaaz tucked his wings and plunged through the upper canopy. It was like diving through the algae of a deep pool. Sunlight failed. Wind gave way to stillness. Airy creatures were replaced by giant spiders, staring Kavu, and every skulking thing.

His people descended in a ribbon behind him.

Darigaaz circled the magnigoth trunk. Heat seeped from his skin. Talons dragged through moist murk. Wings brushed the spikes that jutted from the root bulb. There was no true soil here except the humus that ran in a black network among the trees. On that spongy ground, Darigaaz landed. His claws dug in the dirt, and he tucked his wings. With a final flap of leather and a series of soft thuds, the dragon nations of Dominaria landed. They formed a thick ring of flesh around the prison of their ancient lord.

Darigaaz took a deep breath and eyed the tree. It was indeed a mountain. How could he bring this creature out? How could he hope to free a Primeval?

You know how, spoke a voice in Darigaaz's mind. It was a purring voice, feminine and powerful.

Abstracted, the elder dragon reached up to the talismans at his wattle.

No, the answer does not lie there. That is new magic, a distillation of colors. We lived before all that. We lived when power was raw and elemental. You must tap the primeval power, Rhammidarigaaz.

Tap the primeval power? How?

You have been a servant to mortals too long. You have forgotten what it means to be a dragon. To be a king.

Darigaaz bristled. He was the elder dragon of Shiv. He was the lord of the dragon nations. He had not forgotten what it was to be a dragon king.

You're no king. You're a diplomat, a negotiator. You must rule yourself before you can rule these folk. What of volcanic desire? What of volcanic power?

"Have you brought us here merely to stand and stare?" asked the lord of the black dragons.

Darigaaz shook off his reverie. Only then did he notice that Lord Rokun coiled before him.

Rokun was a coal-black beast cast in the very likeness of Tevash Szat, the dragon god who had begun this whole escapade. Rokun's tongue was also the equal of Szat's.

"Did we fly across the ocean only to land here without plan or purpose?"

Yes? Did you?

The fire kindled in Darigaaz's belly grew only hotter. "Our purpose is to raise the second Primeval before the Phyrexians can destroy her. Our plan is to join the strength of the dragon nations to tap ancient power."

Feigning credulity, Rokun said, "Oh, yes. Let's all join in a circle and hold hands—"

Don't coddle him. He is not your child. He is your subject.

"Would you be silent?" Darigaaz snapped, uncertain whether he addressed Rokun or the voice in his head.

"No, I will not," snarled Rokun. His tail lashed. His claws gripped the black soil as he circled the dragon elder. "I kept my silence while many of us were slaughtered at Koilos—and for what, a hunk of sand that is now in Phyrexian hands?"

You fight for men, not for dragons.

"The permanent portal was destroyed. That was the purpose of the Battle of Koilos—"

"I kept my silence as you led us to what little remained of your homeland, to fight for nose-picking goblins and runty Viashino. I kept my silence even as you led us across the world to find this oversized scratching post, but I will keep silent no longer."

Lash out. If you let him speak that way to you, he will rebel.

Darigaaz lifted claws to his ears. "I'm through listening to you."

"No, you aren't. I'm taking control of the dragon nations. We will follow you no longer!"

Lash out! Are you too docile to save your own people?

Darigaaz's claws raked down from his ears and seized the black, hackled throat of the upstart. "You will not take command of this army. Not while I live." He hurled Rokun away from him, into a crowd of black dragons that eagerly watched the confrontation. They reeled back, clearing the way.

Rokun rose menacingly. In the dark forest, his plate armor seemed more insectoid than reptilian.

Through gleaming fangs, he hissed, "Oh, Rhammidarigaaz the Elder, I have longed for this moment." He launched himself at his foe.

Black power scintillated across his horns and coalesced down his arms. Rokun's claws grew preternaturally outward like lines of ink drawn on the air. Those lines intersected Darigaaz's stomach and cut deep parallel furrows through the scales.

The elder dragon reeled back.

At least one of you remembers how to fight.

Darigaaz did not heed the voice, busy remembering something else—the volcanoes of Shiv. He drew the power to him and formed it into a red-hot column of force that poured from his clawtips. He roared and lunged. His talons clenched the black dragon's throat. Incendiary heat ripped through the monster's neck. From the holes torn by his claws gushed a tarry liquid. The acid burned Darigaaz's flesh. More sprayed between the black dragon's clenched teeth. Where it spattered Darigaaz, his own scales dissolved. It burned wounds across his neck and shoulders. Darigaaz reeled back.

Use your native power. . . .

Like a well-stoked furnace, Darigaaz drew a hissing breath. Within his chest, breath transformed. It coalesced into pure energy and roared out. Flame blazed from his mouth. It ate the air between the dragons. A ball of fire broke over Rokun.

Ah, you do remember about volcanic heat! You do remember that you are a dragon and a king!

Rokun thrashed in the searing fire. His wings burned away in an acrid whoosh. His scales curled upward like mud drying beneath the sun. He staggered, going to his knees. Even the acid that dripped from his wounded throat burned.

Still, Darigaaz did not relent. Feral flame poured out of him and laved the rebel lord.

Yes, Rhammidarigaaz! Kill him, and the others will fall in line!

As if awakening from a nightmare, the elder dragon shuddered. His eyes grew wide. Fire ceased in his throat. The last of the flames dribbled between his fangs. Rhammidarigaaz stared in horror at the smoldering figure.

Rokun struggled to rise from the blackened ground where he lay. It was no good. His scales were as fragile as dry leaves. The vital fluids of his being drained whitely from every pore. He would die—that much was certain—but he was not dead yet.

Staggering numbly toward his foe—his victim—Darigaaz called out, "Summon the white dragons! Summon the healers!"

"Don't bother!" rasped out Rokun. "They can only prolong it

now. You have slain me, Rhammidarigaaz. You have slain me because I dared to oppose you."

Yes, Rhammidarigaaz, purred the voice in his head. *That is what you have done. That is what you had to do.*

Staring feverishly at the ravaged figure, Darigaaz said, "You would have slain me—"

"I would have slain you . . . to save our people from worthless wars and old myths," gasped Rokun. "I would have slain you to save the dragon nations . . . from being the tool of planeswalkers."

"Better the tool of planeswalkers than the tool of Phyrexians."

Through smoke-whitened eyes, Rokun looked up past Darigaaz to the other dragons. "Break from him. . . . Escape the doom he brings. . . ."

You must finish him before he turns your people away!

"This quest will destroy you . . . and all of us. . . ."

"Silence, Rokun! You are defeated. Be silent!"

"You cannot silence me. . . . They will rebel against you. . . ."

A self-fulfilling prophecy!

"I said, silence!"

"Rise against him, dragon nations! Rise!"

You must finish him!

Rhammidarigaaz reached down, grabbing the scorched body. Scales shattered beneath his claws. He hoisted the creature overhead. Fury surged through him. Lifting Rokun high, he hurled him through the air. The ravaged body arced outward. Enough life remained in it that Rokun struggled to right himself. His claws and tail lashed.

Rokun crashed atop the root bulb. Nine spikes ripped through his seared flesh, impaling him. The body slumped on those spikes. Air left him in a long, gurgling hiss.

Darigaaz watched, heart pounding in his throat. He looked down at his claws, black from the deed. He looked up at the dragon nations. In their eyes, he saw his mad figure.

Speak to them, Rhammidarigaaz. Threaten them. You are on the verge of losing them.

"Any other traitors—" Darigaaz began, even before he was sure what was coming from his mouth— "will die the same way."

It had been the wrong thing to say. The beasts visible recoiled from him.

It didn't matter. A transformation had begun.

The dead dragon spilled acid and blood onto the magnigoth's bark. The humors did not drip down but up, drawn skyward. They sank into a crevice and pried it apart. The caustic liquids ate through bark into the quick of the tree. The seam peeled back. Year by year, century by century, millennium by millennium, the rings were exposed.

"What's happening?" wondered Darigaaz aloud.

You did it. You remembered what it was to rule your nation. You awoke your volcanic fury and united your kindred. It is enough. You have awakened me.

Rokun had been a sacrifice, Darigaaz realized. To free the Primeval, Darigaaz had had to sacrifice a mortal dragon on the tree.

The sorcery that split the tree had reached to its very core. Instead of deep darkness, the space shone sunlike. From it rolled the scent of dragon life essence. The air seemed liquor—stinging and numbing and intoxicating. It poured out and bathed the dragon nations. They could not remain standing but fell to their haunches and bowed their heads.

Only Rhammidarigaaz kept his feet. He stared with bald eyes at the creature returning to the world.

The blinding cleft widened, taking on a distinctly draconic shape. Long wings raked upward. Talons gripped the wood that once had gripped them. A tail lashed with new life. Scales glimmered like prisms. The creature strode from the wood. As it emerged, the tree closed. The dragon dimmed. It went from white-hot to red-hot, and then to its native color—green.

She was beautiful. Her scales shone like jade. She was powerful. Her claws and legs and wings and tail all spoke of brute strength. She was brilliant. Within her gleaming eyes were stored millennia that modern creatures could only guess at. She approached Darigaaz.

His heart pounded. The enervation of the fight was gone. Bathed in this creature's glow, Darigaaz felt as beautiful and powerful and brilliant as she.

When she spoke, her voice was just as it had been in his mind. "You found your fury, Rhammidarigaaz. You found your dragon's soul, and you awakened me. I am Rith, Primeval of Yavimaya."

He could only nod in response.

"The circle is begun again. It is but a short arc now. When it is complete, no one will be able to stand before the nation of dragons."

* * * * *

The dragons did not remain long. They followed the gleaming green Primeval skyward. The last of them lifted off before the forest's defenders could rally.

En masse, Kavu bounded down the three-thousand-foot trunk of the magnigoth tree. They reached the root bulb below. Massive and horn studded, the great lizards circled the tree and sniffed the air. Dragon stench lingered. It stung their eyes. Nictitating membranes drew across them. Nostrils pinched shut.

These dragons had been foes as surely as had the Phyrexians. They had stolen one of Yavimaya's most ancient treasures. The Kavu had defended the forest against Phyrexians, but they would have to marshal greater defenders to reclaim the lost serpent.

Circling the wounded magnigoth, the Kavu placed their claws on its root bulb. They threw back their heads and filled their wattles with air. From fangy mouths emerged a deep, mournful bellow. The song resonated among millennial trees.

In time, the magnigoth guardian awoke. With terrific motion, it drew its roots up from the tangle of others. The cleft that once had held Rith split into an enormous pair of legs. A mouth gaped open beneath pitlike eyes. Most important of all, though, was the great canopy of leaves overhead. They nourished the beast, and through billions of stomas, they sniffed the air.

The Kavu ceased their song. Their message had been conveyed. Rith had escaped. The treefolk lord must lead its people to bring her back.

The magnigoth guardian drew in air all across its dome of leaves. Ah, Rith had headed out across the sea. It would follow her scent trail, the unmistakable smell of draconic power.

The treefolk lord strode from its spot in the forest of Yavimaya. Kavu in their hundreds climbed onto it. They too would go seek Rith. Even if they must hibernate beneath chill oceans, they would go. They were not the only ones. As the treefolk lord went, it awoke others of its kind. In the scent language of plants, it conveyed the news. Rith had escaped. She had headed over the sea.

By the time the magnigoth guardian had reached the shores of Yavimaya, a hundred of its kin followed. Kavu filled their boughs. The Yavimayan army strode out to sea. Their roots churned the sandy shallows. Faster than any sailing ship, they pursued their lost Primeval.

CHAPTER 13
The Warrior's Feast

How like Thaddeus he is, this Lich Lord Dralnu, thought Agnate. He hefted his torch and glanced sidelong. Yes, he could almost be him—Thaddeus's face, his eyes, his hands. More than anything else, it was Thaddeus's voice. These were his words.

"When I lived, I was as you—a great warrior. It is the province of men to make war, to kill, as it is the province of women to make life."

Agnate and Dralnu descended through a black and twisting cave. Their companies followed—the five hundred Metathran who had fallen into the quicksand and the five hundred undead who had saved them. Boots and bones pattered in a stream at the base of the cave.

"I suffered a likely enough death for a warrior—slain by a greater foe," Dralnu continued. "That is when my story became unlikely. At that time, there was a lich lady in Urborg who collected fallen warriors. She raised them and restored their armor, their clothing, their very flesh. She raised me and put me in her collection."

Agnate nodded. "Not a fate worthy of a great warrior."

"No indeed. The ultimate sacrifice should not have been so meanly repaid," Lord Dralnu said. "I should have been burned or buried or left to rot in the swamp. I should not have been raised to dance on wires, but I bided my time.

"I learned all I could from the lich lady. She even taught me her necromantic spells. I used them first to enhance my body and mind. I used them next to destroy her."

"Destroy her?" Agnate echoed, surprised.

"It was a brutal act but an act of war. I was liberating the occupied nation that she ruled. I was taking her collection to turn it once again into an army."

Agnate's eyes gleamed like sapphires. "These troops, who saved us—these were her collection."

"Some," Lich Lord Dralnu responded. "Most are mine. I've become the equal of my mistress. I can raise even ashes to do my bidding."

A fragile question came to Agnate's lips. "How far does your power reach?"

"Throughout Urborg. My troops stand guard all across the island. The dead can wait indefinitely, whether within a shattered tree or a quicksand slough."

"I mean your magic," Agnate clarified. "How far can it reach? Can you touch other lands, distant battlefields?"

A dry smile formed on Dralnu's pallid lips. "There is someone you wish to raise. Every mortal has someone."

Agnate's gaze darkened. "Forgive my presumption."

"Forgive my inability to aid you," Dralnu replied. His breath had a dry, unwholesome quality. "My powers do not reach beyond this isle." He paused, seeming to consider. "Was this someone a great warrior?"

Blinking, Agnate said, "Yes. A great warrior slain by a great warrior—me." With a shuddering breath, Agnate changed the subject. "Why did you save us?"

"What?" asked Dralnu, seeming surprised.

"Why did you save us? You could have had a whole new division in your undead army if you'd allowed us to die."

"Unlife is no substitute for life," Dralnu responded without pause. "You forget, Agnate. I was once a warrior. No true warrior should die before his time. The world needs you and your troops, and it needs you alive. I would rather have you as living allies than undead minions. I do what I do for the good of war and warriors."

They were the sort of words Thaddeus would have spoken. It was more than that. Agnate and his troops owed this lich their lives. When Dralnu had invited them to his underworld kingdom to feast the new alliance, Agnate had been honor bound to accept.

Ahead, the pathway descended through its last, snaking turn. It opened into a large, deep cavern. Water led the way. From the moment they had left the world above, the troops had marched down through the trickling stream. It guided them to a world below.

Side by side, Agnate and Dralnu peered across the yawning spaces.

The cavern before them was immense. All around the perimeter of the space opened caves like the one where Agnate and Dralnu stood. Some of these passages emptied mere trickles of water across the sloping floor. A few to the right gushed regular rivers. The streams wended through deep channels, joined with other streams, and at last plunged into the wide pit at the center of the chamber.

All the light in the cavern came from that pit. It glowed crimson, the color of bare magma. A constant column of steam gushed upward from it. No doubt the waters that poured into that well fell until they stuck the world's hot soul. The incessant steam had built up a massive collection of stalactites above the pit. Even now, sultry winds coiled about the stalactites, adding minutely to them before slipping upward through cracks in the ceiling.

"Behold, Agnate, the city of Vhelnish."

Within the stalactites, lights glowed. Yellow and green, orange and purple, windows shone in their thousands. No solid fingers of stone, these structures were inverted towers. Instead of yearning skyward, they plunged toward fiery depths. Within their dripping walls would be chambers and stairways, libraries and staterooms, garrisons and guardhouses. Walkways stretched from tower to tower. Balconies perched above the reeling deeps. Here and there, just visible in shifting shadows, were the unliving inhabitants of this city.

"Vhelnish," whispered Agnate in awe.

"Yes. It is my city. Once it had been only a showcase for my mistress's collection. She kept warriors in niches as if they were statues. I have given them quarters of their own. She wished them to do nothing but stand. I have given them duties. I have made a life here for the dead. We work. We guard. We fight. We feast."

"All in mockery of the cities above," Agnate murmured before he could catch himself.

Dralnu did not bristle. "Not mockery but reflection. Throughout the world are priests who say death is not final, that we will live again in glory. I have died, Agnate. I tell you, there is nothing after death, nothing except oblivion. I have made a bargain with death to live again, to make a haven for virtuous souls that have gone before. No, it is not paradise, but neither is it oblivion."

A deep sadness moved through Agnate. Here was a righteous warrior who, in the absence of a loving deity, determined to provide an eternal reward to those who deserved one. Yes, he was a necromancer. Yes, Dralnu had made a dark bargain, but all mortals try to bargain with their killers. This was not the inevitable end of a perverse soul but the inevitable end of a righteous one.

"Come," Dralnu said.

He gestured toward a wide walkway that stretched from a nearby knob of stone up to the hanging city. Though wide enough to accommodate ten warriors abreast, when glimpsed against the yawning spaces, the path seemed a mere cobweb. Agnate had not even noticed it before. Now he glimpsed numerous other threads, ascending from distal points around the cavern.

Dralnu motioned Agnate upward.

"Are we the first living beings to walk this road?"

"Yes," the lich lord said. "But I hope you will not be the last, and I swear that all of you will return living to the daylight."

That was assurance enough. Agnate stepped onto the broad path. It was fashioned of braided cables, solid and flexible. With Dralnu beside him, he ascended the silken road.

If only this path had extended to Koilos, Agnate thought, perhaps Thaddeus could have climbed it.

A cold thrill went through Agnate. The sensation passed as he rose into misty heights. Water beaded on his tattooed forehead. He drew steam into his lungs. It wrapped his heart in a hot hand. Agnate's steps became numb things. He strode forward in happy bliss, a spirit entering the cloudy afterlife.

His troops followed more reluctantly. Hands were ready on weapons. Confusion and impatience showed in their eyes.

They do not understand death, Agnate realized. They deal it to others without hesitation, but they do not understand it. Death is not a thing that can be grasped. Death does the grasping.

From the time Agnate had slain Thaddeus, death had had its hold on him. Only here, on this strange highway, did he at last feel free.

Clouds rolled back. Vhelnish appeared, sudden and beautiful before him. Water-smoothed curtains of rock draped down around vast stalactites. Lantern and tallow set warm squares of light in the red mists. Monoliths jabbed down, their tips silhouetted against magma. The pit seemed almost an enormous sun at noonday.

Agnate swooned with vertigo.

A strong, cold hand steadied him. "Come, my friend. My people await. You are more than our guest. You are an avatar of all we once were."

Nodding, Agnate turned and exhorted his troops. "Do not fear, my people. We do not enter Vhelnish to remain. We come only to honor our host and his people, the warriors who went before. We come to honor those we have lost, those we had never known, those who live on in the weapons we bear and the knowledge of how to wield them. Come, my people. Do not shrink from death. Let us befriend it today! One day it comes for us all!"

Once again facing the city, Agnate strode with Dralnu inward.

Great gates stood ahead, massive in stone. Perfectly balanced, they pivoted easily aside, pushed by a ghastly pair of gate guards. Though dressed in fine livery, the men were gray skinned and mottled in rot. Rips in their flesh emitted light. The ravages of time had brought one guard's cheekbones through his skin. The other left oozy hand prints on the door.

Agnate's natural response would have been revulsion, but the way those men snapped to attention at their posts and stood in earnest solemnity made him feel only sorrow.

These were only the first such creatures Agnate encountered. In the arched passageways beyond, soldiers stood or bowed according to the customs of their lands. They saluted if they had arms to do so. They averted their gaze if they had eyes. In every way possible, they honored their living guests. Human, minotaur, dwarf, elf, Viashino, goblin . . . the undead minions of Dralnu bowed before Agnate and his troops.

It was a gauntlet to walk between the lines of pathetic creatures. Agnate did not fear physical injury, but each new horror wounded his soul. These could be his comrades, his foes. Here was the undeniable end for all warriors.

At last, the procession reached a great hall. It was a glorious space, carved out of jet-black stone. A vaulted ceiling above hung with the banners of hundreds of nations. The polished floor below held table after well-set table. All about stood Dralnu's finest warriors. They bowed as Agnate appeared at the door.

"Enter please, my lord. My folk have prepared a feast of real food for you and yours."

"You do us honor," Agnate said, bowing low.

Dralnu led him to a lofty table at the far end of the chamber. He showed Agnate his seat and directed his troops to theirs.

Dralnu approached, bearing a basin filled with black waters. He bowed deeply to the Metathran commander and set the basin at his feet.

"Allow me to do you one more honor. This is an ancient rite, from commander to commander, that will make us allies forever."

Agnate nodded, uncertain.

Kneeling, Dralnu deftly removed Agnate's boots and dipped his feet in the black tide. He washed the commander's feet, from toes to knees.

"I am your servant, Agnate of the Metathran."

"And I am your servant, Dralnu of the undead."

Revenants arrived, carrying between them a roast boar, steaming and succulent on a giant platter. Another servant emerged, wine flagons in his skeletal hands. He filled the goblets set there with a libation as red and thick as blood. Baskets of bread, trenchers of stew, bowls of fruit—the foods could have been acquired through only the most extreme efforts. Still, the banquet was plentiful and fragrant.

Such foods would have been poison to the undead warriors. Creatures such as they subsisted on worse fare—rotting flesh, organ meats, brains, pitchers of blood, and mounds of filth. Even as they sank their desiccated fingers into the horrid food, they glanced up with apologetic eyes.

It was more than Agnate's troops could take. They did not touch their food, instead sitting solemn and still at their places. Only Agnate ate, not wishing to offend.

Dralnu seemed to appreciate his efforts. Having completed the foot-washing ceremony, he had taken his place beside the Metathran commander.

He raised his goblet and said, "I drink to you, Commander Agnate."

Lifting his own goblet, Agnate replied, "And I to you."

Their goblets met. The allies drank, one of wine and the other of blood.

CHAPTER 14
The Battle on the Ice

The charge across the ice was a thing of glory.

Eladamri rode his colos at full gallop. The horned beast pounded across the glacier and leaped fissures with the ease of a child jumping puddles. To one side of Eladamri rode Liin Sivi. She held on with her legs while her toten-vec whirled overhead. To Eladamri's other side rode Warlord Astor. Eladamri was glad for his presence. The young warlord had an uncommon knack for word and sword and for finding his own path. Farther out along the line of charge rode Doyen Olvresk and Doyenne Tajamin. Their troops swarmed behind them, just able to keep pace.

Eladamri's own nations could not have run so far so fast. Instead, they crowded the decks of the Keldon long ships. Ice crackled beneath the surging blades. Longbows fought for space under full-bellied sails. Wind barked in canvas. Catapults strained against mountings.

Emerging from the wind-shadow of the mountains, the armada caught a gale. Warships rushed forward. They overtook infantry and cavalry both. Breasting through waves of charging muscle, the ships took the fore. Once ahead of their own lines, prow lances splayed. Archers nocked pitch-soaked arrows. Grenadiers lit oil bombards. Catapult captains called out launch signals. Rams drove eagerly toward the Phyrexian hordes.

"Keld!" It was the word for fuel and flame, for the people and their courage. This time, though, the word came from the mouths of catapult captains. It meant, "Fire!"

With a series of shuddering thumps, catapults hurled their payloads. From a hundred warships, black bombs rushed skyward. They trailed fire like awful wings. They arced down toward the Phyrexians. Bombs staved skulls and crushed thoraxes and ripped muscles. Fires ignited oil-blood, and Phyrexians exploded. Hunks of scale and claw bounded out to slay more monsters.

Another onslaught came from the ships. Torches ignited pitch-soaked arrowheads. Elf archers lifted their bows skyward. Strings grew taut.

"Keld!"

A thousand arrows flocked from the war vessels. Fire rattled as it tore through the air. Shafts reached the peak of their flight and dived downward. The ships' momentum carried the quarrels deep into the charging line of monsters. Arrowheads cracked off armor. They plunged into throats. They pierced eyes and the fiend brains beneath.

Even as catapults thudded with new loads and archers nocked new salvos, the lines closed. Long ships plunged through the burning remains of the Phyrexian front lines. Living beasts converged from ahead. All along the rails of the warships, infantry prepared pikes and swords.

With an inhuman roar, the main Phyrexian line crashed into the long ships. Prow pikes impaled many monsters. Great swords decapitated others. Grenadiers hurled bombs into the pelting mob. Archers turned their longbows from the skies to slay at point-blank range.

Still, Phyrexians clawed their way up the gunwales of the ships. They did not seem individual monsters but one monster with countless fangs and endless horns.

The ships with Keldon crews fared best. Their cudgels and axes pulped the beasts that tried to climb aboard.

The elven ships were worse beset. One was already overwhelmed. Its crew had come to pieces in Phyrexian claws. What remained of them fell in red tatters from the rails. The victors took what spoils they could use—grenades and weapons—and abandoned the ship to wind and ice. It veered, rattling along emptily before tipping into a broad crevasse.

"That was one of ours!" Eladamri shouted above the hoofbeats of his mount. His sword clove a Phyrexian trooper that had won past the line of long ships.

"They're all ours," replied Warlord Astor. His sword struck a scuta and cracked its shield like an eggshell. The colos bounded over the burning dead of Phyrexia. "They've paved our way. The true fight is ahead."

Liin Sivi yanked her toten-vec from the chest of a bloodstock and deftly caught the oily blade. "Let's get up there."

Bending toward the necks of their colos, the three warriors drove onward. Phyrexians loped toward them across the corpse-strewn ice. The three killed all those in reach and let the others go. They would be nothing against the Keldon hordes coming behind. Astor was right about the battle. A dense wave of scale and claw broke just ahead.

The great mountain yaks slew first. Their hooves were hardened and sharpened on ice itself, and they fell with a half-ton of weight atop them. Carapace cracked. Organs oozed. Phyrexians died. Colos bounded on, trampling the beasts beyond.

Their riders did killing work above. Eladamri's sword chopped through a powerful arm that clutched his neck. He kicked the huge monster back and peeled dead claws from his throat.

The monster lunged. It opened its mouth, intending to take with fangs what it couldn't with claws.

Eladamri gave the thing its arm back. He rammed the grisly end down its throat. It tried to swallow, but Eladamri twisted the limb. Bone caught in the beast's windpipe. Gurgling, it fell.

Another menace approached. Green and huge, the mogg goblin hurled itself onto the colos's back.

Eladamri's sword was too slow. It sliced the goblin shallowly across its belly, but the creature pounded down on him. Scaly fists smashed the elf's armor.

It had been a while since Eladamri had fought one of these natives of Rath, but the smell brought back memories. Eladamri swung his elbow up to crack the goblin's jaw. That gave him enough space to draw a dagger with his off hand. He rammed it into the cut his sword had started.

Cursing, the mogg leaped away from the stinging blow.

At last, Eladamri's sword had room. He slashed. The goblin came to ground in two pieces. It joined two more of its folk, slain by Eladamri's colos.

Beside him, a clutch of Keldons fought a gaunt creature that reared on a serpentine tail. White armor turned Keldon axes. Six long, barbed arms plucked up the fighters. A mouth of shifting plates bit away heads.

Eladamri drove his colos toward the brutal fight.

Something flashed out before him, and he reined in. Liin Sivi's toten-vec whirled toward the beast. Her blade reached where axes could not. The head soared perfectly into the monster's mouth. Metal bit into flesh. The chain went taut. With a roar, Liin Sivi yanked. The weapon came free, dragging mouth parts and membranes with it.

Unable to bite its foes, the Phyrexian began a retreat. It was too late. Keldons climbed it like ants devouring a worm. Their blades at last found chinks in the thing's armor. It fell to chunks beneath them.

Nearby, Astor fought aback his stamping steed. His eyes shone with the battle gleam of true Keldon warriors. A ring of bodies and oil surrounded him. Any creature that ventured into it ended up among the dead. Just now, a Phyrexian trooper charged him. Astor's axe chopped down between shoulder spikes and clove deep into the thing's ribcage. There, the blade jammed. Astor seemed not to notice. He hauled hard on the haft, lifting the trooper from the ground. The wriggling creature struggled to claw him, but he flung it off.

"They're breaking through!" Astor shouted, leveling his axe toward a spot on the distant battlefield.

Eladamri and Liin Sivi turned to see.

A Keldon long ship that had cruised deep into the Phyrexian lines had been captured. The beasts had turned the vessel, harnessing the winds and loading the catapults. With their own dead draping from the prow pikes, Phyrexians sailed the ship back toward the front lines. A monstrous infantry formed up on the ship. Already they reclaimed ice where their own troops had burned away. The vessel beat toward the heart of the Keldon army.

Oil bombs vaulted from its decks. Shrieking through the air, they dropped in a brimstone rain on the allies. A bomb that could kill a single Phyrexian could annihilate a whole elven squad. Even Keldons fell in the holocaustal onslaught. Those who fought on did so with their skin hanging in rags from their shoulders. They folded like paper before the Phyrexian charge.

"*That's* where the battle is!" shouted Warlord Astor.

He sent his colos bounding out across the ice, toward the skating ship. Astor's axe whirled in fury. He left behind a trail of twitching beasts. Liin Sivi widened that trail with the spinning reach of her toten-vec. Eladamri brought up the rear. He stood in the saddle and peered out across the glaring field.

As that black warship had drawn Phyrexians into a charge, it also drew Keldons into a counto a counter the battlefield, mounted warriors converged on the vessel. Eladamri glimpsed, in varied livery, the colors of Doyen Olvresk and Doyenne Tajamin. They came not only because the ship was breaking through their lines, but also because it was *their* ship, turned against them.

"Form up!" Warlord Astor called over his shoulder. "We'll go in tight! We'll take it back!"

Tucking her toten-vec, Liin Sivi drove her colos up beside Astor's. Eladamri came up the other side. More mounted warriors joined them, fanning out in a wide wedge.

The colos lowered their curled horns. They smashed into the Phyrexians before them. What monsters were not unmade by the horns were destroyed by blades. The colos cut through the flank of the Phyrexian charge and drove on toward the captured ship.

Astor bore down on the bloody gunwales. He did not slow. The ship loomed up. His mount's hooves bounded twice more before it launched from the ground. The mountain yak soared through the air. Wind ripped at its white fur. The colos cleared the rail. It came down atop an unwary Phyrexian. Hooves hammered the thing to the deck. Astor stood in the saddle and chopped another beast through the middle.

Two more Phyrexians died before the monsters recognized they had been boarded. By then, Liin Sivi's mount was landing and Eladamri's as well. The three warriors drove across the deck, hewing as they went. More yaks pounded onto the ship, bringing more Keldon warriors. The planks ran with glistening-oil. Shattered corpses fell from the rails. In moments, Astor and his warriors had taken back the deck.

"Get below! Cleanse the hold!" Astor shouted to Liin Sivi and Eladamri. They dismounted and went.

Astor meanwhile rode his mount up to the stern castle. He leaped from the saddle. Grabbing the ship's wheel, he turning it hard to windward. The ship lurched upwind, cutting into a bare section of ice.

"Back the main!" he ordered. Below, warriors hauled on the mainsail lines, cleating them off. The face of the sail caught wind and the ship slid backward. Spinning the wheel, Astor brought the long ship about. "Trim the main for a westward run! Load the catapults! Man the bows!"

Even as the sail caught wind again, the catapults were hurling fire back into the heart of the Phyrexian forces.

Eladamri and Liin Sivi returned from the hold. Their eyes glowed.

The elf commander said, "Not a beast remains below."

"Excellent," said Astor through clenched teeth. It wasn't clear whether he smiled or grimaced.

"Yes, excellent," came a new voice. Doyenne Tajamin rode her colos onto the stern castle and dismounted. Despite her words, her face was grim. "We need this ship. We need every ship, every grenade, every oil bomb."

The meaning of her words was plain. The allies were losing. Though Keldons and elves fought with furious valor, the Phyrexians were simply too many. Their lines stretched back across the glacier to the distant peaks. They flung themselves into the front with no regard for survival. Keldons could stand against almost every kind of warrior, but not this kind—not warriors without honor, without end.

In a voice of command, Doyenne Tajamin shouted, "Set a course for the Necropolis!"

Even as Astor turned the ship, the comrades saw the reason: the prize for which they fought was already in Phyrexian hands. Monstrous troops fortified their positions around the base of Necropolis Peak. The long ships that had driven toward that spot were mired at best and burning at worst. Colos riders could not smash through. Infantry could not slay them fast enough. All the while, out of reach of sword and catapult and spell, Phyrexians swarmed up the black cliffs beneath the Necropolis.

The monsters climbed with preternatural speed. They surrounded the peak. They poured into the halls of the guardians.

"Atrocity!" spat Doyenne Tajamin. "Before this battle is done, we will all lie in ice graves." Her hand tightened on the grip of her cudgel. Something changed on her face. She lifted the ancestral weapon before her.

Blood—Phyrexian and Keldon and elf—draped the ancient runes. The tales of Twilight were obscured beneath the gore of battle. Indeed, the glistening-oil even seemed caustic to the symbols. It hissed. Tendrils of white steam crazed the air. Heat trembled through the weapon.

"What's this?" Doyenne Tajamin wondered aloud.

"Look!" said Eladamri, pointing.

Sudden light flared from the Necropolis. Fires blazed. They roared out of every window and door. The very mountain shook with that initial blast. Then came a second. A ring of force spread from the summit across the sky. The third blast was the most powerful yet. Blinding light beamed from the dead city. It swallowed fire, so intense it was, and swallowed the disk of cloud. All dissolved before its brilliance.

Doyenne Tajamin watched a moment more before she fell to her knees. She clutched the sizzling cudgel to her breast. Breathless, she recited the words of the *Book of Keld*:

> And there shall come, in the darkest corner of Twilight, a light that will scour away the shadows. A new sun will dawn over Keld and draw into its compass all the clans and nations. As the warriors of Keld were firstborn from the hearth fire, so the new and true warriors of Keld will be secondborn from the burning sun. They will ride her golden bow from the world before to the world thereafter, and they will fight the final battle of Twilight.

As if in answer, dark figures emerged from the beaming windows and doors of the Necropolis. They were almost unseeable in that ferocious glare.

"The honored dead of Keld," Tajamin murmured worshipfully.

More plentiful than the monsters that had swarmed the peak, the ancient warriors of Keld emerged. They descended to do battle.

"Now we have our army! Every great warlord who ever lived joins us. They join us to fight the final battle of Twilight!"

Swarming downward, the first of the ancient warriors reached the base of the cliff. They drove the Phyrexians before them.

Rising to her feet, Doyenne Tajamin stared in awe. "With the eternal champions fighting for us, we cannot fall!"

Eladamri spoke, his voice quiet with dread. "But . . . they do not fight for us."

Doyenne Tajamin stared toward the front lines, where the ancient dead of Keld slew their own living warriors. "Atrocity. . . ."

CHAPTER 15
New Troops for Urborg

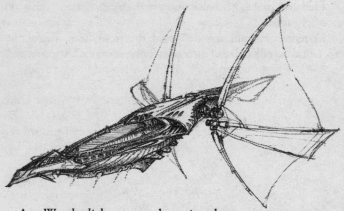

As *Weatherlight* tore the air above Urborg, Tahngarth tore the ground below. His ray cannon laid a highway of fire across an Urborgan slope. Beams ripped up grasses and dirt before striking the first Phyrexian bombard embrasure. It flared and melted, its crew buried in molten metal.

Across the forecastle, Gerrard was ranting. "Where the hell is Agnate!" he shouted. His cannon echoed the sentiment. Rays darted down into a swamp. Light ignited gases, which burst in a sudden blue glow. Azure fire wrapped a contingent of Phyrexians. They burned, white smoke pouring from beneath peeled black armor. Gerrard gritted his teeth in satisfaction. "We can't fight

128

the land battle too. These Metathran are worthless without him. Where the hell is Agnate?"

Weatherlight vaulted on, above a slough of skeletal trees.

Tahngarth considered grimly. "Perhaps he has fallen."

"Then the land battle is lost," Gerrard roared. "Look at them!"

As *Weatherlight* shot out beyond an ancient brake of thistle, Tahngarth looked down. Lowlands opened before the ship. There, a contingent of ten thousand Metathran crouched in shallow trenches. Their battle-axes lay idle beside them. Instead, they set powerstone pikes against impending attack. The woods beyond teemed with monsters, gathering to charge.

Gerrard sent a blistering shot down among them. It blasted a few Phyrexians but did little more.

"The damned Metathran entrench and wait! They brace for attack! Who's commanding them? With Agnate, they advanced."

Tahngarth snorted. "Without a great commander, the Metathran are nothing. We need new troops. Another army. Too bad *Weatherlight* can't carry more than a thousand." He loosed a single shot that moaned as it descended toward the trees. "If you found the right army, where every warrior was worth ten . . ."

Casting a wicked glance over his shoulder, Gerrard said, "Excellent idea, Tahngarth!" He leaned to the speaking tube. "Sisay, prepare to planeshift."

Her voice answered from the tube. "Where to?"

"Tahngarth's homeland."

Tahngarth sagged in the traces. Ever since he had been tortured in the Stronghold, he had dreaded returning to his people. To minotaurs, appearances mattered. A handsome beast was a virtuous warrior. A twisted creature was a monster. Under the torments of Greven *il*-Vec, Tahngarth had become a monster. He was certain his folk would reject him. His hands went numb on the fire controls. Urborg scrolled, watery and black, beneath him.

"I've got the coordinates laid in," Sisay replied.

"Take us there," Gerrard said. "The rest of the fleet and the Serrans can hold the skies while we're gone. Do it."

Sisay sent *Weatherlight* in a long, steady climb up the skies. Her engines roared. Her airfoils tucked. The Gaea figurehead drove up through racks of cloud. In moments, the island shrank to stern. The prow carved a hole in the heavens.

With a clap like thunder, Dominaria vanished. Blue sky dissolved into gray chaos. It buzzed in deadly disarray just beyond *Weatherlight*'s power envelope.

Tahngarth stared bleakly out at the Blind Eternities. This nowhere place somehow soothed him.

The planeshift was done all too soon. The envelope around *Weatherlight* turned to sky and water. Suddenly, all the world was blue and white. Above the hurtling ship arced a cerulean dome. Below it stretched an endless sea. The two were halves of each other, brilliance and darkness. *Weatherlight* slid between them, her prow pointing toward the arrow-straight horizon.

"Where is it?" rumbled Tahngarth.

"I don't know," replied Sisay. "The coordinates are correct." Her words faded away to the roar of the engines.

"What do you mean?" Tahngarth asked. "How can a whole continent disappear?"

Gerrard snapped his fingers. "Teferi!"

"What?" the minotaur barked.

"Urza said something about his phasing out Zhalfir—magically taking it. He said only the sea remained. He must have taken the Talruum mountains too."

Tahngarth stood and peered at the choppy sea. He couldn't believe it. "He took the whole continent?"

Gerrard shrugged. "That's what Urza said."

It was a brutal irony. A moment ago, he feared rejection from his people. Now, they didn't even exist.

Faltering, Gerrard added, "Urza said something about refugees. He said a contingent of Talruum minotaurs went to Hurloon."

"Next stop, Hurloon?" Sisay asked.

Eyes blazing with fire, Tahngarth growled at Gerrard, "Why are you doing this?"

Gerrard cast a glance behind him. "You said we needed another army."

Eyes darkening, Tahngarth crossed his arms. "How are you going to enlist their aid?"

Gerrard shrugged. "I don't know. Honor? The promise of a brutal fight? What do you suggest?"

"Don't expect me to be your liaison, Gerrard. They will hate me."

Gerrard shot back, "They just don't know you like I do." Turning to the speaking tube, he said, "Captain Sisay, take us to Hurloon."

"Aye, Commander."

Tahngarth closed his eyes as the engines took hold of his stomach. He felt the beaming sun go out of existence. His shoulders grew cold. The tearing winds of the deck died to nothing. The whine of *Weatherlight*'s power core was dampened, sound slipping away into the Blind Eternities. Tahngarth did not watch. He could not bear to see the world dissolve again.

Sound changed. The engine's clamor rebounded from ground. Sudden wind tore at Tahngarth's hide. The cold of evening wrapped him, the wet of alluvial plains. Wood smoke hung in the air. This would be Hurloon. He opened his eyes.

Immediately he wished he hadn't. Below, in the last glow of the day, stretched an enormous wasteland. It had once been the city of Kaldroom, a garrison ground for centuries of minotaur warriors. Now, the city was in ruins. Every roof, every fence, every wooden thing had burned away. Only stone foundations and rubble walls remained. They twisted away to the horizon. Within them lay bodies, minotaur bodies—bulls and cows and calves. They had died where they had stood, slaughtered by the same fire that had destroyed their city. The streets of the city were lined with craters. Smoldering fires lit the darkness. They sent gray smoke skyward. *Weatherlight* shot among them, stirring the smoke in twin vortices.

Tahngarth pulled himself from the gunner traces and stood at the rail. He stared with bald horror at the scene below. These had not been warriors. These had been merchants and teachers and families. The fire that had slain them had not fallen from the sky. It had burned on Rath as the world overlaid. With utter precision, the Phyrexians had turned a whole city into an oven.

Lifting his head to the skies, Tahngarth released a roar. It mixed with the thrum of the engines and the shout of the air. Long and furious, the sound pealed out across the plains.

The minotaurs of Talruum were gone, and those of Kaldroom were slaughtered wholesale. Better to have disappeared into the ocean than to have died like this. And what of the other cities? Was Tahngarth the last of his people to live? Twisted into the semblance of Phyrexian monstrosity, was he all that remained of the once-proud race?

Weatherlight shrieked out across the city to the garrison grounds. Half the population of Kaldroom had dwelt within the barracks of that place. They remained. Minotaur warriors were laid foot-to-head, row on row across the ground. Their bodies were pristine, untouched by the fire that had destroyed the populace. Even their armor was polished, even their uniforms. Not one showed the wound that had killed him. Their eyes had all been propped open as hunters do to the creatures they stuff. What were these corpses? Trophies? Why would Phyrexians bother to chain corpses together?

"They're alive. . . ." Tahngarth whispered breathlessly. The realization prickled his hide with a memory.

He is trapped. A red beam stabs down at him from a panel above. It strikes his flesh. It twists his horns and swells his muscles and transforms him into a monster.

Shaken by the flashback, Tahngarth suddenly knew why the Phyrexians had kept these warriors alive.

Without bothering with his gunner's harness, Tahngarth swung his cannon to the fore and was squeezing off his first shot before he had even glimpsed what must lie beyond. Red rays ripped the air, plunging toward a huge black building, as amorphous as a mountain. It was a flowstone laboratory, grown on Rath and overlaid on Kaldroom. Tahngarth's shot struck the side of the structure. It lit up a portico and bathed the scabrous priests that stood there. They burned like paper. The portico collapsed. A hole opened in the wall. Through it, Tahngarth glimpsed what lay within: torture chambers, vivisection tables, vats of glistening-oil. It was only a moment's glimpse before *Weatherlight* hurtled above the black rooftop, but it was enough to convince Tahngarth.

"We must destroy that building!"

"What is it?" Gerrard shouted as *Weatherlight* entered a long, sweeping turn to port.

"A Phyrexian incubation ground. They've killed the citizens and have somehow drugged the garrison. They're going to turn them into monsters. They're going to make them all like me. We have to destroy that factory."

A beam stabbed up from the structure and sliced across the sky. It howled so close overhead that the hairs on Tahngarth's head curled. Two more shots roared from other guns.

"They're on to us!" Sisay shouted.

Weatherlight dropped out from under the bolts. She spread her wings to catch the air. A sudden flare of her engines skipped her out along the lowlands. Flack burst in a tight trail behind her.

Gerrard, the amidships gunners, and Squee at the tail filled the skies with answering fire.

Tahngarth meanwhile clambered into his traces. "Bring us about so I can draw a bead!"

"I'm still being evasive!" Sisay hissed.

A plasma blast from the laboratory swarmed up toward Gerrard's gun. The energy did not seem to move, only to grow wider. Cursing, Gerrard shot a volley down the throat of the attack.

Energy met energy. The center of the plasma ball was ripped away, but its mantle still struck the ship. Plasma ate through the port gunwale and two of the ribs. It dissolved the rail on either side of Gerrard's gun, and flack arched over his head.

The speaking tubes were suddenly jammed with voices:

"Multani, hold us together!"

"Target those guns, Squee!"

"Tuck the wings!"

"Full power!"

"Bring us about!"

The shouts were echoed in blazing rays from the guns and roaring fire from the engines. Like an angry hornet angling toward its tormentor, *Weatherlight* shot above the trailing fire. Her port-side guns bled the sky. She turned her bow hard toward the laboratory.

At last Tahngarth could draw a bead. He unleashed a barrage that lit up the fields below. Flares overwhelmed Phyrexian fire and pulverized the gun that had flung it. A second blast obliterated another bombard along the structure's edge. Tahngarth shifted his aim toward the roof line. The other gunners could take out the weaponry. Tahngarth would destroy the factory.

A blast ripped a long hole in the roof. Another burned away rafters and gantries. The third punched past, to row on row of vats. The golden stuff in them was glistening-oil, the placental fluid of newts. The volatile liquid made one strike work like five.

Vats exploded. The miserable creatures within died in an instant. They would not bear Tahngarth's shame. Blasts rocked the structure and hurled metal and glass outward. Blazing oil lit more vats. They flamed and burst. A chain reaction swept through the incubation chambers. In manifold explosions, the core of the building went up.

Not pausing to admire the conflagration, Tahngarth hurled bolts of destruction into the adjacent rooftops. Vivisection laboratories were laid bare. Their inhabitants glared upward in startled dread in the moments before they were broiled alive. More shots ripped open the torture chambers.

Tahngarth stared feverishly down. A strange abstraction contorted the scene before him.

His gun is a flat panel in the ceiling. It pours a red ray down onto his flesh. The stinging strokes repair his deformity. They return his soul to its former, beautiful state.

Yes, he felt the shuddering of *Weatherlight* as she took blast after blast. Yes, he knew that by the time the factory and its defenders were destroyed, the ship would not be battle worthy, perhaps not even sky worthy. It didn't matter. Tahngarth would save them. He would save his people the fate he had endured, and in saving them, he would save himself.

CHAPTER 16
In Yawgmoth's Workshop

Nine titans towered above a blasted underworld.

The second sphere of Phyrexia was a scrap heap. The ground consisted of rusted iron and corroded brass. Inert machines lay like dead giants on the horizon. Here and there, smokestacks jutted from the ground. They spewed constant pillars of soot high into the air. The metallic waste spread into a churning black firmament miles overhead. Among columns of soot rose columns of metal. Girders and pipes ran like veins on their outer edges. As wide around as whole cities, the pillars extended from the ground to the smoggy firmament above. Here and there, the clouds parted to show not an open sky but a closed vault. It was the underbelly of the first sphere. Enormous trusses stretched column to column. Their metal was encrusted with carbuncles. There was no sun here, no stars. Were it not for occasional blasts of fire from the smokestacks, there would have been no light in this sphere at all. As it was, the red glares leant a flickering and lurid aspect to the landscape.

Planeswalkers did not need light. They could see heat signatures, and there were plenty of those. There were other signatures here too. Dead ahead, some five miles from where the titan engines stood, the bomb production facility lay. Each of the stone-charger shells in that factory gave off a null signature. Its mana-voided core warped natural energies. The total effect, even at five miles, was unmistakable.

Each of us has the capacity to take twenty warheads, Urza told his immortal comrades. *Gather that number, 'walk to the master columns, set the charges, and rendezvous on the third sphere.*

Taysir remarked, *A simple plan—*

From a simple mind, supplied Szat, kicking a shattered mechanism with the claw of his black dragon suit.

—but Phyrexia is not a simple place, Taysir finished. The multi-colored gemstones of his suit scintillated in the eerie darkness.

Within the pilot orb of his own titan engine, Urza made final adjustments. Small lightnings scintillated on the energy fork at the peak of the suit. *This sphere is a habitat, just like the first, except here there are only predators, only mechanical watchdogs—the Devourer, the Dreadnought, the Diabolic Machine. . . .*

Holding a rusted cog in her ivy-vined hand, Freyalise said, *You seem all too impressed by those names, artificer.*

Urza's titan engine almost shrugged. *And why not? They are masterworks of design. Where Thran artifice ended, Phyrexian artifice began. Engines such as these have never been equaled on Dominaria— except in these suits, of course. And you would do well to show a little appreciation yourselves. Without these suits, the caustic atmosphere would rip your nerves to rags.*

Daria coyly crossed the legs of her lithe and perfectly balanced titan suit—a feat none of the other engines were capable of, and said, *And I suppose if we get killed, it's our fault, not a design flaw.*

Urza peered out of the cockpit dome and gave a rare smile. *And I thought you didn't understand me.* With that, he turned toward the distant bomb factory. *Let's go. Every moment we wait is another moment for the Dreadnought to find us.*

Above his piloting bulb, the energy fork flickered with an impending storm. Its blue reflection crazed the glass below. The bulb seemed a mad, glaring eye. Tripod feet crunched down atop piles of twisted scrap. Metal shrieked against metal. Two more steps, and Urza was at a full run.

Bo Levar surged up to one side. Clumps of Urborgan mud fell from the pounding legs of his titan engine. Tatters of tobacco dropped from the joints in his hand as he clawed past a metal pillar.

You ever done this before, Urza?

Attack Phyrexia? he asked curtly over the noise of the engines.

No, attack an ammo dump, Bo Levar replied idly, *because you're doing it wrong.*

The words that returned were snide. *And you're an expert because—?*

The foes of free trade are known to assemble vast arsenals. I've made quite a few raids in my time.

And what am I doing wrong?

Bo Levar reached down to the mud-encrusted knee joint of his suit and grabbed a clod. He shoved the wet stuff onto Urza's energy fork, diffusing the lightning storm.

First, you've got to remember that the ammo's not your enemy, the guards are. You go in there blazing lightning and rockets, we'll all be blasted to oblivion.

Stone chargers can't be set off that way.

But you don't know what other munitions can. Bo Levar let out a satisfied sigh, and the interior of his pilot bulb grew momentarily blue-gray. *Windgrace and I will take point. Follow and learn.*

With a sudden burst of speed, Bo Levar outpaced Urza. Lord Windgrace's engine bounding up beside him. On all fours, it was the fastest titan. Side by side, Bo Levar and Lord Windgrace raced toward the installation. Urza followed shortly behind, with the other six in company.

It was only a mile away now, a roofless assemblage of demonic machines—toothy cranes, cobweb gantries, smelting buckets, smoking furnaces, rivers of molten metal, mounds of shattered crystal, and droves of artifact drones.

In their midst stood row on gleaming row of stone chargers, the most powerful bombs developed by the Thran. One stone charger could annihilate a huge city, scouring soil to bedrock and irradiating a hundred miles with deadly concentrations of white mana. It was rumored that Yawgmoth had used such devices to eradicate his rivals in the Thran-Phyrexian war. Now, those bombs would be used on Yawgmoth's own world.

The drones are no concern, Bo Levar advised. *It's whatever watchdog guards the drones—*

A huge and toothy mechanism rose suddenly before the titan engines. It had lain dormant amid piles of scrap, waiting for intruders. Now the thing lunged up from its well of metal. It had the configuration of a sea urchin, rods bristling outward from a central body. Each rod was tipped in a pair of jagged bear-trap mechanisms, ratcheted open. The vicious things swung out to clamp onto Bo Levar and Lord Windgrace

Without breaking stride, Bo Levar said, *Here's what I meant.* He leaped over the snapping jaws of the Phyrexian defender. Lord Windgrace did likewise. Both titans sailed through the smoky air.

Eschewing the advice of his lessers, Urza halted before the monstrous machine and loosed a pair of rockets. They surged from their wrist housings and corkscrewed toward the beast. The first missile struck a pair of snapping jaws and deflected upward to explode in clear air. The other passed perniciously through the forest of rods, screamed out over the intervening space, and struck a blast furnace. The detonation cracked away metal and brick, loosing a great river of molten steel. It gushed across an adjacent array of stone chargers, liquefying their shells and rendering them useless.

Clucking quietly in his piloting bulb, Bo Levar said, *That wasn't so well done.* With a nonchalant kick, he struck the back side of the defender mechanism, where none of the rods jutted. Like an urchin pried from its rock, the thing folded to one side.

Windgrace administered the killing blow. Blue motes swarmed from the eyes of titan suit, struck the drive mechanism before him, and liquefied it. The mouths snapped a few more times spasmodically before they lay still.

Brushing the hands of his titan suit, Bo Levar said, *Let's see what they've got for us next.*

Look out! sent Kristina. Her weighty engine hurtled through the air above the destroyed mechanism and the other titans. She came down on the next guardian.

This monster was more muscle than machine. Like the dragon engines of the first sphere, its flesh was living metal. Unlike them, the thousand-legged giant millipede was too ferocious a predator to have free run of the first sphere. Its fang-studded mouth reared into the air.

Kristina ducked beneath the striking head. The titanium toes of her engine cracked into the back of the great beast. A quick spell made those toes razor sharp. Feet slid between folding plates of metal. With similarly honed fingers, Kristina crouched and grabbed handholds. She heaved, ripping open the back of the monster. Sparks spewed from ruptured wires. Pneumatic muscles groaned as she yanked again. Steel cables separated beneath the millipede's plates. Cords lashed.

Kristina was dauntless. She plunged her hands deeper. Titanic fingers grasped adjacent ribs along the millipede's torso. Spells heightened the tensile strength of her own gears. She pulled. With a pop and an acrid gray cloud of smoke, the nerve center of the beast separated. Severed halves of the monster flopped in biomechanical agony. Kristina continued her grim work until she had completely ripped it in two.

The joints of her suit steamed with exertion. Kristina rose triumphantly in the breach of the worm.

Commodore Guff arrived, his titan engine striking a dignified pose. Through a haze of smoke, he peered out of the pilot capsule and stared appreciatively at Kristina's handiwork.

By Belinus! You've got a way with bugs. We'd had critters like that back when I was a kid, and we ripped 'em in half too, but just to watch 'em grow a new mouth on both ends—

Kristina was too slow—they all were too slow. Both new mouths lunged for her engine. It seemed Yawgmoth had known the signature defense of living millipedes. The first mouth bit straight through Kristina's pilot bulb. Glass shattered and metal sheered. The bulb crushed like an egg. The second fastened onto the torso of her engine. In dynamic opposition, the two mouths ripped the head away from the body.

Had she 'walked? Had she 'walked? came Taysir's anxious thoughts.

With an animal shriek, Szat hurled himself between the two halves of the beast. He had learned from Kristina's mistake. You couldn't tear this beast apart. You had to kill it from the inside out.

Swallowing, one mouth lunged for Szat. He caught its jaws and roared, pouring fire down the metal throat. While the flame went from red-hot to white-hot, Szat also sent a cloud of corruption down the beast's gullet. Millipede teeth wept like candles. Metallic flesh melted from metallic bones. Neural networks turned to sparking goo. Szat's attack killed the brain of the thing. It went limp, settling like a long, deflated balloon.

Hurling the dead creature down, Szat whirled to attack the other millipede at his back.

He breathed fire. He poured out corruption.

But it wasn't the other half of the millipede that he slew. It was already dead, smoldering in blackness beneath the angry figure of Kristina. She had planeswalked away from her titan engine just as it was dismantled. Reappearing aback the second beast, she marshaled her full arsenal of planeswalking spells. The monster lay in dead runnels beneath her, but every last spell was gone from the woman. Battling the caustic air all around her, she had no time to 'walk again.

Szat's firestorm dismantled her. Skin, skull, and brain—brain was the thing, whether with a millipede or a planeswalker. If she couldn't think, she couldn't step away from danger, couldn't reassemble a new body. She was gone. Obliterated. An eternity over in an instant.

Szat stood gaping while another beast attacked. This was no Phyrexian but a more deadly mechanism—Taysir, onetime love of Kristina. He fell like a mountain on his fellow titan, hurling him to the scrap heap and landing on top.

You careless bastard! You damned vicious monster!

Taysir was proving himself little better, furiously battering the titan engine of his foe. It was his mistake. Szat was not helpless like Kristina.

Flipping over, Szat hurled Taysir's titan off him. *She killed herself. She got in my way.*

Both titans were knocked back by a sudden presence between them—Urza Planeswalker in the largest, most powerful engine of all. *Hold, both of you. Have you forgotten our mission?*

Taysir's suit flashed in rage. *Have you forgotten Kristina?*

Szat sneered. *Urza always forgets the dead.*

You're implicated in this, Urza. You're the one who insisted on bringing this . . . this . . . murdering monster. Maybe you needed somebody else who would love this place, Taysir roared.

Urza stared from his pilot bulb with bald incomprehension. *What are you talking about?*

Oh, don't kid yourself, Urza. You love Phyrexia like a man loves a woman. You love her lines. You love her machines. You love the perfection of design through constant war. You don't want to blow up this place. You want to take it as your own!

Enough! Urza shouted. *Enough! This was an accident. It shows how vulnerable we all are without our titan suits. Keep them on. In the meantime, I will prove to you what little love I have for this world. On! On to the stone-chargers!*

The three had been so immersed in their argument that they hadn't realized the other five had fought on toward the munitions factory. Bo Levar and Commodore Guff led the charge.

Have you seen this one? Bo Levar asked as new defenders rose in a swarm about him. The mechanisms had the configuration of tadpoles, though instead of tails they had single lashing wings. Their main body consisted of gnashing teeth. Bo Levar easily grabbed the wing of the first creature and swung it in an arc before him. The titan engine's glove glowed with a blue radiance that proliferated out across the body of the defender. It seemed to draw the other defenders magnetically inward. They converged around the first beast. The chattering jaws chewed each other to shreds of metal. *Twenty in one blow.*

I'll be jiggered, said Commodore Guff in genuine amazement. *Combining martial sciences with magical ones.* . . .

The wave of the future, Bo Levar said. *You watch. Once this business is done, this kind of stuff will be huge.*

Let me have a go, the commodore replied. He grappled a huge, spidery construct that rose in his path. Various colors of magic flashed from the titan and raced along the rodlike legs of the beast. The first spell managed to produce an odd odor, the second to cover the spider in rampant ivy, and the third to send it floating away toward the smoggy ceiling of the sphere. *Ah, perfect. I'll be happy to write about that one.*

As Bo Levar and Commodore Guff blazed the trail forward, the other titans loped afterward, Urza last of all.

Taysir had sounded so like Barrin. The mage master had once joked that the only difference between Urza and Yawgmoth was a four-thousand-year head start. Such comments were not helpful, and Barrin had been full of them.

Taysir and Szat had been wrong. Urza didn't forget the dead. Every day since he'd killed his brother Mishra—it was a mercy killing, yes—Urza remembered him. He remembered Xantcha and Ratepe, who had been Mishra for him and had helped him reclaim his mind. He remembered the students and scholars of the first Tolaria and of New Tolaria. Most of all, though, he remembered Barrin. That was a loss Urza would never recover from. Barrin, Xantcha, Mishra—they had all become a single beloved other lost for all time. Urza remembered all too well.

His dark reverie was broken by a bright vision. He and his team had reached the ammunitions factory. Before them, row on glorious, gleaming row, stretched thousands of stone-charger shells.

Beautiful.

CHAPTER 17
The Twice Dead

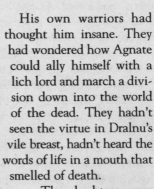

His own warriors had thought him insane. They had wondered how Agnate could ally himself with a lich lord and march a division down into the world of the dead. They hadn't seen the virtue in Dralnu's vile breast, hadn't heard the words of life in a mouth that smelled of death.

The doubters were proven wrong. In sunlight and cypress break, they saw the truth. The five hundred troops Agnate had led down among the dead had emerged again, accompanied by a hundredfold allies. Agnate's forces now marched with an undead army of fifty thousand. Dralnu had taken Thaddeus's portion. His ghouls and skeletons and zombies and revenants had replaced Thaddeus's warriors. At last, Agnate had a counterpart toward whom to drive in the deadly Metathran pincer.

How right he had been. How perfect this felt, to fight so.

Reaping Phyrexians like grass, Agnate and his vanguard topped a low ridge. Beyond it opened a wide mudflat beside the sea. Phyrexians in their multitude crowded the spot. They had nowhere left to flee. Voda warriors tore apart any who sought escape in the water. It was a fitting trap for the arrogant beasts.

Agnate peered down the ridge. It swept in a long curve around the flat. On the opposite side, a mere mile distant, appeared Lich Lord Dralnu with his contingent. The timing could not have been more precise if it had been Thaddeus who stood there. It was time for the pincers to close. Agnate gave a sharp hand signal. As one his Metathran and the armies of the dead descended the ridge at a charge. They crashed into the mud-caked Phyrexians.

There was pure joy in this. Agnate's battle-axe batted away a bloodstock's raking claw. The Phyrexian centaur reeled back. Following through, Agnate brought the axe downward to sever the beast's forelimbs. The bloodstock fell before him but still clawed. Agnate's axe ended its struggles.

Agnate stared down at the split head of the thing. He had delivered Thaddeus's mercy blow the same way and for the same reason. The work of vat priests was irreversible and unbearable. Agnate's axe was not a destroyer but a liberator.

That was the joy of this battle. It was not war but salvation. He was not slaying souls but freeing them. When he and Dralnu were done this day, even the mud would be clean.

Such are the fleeting fancies of warriors between axe blows.

Agnate's weapon swung toward a Phyrexian crab. On a tripod of bladelike legs, the mechanism had only one vulnerable spot— a trio of fleshy heads grafted to its back. The heads were fused in back, three sets of eyes staring in three separate directions. Agnate's axe fell. It bisected two of the heads, but the third lived. One of the thing's claws flung back the axe. Another grabbed Agnate's free hand. The last gripped his weapon arm, dragging him toward pelvic scythes.

Agnate had one option. Instead of struggling to break free, he hurled himself inward and head-butted the remaining face. It collapsed like an egg. Agnate reared, his head flinging glistening-oil, but he could not break free. He butted the creature again. This time, something gray mixed with the gold, and the creature slumped.

Agnate escaped. He wiped oil back along his pate.

To either side, Metathran troops formed a blue wave across the mudflats. Where their tide rolled, monsters fell. In muddy graves and thrashing seas, Phyrexians lay dead.

Agnate's axe sang above the heads of his foes. Here it clove the skull-shield of a scuta. There it chopped through the waist of a Phyrexian trooper. It bashed back claws and bashed in teeth. It liberated scores of souls from the Phyrexian prisons they called their bodies.

Then blade met blade. Agnate's axe rebounded. A Phyrexian slasher advanced to kill him. He couldn't do likewise. There were no soft spots on the artifact engine. It was all razor edges. Three knifelike legs supported a body that bristled with whirling steel.

Agnate backed away, swinging. His weapon only clanged on the foremost scythe. The machine scuttled toward him. Agnate swept his axe downward but nearly tripped over a dead body. The axe bit deep in the mud and was mired. He yanked on it. The machine leaped at him. Agnate released the weapon and retreated beyond the corpse.

Reaching down, he lifted the body he had stumbled over—a Phyrexian trooper. Hoisting it overhead, Agnate hurled it down on the slasher. Its main blade impaled the corpse, while side blades shredded the body. The Phyrexian's weight shoved the slasher's legs into the mud. Hefting another corpse, Agnate flung it down atop the machine. Deeper the thing went. Two more bodies, and the slasher was hopelessly stuck.

He had to laugh.

Striding past the machine, Agnate worked his axe free from the mud. The battle raged ahead of him. Only a narrow wedge of monsters remained between the closing halves of the army. Eager to deal the final blows, the Metathran commander leaped back into battle.

He reached the front lines at a run, axe lifted high. It came down with a profound stroke that entered the crown of a blood-stock's head and exited its belly. The cloven monster fell before him as if in a deep bow. Agnate's axe decapitated a monster beyond—a ghoul with dripping sores across its flesh. Like a man hewing wood, Agnate swung again, slaying a zombie in rotten rags. He raised his blade and began another attack, but something stayed his hand.

Thaddeus. No, not Thaddeus—Lich Lord Dralnu.

The necromancer gripped Agnate's forearm in an implacably powerful claw. His mouth opened, and words that smelled faintly of rot emerged.

"Hold, Agnate. You do not slay Phyrexians but your own troops. The foes are gone. The day is won."

Beneath a brow that streamed sweat, Agnate blinked. "What?"

"The day is won," said the lich lord simply.

Agnate lowered his axe and took a deep breath. He looked at the zombie and ghoul he had destroyed. "I did not realize—"

"War has its casualties. I have lost ten thousand in this fight, and you perhaps five thousand."

"That many?" Agnate wondered aloud. He glanced back at the battlefield. Most of the corpses there were Phyrexian, but there were many Metathran among them. The thought grieved Agnate. The bloodlust of battle was draining from him. "We've slain many Phyrexians today. I would guess thirty to forty thousand. The five and ten thousand that we lost died valiantly."

"Oh, your troops are not lost, my friend," Lich Lord Dralnu said. A strange smile showed on his face. "Not while we are allies. I will merely raise them to fight again. They are perhaps lost to you, but they are gained by me. That way, each of us has lost only five thousand."

Agnate nodded, feeling vaguely unsettled. "Will you raise also these?" He pointed to the zombie and ghoul. "And your other slain troops?"

"No. The twice dead can never rise again."

* * * * *

Bone fires burned high along the mudflats that night.

Fatigued Metathran and indefatigable undead had worked side by side to drag the corpses into funereal pyres—nine for the Phyrexians and five for undead. The latter had been laid out ceremonially on wood soaked in glistening-oil. The former had been tossed in heaps on the mud. Even now, the monsters' bodies burned with alacrity. Fires melted the metals within them. Hearts sizzled and burst in sudden gushes of oil that made flames leap and pop. The undead gave their bodies to the wind more gradually. Lying decorously on their pyres, they surrendered to flame. It licked away their hair and skin and muscle down to bone.

Not so the Metathran dead. On litters fashioned from nearby trees, they rode toward Vhelnish. Lich Lord Dralnu went with them, eager to restore them to life.

Agnate wished the lich lord had remained. He peered out the flap of his command tent.

The ocean was steel-blue beneath a sky veiled in sunset. The tide had crept slowly in across the mudflats. It had slid a mirror of water beneath the burning pyres. Pillars of fire stood on the waters and sent their reflected blaze down in them. It was a beautiful, feral scene, the dead giving light and heat to the living.

Agnate peered out along the ridge where his troops camped. Their fires were pale imitations of the pyres, flickering like lightning bugs. In the woods beyond, undead stood guard. Ever vigilant, ever faithful, those ancient warriors would keep Agnate's troops safe tonight.

Still, he felt uneasy. Withdrawing from the tent flaps, he sat on a camp chair. It was time to shuck the weary armor of the day. Agnate drew the boots from his feet and the shin guards from his legs. He removed his breastplate and the sweat-soaked tunic beneath. Everything itched. That was the cost of hard-fought battle in good armor. The salt water would cleanse his skin. It would sterilize his wounds.

Stripping bare, Agnate emerged from his tent. He strode down the embankment and onto the mudflats. Water splashed about his ankles. It stung his feet, but the sensation was warm and good. He strode out among the still-burning pyres. Their radiance bathed his skin in heat and light. Through the flames, he glimpsed Phyrexian skulls. Eyes of fire flickered in their sockets. Agnate nodded to them. He'd grown comfortable among the dead.

Always before, death had been inviolable. Lich Lord Dralnu had changed all that. Warriors brought death, and lich lords brought new life. The walls of eternity were breached, and Agnate and Dralnu marched through.

The Metathran commander strode out beyond the pillars of fire, toward the dark and deep waters beyond. No longer did the water sting. Now it welcomed him. Sand replaced mud beneath Agnate's feet. It sloped quickly away. He descended the bank. Water rose to his shoulders. It slid up his neck, across his bald scalp, into his pores. It closed over him.

The roar of fire was gone, the camp sounds, the night noises of the jungle. . . . A numb silence settled over Agnate. He felt only the nudge of waves as they dragged over him.

This must be what it is like to be dead, truly dead—dead for the second time, as Dralnu had said. Numb silence. Darkness. Nothing. It would be welcome after all the striving. It was a mercy that even Dralnu could not reach past the second death.

All too soon, the breath in Agnate's chest grew hot. It ached to be expelled. His lungs pleaded to breathe in. Life was insistent, impatient. Agnate turned reluctantly back toward the shore. He walked upward. His head broke the surface. He breathed. Water rolled from his ears, taking the placid silence with it. Angry flames and muttering men and nocturnal cries intruded on his reverie. It was not his time to die. Not yet.

The steps were few between total immersion and ankle-deep water. The dead blazed to every side. Fire dried Agnate's skin. Salt left fine lines of grit across his muscles. Every cell seemed to ache. It felt like Agnate's own flesh burned. Had he been stung by jellyfish while he waded?

Spreading his arms out, Agnate peered down at his body. Only then did he see the dark spots on his legs. They began at his knees and thickened as they descended his calves. Lifting one foot from the water, he saw that the blemishes covered his feet. Mud?

Agnate reached down with his thumb and rubbed a large black spot on his ankle. The darkness bunched up before his thumbnail and tumbled away, as if it had been mud, but it left a deep divot in his flesh.

It was his flesh, turning to rot.

Agnate knew every ailment that could afflict a soldier. This was different. This was no simple gangrene, eating away dead flesh. This was a disease that ate away healthy tissue.

Amputation. It was the only solution. He could do without his lower legs. He could even rig stilts to let him run and fight. It would save the rest of his body.

Except that, when he looked closer in the firelight, he saw smaller spots had spread up his thighs, and pinpoints of corruption rose even to his ribs.

The walls of death were not meant to keep the living out but to keep the dead in. Soon, all too soon, Agnate would be among the dead.

CHAPTER 18
Twilight Falls

The Necropolis blazed, a second sun beneath the first. Its light erased the basalt cliffs on which it sat and fused the citadel with the sky. From horizon to horizon, the heavens were the color of lightning. Nothing impure could remain in them.

Everything impure covered the glacier below. They were all the same—living Keldons and dead Keldons, Skyshroud elves and Steel Leaf elves, doyen and doyenne and Phyrexian—all killers. Blood and oil gushed across dazzling ice. Bodies plunged into mile-deep crevasses. Keldon warlords battled Keldon legends. Phyrexians slew elves. All fought in the blind fury of the end of times.

Into the sea of death sailed a long ship with full-bellied main. Keldons and elves swept aside gratefully as the warcraft roared up in their midst. The ship surged on into Phyrexians. Prow spikes impaled the bugs and their undead allies. They writhed, struggling to pull themselves free.

Other monsters clawed the gunwales. The first were dragged beneath its skating keel. Their severed bodies clung on and became footholds for the next, and they for the next, until at last the great ship was swarmed with beasts. It ground to a halt. Phyrexians and undead climbed. They reached the rails only to have colos on deck ram them. Phyrexian heads cracked. Their bodies slumped but were borne upward as shields for the next killers. The monsters gained the deck.

There they met even more ferocious resistance.

Eladamri brought his sword down in a moaning, overhand blow. It caught a snake-headed beast in one eye. The cut opened that orb and the socket that bore it, the nasal structures beneath, the throat, chest, and all three of the serpent's hearts.

The tip of the sword cleared the dying form only moments before Eladamri rammed the blade in a vicious thrust into the belly of another monster. He felt the slimy cascade of innards as he turned to kill again. In a powerful lateral blow, Eladamri's sword sheared through the shoulders of a Phyrexian trooper and lopped off the monster's head. A shadow at his back brought him whirling around but too late.

A bloodstock reached with four arms—two mechanical and two biological—to grab Eladamri at neck and shoulders. The grip was unbreakable. His arms were pinned to his side. His throat was squeezed shut. As blackness shaded his vision, Eladamri felt his feet lift from the planks. The bloodstock hoisted him high to dash him against the deck. A brutal gleam showed in the monster's eyes.

It sprouted a metal crest between its eyes—not a crest, but a blade. Eladamri knew that blade—the flying cleaver of Liin Sivi's toten-vec. Just beyond the bloodstock, she wore a brutal expression of her own. Never before had Eladamri been so happy to glimpse his comrade. She yanked the chain of her toten-vec, chucking the blade free. The Phyrexian fell, with Eladamri atop it. He struggled from the double embrace and stood.

Liin Sivi gave him a moment to breathe. She staved off the foes, fighting in a whir of steel. Her toten-vec leaped from her hand and struck with the speed of a falcon. It was not so much battle but dance. Liin Sivi's natural beauty was only augmented in a fight.

On Eladamri's other side, young Warlord Astor battled alongside Doyen Olvresk. The two warriors fought as one. Their scythe and axe gleamed in a tandem attack, entering either side of a trooper's rib cage and meeting at the creature's heart.

Beyond them, most furious of all, fought Doyenne Tajamin. No blade for her, but her ancestral cudgel. It glowed with the preternatural light of the sky. Its runes bled fire. The head of the club struck the head of a Phyrexian and opened it. Oil streamed from the cudgel. The club's metal prongs rammed into the teeth of another Phyrexian. It bit her with bleeding gums, but she staved its head, and the beast went down in a mess.

Another foe charged her. She struck it between the eyes. This was no Phyrexian monster. This was one of the Keldon dead. The moment she hit it, she knew. The moment metal smashed dead flesh, the cudgel itself knew.

It was an abomination that the Twilight Cudgel should slay a Keldon legend. It meant that the bearer had turned traitor against her own people, or worse, that the dead had turned on the living. It meant life was death, evil was good, and Twilight was blinding bright.

The runes of the cudgel flared brilliantly. They projected their figures out on the black mountains. The ancient truths of Twilight shone in contradiction to the battle on the ice below. The cudgel moaned. Its complaint grew louder. It sang. It roared like warriors in full charge—the shriek of outrage.

Metal shuddered in Doyenne Tajamin's grip. Sound turned to heat. Fire formed a corona around the cudgel's head. Flames blistered the doyenne's hand and face.

She was no stranger to pain nor to death. She could have borne death by fire, the most honorable for a Keldon, but not death by falsehood. To think the ancient prophecies of Twilight were lies was enough to slay the Keeper of the Book of Keld. If she held onto that false and furious artifact a moment more, it would destroy her and everyone on the ship.

With a despairing shout, Doyenne Tajamin hurled the cudgel out before the bow. Like a shooting star, it soared through quicksilver heavens. Its fire lashed Phyrexian heads. The cudgel came to ground with the weight and force of an asteroid.

Ice shattered. The glacier shuddered. Razor shards blasted up in concentric rings. Nearby beasts were torn to shreds. A huge crater formed. In its center, the fiery cudgel sank through ice. Steam and water geysered upward. The deeper the cudgel sank, the higher and more ferocious the geyser became. Already, boiling water made a hundred-foot column.

The crater widened. Phyrexians fell into it. They slipped down the icy slope and into a boiling lake. Currents surged. Thrashing, the monsters were dragged below only to rise again, dead, in the geyser.

"What is happening?" Eladamri shouted above the hiss of water and the roar of retreating soldiers. No one fought now—not Phyrexian, not Keldon, not elf. All fled back from the widening crater. Instead of climbing aboard the long ship, Phyrexians and their allies streamed away from it. "What did you do?"

"Prove it!" Doyenne Tajamin barked in sudden realization.

"Prove what?" asked Eladamri, uncertain.

"That is what the cudgel is doing. It is accepting the most ancient challenge of the Keldon people. It is proving the prophecies it bears."

Staring out past the bow, Eladamri said, "What?"

"The cudgel is turning the false Twilight into true Twilight."

The glacier leaped. It was as though a gargantuan creature beneath the ice shoved upward. The geyser spewed higher. Its superheated waters rose to the height of the Necropolis. Then, as though the world itself bled, the watery column turned from white to brilliant red. Crimson stuff spattered across the ice, eating it away.

"Lava!" Eladamri realized.

The cudgel had sunk right down through the glacier, even through the rock beneath, to awaken the fire of the world. It had ignited a volcano. The searing lava that jetted from the crater was only the smallest portion of the stuff that gushed out below. In moments, the ice would lose its integrity. They all would plunge into the volcano.

The true battle of Twilight had begun—not a fight between Keldons and Phyrexians, but a battle of ice and fire.

Sheathing his blade, Eladamri strode toward Warlord Astor. "Turn the ship around! Get us out of here!"

The young warlord stared fore, a strange light in his eyes. "This is Twilight. This is our battle—"

"It will be your grave, a mass grave, unless you turn this ship around!"

Astor did not seem to hear. He spoke in a faraway voice. " 'All the warriors of Keld will fight in the Twilight, but only the true warriors of Keld will survive.' "

Growling, Eladamri turned toward Doyen Olvresk. He too stared with the blindness of belief. Doyenne Tajamin and every other Keldon wore the same beatific expression. Even the dead Keldons watched in awe. It was as though they hoped to be consumed by fire.

"Sivi!" called Eladamri.

She tapped his shoulder. He spun, startled. Always she knew what he was thinking.

"Gather up the elves who live. I'll bring our colos. We've got to get our people out of here," Eladamri said.

"Yes," Liin Sivi said simply as she headed out across the deck toward a pair of elves.

Eladamri meanwhile climbed to the stern castle. There a steep-pitched roof covered a colos barn. The beasts had naturally wandered to it in the confusion. Ten mounts milled within. Eladamri strode purposefully in among them, grabbed the reins of the first, and spoke the words he had heard from countless riders: "You will bear me." Swinging into the saddle of the mount he stared at the others. "You will follow." Setting heels to his colos, he rode out of the barn. He drove his beast down to the amidships deck. The other colos followed.

Liin Sivi had gathered the seven remaining elves. They eagerly climbed onto the beasts behind Eladamri.

"We've got to reach the main elven contingent," he instructed. "We've got to lead them out—"

A new eruption drowned his words. Beyond the prow, the crater had quadrupled in size. At its center, the lava column had collapsed, giving way to a boiling mound of water and rock. Deep concussions shook the ice. It cracked in a thousand places. Faults opened beneath catapults. Crevasses swallowed ships and platoons. Cracks even raced up the black mountains all around.

Still, the Keldons stood, unmoving.

"Let's go!" Eladamri ordered.

He kicked the sides of his colos. The great mountain yak bounded toward the rail. Touching down once more, it leaped from the ship. Liin Sivi's steed soared through air just beside it. The seven elves followed on their own mounts. All the colos were airborne before Eladamri's landed. Ice flew out in a sharp spray. The glacier trembled beneath the hooves of the beasts, but they were surefooted. They thundered across the battlefield.

The scene before Eladamri was grim. A mile ahead, the main elven contingent struggled amid cracks. Bodies lay strewn across the intervening ice, and new crevasses opened.

Behind Eladamri came a bellowing groan, like the sound of metal failing. The ice lurched backward. Eladamri glanced over his shoulder.

The scene was even worse. The crater grew faster than soldiers could run. Armies disappeared under its advancing lip. Siege engines toppled and sank. Even the long ships were caught. At least they stayed upright, though the currents dragged them sideways like toy boats. A maelstrom had begun.

It whirled in a wide and irresistible arc through the crater. All the detritus of the lake spiraled toward the churning mound at its center. A long ship plunged into that space. It dived prow-first into the flood. In a moment, it was gone.

Warm water struck Eladamri's face. His colos's hooves splashed in a steaming tide. The flood was overtaking them. It raced out atop the glacier faster than the steeds could run. Just ahead, the water poured into a deep crevasse. Beyond, the ice was dry and solid.

Driving his mount toward the crack, Eladamri waved for the others to follow. Hooves came down on the edge of the crevasse. The colos leaped. It hurled itself off the cascade. Water plunged to darkness. Wind whipped the pelts of the leaping beasts. Even as they soared above the crack, the water at its base rose alarmingly upward. The colos stretched their hooves for the far side.

Eladamri's mount touched down with a crackle of ice, just ahead of Liin Sivi's steed. They bounded forward, away from the flooding canyon. The other elves had made the leap as well. At last, they had solid footing. Only a quarter mile ahead fled the rest of their people.

The loudest blast yet rocked the glacier. It made a sound like thunder. Ice dropped away beneath the colos's hooves, stranding them in air. They jolted down upon a steep slope and managed one more leap.

Cracks ripped across the ice. White chunks spun into the air. Water gushed up the empty spaces. The ice disintegrated. When next the colos came down, there was nothing to stand on. They plunged into a deep, hot sea. Water closed over their heads.

Churning huge hooves, the beasts drove themselves toward a surface crowded with ice shards. They butted the stuff aside and lifted their heads above the flood.

Shaking water from his hair, Eladamri saw there would be no escape.

The churning sea was surrounded by sheer ice walls. Huge chunks of glacier calved off, crashing into the flood. The dead and the dying were shoved among icebergs in a current that spiraled inward. No longer was there a mound of water at the center of the sea but only a great, sucking blackness. It drew everything down—siege engines and ruined ships and hunks of the shattered Necropolis. It drew everyone. Phyrexian and Keldon and elf. . . .

"Sivi!" Eladamri yelled. Once again, she was right beside him, her mount treading water. He pointed to the whirlpool. "Any ideas?"

"Drive these beasts toward shore."

With a nod, he indicated the ice cliffs. "That's shore, and they'd never make it against this current."

"We've got to try. We've got to stay together."

"Yes," Eladamri said, reaching across to grip her hand. "We've got to stay together."

CHAPTER 19
Homecomings

Smoke rolled into the black sky over Kaldroom. Even the burning Phyrexian laboratory did not light the darkness. Its glow was sucked away into soot.

Only *Weatherlight*'s ray cannons lit the scene. Docked on the garrison grounds, she hurled fire to the distant hills. The blasts cooked Phyrexians wherever they gathered. Between ship and Phyrexians lay a minotaur army. They were not dead nor truly alive. Their wide-open eyes glowed with cannon fire.

The crew of *Weatherlight* rushed among them like ants. Pairs of workers rolled minotaurs onto litters and carried them up the ship's gangplank. Everyone except the gunners worked—even Multani and Karn and Tahngarth. Multani configured his body into a kind of ambling stretcher. Karn carried a minotaur slung over either shoulder.

Most effective of all was Tahngarth. The minotaur could not be kept in gun traces while his people lay below. He carried a compatriot over either of his massive shoulders and a third draped in his arms. It was a feat made possible only by his Phyrexian physique— a feat performed as penance. Each time Tahngarth approached a warrior, he bowed to the perfect form of his people. Each time he lifted one, he put himself beneath. Each time he laid one on the deck, he rescued a minotaur from Phyrexian transformation.

Sweat matted his forelocks, stung his eyes, and flowed like tears.

Minotaurs filled every space on *Weatherlight*. They lay like fish spilled from a bursting net.

It was unwise. *Weatherlight* was torn from stem to stern. Breaches riddled her hull. Her airfoils hung in tatters from folded spars. Heat stresses formed a fine network of cracks along engine manifolds. She was not battle worthy, perhaps not even sky worthy, but even so, she was overloaded with a thousand comatose minotaurs.

Gerrard and Sisay had tried to broach the subject with Tahngarth, but the minotaur wouldn't listen. Tahngarth wasn't just saving his people. He was saving himself.

At last, he hauled the final three minotaurs on board.

"All right, that's it!" Gerrard punctuated the words with a pair of blasts from his ray cannon. Monsters advanced across the garrison grounds. Into his speaking tube, he shouted, "Posts, everyone. Ignite the engines. Prepare for liftoff."

"I'm not sure we can lift off," Sisay said from the helm. "Not this heavy. Not without airfoils. Not without Hanna."

"Yeah," Gerrard responded grimly. He felt the absence of the ship's navigator every day, every moment. "Well, we can't do anything about Hanna or the airfoils. The only other option is—" Gerrard glanced over his shoulder at Tahngarth, who gingerly stepped among his country folk. The look in the minotaur's eyes was both intent and fragile. "The only other option is to planeshift without taking off."

"What?" Sisay asked.

"How far do you need to reach planeshift velocity?" Gerrard asked.

"How far?"

"Yes, how far—skating across the ground on our landing spines—do you need to reach planeshift velocity?"

"I don't know," Sisay replied. "A thousand yards."

From the speaking tube came Karn's voice, metallic and dour, "We have five hundred yards to the garrison wall and three hundred more to the hills beyond."

Gerrard nodded. "We can blast through walls but not hills. You'll have to do it in eight hundred."

"There are Phyrexians in the hills," Sisay pointed out.

"We can blast through them as well," Gerrard said, proving the point by unleashing a barrage that vaporized a charging contingent. "But whatever we do, we've got to do it soon."

"Planeshift where?" Sisay asked. "We'll be destroyed if we return to Urborg."

"Lay in a course for Yavimaya," Multani suggested. "It's the only place where I can heal the ship's hull."

"That'd be a great idea except that we'd be smashed to pieces against the trees. We can't steer the ship."

"No, but I can steer the forest," Multani responded. "Just lay in a planeshift along the Mori Tumulus in the center of Yavimaya. I'll do the rest."

Gerrard smiled grimly. "Now I remember the lesson you taught me, Master Multani."

"And what was that?"

"How to be damned reckless," Gerrard said. "You heard the man, Sisay. Lay in the course."

"It's already done," she replied.

"Karn, full power to the—"

The command was cut off by a massive surge of the engines. Weatherlight grated forward on her landing spines. Metal shrieked across flagstones. The hull shuddered angrily, but

Multani surged within every remaining fiber of wood. In moments, *Weatherlight* ground forward at a horse's gallop. The Phyrexian armies ahead closed in at redoubled speed.

"Tahngarth, clear the way."

Radiance rolled out from Tahngarth's gun and smashed into the black-scaled figures. The front ranks dissolved altogether. Those behind exploded as their oil-blood boiled.

"Guess I should just shut up and fight," Gerrard mused, firing his own cannon.

Together, Gerrard and Tahngarth laved the ground in fire. Still, their incinerating rays could not blast Phyrexians quickly enough. Burning hunks of monster cracked against the landing spines. More bodies struck the keel.

The gunners had more to worry about than bodies. A solid wall approached. The cannons fired a synchronized blast. Red energy smashed into the wall. It cracked outward. Stones crumbled to rock fragments. A second salvo punched a hole through the wall. A third turned the stones molten.

It was enough. It would have to be. *Weatherlight* rocketed through the gap. Lava splashed before the ship. Her landing spines tore out across grassy ground. Another wall approached ahead— a hillside. There was no blasting it away. Nor could *Weatherlight* be stopped now. She shot forward like a crossbow quarrel.

"We're not going to make—" Gerrard stopped himself this time as the stony cliff vanished, replaced by the Blind Eternities.

The shrieking was done. The splash of molten rock, the thud of bodies—it all was gone. *Weatherlight* was bathed in the humming crackle of the world between worlds. She glided in a placid envelope amid spinning energies. Gray light spilled over the strange cargo of warriors.

Gerrard breathed. The whole crew breathed. Never before had they planeshifted without flying. It was a miracle they had survived. It would be a miracle if they survived their landing.

Like a silk veil ripping away, the Blind Eternities crumpled and withdrew. Heat and green replaced it. Trees as tall as mountains and as wide as cities flashed past the ship. The sky was an uneven blue ribbon threaded among treetops. The ground was a rumpled scar—a steaming fault in the world. Enormous roots sought to straddle that broken line, but even magnigoth trees were impotent to close the wound. *Weatherlight* flew along the fault.

"All right, Multani, what now?" Sisay asked.

"Now you land," came the placid reply.

"Where?" she asked.

"Anywhere atop the fault."

Her snort traveled down the speaking tubes. "If I slow down, we'll augur into the root bulbs."

"Hmmm," replied Multani.

Tahngarth shook his head miserably. "Oh, this is great."

Gerrard said, "This is a little *too* reckless, Multani."

"Take us up, Sisay," Multani suggested.

"Up? I thought we wanted to land," she said.

"We do. The best place for us to land is up."

Weatherlight's ravaged bow rose. The ship labored skyward. Above, treetops hovered like green thunderheads. *Weatherlight* climbed three thousand feet and vaulted through the leaves. Sunlight broke hot and bright across the ship. The canopy fell away in a sea of green.

"Where do we land up here?" Sisay asked.

"There," replied Multani.

The bow swept around, showing a magnigoth tree that was twice the height of those around it. This single tree was a world unto itself, with four separate levels of foliage above the main canopy. Each was a different biosphere, each a different hanging garden of plants and animals. Kavu, the guardians of Yavimaya, clung to the side of the tree and stared querulously at the ship.

"You want us to land in that tree?" Sisay asked incredulously.

"No," Multani replied. "I want that tree to catch us."

"Catch us? Why would it catch us?"

"Because I'll be in it. Besides, the ship came from that tree."

"What are you talking about?"

"That is the Heart of Yavimaya. From its center came a wedge of wood called the Weatherseed. It was that seed that grew into the hull of this ship."

The human members of the crew only stared in astonishment, unsure what to say.

Multani continued, "Just bring us in a spiraling path across the top layer of foliage. Take us low enough that the hull touches the leaves. I'll take care of the rest."

Even as she angled the ship toward the Heart of Yavimaya, Sisay asked, "Well, Commander, what do you think?"

He shrugged, sighing deeply. "Reckless, yes . . . Take her in."

Without airfoils, *Weatherlight* shot like a flaming arrow across the sky. She closed the distance to the Heart of Yavimaya. It grew. Worm holes in the smooth wood swelled into caves and into huge caverns. Bark became a vertical world, with sideways forests of moss. The ship climbed higher, where saprolings covered the upper boughs of the tree. At last, *Weatherlight* reached the mountainous crown. The air here was cooler, drier than below. Foliage spread in what might have been a mountain meadow above an incredible plunge. The tip of one long branch brushed the ship's keel.

Weatherlight shuddered as Multani went out of her. The hull suddenly rattled. Wind whistled in countless holes. She seemed to be breaking up.

"Spiral inward!" Gerrard ordered. "It'll slow us down."

"It'll tear us apart too," Sisay replied, but followed the order.

Weatherlight banked into a tight turn. A huge bough rose like an arm in front of the ship. Leaves slapped at the prow. Twigs lashed the rails. The bough swayed outward, following the ship's motion. Vines tightened. *Weatherlight* strained against the dragging weight.

"Cut engines!" Gerrard called.

Immediately, the roar of the power core died away. *Weatherlight* sloughed forward in a cradle of branches. She sank slowly in green arms and descended amid rustling leaves and crackling twigs.

Heart in his throat, Gerrard breathed a deep, thankful breath. He stood in the traces and lifted a joyous shout. The crew answered. Laughter followed. Relief flooded the deck.

Looking out at the primordial tree, its twisted wood rising to the sky, Gerrard said to himself, "This is a powerful place, a good place. Multani will heal the hull. He'll make it stronger than it ever was."

Slowly, a network of boughs eased *Weatherlight* down beside a huge arboreal lake in one wide crotch. The ship docked on battered landing spines. She groaned as her riddled bulk settled. At last, *Weatherlight* was at rest.

Kavu emerged from the undergrowth and formed a solemn circle around the ship. For a moment, Gerrard feared they might attack. Then he saw, on one of their backs, the figure of Multani.

Gerrard smiled to his onetime mentor. Waving, he whispered assurances to himself. "Multani will heal the ship, and we'll fight again at Urborg."

* * * * *

While Multani reworked the hull and Karn reworked the engine, Tahngarth descended from the crowded ship to rework himself. He who had saved a thousand minotaurs was not willing to be among them when they awoke.

Already they were shaking off their stupor. Perhaps Orim's ministrations brought them out. Perhaps it was only the healing magic of minotaur muscle.

The healing magic of minotaur muscle. . . . Tahngarth snorted. He looked at his own twisted form. That magic was gone from him.

At the lake, he dived. He dived deep. He remained down long. The cold water felt good on his tortured flesh. It washed away the dust of Kaldroom, the sweat of Urborg, the stink of every tormented place.

When he rose again toward the surface, his eyes made out a strange assemblage on the shore. He broke from the water. It streamed from his horns and hair.

Before him, all along the bank, stood minotaur warriors. The line of them stretched back to *Weatherlight*. More warriors poured down the gangplank. All headed toward the water and the single figure bathing there. All looked at Tahngarth, their eyes grave as they traced his deformations.

Gritting his teeth, Tahngarth strode from the lake. He would not turn from them. He would not skulk away. He would walk through their accusing midst, back to his friends. He only hoped the minotaurs would let him pass.

They did not. Shoulder to shoulder they stood.

Tahngarth stopped before them. He returned their stares. Words failed him.

Then the beasts before Tahngarth moved. They dropped to their knees and bowed low. So too did the warriors behind. One by one, the minotaurs of Kaldroom knelt before the noble warrior who had saved them.

CHAPTER 20
The Dragon of New Argive

At the head of the dragon nations flew Rhammidarigaaz of Shiv and Rith of Yavimaya. She flew in glory, the unquestioned ruler of the serpentine races. At her side, Darigaaz was but a doubtful shadow.

Was he a murderer? Was he a tyrant? Rokun had not been a traitor, not really. He had defied Darigaaz, but before that moment, Darigaaz had suffered defiance. Something had snapped in him. He had killed Rokun and hurled him against the root bulb. He had destroyed the dragon nations' faith and replaced it with fear. He had sacrificed Rokun to gain power.

Fear and power—they were halves of a whole. The more the dragons feared him, the more powerful he became. The more powerful he became, the more he feared himself.

There was but one antidote for fear—rage—and when Darigaaz glimpsed the ruins of New Argive, he had plenty of rage.

Not a building stood. The white glories of the ages were shattered eggshells. Not a soul survived, only bodies—bodies and soulless Phyrexians. Monsters scuttled among smashed walls and collapsed roofs. They feasted on bodies and pillaged metals and burned books. They killed living Argivians and obliterated the knowledge of the dead.

And you wondered why you needed such power, Rith said, speaking directly into his mind. *And you wondered why you needed Primevals*. Before he could answer, she tilted in a steep dive.

Darigaaz followed. His wings tucked. He plunged. The ruined city roared up to meet him. The dragon nations stooped into the dive as well. They headed for the central thoroughfare, flooded with Phyrexians. Dragon shadows swept over scaly heads.

Monsters looked up. Into their eyes poured death.

Rith's teeth parted. Green spores roared from her mouth. Where they struck, they rooted and grew. Parasitic plants drank Phyrexian blood. Vines coiled about arms. Tendrils cracked joints. Monsters dropped beneath rampant gardens.

Darigaaz breathed fire—a simpler but no less certain death. Flame bled from him. It baked brains and fried muscle and burned oil.

More attacks poured down on them. White serpents keened a sound that cut like knives, separating flesh from bone. Black dragons belched acidic sludge that ate scale and metal. Blue lizards breathed winds that dashed creatures to cobbles. The dragon nations strafed New Argive like a fivefold plague.

Rhammidarigaaz and dragon lords, come with me, Rith said into the minds of the dragons. *The rest of you, fan out and destroy Phyrexians*.

Without hesitation, the dragon nations peeled away from the main column. They hurled their killing breath into every alley, every ruin, every plaza.

Darigaaz watched them go, proud of their power.

Before him, Rith soared down to a huge ruined structure. Once it had risen multiple stories. Now it was a rubble pile. Sections of marble column lay among shattered friezes. Terra cotta bosses and torn tapestries and mosaic tiles and bodies—plenty of bodies in bloodstained robes.

A temple? Darigaaz wondered.

A kind of temple. A temple to knowledge. This was once the single greatest library on the face of Dominaria, replied Rith grimly.

Rhammidarigaaz studied the wreckage. *A library? Where are the books?*

Rith nodded her head toward the street. Huge black circles showed where numerous bonfires had burned.

The greatest library on the face of Dominaria . . . and they destroyed every last book.

Yes, but they did not find the library's greatest treasure, Rith said as she settled down atop the rubble pile.

Furling his wings, Rhammidarigaaz landed beside the green dragon. Four more beasts came to ground with him, including the resentful black dragon who had replaced Rokun.

Darigaaz turned a level stare on her. He would have to watch her. Swamp dragons were natural traitors. He shook the thought away. Already, he was thinking the way Rith did.

"Dig," Rith said simply, interrupting his reverie. "All of you, dig."

Rhammidarigaaz stooped, grabbing hunks of stone in his massive claws and hurling them aside. The black beast lashed her tail once, and then she set to work with a vengeance. So too did the rest, even Rith.

Darigaaz ignored the others, lost in his own thoughts. With each cornice he grasped, he imagined the walls it had once joined. With each shattered shelf, he read the books that once loaded it. With each body, he lived lives lost.

Rith had awakened something primal in him—something that stretched back beyond his own millennium of life. At first, he had thought it only instinct, but this was more than race memory. This was a longing for former days, when the world was young and humans were only scurrying rats. Then dragons had ruled. In that half-feral mind, Rith's words made utter sense.

The dragons uncovered a wide marble stairway that plunged away through more piles of rubble. They followed it down into darkness. The library had fallen into its basement, but there was a subbasement below it. In only a few places had its ceiling given way. Rith drove them on. They dug deeper. At the fourth turn of the stair, they reached the end of the debris. Another subbasement lay below. With wings tucked, the dragons slithered down through the darkness. More turns revealed a third and fourth level. At last they reached a deep vault.

Humans could not have seen anything in that dank space, but dragons saw the cold air that dragged away from musty walls. They glimpsed the chill drafts that danced like dark spirits across the floor. And in the center of the space, at the precise junction of the building's transepts, they saw that the floor glowed with unnatural warmth.

"What is it?" asked Darigaaz.

"Who is it, you mean," replied Rith. On all fours, she stalked slowly toward the spot. "Everything that mortals have, they stole from us. First, they stole dominion over fire, which they used to capture the Primeval of Shiv. Next, they stole dominion over plants—what they call agriculture. With that power, they imprisoned me in Yavimaya. Their greatest weapon they gained next, dominion over words. Stories, histories, sciences—writing is the magic that allows the dead to instruct the living. Books are no less than the memory of the world. Once mortals tapped that memory, they knew exactly how to trap the third Primeval." Her voice was quiet but imbued with a barely contained rage. "She is Treva, and she lies pinioned beneath the foundation drums of this library."

Darigaaz had crept near enough now to make out the shape of the warm silhouette on the floor—unmistakably that of a dragon.

She was buried deep within the lime mortar of the floor. She had been crucified. Her forelegs were stretched out unnaturally beneath a pair of massive pillars. Her hind legs were similarly splayed. Her tail formed a large curve beneath the feet of the dragon lords. Her head jutted into the apse beyond. A pair of wide, graceful wings swept into each transept.

Darigaaz glanced up to the sweating ceiling. "This level is older than what lies above.

Rith smiled in the darkness. "Perceptive. Yes, this level is the first library, in fact a monastery, no larger than these crossed transepts. It was leveled and rebuilt in the time of the Thran. That library was destroyed in the cataclysm of Yawgmoth. A university then took this site, only to be destroyed in the Argoth event. So have passed the ages. Knowledge comes and goes, but the foundation of knowledge—" she spread her claws toward the warm silhouette—"remains."

Staring at the shape, Rhammidarigaaz said, "Yes, but how do we free her? You escaped your prison only after Rokun was—only after I slew Rokun. I am not willing to make such a sacrifice again."

There was murmured agreement among the other dragon lords.

Rith purred casually, "Oh, you needn't worry about sacrifices. I know the ancient sorceries." Her teeth glinted in the murk. "Even so, I need your help. The spell requires black mana, to break the grip of death, and then green, white, and blue mana to restore life. You, the dragon lords of swamp and forest, plain and sea, must tap the magical power of your homelands and bring it here, into this place. Then Rhammidarigaaz will unleash a red-mana spell to cut through the floor beneath us. Once Treva is revealed, I will channel the mana you have drawn to awaken her."

"That much power could bring the ceiling down on us," Darigaaz objected.

"The other four may stand safely clear, beside the pillars, in case the ceiling comes down. You, though, Rhammidarigaaz, must stand beside me, risking all."

The black creature snickered. "Rhammidarigaaz would risk anything for the good of the dragon nations."

Darigaaz scowled. Rith was singling him out, perhaps intending to use his life force to power the spell.

A hiss came from the black dragon. "Or is Darigaaz willing to require the ultimate sacrifice of Rokun, only to shrink from danger himself?"

"No," Darigaaz replied levelly. He strode toward Rith. The floor felt hot beneath his claws. Treva's power seeped up his legs and into his heart, bringing a fierce longing for ancient times. "I will do it."

Rith extended a welcoming claw toward him. She gripped his talon. Small sparks leaped between their fingers.

"Good. You can trust me, Rhammidarigaaz. Do you feel the power between us? It will be sufficient." Raising her voice, she spoke to the others. "Spread out equally around us, facing forward, and remain in line of sight."

Hissing happily, the black dragon withdrew beside one of the four drums that held up the vault. The three other dragon lords took their places beside the other drums.

"Excellent," Rith said. "Now, to begin the spell, you must tap the power of your homelands. Concentrate. Draw the mana into you."

The air in the chamber changed. There came a smell of lightning. Power crackled. Beside the four pillars, the dragon lords glowed. Energy cascaded through their blood and lined out their arteries. It limned every scale. It shimmered across horns and teeth and even poured from eyes. Visions of deep forests and deeper oceans mixed with scenes of fetid murk and fecund field.

"Cast your spell, Rhammidarigaaz," Rith said quietly.

The power mounting in him lashed downward. Crimson rays surged from his splayed claws. They struck the floor and burned through. With precise lines and jags, Darigaaz traced the heat-silhouette beneath his feet. The beams bit deep. Lime mortar cracked over the silent form.

Rith bowed, pulling up hunks of the loose material and flinging them away. Piece by piece, the Primeval was uncovered. Her wings were manifold, formed of featherlike scales. Her limbs and belly plate were as white as chalk. Her throat and forehead were mantled in gleaming pinions.

Last of all, Rith drew back the shard that covered the dragon's face. The slim snout beneath bristled with teeth, and eyes glowed with beaming magic.

As the red sorcery ceased pouring from his claws, Darigaaz looked up. The four other dragon lords shone with gathered magic. Their eyes glowed. Their teeth sparked. Their limbs shuddered. It was as though they were transfixed on shafts of lightning.

"It is time. Draw off the power," Darigaaz said to Rith. "Draw it off now, before they are destroyed."

She did not seem to hear, gazing at the glowing figures.

"Draw off the power. They will die!" Darigaaz demanded.

"But how many more will live and rule?" Rith replied quietly. "You said there would be no more sacrifices."

She seemed angered, turning on him. "I said you needn't worry about sacrifices."

A quadruple burst of power ended the argument. The four dragon lords erupted in a storm of wild mana. It blasted the flesh from their bones, and then burned bones to ash. It cracked the stone drums behind them. Rock shards bounded outward. The vault itself would have come down except that it was hurled up and away. The energy tore through four subbasements and the rubble atop them and flung it all into the sky. Everything was ripped from that deep pit—everything but Rith and Darigaaz.

They stood untouched in the eye of the storm. Darigaaz could only gape in horror at the destruction all around. Rith meanwhile casually channeled the rampant mana. Her sorceries awoke the Primeval at their feet.

In moments, the white dragon's eyes blinked. Wind riffled among her feathery scales. Muscles twitched. Lungs filled with their first breath in ten thousand years.

As life entered Treva, it redoubled in Darigaaz. He felt the same strange transformation that had occurred when Rith emerged from the magnigoth. His horror at the deaths of his comrades was washed away in this overwhelming surge of power.

He remembered things. He remembered a world before humans. He remembered ruling that world.

Suddenly it wasn't a memory. Suddenly the power storm was gone, and Treva and Darigaaz and Rith stood side by side by side.

CHAPTER 21
A Commingling of Flesh

Agnate strode no longer at the head of his troops. He could not. His legs were uncertain things these days. It didn't matter. His armies were not uncertain in the least.

A tide of commingled flesh—blue muscle and black rot—surged up the volcanic hillside. Living and dead had become comrades in arms. Agnate and his combined armies had scoured the lower reaches of Urborg—every filthy swamp, every festering pit, every sand spit and bone beach. It all was in his grasp. Hundreds of thousands of Phyrexians had ended in fires on the beach. Metathran held the dry land, and undead held the watery reaches.

Only the volcanoes remained. They would fall easily in the next weeks. The Phyrexian garrisons had already been blasted from above. Agnate needed merely to clear out bunkers—just the job for a half-rotten man and his half-rotten army.

Agnate's heart tumbled in him. It had to work especially hard these days, pumping blood through collapsing vessels, driving legs that turned to mush. His heart could do it. It was strong. His secret infirmity didn't matter, for his heart would win the land war of Urborg.

Agnate strode like an old general behind the vanguard. His troops streamed up around him, boys eager to race up a hill. Agnate allowed it. For months, each of these soldiers had fought like ten men. Now they played like boys. After all, there was nothing to fear here in the foothills.

Something huge suddenly eclipsed the sun. Its shadow slid like a leviathan over them. The playfulness left their legs. Soldiers turned, half-crouched away from the shape, and peered up at it with fear.

It was no Phyrexian ship, that was sure, but neither was it a vessel any of them had ever seen before. The craft was headed up with a massive ram, its end carved in the shape of a powerful woman. Spikes proliferated along either side of this figure, leading back to a sleek hull covered in thick armor. The metal shone mirror-bright. At the stern, the armor swept outward in a pair of gleaming metal wings. Long, steely pinions could slide closed across each other like folding fans. Between them jutted a pair of thermal exhausts for what must have been a massive drive mechanism. Fire burned in twin cones of red behind the ship.

Most ominous of all, though, were the Phyrexian ray cannons that gleamed at forecastle, amidships, stern, and belly.

Agnate cursed himself for a fool, but it was too late to recall his men. They were caught in the open, beneath . . . whatever it was, yet Agnate's heart told him not to run.

The ship cruised toward a flat spot on the volcano's side. Steam hissed from numerous ports along its base. Troops below scattered back. Beneath the ship, landing spines extended from metal panels. The vessel eased down toward its perch.

Only then did Agnate see the ship's profile—her needle-sharp bowsprit, enclosed bridge, and slim stern. Joy swept through him.

"*Weatherlight*."

When last he had seen her, she was battered. To see her transfigured by her wounds gave Agnate the hope that perhaps he himself could be healed.

He strode forward faster than his legs wished to go. This was a meeting of champions. Agnate was winning the ground battle, and *Weatherlight* was winning the sky. It was a moment of triumph. Agnate needed a moment of triumph.

He hailed the ship: "Commander Gerrard. It is good to see you among the living!"

From the rail came an answer, "I would say the same of you, Commander Agnate, though you seem among the dead!"

Gritting his jaw grimly, Agnate approached the vessel. It seemed even larger on the ground than it had in the air.

Agnate cupped a hand to his mouth and shouted, "This alliance—strange as it may be—has won the wetlands of Urborg. Soon we will win the mountains too."

Gerrard jutted his head over the rail. His face was handsome and dark against the beaming sky, though his eyes were worried. A humorless smile spread across his lips.

"Yes, soon you will win the land, but at what cost?"

The joy that had flooded Agnate drained away. He suddenly seemed all rot. "Permission to come aboard, Commander."

"Permission granted."

A rumble came above as crew members lifted free a section of rail and slid the gangplank in place. It extended down to crunch on a patch of pumice.

Agnate strode slowly toward it. He did not want to seem overeager. Nor did he want his legs to fail. As he ascended the gangplank, he saw the crew members who had lowered it— minotaurs. They were everywhere, crowding the refitted ship.

In their midst stood Gerrard. The young man's eyes were grave, though he wore a welcoming smile. Agnate remembered that smile—the look of a commander who wins all the battles but loses the war. Agnate wore such a smile himself.

The commanders met. They clasped forearms in a hearty greeting.

Gerrard said, "Welcome aboard *Weatherlight*."

Nodding graciously, Agnate replied, "Welcome to Urborg."

Gerrard returned the nod. He swept his hand out to one side of him. "I have brought you reinforcements. A thousand minotaurs. The elite troops of Hurloon and Talruum. The Phyrexians liked them so well they were planning on recruiting them. I beat them to it."

Agnate took a deep breath and gazed at the minotaur troops. They were the fiercest natural warriors Dominaria had to offer. Urza had used much of minotaur physiology and flesh to design the Metathran. They were cousin races, one conceived by Gaea and the other by Urza.

"Excellent. Minotaurs fight like ten men. You have given me a levy of ten thousand soldiers."

"More like twenty thousand. These troops have lost their homelands. They've sworn a death oath against Phyrexians."

"Yes," Agnate agreed. "Then perhaps even thirty thousand."

Gerrard clapped a nearby bull-man on the neck and drew him over. The warrior wore a solemn expression, despite Gerrard's casual demeanor.

"This is Commander Grizzlegom, leader of the minotaur army."

Agnate dipped his head in greeting, but his eyes remained on the bull-man's face. There was strength in this minotaur but also subtlety, intelligence, perhaps even wisdom. Minotaurs judged each other this way, by the lines of the face and the soul in the eyes. Agnate made a snap decision. It was uncommon for him, but he hadn't much time.

"Commanders, I must speak with you privately," he said in a hushed voice.

Gerrard seemed surprised. He looked around the crowded deck before gesturing toward the stern castle. "We could ask to use Captain Sisay's chambers—"

"No," preempted Agnate. "The sickbay. Your healer should be there too."

Gerrard nodded seriously. "Yes. Yes, of course. This way, Commanders."

* * * * *

The ship had transformed. That was the miracle of Thran metal. It grew.

Karn entered the metal. This was more than peering out the rail lanterns or feeling areas of heat stress on the manifold. This was merging with the ship. Karn's body still crouched beside the engine block. His fists still clutched the twin control rods deep in their ports, but Karn's mind lived in *Weatherlight*.

The feeling was exquisite. Thran metal was more alive than his own silver frame. Oh, to be made of the stuff, to be a Thran-metal man.

That sparked a memory:

He stood in a hot red place, a laboratory where another metal man was being made—a Thran-metal man. Lizard folk took measurements from Karn and added pieces to the mechanism. Jhoira was there. She seemed not to have aged a day since that horrible time of slaughter in Tolaria. Still, her young eyes were sad. Her jaw clenched in consternation as she studied diagrams. Beside her stood a handsome young man with a dark complexion. Teferi? How had he aged decades when Jhoira had not aged at all? Why would they make a new Karn?

The memory was gone. How strange. Another Karn, made of Thran metal? A replacement? His friends would replace him with a better design?

Karn had often wondered about his creation. He knew he was ancient. Many of his components were Thran in origin, even the symbol on his chest. Those facts had allowed him to believe in a lofty creation. This memory told of humbler beginnings. He was almost replaced by a Thran-metal man. He was almost traded to lizards.

Desolated, Karn wandered through the fittings of the ship, a man pacing the decks. He absently adjusted a lantern outside the captain's study, enlarging its parabolic mirror. There was also a misaligned latch on the study door—a fitting that hadn't changed to accommodate the enlarged frame. Karn fixed it as well. Every major change to the ship brought a thousand minor ones. Once Karn was done, *Weatherlight* would be perfect.

Another few months, said a voice deep in his mind, *and* Weatherlight *will be perfect*.

Karn paused a moment within the doorknob to Sisay's chambers. The remembered voice brought another scene to mind—a deep woodland. A tree grew there with unnatural speed. It rose from the Weatherseed. Tendrils reached up around hunks of Thran metal, floating in air. Each new shoot brought the tree into closer configuration with its metal parts.

Well, she won't be perfect, said the voice in Karn's memory. He felt a hand on his shoulder and turned. Beside him stood a man with intense eyes and ash-blond hair. *Nothing's ever perfect. Conditions change and designs must too.* A bemused look came into those glinting eyes. Suddenly Karn remembered who this was—Urza Planeswalker. *Come to think of it, Karn, you're the only machine I ever made that I stopped fiddling with. That's because you're the only machine that keeps redesigning itself.*

Karn was glad he rested in a doorknob. Had he been on his own feet, he would have fallen over.

Urza was his creator. No, that wasn't entirely true. Urza was Karn's originator. Karn was his own creator. That's why he was still around. Karn redesigned himself. Though his metal body did not grow, his soul did.

He suddenly remembered the fate of the Thran-metal man. It had grown until its joints locked up and its plates popped free and it literally burst. It grew outwardly, not inwardly.

The doorknob to the captain's study grew a faint smile.

* * * * *

There were no smiles in sickbay as Orim bent over Commander Agnate. Her coin-coifed hair sent little circles of light dancing across the bulkhead.

To her side stood Gerrard, his eyes intent.

The minotaur commander watched as well. His nostrils flared as Orim untied the Metathran's leg armor.

"I know you do not understand this alliance I have made. It seems cowardly to you, but it is a matter of courage. It seems dishonorable, but at its depth, it is honor," said Commander Agnate. His voice was strained, as if each movement of Orim's fingers brought agony to him. He shook his head and clung to his cot. "You don't understand. You can't understand."

With a sucking sound, the solleret and jambeau came away from Agnate's foot and shin. A foul whiff of air rose from the infection beneath. It was all infection. Rot ran solidly from Agnate's knee to the ball of his foot. His toes were gone. The few muscles that lived under that dark pudding slid along riddled bones.

Gerrard's face hardened. "The Phyrexian plague!" He reached out, grasping Agnate's hand. "No one blames you for this, Agnate. We know about the plague. One of our own died from it."

Agnate gritted his teeth as Orim peeled back the knee piece and cuisse. "There were three plague spreaders . . . in a swamp. I blasted them—burned them away. That's what happened to my hair. That's when this began." His thighs too were mottled with black spots.

"We can stop it. We can make sure it claims no more of you," said Orim. She withdrew from the prone man, retrieving what seemed to be a vial of fish eggs. "This is the immunity serum for the plague, derived from glistening-oil." She opened the stopper on the vial and tipped it toward Agnate's mouth. "Swallow these, and the plague will spread no farther."

Agnate swallowed. "I will not give in until the land war is won."

Orim stared compassionately at him. "You must. Your legs must be removed."

"No. I can still march. I can still fight—"

"In utter agony," Orim broke in.

"Agony means nothing. Victory means everything," Agnate responded. "Don't you see? I have won the swamps with an army of Metathran and undead—a commingling of flesh. I am as my army. Together, we will win the mountains."

A sharp look came to Orim's eyes. "If I do not remove your legs, you will die."

Agnate's eyes rolled in pain. "The walls between life and death are down. I will not die. I will merely cross over."

CHAPTER 22
The Bowels of Phyrexia

Lithe and watchful, Daria crawled atop a huge ceramic pipe. It gurgled with a river of oil. The ceramic was cold beneath her fingertips. Just above her shoulder, stone tubes glowed in a hot tangle. They seared her back. Had she been mortal, she would have been dead already. Even as an immortal, she suffered dreadfully in this caustic place. For the first time since doffing it, she wished she had her titan suit, but it could never have navigated the third sphere of Phyrexia.

The place was an endless jumble of pipes, as deep as an ocean and as wide as a world. Rarely did the tubes run more than a man's height away from each other. In most places, they formed a maze of inescapable cages. Pits held piles of bleached bone. The flesh of those unfortunates had fed monsters that even now stalked Daria.

Metal claws skittered on the pipe behind her. The beasts only waited for her to wander into one trap or another before they converged to feed.

Daria intended to disappoint them.

Ducking her head, she slid through a narrow gap. She would have passed easily if not for the bomb strapped to her back. It hung up on a fitting. Heat poured in a vicious wave over her. Gritting her teeth, Daria flattened against the lower pipe and struggled free. She pulled herself through. There was enough space now to stand. Climbing to her feet, she ran along the pipe.

Ahead glowed a huge column, the confluence of a million power pathways. Daria felt its radiance on her skin and in her mind. The energy in that pillar created a spacio-temporal distortion that prevented planeswalking. It was a natural defense. These conduits were the most vulnerable points on the third sphere. A single bomb, like the one strapped to Daria's back, would destroy a section of pipe a hundred miles in diameter.

It was dirty work, and hot, but it needn't have been. Without breaking stride, Daria thought away the sweat on her brow. This body was only a projection of her mind, but sometimes a distracted mind allowed its body to follow natural courses.

The pipe took a sharp bend downward. Daria leaped from the end of it. She allowed momentum to carry her across the yawning pit. Her feet came down at a run atop a cluster of tubes. She ran into the glowing aura of the power column.

Energy pressed on her and flowed around her. It was like running through hot water. Power dragged her hair backward. Soon the strands would burn away. With a thought, Daria formed her hair into a helmet. Her battle vest thickened and grew to a heat-resistant hauberk. Even her exposed skin darkened and hardened. Nictitating membranes covered her eyes.

The central core was just ahead. Running, Daria unstrapped the bandoleer that held the bomb. She swung the thing up before her. Twisting the conic tip of the device, she activated it. Her feet slowed. The dynamic flux was almost unbearable. She held the bomb out into the streaming energy. There was no need to affix the device. It would cling like a magnet to a construct of such power.

The air became gel-like. Daria consciously ceased breathing. Her scaly hand pressed the bomb inward. At last, it touched the solid edge of the column. There it clung.

She backed away a few paces before turning. It felt good to have the bomb gone from her back. It felt good to have the heat push her outward. She cast a shadow before her. Daria walked, looking at her hands in their black carapace.

"I look almost like Szat," she mused.

Something moved on the twist of pipes ahead, something black and huge. It must have been one of the bone pickers that had been following her. It approached.

In reflex, Daria tried to planeswalk away. She could not, mired in the spacio-temporal fluxes.

It would be a fight then. Daria set her feet in a crouch. She extended her left arm. Her sleeve grew into a long, thick shield. Lifting her right arm, she formed the air around into a blazing sword. The helmet on her head grew a gleaming visor. She was ready.

The beast bounded toward her. It was huge and black—a dragon engine. Its hackled back scraped the pipes. A barbed tail lashed behind it. A fangy mouth gaped before it. Corruption welled up between the creature's teeth.

There was something familiar about that face. Before she could make it out, a ball of acid hurtled from the toothy maw.

Daria raised her shield. It grew to cover her whole front. Acid splashed across it, striking the pipes above and below. The inky stuff dissolve them. Steam hissed from the pipe overhead and oil gushed from the pipe underfoot.

Daria fell back, lest she plunge through the ceramic and into the open channel. Her shield was gone, but it had saved her life—for a moment.

With a thunder of talons, the dragon was upon her.

Daria swung her sword out. Its hilt became a haft, which she rooted on the pipe. Its blade jagged into a huge pike. The edge struck the dragon's breast and cut through scale and meat and bone to organs beneath. This was no dragon engine, but an actual dragon. Ducking under the soaring belly, Daria wrenched her pike sideways. It macerated the monster's liver. Bile sprayed out over her. The beast's momentum carried it overhead. It crashed atop a tangle of pipes. Daria's pike jutted from its heart.

It wasn't dead. That blow would have killed any normal dragon, even a dragon engine, but this was something more. It yanked the pike from its breast. Sinew and scale closed over the wound. The creature sat up. When its head lifted, at last Daria knew who hunted her.

"Tevash Szat," she growled, her eyes narrowing. "What are you doing here?"

Climbing to his feet, the planeswalker stalked forward. His tail lashed fitfully. "I should think that utterly obvious. I'm doing to you what I did to Kristina."

Shaking her head ruefully, she said through gritted teeth, "I should have known." She leaped backward over the break in the oil pipe. Her hand lashed out, hurling a spell. There was very little mana in this sphere—it was the reason she had not cast a spell before—but this effect needed only the mildest of power. Fire rushed down into the pipe. It ignited the oil, hurling up a wall of flame. Daria turned and ran. The flames burst the pipe behind her, introducing more air. The fire redoubled. It would be racing the other direction as well, toward Szat. Flame would force him back toward the power column, would trap him there until Daria could escape its aura and planeswalk to the others.

She ran. There was no other escape. Pipes burst behind her. Fire lashed her feet and blasted against her hauberk. The narrow passage was just ahead. If she could reach it, if she could dive through . . .

Mantled in flame and hoary with wounds, Tevash Szat surged up suddenly behind her. His jaws spread wide. His teeth clamped down. They pierced her through the head and throat and chest. They went straight through her and met. Claws scooped up the severed lower half. Wings surged once more.

Then Szat was gone. He had planeswalked away with his meal. He would take time to eat it, to heal the burns across his body before returning to the others.

Then he would reappear within his titan engine and wait for his next victim.

* * * * *

Urza had chosen this section of the fourth sphere because it was intensely black. There was no better place to hide eight titan engines. The blackness also meant that most beasts avoided the spot. Only stupid things approached. Urza had been visited by twenty-some scuttling gremlins—dog-sized creatures with white claws and red eyes. They crushed just fine underfoot.

Urza's engine stepped on two more. He scraped the tripod sole on metallic ground.

How long before they raise an alarm? asked Taysir. He stood guard with Urza but had allowed his comrade all the stomping duties. *Doesn't the lord of this junk pile know the mind of all his creatures?*

So legends say. But these beasts are nothing to him. They are toenails. Toenails split all the time without their owners noticing.

Lightning cracked out across the sky. It showed up the underbelly of the third sphere—pipes knotted in tight convolutions. Jagged energy probed an enormous flywheel. It illuminated a complex of gears and spindles before disappearing across the sky.

He knows we are here, Taysir said. *Why doesn't he do more to stop us?*

He cannot, Urza replied. *All his forces are committed to the invasion. In his arrogance, he never believed we could assail him.*

You're wrong, Taysir said. He and Urza had never been friends, and since Kristina's death, Taysir made no attempt to hide his animosity. *He is smarter than that. He knows something we don't know. He's luring us in.*

And you accuse me of paranoia, Urza said. *No, Taysir. You are the one who is wrong, about this, and about a great many things.*

One of the vacant titan engines powered up. A bluster of thoughts intruded on the conversation. *Can't believe we have to muck about in pipes and sepsis, putrefying our hands and burning our beards and scratching our—my monocle! How in hell did that damned creeper scratch my best monocle?*

How did your mission go, Commodore Guff? Urza asked.

Huhh? came the thought, flustered at the presence of the other two planeswalkers. *Oh, peachy, my man. Not a hitch. Textbook.*

Textbook? Urza ribbed. *So, you are writing fiction these days?*

The commodore gave a confident chuckle. *That's the beauty. A man in my position writes fiction, and it becomes reality.*

Two more titan engines powered up. Their piloting bulbs glowed faintly in the darkness. Within one sat Bo Levar, happily puffing on a cigar. Blue smoke curled up around him and drew away through fans at the rear of the suit. He waved a greeting to his comrades.

Within the other was Freyalise, settling into the command harness. *Grime and oil and soot. Really, Urza, I don't know what you see in machines. Filthy, loud, vicious things.*

Look at it this way, Bo Levar commented amiably, *you're setting bombs to blow up the biggest damned machine in the multiverse.*

Freyalise dipped her head in acknowledgment. *That's the whole reason I agreed to come. I couldn't blow up all Urza's machines at once, but I could blow up all of Yawgmoth's.*

Do not say that name, Urza warned. *Do not even think it.*

Urza thinks Yawgmoth doesn't know we're here, Taysir explained.

Freyalise gave a snort. *Yeah, that's likely.*

Don't say that name! Urza insisted.

The panther warrior's quadrupedal machine powered up. So too did the draconic machine of Tevash Szat.

Ah, so the animals are the last ones back, quipped Bo Levar, sending a great puff of smoke up into his piloting dome. *I'd think on four legs you could have done the job in half the time.*

Ever laconic, Lord Windgrace spoke only a few purring words. *I ran into some . . . rats.*

189

Did you plant the bombs? Urza asked.

Yes. They are set.

Mine too, offered Szat quietly.

That leaves only my daughter, Taysir said.

Oh, she won't be coming, said Urza casually. *She's dead.*

What? chorused Taysir and Freyalise.

Urza's titan engine began to pace with the same demeanor the man had used in Tolarian lecture halls. *There has been a lot of talk lately about who has underestimated whom.*

What does this have to do with Daria? Taysir demanded. *Where is she?*

The hand of Urza's engine rose. *Let me finish. It has been said I have underestimated our foe. This is not possible. I've spent four thousand years preparing for this battle. It has been said I have underestimated Tevash Szat, that he is untrustworthy and evil. This is also impossible. I constructed these engines with Szat in mind. In fact, the one person in this group who is chronically underestimated is me.*

Szat hissed, *What has any of this to do with Daria?*

Simply that you killed her, and I knew you would, and I now exact your punishment.

Instead of responding, Szat only hung there within his engine. Taysir shouted, *What going on!*

He's dying, Urza replied simply. *I've initiated the kill rubric.*

Kill rubric?

At my command, ten thousand metal fibers emerged from his piloting harness to pierce his flesh. Minute lightnings pass through each of these, creating a local and general paralysis. He cannot move or feel, act or think. He is in a kind of suspension.

Taysir stared in amazement into the piloting bulb of Szat's engine. The dragon hung limply within the harness. *So, you have incapacitated him. You'll punish him. But what about Daria! You said you knew this was going to happen. Why did you let it happen? Why did you let him kill Kristina and Daria?*

Oh, I didn't know he would kill any of us, only that he would betray us. And I had to allow him to betray us so that I could exact punishment. And I had to exact punishment because it was the only way to charge my most powerful weapons.

Have you gone mad? Freyalise demanded.

An uncomfortable laugh came from Urza. *Barrin always use to say that. No, I'm not mad. Come here, all of you, up beside Szat. Come look at what is happening inside the engine.*

They crowded around Tevash Szat and peered into the piloting bulb. Tiny motes of light scintillated across the dragon's form. They emerged from the core of his being and glinted along the filaments that pierced his scales.

Barrin always said that I did not consider the moral implications of my actions. He said it particularly loudly when I developed these soul bombs. You see them there, beneath the piloting seat? They are extraordinarily powerful explosives, able to destroy whole cities. Unfortunately, they can be charged only by capturing a soul. Barrin had said I could never ethically charge them. I pointed out that plenty of traitors and murderers are executed every year, and their souls could charge these bombs. Again, he said I was mad, that no mortal crime deserved an immortal punishment.

So, look what I have done. I have found an immortal to commit an immortal crime—a traitor and a murderer whose soul can charge not one bomb but twenty. Even now, Szat is giving us the means of destroying the fourth sphere.

Can any of you imagine any more moral solution than that? Can any of you imagine any more sane plan? Now you know why I insisted Szat come. He has become my greatest weapon.

The others could only stare in horrified amazement as the last of Tevash Szat's life force seeped out of him and into the soul bombs.

CHAPTER 23

Predator as Prey

In the early morning
light, *Weatherlight* rose from the
encampment. The engine rattled
command tents. Ash from spent logs
fled up the volcanic hillside. Metathran stirred in their bedrolls.
Minotaurs looked up from sharpening strivas. The perimeter of
ghoul sentries turned to see the great ship surge out across the
mountains of Urborg.

In his gunnery traces, Gerrard stared down at the conglomer-
ate army. "Life surrounded by death." Agnate was winning the
land battle but losing his life in the bargain. His pure heart was
surrounded by rot. Even now, he and Commander Grizzlegom
mustered their forces for an assault on the first volcano. At the
summit, they would meet up with Lich Lord Dralnu and a new
contingent of undead.

Gerrard and *Weatherlight* headed to a different mountaintop for a different confrontation.

"How far out are we?" asked Gerrard into the speaking tube.

"Thirty miles," Sisay responded. "We'll be there in a few minutes."

"Aye," Gerrard said with a nod. "Karn, you're sure about the power signature?"

"It is unmistakable," came the resonant voice of the silver golem. The ship's new configuration allowed her not only to sense the presence of a Phyrexian ship but also to identify it. A huge power signature rose from the central volcano in the range. "Without a doubt, that's where we'll find the Stronghold."

The Stronghold. Gerrard and Hanna had fought epic battles in its corridors. Sisay and Takara had languished in its cells. Tahngarth and Karn had survived its tortures. Selenia and Mirri had not. . . . Now the crew returned to face Volrath's successor—Crovax.

Once a member of *Weatherlight*'s crew, Crovax now was Evincar of Rath, lord of the overlay. He had brought the planeshift to Dominaria. The murder of millions was upon his head. There could be no truer avatar of death.

Gerrard was determined to face him down and kill him.

"There it is," Sisay said.

Gerrard peered out past the bowsprit to a huge mountain. It eclipsed the morning sun and cast *Weatherlight* in its shadow. The near face was swathed in blackness. Its rocky rim glowed hellishly.

"It's fifteen thousand feet high, with a five-thousand-foot caldera," Sisay said. The rattle of charts came through the speaking tube. "It'll surely have defenses. If I were Crovax, I'd set up cannonades in bunkers along the crater's rim."

A shaft of sun-colored light cracked past *Weatherlight*'s rail. It soared on, striking a nearby hill and melting rock to lava.

Gritting his teeth, Gerrard pointed his cannon toward the peak. Energy rolled from the gun. It sliced through the mountain's shadow and flew to the bunker. The bolt slid through a low window. It lit the space within. Burning silhouettes went to puddles and ash.

"Those bunkers are set up to fire outward, not upward," Gerrard said. "Sisay, bring us in along the crater's rim. Gunners, watch for more bunkers. Send the roofs down on them."

Tahngarth's cannon barked, ripping down a curtain of fire from another gun.

Gerrard pinpointed the nest. He squeezed off a shot. Plasmatic air splashed into the bunker. Hunks of scale tumbled out. The gun wilted.

Sisay brought *Weatherlight* up. Sunlight flashed across her mirror hull. She rose above the caldera. The crater centered on a black pit. The Stronghold would be below. Once the caldera was secured, *Weatherlight* would plunge down that shaft. For now, she traced the rim.

"Let's make one circle do the job," Gerrard said.

The sky suddenly went red. Cannon fire crisscrossed. From embrasures along the inner edge of the caldera, blasts ripped the air.

"Plenty of targets!" Gerrard shouted, standing in the traces.

He let fly a barrage. Bolts plunged toward the bowl. They stitched along beneath the rim. Rock melted. Bunkers collapsed. Power cores blew. The inner edge of the crater crumbled. Basalt boulders rolled down on Phyrexian crews.

All the guns were firing. Tahngarth and Squee, the amidships men, the belly gunner, the tops gunner—all unleashed their fury. *Weatherlight* seemed suspended on lines of power above the volcano.

Still, they could not catch and fling back all the flack. *Weatherlight* shuddered. Bolts spattered across her new hull. Where before such blasts would have ripped through wood, now mirrored metal reflected the rays. They stabbed downward. Even her new wings were reflectors.

"Take us low!" Gerrard shouted. "Let 'em rip their own eyes out."

"Aye, Commander!" replied Sisay.

The ship plunged toward her attackers. She was a silver phoenix, flying in the midst of fire. Every metal facet hurled back the blasts. Death poured on the head of the killers. She left a molten ring. Nothing could survive there.

Gerrard drew his gun back. "Cease fire! Let them kill themselves."

The sky stormed with bolts. The land burned. Phyrexians and their guns turned to soup. They wouldn't cease firing, even when they saw what the glorious ship did. One circle would do it. As *Weatherlight* came back upon her own wake, the beams ceased below.

"All right," Gerrard instructed, "that's just a prelude. There will be other defenders—"

From the wide pit in the center of the caldera rose just such a defender. Twice the length and six times the displacement of *Weatherlight*, this ship was a monster. It had two hulls, one atop the other. The upper hull seemed a thing of carapace. Its flying forecastle hovered like the claw of a crab. The lower hull consisted of broad plates of armor. From these two structures extended four bony masts, stepped back. The ship bore cannons that were the equal of *Weatherlight's*—in fact were of identical design. But this was not the most fearsome aspect of the new ship. It was the all-too-familiar outline: *Predator*.

In the skies over Rath, *Predator* and *Weatherlight* had fought a vicious duel. Gerrard had battled the ship's captain—Greven il-Vec. The attack had ended badly, with Gerrard thrown overboard and Karn and Tahngarth taken captive. Such would not happen today. This was no mere battle. This was a showdown.

"Take us down to her," Gerrard ordered.

"Greven is mine," Tahngarth announced.

"Fine," rumbled Karn through the speaking tubes. "You take Greven. I take *Predator*."

Gerrard and Tahngarth traded amazed looks. The commander responded, "Absolutely, Karn. *Predator* is yours. You have command."

"Captain," Karn said, "I respectfully request that you steer straight for *Predator*."

"What do you have in mind, Karn?" asked Sisay as she turned the ship. "A ram attack? A keel strike?"

"I have in mind the utter destruction of *Predator*," Karn replied. The engines roared to sudden life. The ship tore down across the crater.

"Quite a turn for a onetime pacifist," Sisay commented quietly.

Karn's reply rumbled like a war drum. "I will kill them now because, when I was a pacifist, they made me kill."

Weatherlight herself stole away anymore words. Her spikes sliced the air with a chorus of eerie whistles. The ship tore vengefully toward the waiting craft.

"*Predator* is rising to engage," Sisay warned. "Rising fast."

"Stay above her. Keep wings spread," Karn instructed. He redoubled the engine's thrust. *Weatherlight* skipped eagerly, weightless on her new wings. "Gunners, lay down a corridor of fire."

Predator only grew larger, turning with arrogant confidence to face the smaller attacker. She was a massive ship, and she brought her twelve guns to bear on *Weatherlight*. Scarlet flares lit the cannon tips. They swelled outward, reaching with greedy hands upward.

Weatherlight's own fire stabbed across the roaring air. Cannon blasts met and flung each other back. *Weatherlight* shot through the breach in them.

"Lift the bow!" Karn called.

At the head of *Weatherlight*, Gaea soared skyward. The mirror armor of the ship's keel breasted across a sea of fire. Red deadliness splashed away to either side. Plasmatic air curled off the ship's outflung wings. She neared *Predator*.

Suddenly, Karn folded the ship's wings and cut her engines. Only the song of the spikes sounded. *Weatherlight* struck *Predator* like a cleaver chopping a crab. Metal shrieked on metal. Supports moaned and failed. The saw-toothed keel cleft the upper forecastle. Carapace slumped and plunged, taking two guns with it. *Weatherlight* cut through the second forecastle. Her spikes ripped another gun from its moorings. Karn engaged the engines. The ship shot forward. Her blazing exhaust burned wood and cracked metal. At last beyond the ship, *Weatherlight* leaped away. She spread her wings and climbed skyward. Angry beams chased her.

"Covering fire, Squee!" Karn said.

The goblin's voice was barely audible above the clamor of his gun. "You gots nerve, tellin' Squee what's what, Mister Commander Man!" His wild shots dragged flack from the air. "You gettin' us into messes 'n Squee gettin' us out. Squee gots half a mind—" His rant was momentarily preempted when a ray from *Predator* slipped his guard. It struck the larboard wing. The shot bounced from its mirror edge and passed over Squee's head. His ear hair curled acridly. The shot struck the opposite wing and bouncing back. Squee ducked again. The blast rebounded five times over the squealing goblin, lower with each pass.

"Dive, Karn! What you tryin' to do? Kill Squee! Kill de hero of Mercadia?"

The ship dived, slipping from beneath the ricocheting beam.

"Well, now, dat's more like it!" Squee said gladly.

Weatherlight changed course, and *Predator* slid from sight behind the starboard wing. "What you doin' now, eh?"

"She's pursuing," Sisay warned.

"Bring us about," Gerrard said, "and keep us high. Their cannons can't do anything against our hull. And Karn's got the right of it. We drop on her from the sky and cut her in half."

"What about Greven?" growled Tahngarth.

"Sorry, pal. See if you can shoot him before we split his ship."

Weatherlight's engines shouted angry approval of the plan. She banked hard to port and rose.

Predator was a distant knot, abeam and below. Though her hull streamed sparks and fire, she still made quick time across the sky. In mere moments, she crossed the wide crater.

Weatherlight was quicker still. She was not the same ship as when first they had met—magnitudes more powerful, with greater armaments. Nor had she the same crew—these handful were a perfectly tuned machine, utterly committed to battle. *Weatherlight* climbed the sky as if it belonged to her.

Predator struggled to rise. She bled beams up across *Weatherlight*'s bow, which only hurled them back. *Predator* slid to keel.

Weatherlight's engines cut. Her wings folded. She plunged. The gunners floated up in their traces. Air spilled up both sides of her hull. It rose in twin walls and curled above.

Then the keel sliced more than sky. *Weatherlight* cracked into the upper hull of *Predator*, shattering the mainmast. It drooped and fell away. Deeper plunged *Weatherlight*. Her gleaming keel cut through the center of the ship. Planks splintered. Beams broke. Deeper, and the saw teeth of the keel scraped across *Predator*'s engine core.

A series of muffled booms came from the stricken ship. *Predator* lurched. Smoke flooded from her lower decks.

Weatherlight's engines spouted fire. She ground forward through *Predator*'s hull. Her keel ripped the power core. More explosions rocked the ruined ship.

Tahngarth, Gerrard, and the other gunners poured cannon fire on the superstructure, hoping to break free.

Weatherlight edged from the blazing gap. Her wings spread happily, and she leaped away.

Except that something dragged at her. Harpoons shot from the ruined deck of *Predator*. They thudded—three, five, eight—into the deck of *Weatherlight*. After them came grapple after grapple. They clasped her rails Cables snapped taut. They dragged *Weatherlight* back toward the listing ship.

Gerrard struggled to swing the ray cannon about, but he could not draw a bead.

"Cut those cables!" he shouted into the speaking tube even as he fought free of the gunnery traces. He turned, drawing his sword, and stepped to a harpoon imbedded in the forecastle. He sliced down. Steel met steel. The cable snapped away. It whipped back and lashed the deck of *Predator*.

Gerrard bellowed into the speaking tube, "Squee! What the hell are you doing back there? You're so proud of saving our butts. How about blasting that ship to nothing!"

The response that came was not Squee's. It was an angry, brutal voice, inflected with the iron edge of the *il*-Vec.

"Squee cannot save you this time, Gerrard. Squee cannot do much of anything. As soon as I get to the fore, you'll be in the same condition."

Gerrard stared back over the bridge to see where a company of *il*-Vec soldiers boarded *Weatherlight*'s stern. There, in their midst, towered Greven *il*-Vec.

CHAPTER 24
Down the Forgetful Tide

A maelstrom engulfed the world. The whirlpool drew every-thing down into its black heart. Ice chunks, war engines, long ships, colos, Phyrexians, Keldons, elves—all bobbed together on the icy current.

Eladamri could not reach solid ice. There was no solid ice to reach. The glacial cliffs forever calved, hurling huge columns into the flood. The impacts made waves that shoved everything toward the whirling center. Whole platoons of elves had been crushed beneath plunging ice or ground to nothing between icebergs.

"We can't get out that way," Liin Sivi shouted as her mount desperately trod water.

"Drive for the shallows," Eladamri replied, guiding his colos toward a long shelf of ice. "When the waters recede, we should be able to stand."

"It's our best hope," Liin Sivi agreed.

The others followed. They were wild eyed. Their mounts were mantled in foam. Bloodshot eyes rolled in sweating hair. The beasts trembled from exertion and cold. The waters froze one moment and boiled the next. Through the depths below came flashes of fire. The liquid was a torrid purple, a bruise on the world.

Eladamri's steed stroked against the current. Clods of ice drifted toward him. A berg shoved up against the colos. It cracked its hooves on a lower ledge of the thing and drove on. These big hunks of ice couldn't float across the shallows, either. They would get stranded. Among them, the elves could shelter, perhaps even climb out of the flood.

The shallows lay just ahead, a streaming shelf. The current dragged against them. Colos paddled hard just to maintain their position. Even if they could reach the flat ice, the beasts would be spent.

Leaning in the saddle, Eladamri whispered into the yak's ears. He spoke the elven language of animals, a combination of sound and emotion.

"Swim, great beast. Swim with all your might. Rest and peace await us there. Rest and peace and solid ground."

The colos leaned toward the cluttered shallows. Its neck bent against steaming water. Hooves churned. Inch by inch, it approached the shelf. Current dragged its matted fur. Liin Sivi's mount swam beside his own. Other beasts crowded up in a long line.

Eladamri's steed caught a hoof on the ice. It cracked away, a fragile edge. A second try gave solid footing. The beast dragged itself forward through a chest-high tide. It kicked its hind legs and leaped. The colos bounded up above the icy waves. It hung for a moment in glittering air before splashing down again in the flood. Another surge of its hooves, and the beast was driving up, clear of the ice pit.

The others followed. Liin Sivi was just beside him, and eight elves came behind her. Their eyes were alight with hope. Bergs gleamed like monoliths all around, the water rushing past. Through the shallows, colos leaped happily.

Eladamri waved his folk forward. "Ahead, it's shallower still—!"

His beast rounded a huge berg only to lose its footing on an icy slope. It plunged into a sucking tide. The others could not see the danger. Liin Sivi also slipped into the slick well. One by one, the elves went too. They floated again in a raging current. The waters drew them down toward another maelstrom. The whirlpool moaned as air escaped its spinning throat. The column descended into a wide crack in the ice.

"Fight for shore!" Eladamri bellowed, hauling hard on the reins. The beast lagged beneath him. It had already given its last effort. Hooves churned the tide but without their previous vigor. There was no strength left in them, only desperation. The other mounts could do no better. Their riders were white-blue with dread and cold. "Fight for shore!"

Even as he said it, he knew it was impossible. Reins lashed the water. The colos bobbed beneath him. It was drawn around the curve of the whirlpool. Eladamri gazed down into the black hollow. He looked up to Liin Sivi, her steed struggling. He reached for her. His fingers came up only with empty air.

Down the maelstrom he went. He sucked a last breath before icy water closed over his head. The crisp sounds of struggle were replaced by a droning thunder. In an instant, rider and mount were hauled down into blue-blackness, then the colos was gone. Eladamri thrashed, reaching for a handhold. His fingers clawed knobs of ice worn smooth. There would be no sharp edges to rip him apart. The waters had taken care of that, but there was no shortage of burls. They pummeled him like fists. One blow between the shoulder blades hurled the breath from his lungs.

That was it. A man cannot live without breath. Eladamri went limp. His body became one with the ripping tide. He tumbled through dark spaces. Down he went. Water sought its level—the deepest, darkest, coldest place beneath the glacier. Soon all light was gone. There was only the incessant roar and the battering world.

This is what it is to die, this blackness.

Then light returned. It glowed red all around. Whatever volcanism melted this glacier gave its angry radiance to the ice. The water's drone became a shout. Thin walls led inexorably, inescapably, to a bubbling shaft. Eladamri plunged through it.

In a great cascade, Eladamri tumbled into a huge ice cave. He dropped through the cracked ceiling. Suddenly, there was air around him—blisteringly hot air. He breathed. His lungs burned, but better to burn than to die. The smell of sulfur stung his nose. For what seemed a whole minute, Eladamri plummeted. How deep could this chamber be? He glimpsed Liin Sivi and the elves in the cascade above him.

Eladamri struck the hot sea below. He sank. The cascade shoved him down. He tried to tread water, but it was so charged with air it would not buoy him. Something solid struck his side. Eladamri swung his feet around and pushed. He shot up through the waters. The surface above was red and rolling. Eladamri's head broke through.

He dragged a deep breath of the brimstone air. He was below the falls. They gleamed with the crimson light of the erupting volcano. The current here was deep and fast. It descended through steep sluices into blackness. Overhead stretched the smooth, gray ice of the glacier.

Eladamri was perhaps a thousand feet deep. There were four thousand more feet down to bedrock.

Another head broke the surface just upstream. It was Liin Sivi. She gasped a breath.

"Sivi!" Eladamri shouted. He reached toward her and struggled to stroke upstream. It was no good. The rush of water flung him down.

Liin Sivi swam with the current and reached him. Their hands met, and they pulled each other close. The embrace took them beneath the water, but they would gladly trade air for another soul.

Something pounded against them. Eladamri looked up to see a dead colos float past. The beast's legs had been shattered in the terrible descent. Its blood made a red veil in the water.

Gripping Liin Sivi's hand, Eladamri stroked toward the surface. Together, they emerged. They gulped greedy breaths.

No sooner were Eladamri's lungs full than he shouted, "Look out!" He pulled Liin Sivi aside as a huge wedge of wood shot beside her. It was the ram from a Keldon long ship.

Instead of shying back, she lunged and grabbed hold. Liin Sivi pulled him to the ram.

"It floats," she said simply. "It floats, and it takes the beating for us."

"Yes," Eladamri replied. He clung to the wedge. It seemed eager to descend. Ahead, the ice cave was a swallowing gullet. "Where are we going?"

Liin Sivi shrugged. "Where everyone is going. Where the water goes."

The heat of the upper chambers waned. Cold gripped their legs.

"No one escaped," Eladamri said bleakly. "No one who fought escaped. Neither the living nor the dead."

Liin Sivi turned. She wore a rueful smile. "It would be comforting to believe in Twilight, that there is a destiny for virtuous warriors."

"Even the Keldons can't believe in Twilight. Even Doyenne Tajamin, Keeper of the Book of Keld," Eladamri echoed hollowly.

Sivi's eyes were beautiful in the failing light. "Then we have the best fate of all, Eladamri, to die valiantly."

Just ahead, the wide river reached a precipice, where it dropped into utter blackness.

Eladamri drew Liin Sivi up beside him. He stroked back the black locks of her hair. He leaned toward her and cupped her cheek in his hand. Their lips met in a single, warm kiss.

They crested the waterfall. It ripped the ram from their hands. It ripped them from each other's arms. Then all was blackness.

* * * * *

Death was not as he had expected. He had expected torments, but there was only numbness and noise. He had expected other souls, but he was alone. The darkness was right, and the moaning—the sudden crash of huge things and the throb of his head—but the rest was wrong. Worst of all, he had expected to care, but Eladamri cared about nothing at all.

Death was easy. Life had been hard. To live in the shadow of the Stronghold, to battle Dauthi horrors, to lose a daughter and lose a world and fight for one that wasn't even his—these were the hard things. To lie here with something dragging at his legs and something else clutching the scruff of his neck, this was easy.

Eladamri lifted his head. His hair was frozen to the ground. He pulled free and felt pain. It awoke sensations across his entire body. He struggled to sit up. His frozen tunic ripped as it yanked free of the ice. His back burned.

Chill waters lapped at his waist. Cold darkness surrounded him. Just ahead, the river roared hungrily, bearing everything away. The ice shuddered with impacts—hunks of catapult and ship and Phyrexian and Keldon.

Eladamri was not dead, but soon he would be, in utter darkness and utterly alone.

His breath caught. Liin Sivi. She had been right beside him before the waterfall. Now—he splashed his hands through the shallows, but there was no one. She must have already been dragged away. She must have been dead.

Sorrow moved through Eladamri. Liin Sivi had fought beside him since the Stronghold. She had been his strong right arm but more than that. She had been his heart. Except for her, he had been alone through it all.

A gloaming light came to the ice cave. It gilded the walls in hues of gold.

Eladamri stood. In the glow, he could make out the wide, deep flood and the high-arching vault. To his left, the waters plunged into unknown depths. To his right, the channel bored straight away into the glacier. It was from that distant place that the light shone.

Something approached, something otherworldly.

Eladamri stared in amazement.

A ship. A golden ship. Through this black underworld, a ship sailed in utter calm. Her main was full-bellied, as if she harnessed the winds of another world. Her hull breasted the waves in perfect trim. Most glorious of all, the lanterns upon her decks gleamed across a crowd of warriors—Keldons and Steel Leaf elves and Skyshroud elves . . . and Liin Sivi.

She lifted her lantern at the bow. Her eyes searched the darkness. She looked for him.

It could not be. This was a hallucination. No ship could sail these waters. No ship in all the world was so huge. This was a delusion, concocted by Eladamri's mind to ease the moment he would leap into the flood.

The long ship neared. Liin Sivi's lantern spilled its light across him. A smile lit her face. "Eladamri, you live!"

"I am not so certain," he shouted above the roaring tide. The ship drew even with him. In moments, it would be past. "Where are you going, Liin Sivi? Where is this *Golden Argosy* bound?"

She hurled a shimmering line out toward him. It splashed into the water by his ankles and dragged along.

"I am going where we all are going, where the water goes." Her eyes implored. "Join us, Eladamri. Grab the line."

Numbly, Eladamri looked down at the snaking rope. If this were a delusion, to grab it would be to plunge into the water, to die. But if the ship before him were a true thing, to grab the line would be to live.

Either way, he would be with Liin Sivi again.

The *Golden Argosy* pulled away.

The tail of rope lashed past.

Eladamri lunged. He seized its slender tip. The line yanked him away from his perch and back into the hungry flood. It dragged him down to darkness.

CHAPTER 25
The End of Bargains

Commander Grizzlegom hated this fight.

His striva laid open the breast of a Phyrexian trooper. The blade severed ten ribs and wedged in the eleventh. The trooper was unconvinced of its death. Claws raked deep wounds in the minotaur's shoulder.

Grizzlegom tilted his head and rammed a horn through the trooper's skull. He flung the body away and yanked his striva free.

The blade would not be quick enough for the next foe. Grizzlegom's elbow did the job. The bloodstock's neck cracked, and it fell.

A scuta swarmed over it, lashing Grizzlegom's hooves. He leaped on its shield and kicked through it. Vaulting from the dead monster's back, he advanced up the volcanic slope.

Grizzlegom hated this fight. It wasn't that he minded killing Phyrexians. That part was splendid. Hurloon's debt of vengeance would be repaid. What he hated was fighting alongside the dead.

A ghoul advanced beside him. The flesh was gone from its fingers, leaving only bony claws. Its lips were ripped away. Yellow teeth opened wide and bit a hunk of flesh from a Phyrexian's face.

The Phyrexian ripped an arm from the ghoul and ran scythe-tipped fingers across its belly. Desiccated organs tumbled free.

Grizzlegom ended the struggle with a chopping stroke of his striva. The blade passed through shoulder of the Phyrexian and bisected its heart. Both beasts fell in pieces at Grizzlegom's hooves.

What honor was there in fighting alongside rot?

Above the dance of blades, Grizzlegom made out Commander Agnate, leading a charge. There was the honor. The man fought on despite the plague that ravaged him. He fought with a fury worthy of a minotaur. That was the honor in this fight. In his very flesh, Agnate rectified the living and the dead.

Next moment, Agnate fell beneath a Phyrexian swarm.

"Charge!" Grizzlegom shouted.

He drove toward the place where Agnate had fallen. He did not so much fight the Phyrexians but fought *through* them like a man cutting cane. A forehand slice mowed the goat head from one Phyrexian. A backhand jab impaled the belly of another. While his blade cleared foes to one side, his fist dropped beasts on the other. Phyrexians had glass jaws. An uppercut to the throat of a bloodstock drove its lower fangs into its brain. A roundhouse felled an infantryman before it could bring its sword to bear. Fist and striva were less deadly than horns. With them, Grizzlegom bulled up the talus slope. One horn impaled a trooper. Grizzlegom pitched his head, hurling the body down. The other horn rammed into a huge wall of muscle.

Hauling the gory tip out, the minotaur staggered back. A gargantua loomed before him. The thing stood on a pair of huge, clawed legs. Massive arms reached for Grizzlegom. An enormous claw knocked his striva away. The other closed over him and lifted him toward a wide mouth lined with curving teeth.

Grizzlegom kicked. His hooves struck nothing. He pitched his horned head. The points flailed in air.

Like a man tossing nuts into his mouth, the gargantua hurled Grizzlegom inward. He landed atop a tongue coated in thick goo. Teeth closed in a cage around him. The tongue convulsed. The gullet opened wide. Grizzlegom slid down into a sac of hot acid. Powerful muscles clenched him. Stones battered him—a gizzard that could grind a man to meal.

Grizzlegom was no mere man. Arching his neck, he drove his horns through the stomach wall. The points shot through muscle and fat, skin and scale to jut from the thing's belly. The stomach clenched tight. With a roar, Grizzlegom twisted his head. The horns ripped a wide hole in the thing's gut.

He lunged toward the light. Bloody and streaming acid, his head jutted free. He drew a deep breath and fought his shoulders out. The stomach contractions only aided him. Amid a grisly cascade of gastroliths, Grizzlegom spilled upon the ground.

Breath burst from his lungs as he landed. He hadn't the luxury of lying stunned. The gargantua tipped toward him.

Grizzlegom clambered aside. His legs barely dragged free of the gargantua's shadow before it struck ground. The beast hit the hillside, which bounded beneath it.

Grizzlegom's momentary triumph ended when a pair of Phyrexian troopers leaped on him. The minotaur gripped one in either hand and cracked their skulls together. Their heads shattered. Glistening-oil poured down on him. It soothed the anguish of the acid. Grizzlegom rubbed the stuff all over himself. Gripping a body in either hand, he pummeled his way to Agnate.

"Push them back!" Grizzlegom ordered. "Secure this spot!"

Minotaur troops rallied to their battle-mad commander. One returned his fallen striva.

Grizzlegom dropped one corpse and took the striva. He held the other body as a shield. "Form a wedge around me and fight forward!"

The minotaurs complied but at a distance.

Grizzlegom glanced down at himself and knew why. Mantled in Phyrexian blood and gastric acids, he was a horrid sight. His once-fine hide was now a mottled white and brown. His tremendous rack of horns had been bent downward. He had been transformed by his passage through the monster, made into a twisted thing.

Grizzlegom reached Agnate. He chopped a charging bloodstock in half and knelt.

"Drive on!" Grizzlegom shouted to his troops. "Drive on!"

They fought forward, moving the battle away from the commanders.

Grizzlegom sheathed his striva and turned Agnate over.

The Metathran's eyes were haunted. "Tahngarth! What are you doing here?"

A sudden flush of pride moved through Grizzlegom. "I am not Tahngarth. I am Commander Grizzlegom."

"Forgive me." Agnate shook his head blearily. "I cannot walk. I cannot even rise."

"Where are you wounded?"

"It is no wound, but the plague."

"You should not have fought on, in your condition." He took a ragged breath and was suddenly weak. His limbs convulsed, and he lost his balance. Grizzlegom slumped beside his Metathran counterpart.

"You should not have fought on in your condition, either."

* * * * *

Commander Agnate awoke in a much different place. A tent roof swayed in dark breezes. From outside came the murmur of conversations and campfires. A soft cot held him.

A minotaur healer moved through the tent. Lantern light cast his horned shadow across the ceiling. He cleaned savage implements—even his healing methods were warlike. He had fire rods for cauterizing wounds, poison vials for killing unnatural growths, spores for inducing fever. . . . Minotaur healers were renown for their effective but none-too-gentle methods.

"Where are we?" Agnate asked quietly. "Who won the battle?"

The healer arched an eyebrow and approached the pallet. "The stimulant has worked. I am glad you are awake, Commander."

"I too am awake," growled a figure on an adjacent cot. Commander Grizzlegom. "I too must know the battle's outcome."

"We are victorious. We have taken the first mountain of the range. Even now, we camp near its summit." His next words told the true story. "Our forces have been met by an army equally large, led by Lich Lord Dralnu. He has taken the farther flank of the mountain, scouring it of Phyrexians."

"Excellent," said Agnate. "From this outpost, we can secure the rest of the range."

"I fear you will be doing no such thing, Commander," the healer said quietly. "You cannot go to battle. You will never walk again. Perhaps you will not even last the week." His bedside manner was as brutal as his methods. The healer drew back the white linen that lay across him. Though Agnate's chest remained broad and muscular, from the base of his ribs downward, his body was gangrenous. "Were I to amputate, not enough of you would remain to stay alive."

Agnate's mind returned to a former time, when another harsh healer worked over another patient. . . . Thaddeus lay strapped to a gleaming table. . . . His body was gone from the ribs down. . . .

"I want to finish this campaign. I want victory at Urborg."

The healer stared in bald dread at the ruined man. "There is something you must know about this plague. It is not Phyrexian in origin. Orim's elixir would have prevented its spread. This is a different disease altogether, a ravenous gangrene. Its origins do not lie with Phyrexia but with Lich Lord Dralnu."

Agnate remembered the feast in Vhelnish. He remembered the brackish basin and the lich lord laving his feet in the filthy water. He had called it an ancient rite, honoring a new ally. An ancient rite indeed—a necromantic rite.

"He is bringing you over, Agnate, making you into one of his minions," Grizzlegom said. "Don't you see? He has literally corrupted you. The reason your legs no longer work is that they belong to him. When at last this corruption reaches your heart, you will be his entirely. Then he will raise you, and you will dance to his bidding. Through you, he will gain your army."

Agnate shook his head. "No. You don't know Dralnu—"

"He is a lich lord! What is there to know?"

"He does what he does for noble warriors," Agnate insisted. "In the absence of a deity, Lord Dralnu has become a deity—"

"Better no god than a false god."

"And he has made an eternity for us, a heaven—"

"He has made a hell for you. He has made you his devils. Don't you see?" Grizzlegom asked, sitting up on his cot. "You have bargained with death, but death wins every deal."

"If you could only meet him, only speak to him, you would see his sincerity," Agnate said.

"A man can be sincere and still be wrong, Commander. What Dralnu has done is wrong. Life and death cannot be allies. They must forever be at war. You must break this alliance, before you are destroyed."

Agnate's eyes traced out the seams in the canvas above. "I am already destroyed."

The minotaur commander swung his legs from the pallet. He had been badly burned by the gargantua's stomach acid, but minotaur healers knew much about treating burns. Grizzlegom leveled his gaze.

"Only one question remains, Commander Agnate—to whom will you grant your army?"

"Yes," Agnate mused. "To whom?"

"If you grant Dralnu your troops, you have given him everything. He will corrupt them as he has corrupted you. He will scour the land of Phyrexians only to claim it all as his own."

"And if I grant my army to you," Agnate supplied, "you will turn my men against Dralnu. You will make our men fight an army of undead."

"Yes, but at least they will be fighting for their lives, not their deaths."

Agnate's face was firm. "I cannot allow you to betray this alliance."

"How can you speak of betrayal? This whole alliance was a betrayal. You lie there, rotting from a plague given to you by your ally, and you wonder about betraying him?" Grizzlegom asked. He stood, hooves firm on the floor. "It is too late to save yourself, Agnate, but save your army."

"Draw it up, quickly now," Agnate said in sudden decision. "I will sign it. I will seal it. Only draw up the order, and my troops are yours."

Grizzlegom nodded a command to the healer, who drew out quill and parchment to write up the order. Meanwhile, the minotaur commander knelt beside the bed of his comrade. He took Agnate's hand.

"Why not convey the instructions yourself?"

"I cannot. You said it was too late to save me, but you were wrong. I do not want to rise again as a minion of Dralnu. The one condition of my order is that you make sure that does not happen." Agnate stared piercingly at his comrade. "It will take two strokes, the first to end my life and the second to end my unlife. The twice dead cannot be raised. Only then will I be free."

Grizzlegom's eyes were full of dread. "Do not ask me to do this. Instead, I shall slay Dralnu myself, and you will be free."

"It is not certain enough. I am done bargaining with death. This must be certain. Two strokes," Agnate said.

The healer approached, bearing the order and a quill. He brought also Commander Grizzlegom's striva.

Agnate reached out, taking the order. He read it, signed it, and used his ring to seal it. Then he handed it back to the healer.

"There, I have made the strokes that will save you. You must make the strokes that will save me."

Grizzlegom took the striva in hand. He lifted the blade. It was golden in the lantern light. "Until we meet in the true warrior's paradise . . ."

Agnate watched the blade descend. He thought only of a long ago time when another blade—his own battle axe—carved the air of a cave room and descended into the face of another great warrior.

CHAPTER 26
Among Immortals

To see them fly that way above a flashing sea—Treva in white and Rith in emerald—was glorious. No dragon could look upon that sight without sensing the raw power in it. To the heart of any dragon, power was beauty.

See how the sun makes Treva an avenging angel? See how the waves make Rith a mosaic of gems? Who can doubt their glory? It sings from their wings and reaches back to snare us and drag us along. How wondrous to be dragged so!

Rhammidarigaaz could not hush the whispers of his wild heart. He desperately wished to, but these dragon gods had taken up residence in his mind. No dragon who flew in the wake of the Primevals could resist their presence.

What of Rokun? Darigaaz asked himself. There had once been a dragon named Rokun who resisted. He dwelt now in a dark corner of Darigaaz's mind, along with the other sacrifices. It was hard to see them. A mind naturally looks toward light.

The dragon nations flew above crystalline waters. Gleaming billows covered forests of kelp. A deep rift cut across the seabed, its base as cold and sere as a mountaintop. Verdant gardens of coral overhung it and spread across the shallows. Fish schooled there, and otters darted after them. On the watery plateau beyond lay the dragons' destination—the ancient ruins of Vodalia.

Once this great merfolk city had ruled a whole ocean. Now, its sunken palaces and pearly halls were ruled by barnacles. First had come caste wars, then cold waters, and last Homarids. The Vodalians had escaped the crab folk by retreating to a kingdom across the sea. They had abandoned their capital city to hammerheads and octopi.

Of course, one resident remained—a beast so ancient that even the Vodalians had thought him dead. From his deep caves beneath the ruined city, the blue Primeval called to Darigaaz and the other dragons. Through rock and water, air and centuries, Dromar called them.

Treva trimmed her wings along white-scaled flanks and dived. Beside her, Rith also plunged. They angled toward the black ocean rift alongside Vodalia. Darigaaz furled his own wings and followed. The dragon nations flocked behind.

As Darigaaz descended, the air around him grew pregnant with light. His medallions rang together in a chorus of bells. The sea rose toward his bent brow. Already, it received Treva and Rith with white-splashing coronas.

Darigaaz closed his eyes and let his crest cleave the waves. He struck with tremendous force. The water parted around him. He dragged air down in its midst. The sea closed, enveloping him.

The water was as warm and salty as blood. It seeped into Darigaaz's scales. His momentum carried him deep into the cleft of the sea floor. Treva and Rith swam below. Darigaaz spread his wings and drove downward.

The water grew tepid. It lost its steamy vitality and squeezed him in an unwelcoming fist. Each surge of his wings propelled him to colder, darker, deeper reaches.

Vodalia disappeared above. Canyon walls rose. Partway down the rift, even the voracious seaweed gave up its hold. Only black rock remained. Darigaaz's wings flung twirling spirals of bioluminescence up behind him.

Deeper still he swam. The sea wanted his air. It gripped his lungs in a brutal fist. He had never dived so deep. He would have turned back now except for the gleaming outlines of the Primevals below.

Then he saw dim light spilling from a cave. It was no mere cave. This was a grand entranceway carved from the very rock—an enormous and elaborate facade. What armies of mortal beings had slaved to fashion the great gates of ivory? What patient creatures had carved the colonnade beyond? How many score years had the Vodalians worked in these killing depths to create this underwater palace? And why?

A blue flash came at the center of the gates. It illumined the two Primevals, their claws clutched about the locking mechanism. Lightning cracked through the metal. It tumbled apart in shards. A compression wave carried the noise. Ivory gates swung slowly outward, giving a clear view of the passage beyond. It was lined with columns. Light intensified toward the end of the passage. Through the gap swam Treva and Rith and Darigaaz. From chill depths behind came the rest of the dragon nations.

This was no palace but a tomb. Between the columns, wide niches were carved, stacked from ceiling to floor. Those spaces held dead merfolk. Their bodies had been preserved by the cold and depth, and even their clothes remained intact. They wore simple tunics, and their foreheads were marked with the sign of servitude. No doubt, they had carved these walls not knowing they fashioned their own graves. It was the wicked privilege of gods that they bury thousands of their people with them.

The god would lie ahead.

Another surge brought Darigaaz up beside Treva and Rith. Three sets of wings hurled the water back. Trailing vortices stirred the bodies from their niches. Corpses tumbled in a frenzy behind them. Darigaaz was grieved at the desecration.

But they weren't corpses. They were living—or unliving—guardians.

Merfolk zombies swarmed the dragon nations. They clawed eyes from their sockets. They pierced eardrums with reaching bones. They swam down dragon throats and gnawed them away from the inside. Suddenly, the water was full of blood, dragon blood.

Though breath was failing him, Darigaaz turned and plunged into the swarm of zombies. His claws sent fiery magic out through the waters. Boiling liquid shot from his fingers, impaling undead.

The monsters converged. They tore at his wings. Darigaaz shot lightning through them. They gouged his eyes. Darigaaz poured flame into them. More zombies attacked.

They were too many. If he remained, they would kill him. Already, scores of dragon bodies lay dead upon the ceiling.

Darigaaz felt something powerful clutch his arm. He whirled with another spell ready.

It was Treva, gleaming white in that bloody channel. *Come,* she sent, mind to mind, *they cannot reach beyond the waters. Come.*

What of these who die? Darigaaz asked.

They are the sacrifice, that Dromar and the rest of us might live. Come, now. There was no arguing with her. She was a dragon god.

With a final flick of his tail, Darigaaz drove himself from the swarming zombies. Side by side, he and Treva shot through the waters. They reached the end of the colonnade. Light streamed down through a dappled surface. The two creatures launched themselves up.

Their mantles sprayed water as they bounded onto a wide, flat space. They stood, gushing. Darigaaz's red scales were only deepened by the blood of his people. Somehow Treva had emerged untainted. Before them, farther in, stood Rith, glimmering.

"Focus is everything, Darigaaz," Rith whispered. Her mouth steamed in the cave air. "Why do you defend dragon mortals, beset for a moment, and ignore dragon immortals, beset for millennia?"

Darigaaz shook out his scales. "They are dying."

"Not the ones who swim through," Rith replied, nodding toward the pool.

Up from it rose dragon after dragon. Most had tattered wings. Some were missing eyes. A few were maimed beyond healing, with only enough will to reach air before they died.

"Come, let us make room," Treva said, gesturing Darigaaz deeper into the wide cavern. He followed her.

This upper chamber had been carved as well, in palatial majesty. Dragons and draconic figures appeared everywhere. Friezes filled the walls, depicting primordial battles. Statuary flanked the main way—two huge sentinel dragons, and lesser serpents beyond. The floor between them was literally paved in gold, a dragon hoard as of old. It cast the shadows of their claws against the breasts of the beasts as they strode inward.

"An opulent tomb," Darigaaz whispered in awe.

Rith shook her head. "This is no tomb, Rhammidarigaaz. This is a trap, a gilded cage. The merfolk created it for Dromar. They lured him here with slaves, with grandeur, with gold. They enthroned him on the seat where he has sat trapped ever since. It was the next science mortals stole from us, the science of desire. They learned our hearts and turned our hearts against us." She looked sharply at him. "Behold." She gestured before them.

A glorious dais in gold and marble presided over the throne room. It was perfectly conceived, a hexagonal platform upon which, in gemstones, was rendered the form of a blue dragon. On that glittering mosaic lay the dragon himself. He was curled as if in sleep. His blue scales were the precise color of the sapphires beneath him. His wings were folded across his body like robes of state.

"What sort of deep magic holds him there?" asked Darigaaz.

"The deepest magic of all," replied Treva. "Desire. The merfolk gave him everything he could wish for. They sated his desire, removing it. Desire is life. Without it, a creature is dead."

Darigaaz strode quietly toward the dais and gazed at the dragon there. He seemed asleep. His claws spread jealously across the mosaic.

"Desire?" Darigaaz asked. "Mere desire?"

Treva spoke in a gentle voice. "There is nothing mere about desire. It drives all action. It brings Yawgmoth to Dominaria. It sends Urza to Phyrexia. It brings us here today to free a dragon god. Desire is the only force."

Darigaaz continued to circle the glorious dais. It was indeed a trove. The ancient merfolk had mined jewels no dwarf could reach, and so had brought together larger, more perfect stones than any Darigaaz had ever seen. Each one would have cost a life's wages, and here they all were—so many lives piled up. They must have hated Dromar even more than they loved riches.

One by one, the survivors of the dragon nations entered the chamber. The stones reflected in hundreds of eyes. Their radiance multiplied upon itself.

"What elaborate spell will return this Primeval to life?" Darigaaz asked.

"No spell at all but the simplest of actions," Rith replied. She approached the dais. Her green scales blended with the emeralds before her. "This action has been performed numerous times since Dromar was first imprisoned, and performed imperfectly, which is why he remains. It was no fault of the countless grave robbers who plumbed the depths, passed the gates, escaped the zombies, and reached this glorious spot. They failed not because of what they did next, but because of who they were."

With that, Rith reached down to the base of the dais and daintily plucked a large jade. She lifted it before her, admiring its beauty.

Dromar shifted. It seemed almost as though the stones themselves had whispered their violation. A blue-mantled neck rose. Dromar's head lifted. The flanges along his jaws trembled. Horns gleamed with predatory light. The serpent's tongue flicked, smelling the air. Lids slid back from angry eyes. He spoke with a voice that resonated like the sea itself.

"Who dares violate the palace of Dromar?"

Rith replied evenly, "It is not a palace but a tomb, and not a tomb but a trap, Dromar. I am the one who violates your trap. I, Rith, your sister god."

The serpent's eyes narrowed as he studied the creatures before him. Quickly, his gaze went to the jade.

"The gem is mine. You cannot have it. I have slain mortals in the thousands for doing what you have done. Always I have regained what is mine and always returned it to its spot. I am the master of this trove. Return what is mine."

"No, Dromar. While you have mastered this horde, the humans have mastered the world. What stone is greater, this jade in my hands or Dominaria herself?"

Heat entered his voice. "I care nothing for Dominaria. I care only for what is mine!"

"That is the crux of your trap, Brother," Rith said, "a trap from which I free you now." With that, her claws closed over the jade. She squeezed. A crackling sound came. Shards of green rained down from her hand.

Dromar rose to his haunches, hate blazing in his eyes. "You think that will bring me out to fight beside you? It will not. You have angered me, awakened me, but you cannot pry me from this place. What would happen to the rest of my trove?"

Treva drew herself up in stately majesty. "We feared you would say as much. Your trap lies not in the whole horde but in every single stone of it. So, there is but one way." Lifting her eyes to the vault above, she spoke a single word of power.

"No," murmured Dromar, but it was too late.

A crack spread like black lightning across the ornate ceiling. Dust sifted down from it, and then spraying water.

"No!"

Hunks of stone plunged from the ceiling. They crashed atop the dais and the bricks of gold. They shattered the gemstone mosaic of Dromar. Jewels cracked and ground to dust.

Dromar clutched futilely at the shattered treasure. "What are you doing? What are you doing!"

"We are returning life to you, in all its agony of desire," Rith said, turning away from the doomed cavern and heading back down the passage. "Your trove is destroyed. You are master of nothing. Come with us, and you shall once again be master of the world."

Still Dromar did not leave his ruined dais. Still he clutched at the shattered stones. All the while, rocks smashed down around him.

Treva and Rith and the dragon nations retreated to the zombie pool. Rhammidarigaaz brought up the rear. Jewel shards washed past his feet. He turned, extending his hand.

"Come, Brother. Live."

.

CHAPTER 27
A Calling Card for Crovax

"All hands on deck!" Gerrard yelled into the speaking tube. "We're being boarded!"

"Greven is mine," reminded Tahngarth from the other side of the forecastle. The minotaur had drawn a striva, one presented to him by Commander Grizzlegom. He had not wielded a striva in battle since Mercadia. How fitting that this new blade be inaugurated with the blood of Greven il-Vec. Eyeing the wicked weapon, Gerrard said, "You'll get no argument from me."

Side by side, the minotaur and the commander descended the forecastle steps. Up from the central hatch streamed crew members. Most were seafarers turned skyfarers. They bore with them cutlasses and daggers. Others were ensigns and engineers to whom combat was an unwelcome possibility. Among these came Orim and her assistants—healers who now bore swords. All hands meant all hands.

Striding toward the stern, Gerrard greeted Orim. "You could stay below, wait for casualties."

She hitched her brow. "You'd be surprised what Cho-Arrim water magic can do to Phyrexian metal."

Gerrard and Tahngarth mounted the stern castle steps. They ascended beneath the port-side sweep of the wing stanchions. Suddenly another comrade was beside them. The stairs bowed toward his bulk.

"Karn, what are you doing? How are we going to break free with our engineer above deck?"

The silver golem reached casually to his side, seized one of the grapples, and snapped its line. The cord whipped loose.

"How can we break free with these grapples attached?"

"True enough," Gerrard affirmed, thumping the metal man on the back.

They hadn't time for more conversation. Greven and his *il-Vec* and *il-Dal* warriors had headed first for the bridge. The sounds of swords confirmed Gerrard's fears. He rushed around the corner.

The rear door to the bridge had been smashed in. Multani worked feverishly to regrow the wood, but he could not prevail against the axes of the *il-Dal*. Now only a single figure blocked their path.

"Get back, Rathi scum!" Sisay growled. Her cutlass bashed away the strike of an *il-Dal* axe and dipped down to open the man's belly. "This is my ship, damn it. Get back!"

Roaring defiantly, the second *il-Dal* swung his axe in a blow that would cleave Sisay's head.

She couldn't raise her cutlass in time.

The blade hummed as it descended. The warrior completed his stroke—but five feet off the deck. His axe clanged against Karn's silvery back. The golem held him overhead in a pair of huge hands.

"You heard the lady," Karn growled, "get back!" He hurled the warrior over the rail. The *il-Dal* and his axe plunged toward the crater.

"About time you guys showed up," Sisay said as she stabbed another warrior.

Gerrard shrugged, the move bringing his sword up to block an axe. "You seem to be holding your own."

"I seem to be holding the helm," Sisay replied with a barking laugh, "which means I'm holding everything."

Gerrard smiled. "I'd never argue with that. Of course, you can't take credit for holding Greven." Gerrard gestured outward with his sword. The motion simultaneously severed the arm of a foe and pointed to where Tahngarth faced down the monstrous captain of *Predator*.

*   *   *   *   *

The two warriors circled each other. This had been long in coming. Tahngarth was Greven's escaped prisoner, intended to be his lieutenant. Greven was Tahngarth's erstwhile tormentor, intended to be his master. Both had a score to settle. Both had warned off their comrades from their prize.

As twisted as Tahngarth had become in the torture chambers of Rath, Greven was more twisted still. Every muscle of his body bulked beyond natural dimensions. The cords of his neck, the sinews of his eyelids, and the muscles of his scalp all bulged beneath gray-black armor, but the most deadly modification was the mimetic spine that had replaced his own. It had made him the absolute tool of Volrath and now of Crovax. The evincar of the Stronghold could see through his eyes and hear through his ears and fight through his hands.

Greven swung his polearm. Its head was a pair of crab-claw blades set among spikes. Its butt was a mace that sprouted curved horns. Just now, those horns cracked Tahngarth's own.

The minotaur snorted. He bulled forward and rammed the polearm back toward Greven's face. Tangling his horns with the man's weapon, Tahngarth brought his striva in a two-hand slash across Greven's waist. Well-tempered metal cut through the thick leather straps that corseted the mimetic spine. The striva laid open muscle, stopping only when Greven hurled himself back.

"Your transformations have made you powerful," Greven said through teeth locked in a grin. "Let me finish what I began, and you will be a creature to be feared."

Tahngarth's eyes flared. "I already am."

He charged. His striva swept downward in a brutal blow.

Greven backed up. He lifted his polearm to block the stroke. Hands clenched and teeth gritted.

There was too much rage in Tahngarth's attack. The striva sparked as it struck the haft of the weapon. It sheared right through. The cleft ends of the polearm dropped away. The striva continued on, striking Greven's rib guard. It cut through that as well and severed the flaps of muscle laced through his sternum.

Tahngarth continued forward, shoving the blade into Greven's chest. "I want your heart, if you still have one."

Braced against the stern rail, Greven brought the two ends of his polearm around before him. The mace dug its curved horns into the minotaur's chest. The crab-claw blades sliced across his shoulder.

Tahngarth backed up. The striva came away from Greven, trailing blood.

"I will trade you wound for wound, Tahngarth, and you will die. I am a Phyrexian. You are a half-thing, a nothing. Surrender, and you yet might serve me."

Bloodied but unbowed, Tahngarth snorted. "Serve you? You don't even serve yourself. You are a man with someone else's spine."

Tahngarth attacked again. His striva sang as it sliced the air. It struck the crab-claw blades and bashed them back. In the same motion, it blocked the horned mace. Tahngarth drove onward. His blade sank into Greven's jaw. It clove skin and muscle to bone, cutting away the lower quarter of his face. "Not so cocky now, are you?"

The mace and the claw blades converged on Tahngarth. One would spike his head and the other sever it.

Tahngarth ducked beneath the blow. The weapons crossed above him. The spikes impaled one of Greven's shoulders, and the claw blades chunked into the other. Tahngarth butted the beast with his horns. One point gouged through the torn leather corset.

Gored, Greven vomited blood on the minotaur's back.

Ignoring it, Tahngarth lifted his foe across his horns and hurled him down.

Greven struck the deck with a boom. His armor dug into the planks beneath him. He bled profusely at shoulders, face, and gut.

"I will never serve you, Greven," Tahngarth said, pointing his striva at the creature. "It is you who must surrender."

Laughing through bloody teeth, Greven barked, "Surrender?" Despite his wounds, he struggled to his feet. "You still don't understand. You do not speak to Greven. You speak to Crovax. You could never best me, Tahngarth, not when we were shipmates and certainly not now. No, you will serve." Greven launched himself at Tahngarth.

It was a suicidal attack. Whether Crovax tossed a useless weapon at his foe or Greven took the final moment of control from his master, Tahngarth would never know.

The striva fell. It clove Greven's head down the middle. The blade did not even cease until it struck Greven's mimetic spine. The captain of *Predator* fell, his split face striking the stern castle of *Weatherlight*.

Panting, bloodied, still full of battle fury, Tahngarth stared down at the riven form. He had his revenge on the man who had so tormented him.

Obscene sucking sounds came from Greven. Something moved within the split brain case. It nosed forward from the cleft. Its head was a collection of bulbous nodules. Its body was a long centipede of armored cords. Metallic cilia undulated along its length, dragging it forward.

Tahngarth took a step back. "Spinal centipede."

Lifting its pointed tail, the thing bounded toward him.

With one smooth stroke of his striva, Tahngarth bisected the mimetic spine down its middle. Sparking from severed conduits, the two halves fell away from each other. They landed on the planks, snapping and convulsing beside the corpse of Greven. Tahngarth chopped them up as if they were snakes.

Even when Greven was dead, Crovax still lashed out. He still hoped to make Tahngarth his own.

* * * * *

While Tahngarth dispatched the captain of *Predator*, Gerrard did the same to the crew.

He bashed a battle axe aside, deflecting it to the head of an *il*-Dal warrior. While the owner of the axe struggled to haul the thing free, Gerrard felled him with a thrust. He climbed over that warrior to the next and the next. He had one goal in mind—Squee.

The goblin lay beneath his gun. He bore a horrid wound down his back, from shoulder to hip. Muscle and bone were laid bare. The fact that it still bled meant Squee still lived. The fact that it bled so profusely meant he would not live much longer.

Gerrard blocked another *il*-Vec axe and shoved its wielder over the rail. A severed grapple line told that Karn had been along here. Soon he would snap the last lines, and the ship could pull free of *Predator*. The final few cables whined with tension. As long as they held, more invaders could cross over.

Gerrard's sword made quick work of the *il*-Vec. Two more toppled, and he reached Squee.

Gerrard knelt beside the goblin and stared in uncertainty at the long gash. How could he bind it? Reaching to his shoulder, he ripped the sleeve from his shift and dragged it off his hand.

"Here, let me," came the voice of Orim. Word of Squee's injury had reached her, and she had fought through the gauntlet. "Cleaner this way," she said, pressing her hands to the wound. Silvery magic glowed beneath her fingers.

"Thanks!" Gerrard said heavily. He stood in time to stab another *il*-Vec who had clambered over the stern. He fell sloppily beside them, almost landing on Orim.

"See if you can't keep the air clear," she suggested.

"Oh, I'll clear the air!" Gerrard growled, gripping the fire controls of Squee's ray cannon. A few pumps of the foot treadle, and the gun hummed with life. "How about some of this?"

The cannon blazed. Crimson destruction belched from its muzzle. Rays ignited the foundering *Predator*. Sections of the vessel exploded. Crew disappeared in the blasts or tumbled in flames toward the volcano's crater. A second barrage ripped the lower forecastle clean away from *Predator*. With it went the grapple mounts. *Weatherlight* ground free of the disintegrating ship.

Gerrard smiled viciously, leaning toward Orim. "See? We were doing it the hard way. Don't snap the grapples. Destroy the ship."

Sisay retreated to the helm, and Karn to the engine room. The last of the *il*-Vec had been dispatched. They covered the stern castle. Crew members busily dumped bodies over the rail.

Tahngarth loomed up suddenly beside Gerrard. He held overhead a massive corpse—the horn-studded figure of Greven *il*-Vec. With a look of triumph, he hurled the body overboard. It arced from *Weatherlight*'s stern to the gunwales of *Predator*.

"Fitting," Gerrard shouted, "that the captain go down with his ship."

"That's a calling card," Tahngarth said, his voice deeply brooding. He watched the fiery vessel plunge away. It spiraled in air, trailing a cyclone of smoke above it. *Predator* plummeted toward the deep pit at the volcano's center. "A calling card for Crovax."

Gerrard nodded solemnly, watching the ship fall. It seemed a blazing comet as it entered the pit. A ring of fire descended around it and lit the walls. *Weatherlight* would follow down that dark passage soon enough.

Breathing deeply, Gerrard released the fire controls of Squee's cannon and peered at the fallen gunner.

"How's he doing?"

Orim's eyes were weary as she looked up. She stroked coin-coifed hair from her face. "That wound would have killed me or you, but somehow, he's survived."

A muffled voice volunteered, "You need Squee to fight Crovax."

Gerrard laughed. "You used to think everybody wanted you dead, Squee. Now it seems everybody wants you alive."

"Everybody's got smart all of a sudden," Squee groaned. He stood up, stretching his back. "Whatcha do, Orim, give Squee a Greven spine? You probly want Squee as servant! Everybody want Squee as servant!"

Orim smiled. "He'll be just fine." She spotted two more crew members in need of healing. "Tahngarth, give me a hand getting those two down to sickbay."

Nodding, the minotaur followed her.

Gerrard watched his two friends carry the wounded away. His reverie was broken by the sound of goblin feet tapping the planks. He looked down to see Squee, arms crossed, staring at him accusingly. Gerrard spread his hands in question.

The goblin scowled. "Maybe commander think he keep gun. Maybe he think he not give Squee back Squee's gun."

"No, no, no," Gerrard replied, backing away from the cannon. "I was just standing here."

Squee advanced a step. "Maybe he think Squee not well enough to shoot. Maybe he afraid more bad guys sneak up his butt."

"Look! Look! They're all gone. There's nobody here. I was just standing near the gun. It's yours. Fine. Take it back. I don't need it."

"Yes, you do," came a voice out of nowhere. "Greven left one soldier behind."

Invisible arms clamped tightly around Gerrard, and then turned visible—Phyrexian arms. Their grip was implacable.

They pinned his weapon in place. Gerrard thrashed his head to see who had grabbed him, but he could not even turn.

Squee lunged toward them. "Ertai!"

With a thought, the wizard who had once served on *Weatherlight* disappeared from the stern castle, taking Gerrard and Squee with him.

CHAPTER 28
The True Warriors of Keld

Never before had the armies of Keld retreated. When over-matched, Keldon warlords descended bravely into death, grinding away at their foes all the while. Any adversary who would dominate the Keldons would pay for victory in blood, oceans of it. Superior forces often surrendered to Keld for this very reason. The wisest enemies avoided war altogether, knowing they would face an all-out and endless battle.

This adversary was no rival nation. Who can battle a glacier? Who can war with a volcano? Who can stand against the coming of Twilight, the night of wrath?

The Keldons had stood as long as they could. Here was the culmination of history. Millennia of battles since the descent from Parma had led to this moment, this blasphemous moment. Twilight had come. The honored dead of Keld had returned to life. They had emerged from the Necropolis only to join armies of Phyrexians. Dead Keldons had slaughtered live ones. Keldon history had bowed in service to a foreign god. Still, living Keldons had battled bravely on.

Then the very world turned on them.

Beneath the army's feet, ice turned to water. Around their shoulders, water turned to steam. The Keldons in their hundreds of thousands descended through ice and fire into the heart of the world.

Only a single scant legion escaped. They had been farthest out from the fighting—young camp runners and old warriors cursed to survive their battle careers. All of them fled. There was no honor in this retreat, but there was less honor in letting the flood claim them. Keld needed warriors, even if they be only whelps and curs.

Across disintegrating ice, the army retreated. Their colos leaped over widening crevasses. Infantry splashed through new warm streams. Warriors struggled to navigate the calving ice cliffs. They rushed toward the black basalt mountain on one side of the terminal glacier. Even when they reached that rock-solid ground, it too shuddered under them. It was as if the fire gods below pounded the over world with massive hammers.

Now the survivors of the Battle of Twilight camped on a chill ridge of black stone. It was a defensible spot—no Keldon would camp anywhere else—though no Phyrexian foe remained. All had died in the world conflagration. The only foe was the flood itself.

At first, the towering terminus had sprouted countless jets across its surface. Water that had fought through twisted passages shot in straight lines from the glacier. Pressurized streams widened and joined. Centuries of centuries of water burst out into a gray river. Enormous hunks of ice bounded free. They bobbed through deeper stretches and rolled among rapids. The serpent of Twilight muscled its way toward the sea.

The flesh of that serpent was filled with bodies. Keldon, Phyrexian, elf, colos all tumbled in a confused mass. The wurm had swallowed them. A Phyrexian's spikes impaled a Keldon's back, and the two bodies formed a new creature. An elf was tangled in the reins of his colos, and with six legs and two arms and two heads, they floated together. Dead fingers clung to shattered rams and hunks of mast. In places, the bodies had gathered in a ghastly Sargasso.

The Keldon survivors looked down with solemn despair. These dead were the finest warriors in the land, slain not by swords but by fire and ice. Every camp runner and warlord felt instinctually that he should have tumbled in that flood with them.

They did their best to make amends. Warriors stood at the edge of the flood and reached in with polearms to snag whatever soldiers they could. They lifted Keldons and elves out and laid them in orderly rows below the camp. They dragged Phyrexians free and tossed them into bonfires. Even so, most of the corpses were out of reach, even out of sight, schooling along beneath the waves. For every body they hauled from the river, fifty others bobbed past. Even so, the dead below the camp outnumbered the living in it.

"There will have to be a new Necropolis," said camp runner Stokken to himself.

Doyen Lairsen stood nearby, watching the awful tide. His plaited hair and beard were pitted with soot where smoke sticks had burned to their nubs.

"Why? What is the point?"

The young man was startled by his doyen's jaded assessment. "To honor the dead, of course. To renew our hopes for Twilight—"

"Twilight has come and gone," snapped Doyen Lairsen. His hands gripped the hilts of his brutal swords. "It has turned daylight to darkness. What is the point in hoping for another Twilight?"

Blinking incredulously, Stokken said, "The fire of Keld has

burned brightly throughout the day. How much more must we stoke it to make it last the night?"

"Youth!" Lairsen spat angrily. The word was a curse. "Hope is the delusion of the young."

In a low voice, Stokken murmured, "And despair is the delusion of the old."

"What was that!" Lairsen barked, drawing steel. A moment later, the sword was returned to its sheath, and blood wept from a long gash on Stokken's face. The slash was so quick, the sword so sharp, that Stokken did not even feel the attack until his neck grew warm. Doyen Lairsen repeated, "What was that?"

Stokken bowed deeply, dropping to one knee. "I have spoken out of turn, Doyen. Forgive me. I was not responsible for my words, deluded, as I was, by hope."

Lairsen's brow furrowed. The implication was clear—the doyen had done himself a dishonor by striking a deluded man. Still, if he admitted Stokken was not deluded, the doyen would have lost the previous argument. This young man bore watching.

"A delusional man should not bear a sword. Surrender yours to me." Doyen Lairsen smiled, knowing he had won.

Stokken was wise enough not to resist. Even a word at this juncture could be construed as a refusal, as grounds for summary execution. He slowly slid his sword from his shoulder harness.

Receiving the blade, Doyen Lairsen gritted his teeth viciously. "Next you will be seeing visions—the army resurrected beneath a midnight sun—" The grin melted from his face, replaced by a strange golden glow.

Stokken studied his doyen's scarred face some moments before turning to gaze where he did. Forgetting his penance, Stokken rose to stare.

Aback the gray serpent of Twilight rode a dreaming thing. Its hull gleamed golden. Its masts were full-rigged in white-bellied sails. It was queer and glorious and unbelievable, the *Golden Argosy* from the Necropolis.

Could it be that the ship had tumbled with the rest of the destroyed citadel? Could it be that like its people, the ship had been dragged into the boiling maelstrom? It seemed impossible that the *Golden Argosy* could ride now, whole and beaming upon the serpentine tides. And who did she bear upon her crowded decks?

"What is this delusion?" Doyen Lairsen wondered aloud before he could stop himself.

"Hope," breathed camp runner Stokken, taking back his sword. "That delusion is hope."

* * * * *

Eladamri had never seen so beautiful a sky. After three days in the bowels of a glacier, any sky would have been splendid. But this boreal blue, with its ranges of cloud above a tossing sea, this was magnificent. Its glory was second only to that of the *Golden Argosy* herself.

She was a strange ship, stranger even than *Weatherlight*. There was not a stick of furniture in her, no stores, no ballast, no heads, no crew. There was not even a helm. The ship sailed according to her own will. Indeed, she had a will. She had navigated the tight confines of the glacier with an expert rudder, sliding through impossible spaces. Her masts never ground upon the ceiling, her gunwales never scraped the walls. She made sail and reefed sail not according to the torrents of wind beneath the ice but according to the winds of another world. Always, she found the fastest path. Always, she drew up the thousands upon thousands of Keldons and elves who survived beneath the ice. Though her hull was commodious, it could not truly have held this many, and yet each new arrival found room among his or her fellows. Within her hull, they were warm and dry, neither hungering nor thirsting—healed of all they lacked, clothed and rested, even given to understand the speech of each other.

She was an odd ship, constructed not from material but from ideal. She did not sail true seas but rather the seas of dream.

Amid impossible thousands of others, Eladamri and Liin Sivi stood on deck as the *Argosy* emerged from beneath the ice. Together they saw the aching blue sky. The sun broke upon the two of them but cast down a single shadow.

"Once again among the living," Eladamri said gladly.

"Once again," Liin Sivi echoed. Her hand found his, and she slid her fingers between his. "I hadn't doubted it, not from the moment I saw this ship."

Drawing a deep breath of the bright air—no more the wet chill murk—Eladamri replied, "Oh, I doubted. I thought we would never see daylight again. I thought the ship itself a dream. I am not certain it is not."

"*They* are not a dream," Liin Sivi said, pointing to a nearby shoulder of stone. A Keldon camp perched there. Warlords and lackeys crowded the cliff, gazing in wonderment. "Nor is Port Bay a dream." She gestured toward the great Keldon city, its domes and spires jagged against the sparkling sea. "How can this be a dream?"

"This *is* a dream," came a voice in High Keldon, though both Eladamri and Liin Sivi could understand. They turned to see Doyenne Tajamin, Keeper of the Book of Keld. "But this dream is more true than truth."

"More prophecies from your ancestral cudgel?" Liin Sivi asked.

Tajamin shook her head slowly. Her eyes were twin embers, and her teeth gleamed in a scarred smile.

"No, these words are written nowhere except on my soul. I have learned the power—and the limits—of written revelation. It can be misquoted as easily as quoted. The truth of figures is always figurative truth."

The doyenne's smile spread to Eladamri. "These are strange words from the Keeper of the Book of Keld."

"These are strange times," she replied. "It was written that the true heroes of Keld would descend from the Necropolis to fight the true foes of the land. I had always believed that this meant the honored dead would join us against the Phyrexians. In fact, the dead are the dead. They are closer allies to Phyrexia than to us.

"But that does not mean the prophecies are false. The *Golden Argosy* has descended from the Necropolis, gathering the true heroes of Keld to fight the true foes of the land," the doyenne said, fire shining in her eyes.

Eladamri's eyes narrowed. "Our fight has only begun, then?"

She nodded with deep certainty. "The fate of Keld, and all the world, is being decided across the sea. The Battle of Keld is won. Every last soldier who fought was dragged down to death. Only we—the true heroes of Keld—rose again." There seemed nothing more to say.

The *Golden Argosy* breasted the gray waves with the same divine grace she had exhibited in the glacier. The thousands in her hull felt only gladness as she bore them through the tide. On the banks of the flood stood their folk—Keldon and elf—staring. All wore the blank and blind and somewhat worried aspect of sleepwalkers. They could not understand what they saw. It was a spectacle, a phantasm.

To those aboard the *Golden Argosy*, it was more real than real. Eladamri, Liin Sivi, and Tajamin stood in company with two hundred Skyshroud and Steel Leaf elves. Nearby, Doyen Olvresk and his ten "fists" watched among the rest of his war band. Even Warlord Astor had survived the icy torrents. He shouted a greeting to the Keldons on the bank but got no response.

"They cannot understand you," Tajamin called to him. "They are in a mortal place. We are in a divine one. They are subject to want, to hunger, to fear, to confusion. We are not. They are sleepwalkers, only half aware of eternal things. We will return among them and be like them—some of us."

Eladamri was honestly surprised by this. "Return among them? What of the great battle that awaits us? What of the battle across the sea?"

"It is a battle for some of us but not all," Doyenne Tajamin replied. "The Battle of Keld may be done, but there is much to rebuild—whole societies. We have not won back our land only to abandon it. Some of the heroes of Keld must fight our battles here, at hearth and fire. Many of your folk must remain as well." She moved toward the rail and gripped it with powerful fists.

Suddenly understanding, Eladamri came up beside her. "You cannot leap from the ship. The icy flood will kill you."

Tajamin did not smile, but her teeth made a hopeful line. "No. It did not kill me before and will not kill me now. I must plunge into the waters as a sleeper into dream. I will rise on the far bank remembering this ship as if it were but a delusion—I and the thousands with me. We will climb, muddy and shivering, from the flood, and we will turn around to glimpse this ship. We will see it with the same unbelieving eyes as those on shore."

Staring levelly at her, Eladamri said, "If you cannot remember anything else, Doyen Tajamin, remember this. The folk of the Skyshroud are your allies, now and forever."

"Yes, Eladamri, Uniter of Keld," the doyenne said formally, "I will remember."

With that she hurled herself over the rail. She dropped away into the gray flood and was swallowed up. After her went another and a third. Warlord Astor soon followed, and Doyen Olvresk as well, and then more than Eladamri could count. Each one disappeared in the bow waves, each reappeared, drenched and struggling in the cold tide at the ship's stern. All swam for shore and for their folk, who waded in to bring them back to the land of the living.

Eladamri rode on. He, Liin Sivi, some hundred elves, and some ten thousand Keldons rode on. From the banks, their companions watched with bald disbelief.

Only Doyenne Tajamin wore a different look. The forgetful tide had not washed away one memory. She knew.

The sight of it in her eyes gave Eladamri great comfort. His people had found a home in this land. He smiled as the *Golden Argosy* bore him and the heroes of Keld out into the churning sea.

CHAPTER 29
Life Must Ever Battle Death

Commander Grizzlegom emerged from a grim scene. Agnate lay within the tent, unmade by an axe. There wasn't much blood; he had been nearly dead before the weapon fell. The axe strokes—one for Agnate the man and the second for Agnate the undead—had been the only mercy in that awful place. The rest was grimness: the failed philters, the pus-covered bandages, the cot marked with finger-scars, the body that had died weeks ago but rested only now.

These were the foul provisions of a covenant with death.

In his four-fingered grip, Grizzlegom bore the provisions of a new covenant, a covenant with life. Commander Agnate's signed and signeted orders gave the Metathran army to Grizzlegom.

The Metathran guards outside the tent snapped to attention as Grizzlegom appeared. These two towering warriors would have to be his first witnesses, else they would enter, discover the scene within, and spread the wrong story.

"Warriors, stand to. I have something you must see."

The soldiers turned toward him. Starlight shone against their silver hair. One wore shackles at his belt, the equipment of a guard captain.

Grizzlegom presented the orders to him. "Note your master's seal. Open it. Read it."

The soldier's blue eyes studied the seal, seeing the warmth still within the wax. He cracked the wax and read. His face grew grim.

"What has happened to Commander Agnate?"

"He is dead. The plague had destroyed him. He begged me the mercy of ending his pain. I did. My healer is within, preparing the body." Drawing back the tent flap, he allowed the two Metathran to gaze within. "Agnate signed this before I dispatched him."

"This is not written in his hand," the guard captain said.

"No, he was too weak—but this is his signature, and this his signet stamp." Grizzlegom allowed the guard captain a moment before he said, "You now take orders from me. Corporal, close this tent and prevent anyone from entering. Captain, lead me to General Rilgesh."

Nodding, the guard captain said to his comrade, "You heard the commander." Then to Grizzlegom, he said, "Follow me, Commander."

They set out through the night-swathed camp. Old foes—the people of mountain and island—soon would be allies against the forces of death.

Along the near flank of the volcano, Metathran crouched in their dark circles, chewing the rock-hard fare that had come up the supply lines. They needed no fire, no light, and not even the comfort of conversation on that savage slope. These creatures were bred for war, happiest in battle. It was all they needed.

Along the opposite flank of the volcano sat minotaurs at blazing bivouacs. They needed fire and light and stories—and better food. Though they all ate their rations of jerked pork and flat bread, they also feasted on frogs and mushrooms harvested from the swamps below, along with the occasional marsh deer. A small platoon of minotaurs hunted wild game, sending it and firewood to Grizzlegom's troops. Minotaurs loved battle, yes, but they loved life as well.

The gulf between the two armies seemed almost unbridgeable, especially by a slender slip of paper. Still, Agnate had bridged life and death. Perhaps enough of his power remained to unite these old foes. It would have to, or both armies were doomed.

Beyond the camp, Lich Lord Dralnu's forces—ghouls, zombies, revenants—patrolled the outer darkness. No fire, no stories, no food, they needed only unwavering devotion to their master. Though now they guarded the living, in mere hours, they would be slaughtering them.

Grizzlegom clutched Agnate's orders. The Metathran second-in-command, General Rilgesh, dwelt in a tent nearby, among the other generals in the command core. Though Metathran did not need tents, they did need hierarchy, and tents were signs of ascendancy.

Ahead of Grizzlegom, the guard captain approached the soldiers outside Rilgesh's tent. They traded quiet words. The soldiers stood back, holding up the tent flaps and making way for the minotaur.

"Announcing Commander Grizzlegom," the guard captain said solemnly.

Grizzlegom stepped through their midst.

Rilgesh was a Metathran general like any other—sleeping on a cot only because his rank required it. There were no adornments in the tent, nothing beyond a cot, a lantern, a small table where the evening's meal lay untouched, and a strip of velvet that held the general's polished and sharpened arms. Rilgesh had cleaned his arms before cleaning himself. He still sat in battle-scarred armor.

Rilgesh stood, wiping his hands on the weapon rag before tossing it away. He bowed his head in greeting to Grizzlegom.

Nodding in return, Grizzlegom handed the slip of paper to Rilgesh. "Commander Agnate issued these orders, to which his guard captain is witness."

The guard captain nodded his confirmation.

Silently, Rilgesh took the sheet, studied the broken seal, opened the page, and read. There was no surprise in his eyes, not a moment of insurrection. He folded the note and handed it back.

"What are your orders, Commander?"

"Guard Captain," Grizzlegom said, gesturing the Metathran farther into the tent, "sit there, upon the floor. General, sit there, upon the cot. The rest of you, leave us."

The two officers found their seats, and the guards withdrew.

Grizzlegom crouched down near the two Metathran leaders and said intently, "At first light, we will attack the troops of Lich Lord Dralnu."

The unflappable warriors showed a moment's hesitation.

General Rilgesh said, "Dralnu is our ally—"

"No longer," Grizzlegom preempted. "Life can never ally with death. Life must ever fight death. We must fight Dralnu and his legions."

Rilgesh's mouth gaped. "But to turn without warning on a friend—"

"Dralnu has already turned on us. He infected Agnate with plague, hoping to raise him again as a minion. He planned to gain the whole Metathran army by gaining its commander," Grizzlegom replied evenly. "And don't think my axe has stopped him. If he cannot gain this army through Agnate, he will gain it by infecting us all. Unless we act now, all is lost."

Rilgesh's eyes steeled with belief and duty. "We are yours to command."

"Good," Grizzlegom said. "We will send word among our troops to muster quietly. Meanwhile, the three of us will strike.

We will visit Dralnu, catch him off guard, surround him, and slay him."

"How does one slay a lich lord?" Rilgesh asked.

"Destroy the brain first," Grizzlegom said. "Next, shatter the necromantic implements on the body. Then dismantle the body, separating its parts and smashing any crystals imbedded within. Lastly, battle his host and slaughter them, every last one, so that none remain to return to his lair and provide him a new body."

"An elaborate assassination," mused Rilgesh.

"An elaborate foe," Grizzlegom replied. "Will you do it?"

"We are yours to command—"

"I don't mean as subordinates," Grizzlegom interrupted. "I mean as warriors. Will you do what must be done? Already tonight, I have slain a noble comrade. I slew him twice. It was no easy thing, but it had to be done. Now we must slay an ally. I don't want soldiers following orders. I want heroes who believe in each stroke of their blades. If you do not believe, we will die tonight. If you do believe, we will live. So, how say you? Will you do this thing?"

Before they could answer, a voice came from the guards at the head of the tent. "Announcing Lich Lord Dralnu." The flaps drew back, and the beast himself entered.

In bright armor, the lich lord was an amazing sight. He might have been a living man. Gleaming boots drummed to a halt. Cuisses glinted beneath the silk tassels of his tabard. Only his head rose free of the pristine armor—his scabrous and horrid head. The lines of nobility remained in his high cheeks, though here and there the flesh split to show bones. The once-aquiline nose was sunken. Desiccated lips parted above teeth like dry corn. Only the eyes lived, and they burned with anger.

"There is an assassin in the camp," Lich Lord Dralnu said.

The other three warriors had risen. Rilgesh stared in mute frustration at his weapons, lying out of reach on the floor.

It was Grizzlegom who spoke, "What? An assassin?"

Dralnu's eyes were unblinking—his lids long since gone. "I just went to visit Commander Agnate in his tent, and when I got here—" he paused, seeming to eye the minotaur's axe—"I found Agnate slain."

Grizzlegom feigned surprise. "Slain! In his own tent! What of the guard?"

"Yes," Dralnu continued, watching closely. "What of the guard? He would not allow me near the tent. He tried to force me away. I slew him, entered, and found Commander Agnate lying there, his head in pieces."

The two Metathran shifted their gazes from the lich lord to the minotaur.

Dralnu continued. "There was a minotaur wrapping the body. He said he was a healer, though there was no hope of healing Commander Agnate. I ordered him away from the body, but he would not relinquish Agnate to me. I accused him of the murder, and he attacked me. I killed him as well."

Grizzlegom's hackles rose. "It sounds as though you have found your assassins."

"Two of them, but the axe that slew Agnate was nowhere to be found. There must have been a third."

The Metathran gazed at the axe.

Grizzlegom gritted his teeth. "You mean an axe like this?" He drew the weapon with a sudden, angry movement. "A minotaur's axe, with a broad enough curve to cleave a man from pate to throat?"

The lich lord warily watched the blade. "Yes. That sort of blade exactly."

Grizzlegom continued. "Good. Means and opportunity link me to the death of Commander Agnate. Perhaps even witnesses, for you have the power to question the dead."

"I am questioning you, Commander Grizzlegom."

"All that remains is motive, yes? Motive is what makes a killing an assassination or a murder or the normal course of war—or perhaps even a matter of honor."

"There was no honor in this killing. You slew him in order to take command of his troops," the lich lord hissed.

"Are those my motives or yours?" Grizzlegom asked, studying the notched blade. "Your gangrene slew him, not my axe."

"You have as much as admitted your guilt."

"As have you!" the minotaur retorted. "But we argue because we each need these men—Agnate's men. They are our judges. Let them judge. Let them strip away our arms. Let them shackle us in iron—for even a lich lord cannot escape iron. Let them hood our heads, and once we are incapable of striking back, let them choose which they believe and which they kill."

Through rictus lips, the lich lord said, "Why should I submit to such a disgraceful act?"

"If you speak the truth, you have nothing to fear."

"I speak the truth. It was your axe that slew the commander."

Grizzlegom dropped his axe. It clattered to the ground beside General Rilgesh's own weapons. He drew his arms behind him, presenting them for the shackles.

Simultaneously, Dralnu drew the gauntlets from his emaciated hands and positioned them at his back.

The iron bands locked simultaneously in place. The two commanders were turned to face one another. Hatred sparked between them.

"These warriors are honorable," Dralnu said. "They will not believe the murderer of Agnate."

"That is my hope."

Thick woven silk descended over their heads. It wrapped them tightly in blackness. Though he could see nothing, Grizzlegom could hear the guard captain's sword grate from its sheath. Metal clanged as the general retrieved his blade from the floor. One of the Metathran positioned himself behind Dralnu, and the other behind Grizzlegom.

The lich lord whispered, "Fool, they will kill us both, but I am lord of the dead."

Steel whirled. It sliced through silk and skin and skull and brain. A second blade crashed down atop an armored breastplate, shattering the stones inset there. Lich Lord Dralnu had not even struck the ground before his black heart was impaled.

Shaking the wrap from his head, Grizzlegom joined his horns to the gruesome work. Each shattered crystal blazed with searing fire. The lich's sacklike belly held a score of them. They spilled out on the ground like obscene eggs. Dralnu had hoped to hatch himself again and again and again.

* * * * *

When the first rays of sunlight raked across the undead that morning, they knew their master was gone. Without Dralnu, sunlight was a searing thing. In camp, a trump heralded the dawn.

Like minions of that hated morn, Metathran and minotaurs charged suddenly from their tents, their eyes ablaze.

The undead fled. They wished for pits and grottoes and sloughs, but here on the volcano there were none. There was only the beaming sun and the cold blue of Metathran steel and the hot red of minotaur eyes. Commander Grizzlegom led the charge.

The living betrayed the dead. They fought with vicious fury. They sent their onetime colleagues down to the second death.

CHAPTER 30
The Soul Bomb

The Steam Beast was a crude nightmare, ten times the size of a titan engine. Driven by coal and oil, it streamed soot from a thousand knobby joints. Pistons shot explosively from pressure chambers. Drive shafts propelled the monster on six enormous legs. Its central body was a framework packed with hissing boilers. Foot-thick armor guarded the power plants from attack. The beast had no head but shoulders that sported hundreds of reaching arms. Each was tipped in huge titanium shears. Each could dart from the beast to rip apart whatever challenged it.

Urza and his five remaining titans—Taysir, Freyalise, Bo Levar, Windgrace, and Guff—challenged it. They seemed badgers before a bear, except that this bear had hundreds of arms.

Rockets blazed from Urza's wrists. They shot toward the beast, cracked off its armor, and spiraled away. Trailing gray smoke, the rockets rose into the murk of Phyrexia's fourth sphere. One by one, they impacted the pipe-lined ceiling and exploded. Oil and fire rained down.

The Steam Beast's shears lashed out. Blades gnawed one leg of Urza's titan engine and cut through its power conduit.

Growling, Urza invoked a distortion field. Blue magic crackled from his fingertips to trace along the nearest shears. Energy mapped them, lines on a schematic. Urza twisted the lines. Metal shrieked and bent. Blades ground against each other. Joints failed. Bolts popped. A dozen metal arms clattered to the ground.

Still, there were hundreds more. Shears etched scars on Commodore Guff's piloting bulb. They worried Taysir's powerstones. They gripped Lord Windgrace's foreleg.

Urza planeswalked from the battleground and instantly reappeared. His titan feet came down on the back of the Steam Beast.

The iron armor was soot black and slick with oil. Urza's engine lost its footing. He slipped and fell to one knee. The fall saved him, for scores of scissor-tipped arms snapped overhead.

Urza rammed one fist down into the superstructure. Boilers crowded below, organs in the monster's torso. Blistering heat peeled from them. Urza spread his mechanical fingers. Sorceries sprang from the ends of them and fanned out through the beast. The spells struck adjacent boilers and bored through their thick metal. Steam shot angrily from each hole, and then fire. Metal bounded out, swelling before breaking.

Urza yanked his arm back as shrapnel flew. He crouched upon the greasy back plate, saved a second time. Hurtling hunks of boiler rang the armor like a gong. Anything within the beast's torso was doomed.

Shrapnel penetrated adjacent boilers, setting off a chain reaction. The beast rattled and boomed. Its arms trembled and went slack. Creaking, it tipped forward and collapsed to the ground. Steam poured in a storm cloud from it.

Urza rode the beast to ground. Once it was still, he caught his breath and stood, wreathed in mist. It parted, showing him to the other five titans. They stared in amazement.

There will be more, Urza told them. His mind worked to fuse the severed conduits in his leg. *Make what repairs you can immediately, and then fan out around the vat yards. Watch for dragon engines. I will meanwhile plant the last soul bomb in the reactor at its center.*

Bo Levar snorted, flinging away the arm that had almost shattered his helm, *Great. I'm sick of this place. What's the fifth sphere like?*

Huffing in his pilot bulb, Commodore Guff paged through a book. *A nasty sphere, by all accounts.*

Shocking! replied Bo Levar in imitation of the commodore.

Ignoring him, Guff said, *A great sea of boiling oil, thickening below to sludge and then to rock. The firmament is more pipe work, with large ports that suck.*

The sky sucks, the ground sucks . . . sounds like all the other spheres, Bo Levar griped.

Are you a vacuous idiot? raged Urza. The blank looks on his companions' faces only spurred him on. *Are you all so soulless that you cannot marvel at mile-high furnaces and steam-powered magnabeasts? At living metal and mechanisms that reproduce and grow? At the absolute blend of biology and physics, artifice and magic?*

Bo Levar had had about enough. *You speak as though you love this place—and here we are to destroy it.*

Yes, we will destroy it, Urza agreed, *but we are destroying a masterpiece. You must understand that.*

None of us understands that, Urza. To us, this place is a living hell. We can't understand why you think it's a heaven or why, in thinking what you do, that you still want to destroy it. We figured it was just another part of your whacked-out mind—the same part that made you love Mishra and destroy him, and love Xantcha and destroy her, and love Barrin and destroy him. The one thing we do understand is that Phyrexia's got to go, and you're the only one who knows and loves it well enough to destroy it. That's it. That's the totality of our agreement. We're not on board with your perverse little pleasures. We're not on board with your sacrificing planeswalkers. We're not on board with any of this except destroying Phyrexia.

Freyalise, Taysir, Windgrace, and Guff nodded.

Urza felt a stab of panic. Why had he put his trust in such worthless comrades? Why had he brought them to this jewel box, swine to trammel treasure? Wallowing beasts. They could think of nothing but the mud of Dominaria. If they could only follow their brains and eyes and hearts, they would know the glory of this place. They were pigs in a temple.

At last, Urza said, *Are you . . . turning on me?*

Waving a damaged arm outward, Bo Levar said, *Just plant your damn bomb and take us to the fifth sphere.*

We'll skip the fifth, going straight to the sixth—

Whatever, Bo Levar interrupted. *Just go. We'll hold the perimeter.*

Nodding numbly, Urza turned.

His titan suit trembled. It was no longer the power conduit that caused the weakness. It was uncertainty. Ever since the death of Barrin, there had been a creeping weakness in him. It had grown more pervasive each day. It jangled his fingers and hands, and now his whole being.

They would betray him, these five. They had come along to advance their own aims, with no true interest in the fate of Phyrexia. What a fool he had been! Of course, when they rebelled, he could kill them. It was just that he had not planned on killing them. He had not planned on descending to the ninth sphere alone.

The thought was like a fresh breeze. It calmed him, stilled the center of his being. The creeping weakness solidified into something new. *Descend to the ninth sphere alone.* That would be glorious, to stand there before Yawgmoth, to slay him, to see Phyrexia as Yawgmoth saw it.

Under Urza's titanic tread, glass shattered. Oil gushed. Naked creatures thrashed. Newts. Phyrexian newts. Urza had reached the vat fields without even realizing it. He lifted his foot. Oil and glass dripped away. Creatures writhed. Before him, to the distant horizon, vats extended in golden rows. Causeways topped them, and vat priests ran atop the causeways.

Urza smiled. He took another step. Catwalks buckled under his weight. Vats cracked. Oil burst out across the ground. Newts died in tens and twenties. He stepped again. It was like splashing through rainwater. It was like playing in a golden brook.

Ahead, the rows converged on a large central structure in a huge circular well. Radiance flooded out of that pit. Power held aloft the main reactor core. It seemed a beehive, its globular outer walls filled with openings. Raw energy swarmed it. White-hot tracers buzzed up from the well and entered the reactor holes.

A single soul bomb positioned at the edge of that energy storm would unbalance the core and send it toppling into the pit. It would unleash the native power of Phyrexia and gut much of the fourth sphere.

Urza approached the pit and knelt. The knees of his titan engine drove glass spikes through the newts beneath him.

He took another fortifying breath. This destruction. This mad destruction. What could justify it? Fear? Fear that Yawgmoth would do to Dominaria what he had done to Phyrexia? Urza would have been glad to see such magnificent living machines roaming the planet. It would have been like the dragon epoch, an age of power and physics, before humans had muddled everything with their metaphysics, their morals.

Reaching down, Urza cracked loose one of the vats. It came away intact, like a crystal goblet. Urza lifted the vat up before his piloting bulb. He peered out of his glass bubble at the naked creature in the vat.

Urza saw himself. He was that formless newt, pathetic and pitiable. He was the weak raw material from which Yawgmoth would make something powerful. The premonition faded, and Urza was again in his titan suit.

The newt convulsed impotently in the tank of golden oil. It could sense its imminent demise.

Urza slid the tips of his claws through the top of the vat. Gently, he clutched the newt's head and lifted it free. It seemed a sardine in his fingers, flapping back and forth and flinging oil.

Urza laid the creature in the metallic palm of his titan suit. It gulped helplessly. Urza prodded it.

Here was the weakness at the heart of strength—this unformed pupae, this human.

It died in his hand, suffocated. The sardine-man lay still. It was just as well. All these newts would die in the blast. Urza hurled the thing out toward the beaming pit. The body caught fire even before it struck the mantle of energy. Then it was gone—a better fate than lingering in that helpless putrescence—though not as good as final compleation.

Urza unshipped the last soul bomb from its armored compartment. The device shimmered. The stone at its center glowed with the life force of Tevash Szat. Urza kicked clean the edge of the pit. A few blasts of the ray cannons on his hand vaporized the oil. Pivoting the spikes from the side of the device, Urza pressed it into the ground. The spikes sank away and clamped on. It would take a hundred Phyrexians a whole week to dig it out. By then, there would be no Phyrexians left at all.

What am I doing? Urza wondered suddenly, staring at the sun-bright blaze before him. Why am I destroying this masterpiece? His metallic digits turned the top of the soul bomb, setting the charge. Now the device would be triggered with all the rest. Nothing could disarm it, not even Urza Planeswalker.

The sound of distant battle came to his ears. The others must have been fending off an attack. They had slain the Steam Beast. Perhaps now they fought the Walker. They acted like big game hunters gathering trophies.

Urza's titan engine rose from its knees. Glass and oil dripped from him. He turned on his own path—"repented" was the word the ancients would have used. There before him, he saw his trail of destruction. While vats glowed in a golden garden all around, where he had walked was only ruin.

It wasn't too late to end this destruction. It wasn't too late to join the quest for perfection.

CHAPTER 31
Before the Throne of Crovax

Gerrard whipped his head around and glimpsed angry, haunted eyes.

Ertai held him. It was none other than Ertai, onetime spellcaster aboard *Weatherlight*. He had been left behind in Rath. This was his revenge.

The eyes were all that remained of the old Ertai. He now had a mimetic spine. It had twisted his body, bulging every muscle, cinching his waist in a slave corset, turning flesh an angry red. From his elbows sprouted two new sets of arms. All four grasped Gerrard implacably.

Ertai's teleport spell took hold. The stern castle of *Weatherlight* disappeared, taking with it the bright skies over Urborg. In their place, a hot darkness formed.

Gerrard blinked, wondering where they had gone. The brimstone air told him—Crovax's throne room. It was large, grandiose, and mad. Twisted columns rose up the curved walls, giving the impression that the room was melting. The vault dripped stalactites that held impaled bodies. Huge dogs with vampiric teeth trotted around the floor, cleaning up the steady drizzle of blood. Beyond them, watching in mute disinterest, stood *il*-Vec guards.

The centerpiece of the room was an enormous throne of black basalt, carved with a riot of tortured figures. Ensconced in their midst was the tormentor himself—Crovax.

Crovax was another lost member of *Weatherlight*'s crew. In his defense of the ship, he had slain the only creature he had ever loved—his angel, Selenia.

That single desperate act had begun his transformation. Now Crovax was a monster. Talons clutched the throne. Huge forearms and biceps rose to a barrel body in steel. A wide head was crowded with shark's teeth. Even Crovax's eyes were changed, irredeemably mad.

"I knew you would return," Crovax said simply.

Gerrard fought against Ertai's arms, but he could not escape. "Of course you knew. You sent your lackey after me."

Crovax laughed, a sound like teeth on slate. "You have brought your own lackey, I see." He gestured to one side.

Gerrard glanced down, only then remembering Squee. The courageous goblin had hurled himself onto Ertai the moment before the teleport.

"Hiya, Crovax," the goblin said, stepping away from Ertai. "Nice teeth."

There was no humor in the evincar's reply. "Nice everything." He stood, a black cape sweeping out around him. He was stoutly muscled, seeming a spring wound overtight. "I have become the lord of all you see and of much else. I brought this overlay to Dominaria. You might even say, I have become the lord of all the world.

"What about you? Are you still flying your little ship, Gerrard? Are you still cooking grub for the crew, Squee? Or should I say grubs? I always wondered why you made a bug-eater into the ship's cook."

J. Robert King

Gerrard ignored the taunting and smiled. "Didn't you receive our calling card?"

"Calling card?" Crovax asked, eyebrows lifted.

Gerrard dipped his head. "Wait for it."

A huge crashing sound came above. The Stronghold rocked. Bodies jiggled loose from stalactites and spattered on the floor. Cracks raced down one wall. A pillar tumbled in sections. Guards looked up in suspicion but feared to move from their posts.

For his part, Crovax stood rock solid in the midst of the assault. The rumbling stopped. Final shards of rock smacked the floor. Like a man checking for rain, Crovax spread an eloquent claw. "Oh . . . *that.* Yes, I knew *Predator* would fail against *Weatherlight*—now that your ship bears Phyrexian arms and a woodland god. Still, *Predator* did what she was meant to do— she delivered Ertai to you, and Ertai delivered you to me."

Gerrard growled, "You're fixated on me, aren't you. Me and *Weatherlight*—"

"And Squee too," piped the goblin from where he had wandered. One of the fallen corpses had spilled hundreds of maggots, and the white worms were irresistible. Three moggs followed Squee's every move.

Ignoring the goblins, Crovax strode up before Gerrard. The evincar's breath reeked of unwholesome things.

"Fixation is too casual a word for what I feel for you. Obsession even falls short. Don't you see, we are bonded, Gerrard. We are brothers."

"What are you talking about?" Gerrard hissed. He turned his face away from the putrid breath. "Volrath was my brother."

"By adoption only. You and I have the same true parents— Urza and Yawgmoth." Crovax stared into Gerrard's eyes. "Urza always doted on you, Brother, and Yawgmoth on me, but they both made us. They are Daddy and Mummy." He smiled at his joke, but his gaze was lethally serious. "Ah, yes. You know it. You know of Urza's eugenics programs, how he bred and crossbred to create the Metathran. He did the same with human stock. He wanted the perfect hero to fly his perfect machine. You came from his experiments, and I came from Yawgmoth's—"

"Yes, and look how each of us turned out," Gerrard interrupted.

"About the same, as far as I can tell," Crovax said. "Both of us fought for our creators. Both of us sacrificed our one love—"

"I didn't sacrifice Hanna," hissed Gerrard.

"You did, Gerrard, and you know it. We each killed our beloved."

"Yeah," put in Squee around a mouthful of maggots. He'd made a feast of them and idly flipped a few stragglers into the mouths of the moggs. "But least Gerrard didn't stab her through the gut. Aieeee!" He pantomimed an eviscerating thrust then flapped his arms like Selenia in her death throes.

Through bear-trap teeth, Crovax snarled, "Kill him!"

The moggs looked up in surprise, their lips wet with maggot flesh.

Crovax roared, "Do it!"

"No!" Gerrard shouted, struggling against Ertai's grip.

With an almost casual gesture, a mogg gripped Squee's neck. Something popped. Squee went limp. He rolled quietly forward, his knobby head lolling against the floor.

"You monster!" Gerrard roared. "You inhuman monster!"

Instead of evoking anger, the comment pleased Crovax. "Precisely. Inhuman. Monstrous. That's the difference between us, Gerrard. We each sacrificed our beloved, but I realized I had been a fool to do so. I've done everything to bring back Selenia, to win her from the grave. You have done nothing for Hanna."

Gerrard stared incredulously into those mad eyes. "You think this will bring her back? Killing innocent creatures? Impaling bodies on stalactites? Feeding gore to vampire hounds? You think your ridiculous getup will bring her back? Crovax, you're in this hell because when you killed Selenia, you killed the only good in you."

Crovax's taloned hand lashed out, gripping Gerrard's jaw. Claws sank in. Blood snaked down his fingers.

"Don't you understand? I've descended to this hell to bring her back. I've become the keeper of hell's keys, so that I could have dominion over the souls of the dead. I've sacrificed every-thing—and I have succeeded."

"What are you raving about?"

Crovax released Gerrard's jaw and went to one knee. He bowed his head and clasped his hands together. His pate riled with exer-tion. His mind reached out, seeking a distant place, a distant lord.

"Great Yawgmoth, I have brought him, as you commanded. I have captured Gerrard for you and slain one of his crew. I offer them to you now. Let this complete my sacrifice. Release her soul to me—or if you will not, at least send her in solid form, that I may display your power."

Gerrard stared in wonder at the evincar, bowed like a pen-itent toad.

A smile jagged across Crovax's face. He lifted his eyes toward the vault.

Something moved among the bodies. It was a gossamer pres-ence, like weaving souls. A misty figure coalesced. At first she was no more than a dream—white wings beneath black stalac-tites. Between those wings formed a body, powerful and perfectly feminine. In purple shift and turquoise skirts, she could no longer have been a vision. Her beauty was matched only by her sadness. Mournful eyes shone beneath a leather skullcap and long blonde hair. The world took hold of her solidified form, and her wings surged as she descended.

The Evincar of Rath did not rise from his knee, only extend-ing a talon in welcome. It was as though all the horrid days fell away from Crovax, and he was once again a young man in love. His hand received her palm. Gerrard's blood drew red ribbons on her skin.

Selenia lighted upon the ground. Her wings furled.

Crovax kissed her hand. Lips did not entirely close over his teeth. It was a pathetic kiss, leering and hopeless. Crovax shut his eyes in bliss.

"Do you see, Gerrard? I have followed her to hell, and I have reclaimed her. Soon, when I have given all of Dominaria to Yawgmoth, he will give her to me. Until then, I can call her spirit here."

"She's not real, Crovax. She's an illusion," Gerrard insisted. There was more pity than anger in his voice. "Yawgmoth has learned how to twist you. With a simple glamour, he keeps you here."

"Touch him, Selenia," Crovax said. "Let him feel the pulse in your fingers, the warmth of your skin. Show him you are real."

She strode toward Gerrard. Her eyes pinned his. She ran knuckles gently over his cheek. Gerrard's blood smeared from her fingers onto his face. There was solidity to her touch. More than solidity, there was life, even the sweet scent of flesh.

In a voice both wise and sad, Selenia said, "He is freeing me. He is ransoming my soul with a whole world. Death cannot stand before such love."

Closing his eyes, Gerrard said, "Crovax, Yawgmoth doesn't have dominion over the dead. He is not the lord of souls. He could not return your lost love to you."

"Show him," Crovax said. The evincar's head was bowed again, his hands clasped. "Show him, Yawgmoth, that you are lord of the dead."

Gerrard's eye was drawn by movement among the maggots. In their midst, Squee's body shuddered. The green tissues of his neck compacted. Beneath them, fragments of bone slid together to assemble knobby vertebrae. The spinal cord fused again. Fingers convulsed with life. Toes curled and uncurled. Knees drew up beneath an aching body. Elbows trembled as arms pushed the figure upright. Squee's brown vest expanded with breath. He looked up, blinking.

"Gerrard?" Squee muttered absently. He picked a worm from his shoulder. "How'd Squee get down here with dese maggots?"

Gerrard couldn't answer. He stared, unbelieving, at the risen goblin.

Crovax said, "Everyone ends up with the maggots, but not everyone rises again."

"Is it really you, Squee?" Gerrard managed at last. "I'm sorry I couldn't save you."

Indignation reddened the goblin's eyes. "You? Save? Squee? Squee no need saved! Squee save your butt a hundred gabillion times. He save your butt here too." Yawgmoth could not have faked that reply.

Mind whirling, Gerrard shook his head. "What is the point of all this?"

"Yawgmoth is the lord of death," Selenia said. "Yawgmoth can kill and bring life."

Crovax rose and gestured toward Squee. "Look what Lord Yawgmoth has done for this pathetic wretch." His other talon extended toward Selenia. "Look what he has done for me. Think of what he can do for you. Think of whom he could reunite with you."

Gerrard understood at last. "Hanna?"

"Yes," hissed Crovax. "Yawgmoth has her too. Yawgmoth has Hanna. He can return her to you."

CHAPTER 32
When Gods Awaken

Seas spread beneath Rith's scales. Clouds beamed upon Treva's wings. Skies glowed across Dromar's mantle. The three Primevals were beautiful in flight, a glorious arc before the dragon nations.

Rhammidarigaaz flew just behind them. His wings were weary, and his mind was worse. The Primevals emitted a blinding glory. For a time, Darigaaz had seen nothing but its dazzle. Eventually, though, divine light blinds a mortal eye. Then only darkness remains. Darigaaz could see only darkness now.

How many dragons had died to raise these three Primevals? How many more would die to raise the fourth? Once there were four, how total would their hold be on every dragon heart?

"At least there will not be five," he murmured to himself. The red dragon's death would forever prevent a complete circle of Primevals. A complete circle could tyrannize the whole world.

With a fierce surge of his wings, Darigaaz drove himself forward. Crimson scales hurled back the tumbling skies. Another stroke, and he pulled even with the three Primevals.

In the gleaming ocean beyond stretched a line of black islands—Urborg. There raged the battle that would decide the war. Fleets of troop ships stood at anchor around it. Fleets of airships swarmed the skies. Angels fought, and devils, *Weatherlight* and the Metathran. All the world fought there. Soon the dragons would join them.

In Urborg's deepest, darkest slough rested the last Primeval.

Rith watched Darigaaz. Her eyes were slivers of jade. *It is about time you came up to join us.*

Ignoring her comment, Darigaaz asked, *What is the name of the final Primeval?*

Crosis, Rith replied easily. It was an ill-fated name, the root of the draconic word for death. Rith gauged his response. *You needn't be frightened by the name. Rith means childhood, Treva means youth, Dromar means adulthood, and Crosis means death. Together, we Primevals encompass the stages of draconic life.*

And the red dragon? asked Darigaaz.

His name meant conception, the moment of volcanic desire that changes old death to new life. He had the power to be reborn and awaken the rest of us. That is why the Phyrexians targeted him first. Despite their labors, the circle will soon be complete.

Complete except for one, correct Darigaaz.

Of course, Rith replied, *but once Crosis joins us, no one will stand before us.*

Darigaaz studied her. *You mean no Phyrexian will stand before us.*

Of course, she repeated.

Swear an oath. We fight for Dominaria. We fight against Phyrexia.

Turning her head toward him, she drew her jowls back in a predatory grin. *I swear an oath to fight for Dominaria and to fight against Phyrexia.* The look faded. *You mortals and your oaths. Do you realize what we are doing? We are about to awaken not just one god but a whole pantheon. Everything—even an oath—is swept away when gods awaken. Enough discussion. It is time.*

Words and wings brought them rapidly to Urborg. Small blots of land swelled into large islands. Dragons soared over an encircling reef, above briny shallows, and past the shoreline. Beyond rose forests drowned in saltwater.

There was not a living Phyrexian to be seen. The few patches of high ground were marked with fire circles where weird bones lay—remains of the vanquished. The victors meanwhile manned lookout posts of wood and reed. Sentries lifted their eyes to see the great flock of dragons descend on Urborg. Metathran rarely smiled, but these watchmen, each one, waved a glad greeting.

Ahead, Rith sent, *do you feel it?*

Yes, replied Darigaaz. *Yes, I feel it.*

Past the salt marshes, past a wide stretch of quicksand, there lay a deep, black place. It was a tar pit. Nowhere else in nature was there a place as black as that. It seemed a tear in the world, giving view to the nothingness beneath. Any living thing that wandered into it died. Meat and brain and bone all disappeared. Oblivion.

Here, Rith said. *We circle here.*

Rhammidarigaaz and the three Primevals bent their wings. They banked above the tar pit. The dragon nations followed smoothly in their wake. They formed a whirling, multicolored vortex.

The creature in that pit drew Darigaaz. It completed the music in his soul. Open fifths became major chords. Dull drones gave way to symphonies. Music aligned his jangled spirit.

It was more than just music. It was raw power. It magnetized him, aligning the particles of Darigaaz's being. His heart pounded in synchrony with the Primevals' hearts. His muscles ached with energy. This was what it was to awaken a god.

What sacrifice must we make? Rhammidarigaaz asked Rith. Immersed in the soul symphony, he would have sacrificed anything to raise the final Primeval. *How many must die? How must they die?*

Rith's smile glinted like a dagger. *You're beginning to think like us. But no—no mortal dragon must be sacrificed now. Only we four. Only we Primevals."*

Darigaaz stared at her. *We four?*

All this while, you did not sense it? Even knowing your name? My name?

What is the Old Draconic meaning of Rhammidarigaaz?

In dread realization, he whispered, "Conception."

You are the first Primeval. The Phyrexians only destroyed your corpse. They did not know you were already reborn. For a thousand years, you have lived, Rhammidarigaaz. For a thousand years, you could have awakened us. Why didn't you?

Her words pinched the sinews of his heart. *I didn't know—*

Yes, you could not have known. You were hatched as mortal dragons are hatched. You had to learn to eat, to fight, to believe. You could not have known your destiny and should not have known it until the fullness of time. The invasion cut time short. Szat became your teacher. He showed you your grave and taught you the stories you had forgotten. He sent you out to awaken us, and you have.

I am one of you?

Yes. One of us four, who must die to raise the fifth.

Only a moment ago, Rhammidarigaaz had learned he was god. Now, his life—his eternal life—would be required of him. Hollowly, he repeated the thought, *We must die to raise the fifth . . . ?*

In dying, we will awaken our final brother. He is death and has dominion over death. He will raise us all as new creations. As new gods.

Even had he been in his right mind, Darigaaz could not have resisted, but he was nowhere near his right mind. He would sacrifice his life, yes. He would shuck his old flesh and don a new, immortal body. Rhammidarigaaz would become one of the gods.

Yes, Rith, he said. *Let us complete the circle.*

Rhammidarigaaz tucked his wings to his sides, leading the dive. It was only right. He was the first Primeval, the red dragon whose name meant conception. He would lead the four down to death. Wind whipped across his horns and down his red-tasseled back. Rith fell in line behind him, and after her Treva, and Dromar. They dipped downward, away from the cyclone of serpents.

Black tar loomed up. Aloft, it had seemed placid. Now Rhammidarigaaz could see the steamy bubbles that burst upon its surface. They belched heat into the air. This would be no simple suffocation but a burning death. Darigaaz did not close his eyes. He wanted to face death head-on.

His face struck. The tar burned. He plunged into it. Goo encased his wings, his shoulders, his arms. It swallowed his belly and his legs. Darigaaz thrashed. He roared. Sound could not escape his mouth. Tar sucked down his throat. The symphony in his head ceased. There was only the mallet of his heart.

He was dying. He was alone, and he was dying.

They tricked me, he thought. His consciousness poured out like a wineskin. They tricked me into sacrificing myself. I am no god. I'm no longer anything at all.

He tried to drive toward the surface. It was useless, but life always fights, even when the battle is lost. Darigaaz fought.

There was no more time. Rhammidarigaaz was dead. He was suddenly, surprisingly dead.

* * * * *

At first, the notes were scattered and uncertain, as if the players were warming up. A tone here, a trill there, but nothing that amounted to music. Soon, there came a quickening, the pulse of a drum, insistent and irresistible. A drone joined it, the long strident breath of a bagpipe. The basal rhythm invited melody. Strings added their voices, then winds, reeds, and brass. They converged. They crescendoed. They sang.

In all its loud cacophony, life reentered Darigaaz.

He fought again toward the surface. The tar grew watery—slack and tepid. It could not grip him. His flesh was new and slick. He surged upward. Wings hurled back the muck as if it were air.

Rhammidarigaaz's head broke the surface. Tar peeled from his jowls and eyes and horns. It sloughed from shoulders and arms, wings and waist, legs and tail. With a mighty stroke, he shot from the blackness. It closed beneath him.

Darigaaz's roar was a volcano. It spewed straight up into the eye of the dragon cyclone. He followed the fire skyward. Life had returned and brought rage with it. He was done being subordinate. He was done being tricked, done suffering fools.

Darigaaz's body was new—scaled in rubies, youthful and lithe, quick and powerful. His mind was new too, bursting with the sorceries that are a god's inheritance. Even his soul was new, not the suffering spirit of a mortal creature but the unrepentant heart of a god. Darigaaz's time had come to rule—he and his sibling gods.

Rith burst from the black well of death. Her flesh was solid emerald. Voracious clouds of spores fountained from her roaring jowls as she took to the sky. Angelic Treva followed, a creature of white light. Radiance poured up past her teeth. Then came Dromar, who breathed a shaft of distortion that shook matter apart. And, last of all—Crosis.

The black dragon god had bat wings and a cobra's body. His legs were powerful, his talons were tipped in razor claws, and the whole of his being gleamed like onyx. From his mouth came a black column that slew anything in its path.

This was Crosis, the one the other four had died to raise. He had nullified death and raised them all again as gods.

The five Primevals vaulted up through the vortex of dragons, rising faster than mortal wings could have borne them. They owned the heavens.

Except that there, beyond the coiling serpents, a ship dared to fly. She had a massive prow ram and a sleek hull and shimmering wings of metal.

"The skies are ours!" shrieked Crosis.

"Who dares contest them?" hissed Dromar.

"It is *Weatherlight*," said Treva.

"We must drive them to ground," Rith determined.

Rhammidarigaaz was last to speak, but he spoke with the same fury as the rest. "We must destroy them."

Firstborn of the Primevals, Rhammidarigaaz led the dragon gods and their nations across the sky to destroy *Weatherlight*.

CHAPTER 33
Where All the World Fought

"Dragons, dead ahead!" called Tahngarth into the speaking tube. "They're flying an intercept course."

At *Weatherlight*'s helm, Sisay lifted her captain's glass. "One of them is Rhammidarigaaz! They're allies!" A cheer went up across the deck. The crew had needed some good news. They had fought in a shaken delirium since Gerrard and Squee had disappeared. No one knew where they had gone. It was good to see allies in the sky.

Five beasts led up the dragon nations. Red, green, white, blue, and black, the serpents vaulted into the heavens. They climbed with an impossible speed. Their eyes blazed angrily.

"They don't look like a welcoming party," Tahngarth said.

Sisay stayed the course, one hand clutching the helm and the other the captain's glass. Through it, she could see the glint of fangs and claws, the spark of fury in draconic eyes.

"I think you're right."

Tahngarth pivoted his gun forward, drawing a bead on the black dragon. His hands sweat on the fire controls.

"You're the captain, Sisay. You've always been the captain. You have to decide. What do we do?"

Fire roared in a red-hot column from the mouth of Rhammi-darigaaz.

"Hang on!" Sisay shouted.

She swung the wheel hard to port and yanked back on it. *Weatherlight* stood on end.

"Full power!" she called.

Weatherlight's engines hurled their own fire. On pillars of flame, the ship rocketed away. The Gaea figurehead tore through clouds. Her metal wings spawned cyclones in her wake.

Through swirls of mist, the five dragons ascended. They gained on the shrieking engine. As red as ruby, green as emerald, white as lightning, blue as sky, and black as death—the beasts spat killing blasts. They arced up toward *Weatherlight*.

Tahngarth yanked his gun about but couldn't draw a bead past the gleaming wings.

Next moment, those wings were mantled in fire. They would have melted except that the Thran metal was fortified by Karn. Even as flames fell back, voracious spores engulfed the stern. They rooted themselves and grew rampantly. Any other ship would have splintered beneath the parasitic plants, but *Weatherlight*'s magnigoth wood was strengthened by Multani. A white shaft of light blazed out above *Weatherlight*. It dropped to cleave the ship in two. There would be no defense against it—except an expert helmsman.

Sisay rammed the helm forward. The ship plunged. Her wings tucked. She slipped from beneath the killing beam. Engines drove her down toward Urborg.

The hurtling dragons overshot her. They turned in the sky above and folded their wings. Snarling and snapping, they dived.

"Tahngarth, get to stern," Sisay called. "We won't need forward guns while we're running."

Tahngarth nodded his approval and unlaced his gunnery traces. "Let's just hope I can fill Squee's shoes."

* * * * *

How glorious it was to cross Dominaria in the *Golden Argosy*. No hunger, no thirst, no weariness, no wounds—but these were only the beginning of the marvel. The ship sailed with impossible speed. She cut through water as though it were air, and through air as though it were nothing at all.

From the moment that Warlord Astor had debarked, the ship's sails had filled with an otherworldly gale. She had coursed like a comet across the world. Her path was straight and incorruptible. Where islands loomed up before her, she only breasted through them. Her prow clove into sandy beaches, soil, and solid rock. She cut through mountains as though they were but shadows and sailed out the other side.

Never did her company fear. Eladamri and Liin Sivi, the Steel Leaf and Skyshroud elves, and ten thousand Keldon warriors—none of them feared the ship would wreck. They were well aware of the world beyond her rails but knew their role in that world lay far ahead, at Urborg.

Days and nights scrolled away until at last the black island chain opened before them.

Eladamri stood at the prow, clasping Liin Sivi's hand. "The heroes of Keld will fight the final battle of Twilight on that island. There we will turn back the darkness."

Liin Sivi nodded. Her eyes were bright and stern, focused on the island. "That central volcano hides the source of all this evil."

"The Stronghold," Eladamri said, completing the thought. The two had lived all their lives in the shadow of that horrid fortress. They had fought against it, had even invaded it. Now, two worlds away, they rushed toward it again. "We will capture the land and plumb the fiery depths and destroy the Stronghold once and for all."

The *Golden Argosy* surged toward Urborgan shores. She crossed reefs that would have wrecked any normal vessel. She plunged through shallows that should have forbidden her massive draft. The beach swept up. Sand parted before her hull. The *Golden Argosy* clove through palms and swamps. Nothing could halt her.

"What will we do when at last the ship stops?" Liin Sivi wondered aloud.

"We will leap from her and fight," replied Eladamri.

Liin Sivi glimpsed a Metathran guard high in a cypress. He stared down incredulously. "Will we remember this—the ship, the journey, any of it?"

Eladamri gazed at the drowned forest through which they plunged. "No. We will not remember, or remember only as sleepers remember the waking world." He clutched her hand tighter. "But some things even sleepers do not forget."

Without slowing, the *Golden Argosy* suddenly stopped. Volcanic foothills rose ahead of her.

Eladamri peered up the mountainside. "Here is our battleground. Here we must depart immortal realms for mortal ones."

Drawing her toten-vec, Liin Sivi said, "I am ready."

"No," replied Eladamri, reaching across to her. He took her jaw in his hand, leaned slowly in, and kissed her. The heat of mortal desire passed through that kiss. They parted, and Eladamri stared into her eyes. "Now, we're both ready." He drew his own sword, set his foot on the rail, and leaped from the *Golden Argosy*.

* * * * *

One moment, Eladamri had lain half-submerged in an icy sea. The next, he landed on a gnarl of cooled lava. It was black and rough and hot beneath his hands. He couldn't quite catch himself. He tucked his head and rolled around his sword. Rock rasped his neck and elbows. He came up on his feet, his knuckles bleeding.

Liin Sivi rose beside him. Her toten-vec swept before her. "Where are we? What's happened?"

"I don't know," Eladamri responded, edging toward her.

There was sudden motion behind them. They whirled.

From the shrouded forest at the base of the volcano poured elves and Keldons. They weren't wet or bedraggled. All seemed to appear in midair, as if leaping from the trees. Their armor was polished, their skin clean and healthy. Steel Leaf and Skyshroud elves appeared beside Keldon warriors. They stumbled and rose in wary confusion.

"I dreamed of a golden ship. . . ." Liin Sivi ventured uncertainly. "I dreamed we were to fight the final battle of Twilight here. . . ."

"Yes," Eladamri said, taking Liin Sivi's hand. He nodded up the volcano behind them. "This mountain is familiar. Do you remember it?"

A bitter smile lit her face. "This is a Rathi mountain. This is the mountain that holds the Stronghold." She shook her head. "There is no battle I'd rather fight."

Brandishing his sword, Eladamri shouted, "Forward!" With Liin Sivi beside him, he climbed the volcano. Elves and Keldons in their thousands followed.

It was good to march again beneath the sun.

* * * * *

A hundred miles from Urborg, in seas a mile deep, something enormous moved. It might have been a school of whales, though even a hundred thousand leviathans could not have mounded the waters so violently. Whatever coursed beneath the surface was as massive as a mountain and faster than a falcon. In its long trek across the globe, it pushed before it a tidal wave that traveled at awesome speed. It drove toward distant Urborg.

The thing was only seventy-five miles out now. The basin of the sea sloped upward. Just behind the rushing wave, kelpy masses surfaced. They seemed Sargasso. Leaves rattled as the foliage lifted above the waves. Twigs jutted forth, then branches, then boughs. Water cascaded from the widespread crowns of the submerged trees.

These were not just trees. Each was the size of an isle, each the height of a mountain, and they moved. Enormous boughs hurled away water. Vast knotholes glared over the flood. Hollows that could only be described as mouths disgorged the brackish depths. Enormous roots strode along the sea floor at impossible speeds.

The magnigoth treefolk had come all the way from Yavimaya. They were drawn not straight to Urborg but on a twisted path, following their stolen captive: Rith.

In ancient days, the green Primeval had been entrusted to them. For epochs, these treefolk had faithfully guarded their prisoner. Even before the forest of Yavimaya grew, they had kept Rith captive. The Thran-Phyrexian War could not shake her loose, nor the Argoth event, nor even the great Ice Age. Now, though, after ten thousand years, Rith was free. It was a small thing to march across the oceans of the world, seeking her.

At last, they had cornered her at Urborg. She would not escape again.

The treefolk had brought help. All across their bark clustered thousands of Kavu. The gigantic lizards blinked brine from their nictitating membranes but otherwise remained motionless. The cold depths had sent them into hibernation. Now in the sunlight, they slowly awoke. One by one, Kavu opened their nostrils and stretched. Steam rose from armored hides. Blood began to run again. Scaly necks craned for sight of Urborg. Kavu lords—six-legged lizards that easily weighed ten tons—filled their wattles with long-calls. To these eerie battle songs were added the drone of Kavu stomachs. The beasts had awakened hungry and soon would fill their bellies with Phyrexians.

It wouldn't be long now. At fifty miles out, the magnigoth treefolk waded in fifteen hundred feet of water. Boughs dripped their last drops into the turbid ocean. Leaves rustled in sea winds. At twenty-five miles out, roots splashed through the shallows. In mere minutes, they clambered over reefs and up the shore. Treefolk rose to their full height. They were as tall as the volcanoes themselves.

The treefolk strode inward across marshy lands. Saltwater sloughed from their bark. Roots that had traversed half a world tore up the ground of Urborg. They sank in the wet soil and ripped holes through to underground caverns. Seawater poured down these shafts, flooding the caves below. The bubbling channels of water soon were full. Decaying corpses in their thousands drifted from the inundated underworld.

Kavu cared nothing for corpses, but ahead, on the foothills of the central volcano, Phyrexians massed. Battle cries ceased as lizards scrambled down the trunks of the striding trees. They bounded to ground. Claws designed to sink into wood gripped cold lava just as well. Kavu hurled themselves along the mountain side. With mouths gaping, they galloped into the Phyrexian troops. The crunch of the first few only whetted their appetites. This was not battle, but feast.

Heedless, the treefolk strode on. They pursued another foe. Above the volcano flew a great ship, pursued by five roaring Primevals. One of those serpents was Rith.

Striding up the hardened lava, treefolk clawed amid the clouds. Boughs raked the teeming sky. Ships and dragons were but gnats to magnigoth treefolk. They hauled down branches draped with dead serpents. None was Rith. It was easy to kill countless gnats, but difficult to catch a specific one.

The treefolk lord that had held Rith captive all these millennia bellowed with fury. Wind ripped through its core. The exhalation hurled dragons from the sky. The inhalation afterward dragged more serpents in, wedging them in hollows and impaling them on slivers. None was Rith. The Primeval flitted away, along with her pantheon of dragon gods. The treefolk lord pursued its elusive quarry across the sky.

* * * * *

"What in the Nine Hells!" shouted Tahngarth. His barrage of cannon fire ceased as he gabbled at the huge trees that circled the volcano. They lashed out at *Weatherlight*. "Even the flora has turned against us!"

From the speaking tube came Multani's voice. "Sisay, fly closer to them."

"Closer?" she echoed in a near shriek.

"Yes," Multani replied. "They've come not for us but for the green dragon."

Tahngarth shook his head in dubiety. A massive bough swept violently past *Weatherlight*.

"We thought Rhammidarigaaz was on our side too. What's to say these trees don't want their wood back?"

"I'm to say," replied Multani. "I am, after all, their spirit. Take us close. Close enough to make contact. I'll coordinate the attack."

"You're not leaving us," Sisay insisted.

"Only long enough to marshal the treefolk. Then I'll be back. This is a fight I wouldn't miss."

Tahngarth felt his stomachs churn as *Weatherlight* plunged away beneath him. He held on tight to Squee's ray cannon. To port came lofty leaves, thrashing violently along the wing. To starboard was empty sky plunging down to a boiling sea. Directly before him, gaining on the ship's stern, were four angry dragon gods.

Ever since Gerrard disappeared, things had gotten crazy.

CHAPTER 34
In Waving Fields of Grass

Urza Planeswalker wandered through waving fields of grass. The stuff made a shushing noise under his titanic feet. A wind bore past him, eager to cross the hill. On the horizon ranged gray mountains. The sky was a shell in solid white.

It was a serene place, the sixth sphere of Phyrexia. To Urza, it felt like home.

True, it was not grass but twisted wire. Its barbs would rip a person apart before he moved ten paces. Its electrical impulses would cook his flesh instantly. The winds were equally unnatural, spawned in mile-high turbines among the mountains. They would pluck up a person like dandelion down and chop her to pieces and hurl her parts endlessly around the sphere. This was no place for humans, but for an artificer in a titan engine, it was a heaven.

Urza stopped walking. He wished he could crouch here and harvest wires and weave them into a wreath and charge it with the land's own currents. Power was everywhere, but more than power drew him. Beauty did. This place was beautiful.

Urza gazed down at his hand. It held the single ugly thing in the windblown place—an armored device with a riot of its own wires, bound around a powerstone incendiary device. A bomb, but not just any bomb. This was the master. Its blast would trigger all the others. It would set off the destruction of all Phyrexia.

The destruction of all Phyrexia. Urza could little bear the thought.

The place he would plant the bomb lay just ahead. It seemed a termite mound but was the size of a mountain. Irregular towers reached into the beaming sky. Windows glowed with red radiance. The light came from no torch or lantern but from the very inhabitants of the otherworldly city. Yawgmoth's Inner Circle.

While most Phyrexians were creatures of flesh and machine, Yawgmoth's Inner Circle belonged to another phylum entirely. The pneumagogs dwelt between the physical and metaphysical worlds. They had bodies, yes—red-shelled bodies of living metal. Their insectoid legs could gallop across ground, and their rasping wings could slice through air. But these mechanisms were only the loci of their beings, rooting them in time and space. Pneumagog bodies were wrapped in layer upon layer of scintillating spirit. This was the true essence of pneumagogs— brilliant, glowing, empathic souls.

Nowhere else in all the Nine Spheres did pneumagogs exist fully. When they ascended to higher spheres, only their living-metal bodies went. When they descended to lower spheres, only their spirits went. It was here, on the sixth sphere, that they were a glorious amalgam of physic and metaphysic.

Urza strode toward the city of the pneumagogs. They would attack him, of course. He would slay them, as before. Rockets would blast apart their metal bodies. Spells would liberate their fettered souls. Urza and his comrades would extinct them. Even now, the five other titans slew the inhabitants of similar cities and planted charges to exterminate them.

As Urza's feet chuffed through wire, the first pneumagog sentries emerged from the hive. They swarmed toward him.

In reflex, Urza energized his ray cannons. He lifted one arm toward the approaching pneumagogs. They seemed angels in red. Their wings strummed the air. With a single volley, Urza could have cut the figures from the sky, but he hesitated.

In moments, they surrounded him. They did not attack. Instead, the swarm enclosed the titan in a scarlet sphere. Their wings made an assonant drone. Compound eyes stared with sad confusion at Urza.

He marched onward, toward their city.

A few of the creatures darted down to the bomb. With antennae and proboscises, they sensed the device and its function.

Urza lifted it in their midst. He felt their fear. Surely they felt his regret.

Any moment, they would attack. They would rip apart his bomb, his titan engine, and himself. Urza had no will to stop them.

Neither did the pneumagogs will to stop him. They knew what he bore—not only the bomb but also the tremendous reluctance to use it. Instead of impeding his way, the pneumagogs buzzed up alongside him, escorting him. He took another deliberate step. They paced him.

Gentle creatures, why don't you fight this doom? sent Urza to the flock of beasts.

Their answer came in a thousand voices speaking as one in his head. *You are one of us, Urza Planeswalker. You are a creature of flesh and metal and spirit.*

Indeed, they were right. The only difference was that Urza wore his metal body on the outside and carried his metaphysical body within.

But I am going to destroy you. I have devised this bomb for the very purpose.

You would not destroy us, Urza. We know that you see the beauty of this place. We know that your soul is aligned with ours.

Urza sighed in resignation. It was a glorious freedom to be understood. Barrin had understood Urza, but he had not approved of the planeswalker's true self. Always, he had nagged. These creatures, though, they knew Urza and understood him and approved.

How have I been so deluded? I have spent my life defending a world that I hate and that hates me. All the while, I have made war on my true home, my true people.

He knelt in the midst of wires and pneumagogs. Urza lifted the bomb in one clawed hand. With the other, he ripped back the smooth metal casing. The wires within formed an obscene brain filled with an obscene thought—the destruction of Phyrexia. Urza slid the pincers of his free hand in among the circuits. Without these fragile metal filaments, none of the bombs would ignite. Without them, Phyrexia would live.

Urza's claws closed. He yanked. Conduits popped. Sparks showered. White smoke puffed from the case. Urza dragged the ruined ignition device from the master bomb. The powerstone grew dark. He dropped it on the grass at his feet. It lay there disarmed, impotent to slay.

Phyrexia at last was safe.

The pneumagogs fluttered all around the kneeling titan. Their wings made a scissoring song of praise. Their voices spoke into Urza's aching mind.

Welcome home, Urza. Welcome home.

Another titan shimmered into being alongside Urza. Taysir's multicolored engine took form. He lunged, grasping Urza's suit and hauling him to his feet.

Taysir's voice was urgent and full of accusation. *What have you done, Urza! What are you doing?*

Before Urza could answer, the pneumagogs swarmed Taysir's engine. As vicious as hornets, they tore the suit's armor. It would not last long under their assault.

Instead of battling the beasts, Taysir focused utterly on Urza. *You've been seduced. Yawgmoth has done this. You must get away, Urza. Flee, before your soul belongs to him. We will complete the sequence. We will rig a new master and ignite the bombs and destroy Phyrexia—*

Destroy Phyrexia! It was more than Urza could bear.

He triggered the kill rubric.

Ten thousand metal filaments jutted into Taysir's body. Lightnings leaped. The first impulses paralyzed him. He could not move, could not think, could not planeswalk. Stronger currents cooked his flesh on his bones. Other energies extracted his soul. There were no bombs for the planeswalker to charge—Urza had not counted on Taysir's betrayal—and what a fortunate thing! The other traitors might have found the bombs and used them against Phyrexia. No, Taysir's life force was shunted into the suit's oil, which gushed out its arms and legs.

The titan suit toppled backward. Sparks from the grass ignited the oil. It flashed fantastically. Mantled in fire, the titan burned.

Oh, what a terrible scene—so many pneumagogs unmade by that burning oil! They fled up and away, but some were too slow. Pneumagogs flocked around him like burning birds. Even in death, Taysir was a killer. Such a horrible waste.

At least Taysir was dead. The oil had stopped spraying life force. Taysir's suit went dark. It was a waste of good design material. The dome had cracked. The hydraulics systems had shattered. Weapons across the machine were ruined. Perhaps the genius of it was lost.

Yawgmoth would know how to salvage the best parts, the best designs. Taysir's suit was a gift to Yawgmoth.

"What of the others?" Urza wondered to the wind. "Freyalise, Lord Windgrace, Bo Levar, and Commodore Guff? Surely they will try to detonate the bombs. If they are successful—"

A voice in his mind replaced his thoughts. *They are no longer your concern. Leave them to my minions. You must descend toward me. Leave your titan engine here and come to the seventh sphere.*

Urza's breath caught short. "The seventh sphere? It is a place of torments. Why do you call me to the seventh sphere? Have I failed you?"

There is a final test you must pass, Urza Planeswalker. I must know your true heart.

"You *will* know it," replied Urza. "You will *surely* know it."

He planeswalked from the piloting harness of his titan suit. It would stand without him, another gift to Yawgmoth. The sixth sphere of Phyrexia disappeared.

Urza rematerialized in another place, a deeper place. Just over his ashen hair rolled enormous grinders studded in diamond teeth. They gnashed against each other. Were Urza to reach up, his hand would be caught and his whole body ripped away. The ceiling extended in every direction, supported by nothing and tumbling ravenously by. Spatial distortions sometimes lifted the grinders away from the ground and other times brought them into direct contact.

Urza looked at the ground. It was covered with bodies. This was no random carnage, but a calculated thing. Creatures were laid out on their backs. Their legs and arms were bolted to pipes. Some were human, some elf, some minotaur or dwarf—but most were Phyrexian. Their feet and kneecaps had been ground away. Their bellies had been ripped open by the diamond points. Their faces were gone. It was a horrid death to have suffered but fitting for those who had failed the lord of Phyrexia.

As Urza watched, the ceiling nearby warped and descended. Grinders spun, coming into contact with a whole field of bodies. Where they rolled, blood and oil and bits of meat came away. That was not the most ghastly sight though. Worst of all was the jiggling of the bodies, the agonized shuddering that told that these forms were still alive.

Blinking powerstone eyes, Urza said, "Is this the test then? To watch unflinching as you work eternal punishment on your foes?

"This will not shake my belief. I see this and am unmoved. Mortality is no better than this—to lie helpless as time grinds flesh to bone. I have watched mortals—even best friends, even brothers—get ground away like this. It is your right to do this. You are a god."

As if waiting for Urza to finish his lecture, the voice said simply, *Proceed.*

Urza did. He stepped among arms and legs, passing over the flayed figures. They breathed even though their noses were only holes in their faces. They lived even though their hearts were laid bare. The air shivered with agony.

None of this poisoned Urza's heart. Those who pleased Yawgmoth received his bounteous mercies. Those who displeased him received his bounteous wrath. It was the right of gods.

Stop.

Urza did so without hesitation, setting his foot down beside a Phyrexian.

Look at him.

Urza did. Unlike so many others, this creature's head had not been held down. He could turn it to the side when the rollers came down. Both of his ears were gone. The skin and muscle on either side of his head were mere tatters over bone, but his face remained. Black hair, a rumpled brow, sharp eyes, a prominent nose, a mustache, a goatee. . . . It was a familiar face. Even after eons, it took Urza only a moment to recall it.

"Mishra," he murmured, staring at his brother.

When last Urza and Mishra had been face to face, they had sought to slay each other. A fireball had shown Urza what his brother had become—Phyrexian. Metal sinews had strung along beneath the man's flesh. That single spell had also shown Urza what he must do to annihilate the plague he had brought to Dominaria. The sylex blast had made Urza a planeswalker and, he thought, had slain Mishra. He had been wrong.

Your brother failed me. He sought me out in hopes of gaining power. He wanted to use me to defeat you, but I am never used. Mishra failed to slay you. He even closed Dominaria to me for an age. For this, he suffers eternally.

Urza stared down. His gemstone eyes gleamed. One of those stones had been Mishra's—the Weakstone. In the sylex blast, Urza had received both the stones and the power they bore. Mishra had meanwhile received damnation.

He came to me, but I did not want him. I wanted you, and you did not come.

"Until now," Urza said.

Until now.

"Brother," rasped Mishra, "save me." Urza only stared down at him. "Grasp my hand. 'Walk me from this place! We can both escape this hell. Take me to some grassy place where the wind blows, that I may die in peace. Take me away. He will allow it. He has told me. Take me, Brother."

I will allow it, confirmed the voice. *This is your test. I would know your heart on this matter.*

"Brother! Please! If there is any humanity left in you, take me away!" pleaded Mishra. His eyes reflected the violent rolling of the grinders above.

Urza stared once last. "Good-bye, Mishra." He turned and strode slowly away.

"Come back! Help me, Brother!" Mishra's shouts were interrupted by the roar of the grinders descending on him.

Excellent. I know your heart now. You are mine.

"Yes, Lord Yawgmoth. I am yours."

CHAPTER 35
The Mortal Flaw

The damned thing was fast, lightning fast. She skipped across clouds like a stone across water. Her silver hull hid her in plain view. Unnatural, otherworldly, impossible— *Weatherlight* was the monstrous creation of a monstrous planeswalker. She had the arrogance to claim the skies over Urborg. The Primevals would not rest until *Weatherlight* was a shattered hulk.

She was not easy prey. Whenever Rhammidarigaaz and his fellow gods drew near, *Weatherlight* dived among magnigoths. Treefolk shielded her behind thickets of green. They slashed the Primevals with thorns and battered them with boughs.

Darigaaz's fire burned hundreds of magnigoth branches, but hundreds of thousands more fought on. Rith poured rampant spores onto the treefolk, but the resultant growths only strengthened them. Treva's purifying light energized leafy crowns.

Dromar's distortion waves only bent the boughs. Even Crosis's death-word was impotent. The treefolk had no ears with which to hear.

These magnigoths held divinity. A god lurked in the wood and shoved back at them.

Dauntless, the Primevals soared among the magnigoths, intent on flushing *Weatherlight* into clear air. She jittered around a bole just ahead.

Stay on her, commanded Darigaaz.

The Primevals' wings hurled back the skies. They only just kept pace with the dodging machine. A ray cannon blast reached from the ship's stern. It broke over Darigaaz's ruby hide and refracted in harmless beams.

Crosis and I will break away, he sent. *We will linger in the clouds above the main volcano. Drive the ship there. We will stoop upon her from the skies and rip her apart.*

Spreading his wings, Rhammidarigaaz hurled himself high into the sky. As black as onyx, Crosis rose beside him. Never had dragons ascended so quickly. The beginner of life and the ender of it pierced the blue. Stroke for stroke, their wing beats matched. They tore through the clouds and leveled out. The dragons nosed toward the volcano.

Crosis's thoughts brimmed with sarcasm. *These were once your comrades, your friends. You fought beside them in Serra's Realm. Now you fight to destroy them?*

Darigaaz resented the intrusion into his mind. *Serra's Realm was long ago. . . .*

The death dragon coiled through Darigaaz's consciousness. He smelled death and followed it toward its source.

Your mother, Gherridarigaaz, died in Serra's Realm.

Before Rhammidarigaaz could stop it, the image of her death flashed in his memory: Gherridarigaaz rose before a killing spell. She spread wide her wings. She made herself a living shield, guarding Urza Planeswalker. The spell dissolved her, melting flesh from bone.

Rhammidarigaaz shut away the sight of it. *Serra's Realm was long ago. . . .*

Crosis gloated. *Do not feel ashamed. Yes, she made the wrong choice, sacrificing herself. Altruism is a mortal flaw. You are no longer mortal. Your mother chose wrongly, but she could not see all you see. She was not a god.*

Through flashes of cloud, Rhammidarigaaz glimpsed the volcano's caldera below. *Enough of pointless memories.* Weatherlight *approaches.* He tucked his wings and plunged.

Crosis followed.

Darigaaz banked into a perfect intercept course. He watched his shadow jag across the rocky slopes. *Weatherlight's* shadow leaped up an adjacent hill. The dark shapes converged.

Darigaaz landed athwart *Weatherlight's* forecastle. He struck the planks with a profound boom. Claws clasped metal and shrieked. Wood groaned beneath his gemstone bulk. His tail lashed down to amidships and swept the port-side gunner overboard. Clinging to *Weatherlight,* Darigaaz hurtled through the skies.

Crosis swept down to starboard, just missing the ship. It did not matter. Darigaaz was more than capable of doing the job himself.

In one foreclaw, he grabbed the port-side ray cannon. He ripped the machine up from its deck mountings. Metal bolts tore the living wood. Energy conduits ruptured. Green goo oozed across the deck. Hoisting the gun high, Darigaaz hurled it over the rail. The cannon tumbled, sparking and spitting as it went. It impacted the caldera and rolled into shattered wreckage.

It was a satisfying sight. Soon the whole ship would be down there.

Darigaaz turned about. There was no real reason to yank out more guns. The cannons were worthless against the Primevals. Instead, Darigaaz clawed to the amidships deck. Ahead lay the hatch. It led to the engine core. It would be a quick thing, an easy thing, to smash it to pieces.

* * * * *

Grizzlegom's army was not as it had been. A thousand minotaurs and twenty thousand Metathran had begun the war against the undead. Afterward, only six hundred minotaurs and twelve thousand Metathran remained—just over two legions. They were purified, leaner and more ferocious, but the question remained: Could the living warriors take the mountainside?

They faced an endless army of Phyrexians. Monsters flooded over the lip of the volcano. *Il*-Dal warriors, massive in red armor, *il*-Vec fighters fitted with gray cogs, mogg goblins, scuta, bloodstocks, troopers . . . The usual menagerie of monstrous horrors flooded toward them.

Grizzlegom's axe clove through the brain of a goat-headed Phyrexian. It fell. In its place lunged a thing with the mouth of a spider. It tried to snap the minotaur's head off. He interposed his battle axe. The blade cut through the beast's face. Grizzlegom rammed it deeper and twisted. The Phyrexian shuddered in death spasms. Grizzlegom hauled his axe free, only just in time to lop the head from an *il*-Dal berserker.

On either side of Grizzlegom, the minotaurs and Metathran were equally pressed. One blue warrior seemed a figure in a fountain. Oil sprayed up all around him. Nearby, a minotaur advanced with a Phyrexian on either horn. He slew a third foe with his fists. These victories were surrounded by defeats. A bullman roared his fury as he died beneath a scuta. A Metathran clawed toward the front though his legs were gone. For every foot of ground they gained, the army of Grizzlegom lost ten warriors.

The simple math of it meant they would never reach the crest. Still, they fought. Metathran and minotaurs did not need a winning battle to fight on. They needed only a foe.

Grizzlegom gored an *il*-Vec monster in the gut. Its viscera cascaded from a mechanistic cavity.

Dead though it was, the beast clutched the minotaur's throat in four sets of claws. They constricted.

Gasping, Grizzlegom whirled his axe. It took off the thing's head. Its claws only tightened. Dizzy from lack of blood, Grizzlegom chopped loose one arm after another. Still the pincers clung to his neck. Grizzlegom holstered his axe and pried the dead claws from his flesh. He used one straight away, ramming its points into the eyes of the next Phyrexian. The minotaur commander drew his axe and finished it off.

We will never reach the top, he thought as he slew another monster.

With a sudden roar, his lines advanced. A tidal wave of warriors crashed against the Phyrexians. Gray-skinned Keldons were suddenly there in the front lines. They hewed hungrily into the monsters. Just behind them stood elf archers, who filled the air with deadly shafts. The combined forces advanced up the volcano at a run.

Grizzlegom could only stand, stunned into stillness.

A hand clapped him on the shoulder. Grizzlegom turned to see the silver-haired face of an elf warrior."

"From your colors, I assume you command these minotaurs and Metathran?"

Grizzlegom nodded. "And from yours, I assume you command these elves and Keldons?"

The man returned the nod. "I am Eladamri of the Skyshroud elves."

"I am Grizzlegom of the Hurloon minotaurs."

Their hands clasped—glistening-oil sealing their unspoken alliance.

Eladamri nodded to the peak of the mountain. "Let's gain it."

Smiling—an uncommon expression for any minotaur—Grizzlegom said simply, "Yes."

They had taken only a single step up the hillside when more warriors arrived.

Gigantic lizards galloped upward. Claws scrambled over pumice. Scales shimmered atop rippling muscles. In moments, the huge lizards overtook their allies. They launched themselves over the front and landed among the Phyrexians. Lizard mouths gobbled down the nearest beasts. Tongues lashed out to grab those farther away. Fangs punched through armor and carapace and bone. The lizards literally ate through their foes.

"What are they?" asked Grizzlegom, gaping.

"They are Kavu," Eladamri replied in awe. "Guardians of a faraway place." He glanced up the hillside, where magnigoth treefolk battled dragons in the skies. "A friend of mine must have brought them."

"Whatever they are, they are allies," Grizzlegom said. He strode eagerly toward the battle. Eladamri paced him.

Ahead, Kavu feasted. They rolled, swallowing their prey. In their ecstasy, they emitted a metallic purr and seemed almost to laugh.

With axe and sword, Grizzlegom and Eladamri joined the Kavu. They laughed as well.

* * * * *

"Hold on, everybody!" Sisay shouted into the speaking tube. She kept her voice admirably even, given that she was staring a red dragon in the face. "I'm going to shake this snake."

Weatherlight suddenly nose-dived. The horizon line swept from the bow to the tops. The world stood on end. Rhammidarigaaz's legs pulled away from the planks where he clung.

"Full power, Karn!" Sisay ordered.

The engines blazed. They drove *Weatherlight* downward, as though to spike her through the peak of the volcano. Momentum pulled the dragon farther from the deck. Below his dangling talons, a hillside of basalt and obsidian swarmed up.

"Here we go!" Shoving the helm forward, Sisay inverted *Weatherlight*.

Sky replaced ground and ground replaced sky. Upside down, the ship leveled out of her plunge. Her deck thundered above ridges of stone.

Rhammidarigaaz was levered up to dangle beneath the overturned ship. One more yank, and he'd be thrown free.

Sisay gave that yank. She pushed the helm hard forward. The Gaea figurehead climbed skyward. Inverted, *Weatherlight* rocketed after her. Dominaria shrank vertiginously away.

The dragon clung on with damnable tenacity. His back struck the windscreen of the bridge, shattering it.

Glass shards hailed Sisay. She shut her eyes but clung to the wheel. Flying on motion sense, she steered the ship high into the sky.

In moments, the glass had ceased its deadly hail. Sisay opened her eyes. What she saw horrified her. No longer did Rhammidarigaaz obstruct her view. Already he had shattered the hatch and clawed his way down toward the engine core.

* * * * *

With a violent fist, Rhammidarigaaz ripped wide the companionway that led to the engine room. He drew himself down. Talons sank into the inverted ceiling and dragged him deeper into the ship. He reached for the engine room bulkhead. Ruby claws tore the wood asunder.

The room beyond was flooded with power. It limned every metal plate and shone in each mana module. It reverberated through the chamber and sluiced down around Darigaaz. The engine whined as the ship righted itself and struggled skyward. Soon, all this power would be destroyed.

Darigaaz reached toward the thrumming machine.

Suddenly, something appeared in the way. It seemed an animate door—too heavy, too huge to be a living thing. Still, it tickled the corners of his memory. It was not until the thing spoke, its voice like distant thunder, that the dragon remembered:

"What have you become, Rhammidarigaaz?"

Karn. There was but one voice in all time like it. He and Rhammidarigaaz had worked side by side in the mana rig at Shiv.

"You once fought for Dominaria. Now you fight only for yourself."

The answer seemed plain: "I once was mortal, but now I am a god."

The metallic eyes of the silver golem fixed his. "You once were good, but now you are evil." The metal man clomped forward, grasping the dragon's horns. It seemed he wanted to wrestle—a ludicrous thought—but his metallic touch created a mental conduit.

Darigaaz reeled at that touch. What was this? Divinity was awakening in Karn. Power undeniable. The silver man had lived a forgetful millennium, but now that his memories were returning, they were transforming him.

Memory was creating this fledgling god, and with a touch, Karn awoke Darigaaz's own memories.

Into the Primeval's mind came an image of a long-ago time. He was a young serpent. He flew, wings spread, above *Weatherlight*. They struggled to escape Serra's Realm as it collapsed around them. Once a home for angels, the place had become a perfect hell. Its mad ruler saw foes everywhere and slew all those she could. Refugees crowded *Weatherlight*, the final few who would escape.

Once, you would have sacrificed yourself to save another. Now you sacrifice everyone to save yourself.

The Primeval's response sounded hollow. *Altruism is a mortal flaw.*

Karn replied only by dragging forth more memories:

Darigaaz saw Rokun, sacrificed upon the magnigoth. He saw the four dragon lords sacrificed within the catacombs. He saw the hundreds of serpents sacrificed in the watery cave. And now . . . now every last dragon in the world was a living sacrifice to the Primevals.

"What has become of me?" uttered Rhammidarigaaz.

Those words seemed to break the bond that held him in place. The dragon's horns pulled free of Karn's grip. He drifted backward, up the companionway, as if in a dream. *Weatherlight* flipped over again, struggling to be rid of him.

Darigaaz did not fight. He slid effortlessly up the companionway and out the shattered hatch. In battering winds, he hung for a moment beneath the inverted deck of *Weatherlight*. Then he tumbled free.

He could have spread his wings and caught the air but did not. What have I become? He could have saved himself from the volcanic caldera below, but he was no longer interested in saving himself.

One final sacrifice would break the circle of Primevals, would free the dragons from their bondage and make the dragon gods mortal once more.

In his last act, Rhammidarigaaz gathered the power of his ancient homeland. He sent it in a blazing column down into the caldera. He could not awaken a whole volcano, but he could awaken a single molten shaft. It would be enough.

Lava erupted. It rose around him and coated him. It encasing him in a broiling fist and dragged him down. He would be dead before he struck ground.

For all the red-hot rock, for all the agony, he saw not his own sacrifice, but that of Gherridarigaaz.

His mother had chosen rightly. She had indulged the mortal flaw.

CHAPTER 36
To Bow Before Yawgmoth

"What did you say?" hissed Gerrard ferociously. Flexing his shoulders, he almost succeeded in breaking free from Ertai's four-armed grip. "What did you say!"

Crovax leaned toward his captive. A shark-toothed smile broke across his face. "I said, 'Yawgmoth has Hanna.'"

"No!" Gerrard roared.

His elbows swung backward and rammed Ertai's metal ribs. His fists punched forward and broke the man's grip. Gerrard lunged out of his grasp. He swung a brutal uppercut. Good-old Dominarian knuckles cracked Crovax's jaw.

The evincar of the Stronghold reeled back. A triangular tooth flipped from his mouth. Oily pulp dribbled down his lip.

Ertai reached for Gerrard, but his arms were suddenly full of goblin.

Squee wore an impish grin as he head-butted Ertai.

For all the Phyrexian enhancements done to the young sorcerer, none made his skull the equal of the goblin's. His arms shuddered, and he staggered back.

Squee gave him no quarter. He scampered up Ertai's front and slid down his back. Fists pounded the mimetic spine as though it were a xylophone. Each blow sent jabs of rogue energy through Ertai's body.

He convulsed, flailing at the goblin.

"Run for it, Gerrard!" Squee shouted. "Squee save you again!"

"Not likely," Gerrard barked, fists held up before him. "How about it, Crovax? How about an honest fight for once? No angels, no devils. Just you and me."

Claws curling into fists, Crovax waved off Selenia and his guards. "All right, Gerrard. You were willing enough to mop the deck with me aboard *Weatherlight*. This is my ship. Now you're the mop."

"I'm looking forward to this," Gerrard said with a grin.

He faked with his left and swung a right hook.

Crovax caught the punch. Claws spiked Gerrard's fist.

Yanking him down to his knees, Crovax snarled, "All you have is bravado. Bravado is nothing in the face of death." With his free hand, Crovax grasped Gerrard's neck and hurled him toward the ceiling.

Gerrard soared upward. He wriggled like an airborne cat and slid just to one side of a brutal spike. Arms wrapped around the stalactite, and he held on. Legs lashed out to an adjacent corpse. With a wet sound, the body sloughed free and plunged. It spattered atop Crovax and made a sunburst on the floor.

"Bravado is everything in the face of death," Gerrard said.

Squee meanwhile proved it.

Still swarming over Ertai, Squee shouted to the moggs, "Get dis here stinkin' goblin offa me!"

The moggs converged on Ertai. Groping and pinching, their green arms were indistinguishable from Squee's. The canny cabin boy crawled from the fight as Ertai unleashed his first spells.

Fire burned a mogg's arm to ash. Lightning fried the nerves of another. A third withered into a black lump. A fourth liquefied into a puddle.

"He's killin' us. He's turned on us!" Squee shouted as he scrambled behind the moggs' legs. "Stop 'im! He's gone loony!"

As Ertai hurled spells out at his attackers, moggs hurled fists in at him.

Taking advantage of Squee's diversion, Gerrard dropped from the ceiling to stand, fists raised, before Crovax.

"You are a liar. Yawgmoth may have dominion over the souls of his own creatures, but he has no power over others. He has no power over Hanna."

The evincar of the Stronghold circled, just out of fist range. He still dripped the putrid fluids of the corpse that had landed on him.

"You are wrong, Gerrard." He gestured toward Squee. "I returned the soul to your friend here—brought him back to life."

It was true, but there had to be another explanation. "Squee died in your Stronghold, in your grip. Of course Yawgmoth could snatch his soul," Gerrard said. He punctuated the comment with a sweeping head kick. His heel caught Crovax's jaw, cracking loose two more teeth. "Yawgmoth had no hold on Hanna when she died."

Crovax smiled. The bleeding sockets that had held the two teeth folded closed, and the gums rolled outward. Two new teeth ratcheted into position.

"Didn't he? Hanna died of the plague, Yawgmoth's plague. She died in his grip."

Blood swelling his face, Gerrard swung a left hook.

Crovax caught his fist again and grabbed the right cross that followed. Hoisting Gerrard, Crovax hurled him across the throne room.

Gerrard crashed headfirst into the wall. His vision narrowed to a wavering tunnel. He slumped. The wall draped down on top of him. Black flowstone formed into bars that wrapped around Gerrard and solidified. He was trapped.

In that same instant, Squee's fight came to a horrible end.

Ertai slew the final mogg. Squee could no longer hide in plain sight. He dived away. Ertai snatched his ankle, hoisted him up, and swung him over his shoulder like a maul. Squee's head struck the floor. There came a bursting sound and a red spray. Squee's body lay utterly still. His life spread across the floor.

Ertai stared with haunted eyes at the slain figure. Was it hatred that twisted his face, or fury . . . or regret? Whatever it was, when a vampire hound loped up to lick the floor clean, Ertai kicked the beast in the chest, driving it off.

Crovax walked with slow relish toward Gerrard. Over his shoulder, he said, "Nice work, Ertai. Why don't you go recharge yourself? I know you can't resist the mana infuser."

"I'll stay," said Ertai. His voice was feverish. "I want to see this through."

"Suit yourself," Crovax said offhandedly. He reached Gerrard and crouched beside his flowstone cage. "Do you see what has happened to Ertai? Do you see what has happened to me? We have gone the way of all heroes. We have joined the winners."

"You aren't heroes. You never were. Flawed, weak, seduced by darkness—monsters. In your hearts you were monsters all along," snarled Gerrard.

"What do you think of Commander Agnate? Hero or monster?"

"Why do you care?"

A simple hand gesture from Crovax indicated the center of the throne room.

There, as solid as Selenia, stood Commander Agnate. Beneath his battered armor, his flesh was riddled with rot. Two axe clefts split the man's head, but still he gazed at Gerrard with seeing eyes.

"He made a bargain with death and then thought to cheat death of its due. Agnate was clever but not clever enough. He could cheat a lich lord, but he could not cheat Yawgmoth," Crovax said evenly. He cocked an eyebrow. "What do you think of Rhammidarigaaz? Hero or monster?"

"Don't tell me he—"

Suddenly, the red dragon was there beside Agnate. His figure was deformed as if clutched in a brutal fist. Burns covered his skin, but he too seemed solid and alive.

"He sacrificed hundreds of his own folk to become a god. He attacked *Weatherlight* and almost succeeded in ripping the power core from the ship. Your friend Karn paralyzed him with visions, and Rhammidarigaaz plunged down into this selfsame volcano—into the grips of Yawgmoth."

"They were heroes, both of them," Gerrard replied. "Yes, they had made bargains with death, but as soon as they realized the price of those bargains, they ended their own lives. They did everything they could to escape you. The fact that you hold them means nothing."

"What about Urza Planeswalker? Hero or monster?"

Blood fled Gerrard's face. "No, you are lying. . . ."

"Am I?" asked Crovax. A final sweep of his hand indicated a nearby arch. A pair of thick doors slid aside. The scene beyond told that this was no mere doorway. It was a portal—a portal that led to a deep level of Phyrexia.

In floating blackness hung a coliseum. It was not hewn of stone but built up out of pure mind. Glowing lines were etched into the emptiness. They formed rings of seats up from the circular staging ground where the portal opened. At the center of the staging ground rose a round dais. Its perimeter was ranked with countless weapons—polearms, scimitars, staves, axes, maces, daggers—all in fiendish design. Like the rest of the place, these weapons too were formed of thought, not of matter.

"What is this?" Gerrard whispered incredulously.

"This is the mind of Yawgmoth," Crovax replied. "All of Phyrexia conforms to his will, but on the ninth sphere, the thoughts and desires of the Ineffable are all that shape reality. To walk here is to dwell in the mind of a god. Your friend dwells there even now."

Urza Planeswalker lay, prostrate in obeisance, at the center of the coliseum. He was the only real thing there.

"How did you capture him? How did you bring him there?" Gerrard asked, disbelieving.

"He brought himself. He slew a fellow planeswalker and defused the bombs they had planted to destroy Phyrexia. He even left his brother, Mishra, in eternal torment—all to arrive at this deep and sacred place. We did nothing to him, only let him see the glory of Phyrexia, the glory of Yawgmoth. He did what any creature would have done. He bowed down in worship."

Gerrard closed his eyes and dropped his head. "What do you want from me, Crovax?"

"Gerrard, Gerrard, Gerrard . . . Everyone eventually must bargain with death, even you. In the end, death gets us all. The question is what you will get from death." With the air of a schoolmaster whose lecture was completed, Crovax stepped away from the portal.

A figure stood there. Even with his eyes closed, Gerrard could sense her presence. He lifted his gaze, and his heart broke. "Hanna."

She was just as he remembered her—whole and hale, slim and strong. There was not a trace of plague in her flesh, no rotting corruption, no agonized emaciation. Her golden hair was drawn back in a ponytail, the quickest way of getting it beyond the reach of grease and gears. Still, a few strands refused to be contained. They draped down about her slender face. It had been so long since he had peered into her eyes, and longer still since they had looked back with anything but pain. Now, they were full of love—and sadness. Though her lips remained closed, as red and round as rose petals, her eyes spoke to him.

They said, Come, Gerrard. Take me out of here. Take us out of here.

Gerrard wanted to look away, but his gaze was locked with hers. "Hanna," was all he could say. "Hanna."

"You can return to her. You can have her back. You can hold her in your arms again," Crovax said. He withdrew across the throne room to take the hand of his angel love. He bowed to her in grotesque courtliness, and his fangy mouth kissed her hand.

Running a claw along the angel's jaw, he said, "Or is your love not strong enough to conquer death?"

Gerrard rose from the floor. He had not even noticed when the flowstone restraints had pulled away. It didn't matter. For Gerrard, there was nothing but the woman beyond the portal, nothing but her eyes.

"All you must do is step through. Take her hand. Know that she is real. Walk with her to the dais, and there, beside Urza, bow to our Lord Yawgmoth. Then she will be yours."

The words echoed within him. No longer did they come from Crovax. They were the words of his own heart: Step through. Take her hand. Bow to Yawgmoth. . . .

Gerrard reached the portal. He breathed his last Dominarian air. Without pause, he stepped through.

Hanna greeted him with a sad smile. Her arms were real and warm. She breathed in his scent. They stood for an age that way, embracing.

Into his ear, she whispered, "What are you doing, Gerrard? You do not belong among the dead."

He replied with utter confidence, "Once nothing kept us apart except my foolishness. Now everything, even death, stands between us, but we are together." Again, the voice came in Gerrard's head: Bow to Yawgmoth. . . . "Soon we will be together forever."

Clasping her hand, Gerrard strode with Hanna out across the central staging area. His feet walked on nothingness. Only Hanna was real. Reaching the dais, he released Hanna's hand and climbed.

Urza still lay prostrate upon the platform.

Approaching him, Gerrard stared at the black dais. He would kneel on it. He would press his face to it. He would do whatever it took to be with Hanna forever.

One knee kissed the black dais. The other settled into place beside it. Gerrard spread his fingers on the cold surface. Easing himself down to his face, Gerrard lay prostrate.

"Release Hanna—release her whole to me—and I pledge myself to you. I am your servant, Yawgmoth."

* * * * *

In the throne room of the Stronghold, Evincar Crovax swept up his angel in a three-quarter dance. Victory. Yawgmoth had snared the planeswalker, and Crovax had snared the hero. In mere days, all of Dominaria would be theirs.

As the dancers stepped lightly across the floor, Crovax dispelled the illusions of Agnate and Rhammidarigaaz. They had served their purpose. He only wished Yawgmoth owned their souls, but he should not be greedy. Now even Gerrard belonged to Yawgmoth.

"Great lord," intruded a quiet voice into the dance. It was Ertai, standing above the body of Squee. "You had best see this."

On any other day, Crovax would have punished such umbrage with a shock to the mimetic spine. Triumph made him indulgent. Crovax patiently danced Selenia to the spot. He looked down.

No longer was Squee's head spattered across the floor. It was solid again. No longer was his body still. Breath slid into and out of his lungs.

"He lives again. He rises from the dead—again."

Crovax stared down in amazement. "I must have fixed him better than I had thought. Or perhaps this is the work of our lord." Crovax blinked in thought. "That must be it. Squee is a gift for my labors, a plaything I can kill a hundred times each day."

Even as he spoke, the goblin began to cough. He sat up, looking about in confusion.

Resuming the dance, Crovax strode right across Squee. He crushed the goblin to the ground. His claws sank into Squee's belly and ripped it open. Crovax and Selenia continued onward, leaving red footprints.

Once again, Squee lay dead.

CHAPTER 37
A Highway in the Sky

"Tahngarth, get yourself fore!" ordered Sisay. She hauled hard on the helm, bringing *Weatherlight* into the slipstream of the black dragon god. "We've got only one forecastle gun, and it's yours!"

"Aye, Captain," Tahngarth replied from the aft speaking tube. He released the fire controls of Squee's gun and dragged the traces from his shoulders. "But a dozen more dragons are diving on us from the rear."

Through gritted teeth, Sisay shot back, "First, we'll worry about dragon gods, then about run-of-the-mill dragons." She blew a sweaty lock of hair away from her forehead and hissed to herself—" 'run-of-the-mill dragons.' "

The creature that fled before *Weatherlight* was anything but a run-of-the-mill dragon. Hugely muscled, sinuous as a snake, the black dragon was sleek and dangerous. Still, it seemed diminished by the death of Rhammidarigaaz. No longer did its scales gleam like fine-cut onyx. Sisay hoped the beast also was no longer impervious to ray-cannon fire.

Tahngarth reached the forecastle. He strapped himself into the gunnery traces. Swinging the great cannon around, he drew a bead on the retreating dragon. Spittle on the gun's casement sizzled immediately away. With a grim smile, Tahngarth unleashed a barrage. Bolts barked upon the air. They swarmed toward the retreating dragon. The first blast mantled the lashing tail. The second splashed across one wing. The third dug a furrow up the monster's hackled back.

"It can be hurt!" Sisay called. "I'll stay tight. Tahngarth, keep up the attack!"

Karn's voice reverberated through the tube, "It can be hurt, yes, but not killed—never killed."

An incredulous look spread across Sisay's face. "Since when have you been an expert on dragon gods?"

"Since I sifted through the mind of Rhammidarigaaz."

Sisay sent the ship into a dive after the black dragon. "Since when have you been able to sift through minds?"

"I've been changing, Sisay. My memories change me, and so does *Weatherlight*. The *Thran Tome* is my history. I can read it simply by holding it. I know things by touch. I touched Darigaaz's mind and saw his past and mine. I know where these gods came from."

Flack burst from Tahngarth's ray cannon and blossomed into roses beside the dragon.

Sisay struggled to keep the beast to the fore. "Well, Karn, spill."

"When all five Primevals banded together, they had absolute control over the dragon nations. With Rhammidarigaaz's sacrifice, the other four are weakened. If we send this black dragon back to sleep, they will be further weakened."

"Back to sleep? Where does a black dragon sleep?"

"A tar pit on the other side of the main volcano. We must drive him down into it. The ancient magic will take hold. It won't be easy. The other Primevals know the weakness. They'll do everything to stop—"

"Here they come!" shouted Sisay.

Three Primevals—green, white, and blue—surged in an angry **V** toward *Weatherlight*. The black Primeval swooped up behind its comrades and joined their shrieking attack.

Sisay's first impulse was to head skyward, but that would slow the ship and open her belly to attack. There was no room below the dragons. They would drive *Weatherlight* down into the cypress forests. Only one route remained.

"Full frontal assault!" Sisay called. "Bring all guns to bear. Pave a highway through the sky."

From *Weatherlight*'s remaining cannons, fire erupted across the sky. It struggled to outpace the hurtling ship. Beams blazed her trail. A crimson wall of flame broke over the Primevals. Fire blasted eyes and rolled down throats. It curled scales and sent smoke whuffing from mantles. Wings singed. Tails sparked.

The four dragon gods soared from the holocaust. Flames limned them as they came. With impossible speed, they fell on *Weatherlight*.

Sisay spun the helm to starboard. Karn stoked engines. Still, the ship could not escape.

The green dragon clapped talons on Tahngarth's gun. Like an eagle ripping a fish from the water, it tore the cannon from its mounts. Tahngarth shoved the traces between his teeth and bit through. He hurled himself back on the forecastle deck as his gun drew away.

The white dragon strafed low over that deck. Its throat poured out a blinding radiance that ignited everything in its path. Tahngarth's fur burst into flame. He rolled on the deck, but it too burned. Magnigoth planks blackened. The dragon poured light through the shattered windscreen of the bridge. Sisay released the helm, skipping back behind a bulkhead. She saved herself but only just. Everything else on the bridge—maps and desks and even the helm—flamed.

The black dragon shot past next. His mouth spilled the ancient word for death. Tahngarth was spared the killing sound, which was drowned out by his own bellows. Others on deck heard the word. They dropped down dead. Their bodies slid across the planks.

The blue dragon's attack was the worst, though. Azure power rolled out from the thing's mouth—a disruption cloud. It twisted wood and metal, sapped power, shut down engines.

Weatherlight plummeted from the sky.

Sisay flung her captain's cowl over the helm, suffocating the fire. She grabbed hold, but the stick was dead in her hands.

"Let's have some power, Karn!"

In answer, a pair of deep booms came from below. Greenish-black smoke poured from the exhausts. Still, the power would not engage.

"How about stopping these fires, Multani?" Sisay shouted.

Beads of sap welled up and spread across the blackened wood. Where the liquid went, fires guttered and ceased.

Even before they were gone, Orim scrambled across the deck to Tahngarth. The minotaur had suffered serious burns.

"Power, Karn!" Sisay yelled. The volcano below surged up to smash the ship. Lava extrusions reached their gnarled fingers toward the hull. "Power!"

The engines suddenly bellowed. Flame burned black smoke from the exhausts. *Weatherlight* surged. Her keel cracked against a ridge of stone. She bounded free and roared out over tumbled swamps. Four dragons flew directly behind her, their teeth gnashing at her stern.

Sisay yanked the helm toward her. *Weatherlight* hurtled skyward. She was fast but not fast enough. More white light splashed around her, more jittering clouds in blue.

"Out of the frying pan and into the fire," she muttered to herself. Through the speaking tube, she called, "It's no good! We can't defeat four of them!"

Multani replied in a voice agonized by burns. "Take us low. Take us among the forests. We have allies there."

Sisay shoved the helm to fore. "We could use some allies. Feels like we're the only ones left fighting."

Weatherlight skimmed down the slope. Momentarily, she shook the divine pursuers. Ahead, strangled forests reached bone-white boughs toward the ship. Some of the trees ignited with spill-over beams from the white dragon.

"Tahngarth?" Sisay called, "I hate to ask this—"

"Already there," the minotaur responded from the stern speaking tube. He punctuated the comment with a barrage of blasts from Squee's ray cannon. Even as he fired, Orim tended his red and blistered skin.

Sisay nodded grimly. "Where are these allies of yours, Multani?"

"Right here," Multani replied from the helm, which he twisted hard to port. As *Weatherlight* banked, the shattered windscreen swept around to show a huge mountain to the fore—not a mountain, but a mountainous tree.

The lead magnigoth strode with lashing roots across the swamps. A company of grim-faced treefolk followed it.

A bright smile broke across Sisay's face. "Oh, yeah."

Tahngarth's cannon fire was joined by blasts of flame from the engine's exhausts. *Weatherlight* rushed out above the deadwood swamp. Her wake tore the waters below. Dragon gods soared behind her.

"Take us close to the first one," Multani instructed.

The ship sliced across the marshes and flanked the first magnigoth. She turned tightly to port and circled around the massive bole. Ridges of bark flashed past the rail. Sisay dragged on the helm. *Weatherlight* entered a corkscrew climb. She dragged the Primevals in her wake. They slowly gained on the ship.

Clenching her jaw, Sisay said, "Full throttle, Karn."

The engines thundered, hurling the ship higher. It passed a gaping mouth in the side of the tree.

"Stay close. Buzz the upper limbs!" Multani said.

"Right! Right!" Sisay shot back. "You just keep the wheel from falling apart in my hands!" She cranked it hard to port.

J. Robert King

The ship creaked and groaned, wrung by the hands of momentum. "And keep the ship from falling apart too."

An enormous bough swept out before *Weatherlight*. The ship dived just beneath the swiping arm. Dead ahead, a second branch tried to haul her from the sky. Sisay arced above it. Hands sweating on the charred wheel, she wove her way among the boughs.

"These are allies?" Sisay asked.

Multani responded, "Trust me,"

From the stern castle cannon, Tahngarth shouted into the tubes, "I can't shoot through branches!"

"You won't have to," Multani assured.

The largest bough yet swung toward *Weatherlight*. The ship bounded up, her keel barely clearing the thick bark. The limb passed just beneath her, its branches closing.

Muscular grains clamped down around the green Primeval. It writhed in the magnigoth's grip like a frog caught by a schoolboy. The bough bent. It drew the dragon god down to the gaping mouth below. With a casual motion, it tossed the Primeval within and closed its mouth. A profound swallowing sound told the fate of the god.

"It crossed the world to win back its captive," Multani explained.

"The three other Primevals are breaking off!" Tahngarth reported.

Sisay brought the ship hard about. *Weatherlight* shot from the tangle of branches. "We're going after them. We going to put another one of these beasts to sleep."

Weatherlight broke into clear air above the retreating Primevals. She dropped like a hammer from the sky. The Gaea figurehead loomed mercilessly above the beasts. Wind gushed up on either side of her, seeming almost to move her thick-carved hair. Her eyes gleamed fiercely.

Prow spikes rammed into the back of the black dragon. They punched deep, through scale and muscle and bone. Mere spikes could not kill a god, of course, but they did pin him in place as *Weatherlight* drove him toward the tar pit below.

The dragon's tail lashed against the keel. It shouted out the word of death, but the sound could no longer slay. That weapon had been undone. The black Primeval thrashed impotently. It shrieked, only to fill its throat with tar. Muck sprayed up around it.

Weatherlight skimmed along, a scant fathom above the tar pit. Gaea watched with impassive certainty as the dragon drowned in tar. At a precise moment, the spikes that had impaled it shrank and withdrew, letting the beast sink away into oblivion. Death was swallowed up in death.

Sisay drew the ship up from the slough. "Even burned and twisted and spattered in tar, we still own the skies!"

"Not yet, we don't," called Orim from the stern castle. She had just finished her healing ministrations on Tahngarth's burns when she noticed dragon shadows swarming the deck. "Look up!"

Sisay leaned forward to peer out the shattered windscreen. Directly above the ship, circling about the sun, were the dragon nations. There were hundreds of serpents. They formed a cyclone of flesh that reached into the sky.

Sisay groaned. Perhaps *Weatherlight* could prevail against two Primevals, diminished as they were, but she could never triumph over hundreds of dragons. Even as Sisay watched, the creatures peeled away from their circle and plunged down in pursuit.

"Will every last hero be destroyed?" Sisay wondered in dread. "Will all the world be lost?"

Dragons swooped down all around *Weatherlight*. Their clawed wings scraped her burned gunwales. Their scaly tails lashed her airfoils. Not one, though, turned fiery breath upon her. Instead, every last beast flew onward, ahead of the beleaguered ship. They shot out after the final two Primevals.

The dragons nearest them spouted fire across the sky. They fought their own gods. At last, the tyranny of their minds had been broken.

Sisay breathed in deep gratitude. She clutched the charred helm and gazed out over the swamplands of Urborg.

"Finally—hope."

The engine chose that moment to fail. Its throaty howl grew silent. Only the wind spoke, sliding across the ship's airfoils.

The stick again went dead in Sisay's hand. "How about some power, Karn?" She watched the last shred of swampland sweep away below, leaving only rock-hard slopes of volcanic scree. "We're going to need some power, Karn."

Karn's response echoed hopelessly through the speaking tube. "Yes."

Weatherlight lost lift. She burrowed down through spilling air. The mountainside came up below her.

"If not power, how about landing spines?" Sisay asked. "Can you give us landing spines?"

No response came this time.

Sisay wrenched the wheel, but the rudder was dead.

With a heart-rending shriek, *Weatherlight*'s keel sawed across a shoulder of basalt. The impact hurled Sisay against the helm. The ship bounded again skyward. Complaint sounded from every plank and fitting. She soared in air a moment longer before coming down to stay. Scree scraped across the mirror hull of her port side. The ship listed toward the mountain. She slid on her gunwale. Her decks were pitched at a steep slope. Chattering, shuddering, thudding, *Weatherlight* at last hung up on a gnarl of stone. She came to rest leaning against the edge of the volcano.

Sisay breathed a deep sigh. Her fingers were black from the ruined helm, and her knuckles were white. Blinking at the tilted world beyond, she said simply, "Damn."

It took her some moments to extricate herself from the charred bridge and its wreckage. By the time she reached the amidships deck, it was crowded.

Tahngarth stood there, his arms crossed over burns on his chest. He stared in amazement at the ruined ship. Orim worked nearby, tending to scores of other wounded crew members. Multani formed a body for himself out of charred wood and frayed hemp. Even he looked defeated.

The shattered hatchway poured thick white steam into the air. The engines had overloaded. They flooded the lower companionways with broiling air. *Weatherlight* bled her life into the sky.

With angry, sober eyes, Sisay greeted her crew. "Well, I guess that's it."

Tahngarth considered her face. "That's what?"

She spread her hands bitterly. "That's it. That's all we can do. We've lost half of our crew, including Gerrard and Squee. We've lost our ship. We've lost our commanders. We've fought all we can fight. That's it."

Her words could not have seemed truer. That moment, a vast army appeared on the lip of the volcano. They stared down at the ruined ship, and the first platoons began to march toward them.

"Crovax is in his Stronghold," Sisay said, "and all is wrong with the world."

The ruined hatch emitted a new flood of steam. A curling white head of mist rose through the space. It glowed from below. A silver skull appeared, bathed in light. Karn rose up the steps. He bore something in his grasp. It was a book, an open book— The *Thran Tome*. He emerged from the mists, his figure dotted with condensation.

Karn strode toward his friends and looked up. His eyes glowed brighter than even the tome. He spoke in a voice like a distant avalanche.

"I know what we need to do. I know how we can save the world."

Tales from the world of Magic

Dragons of Magic
ED. J. ROBERT KING

From the time of the Primevals to the darkest hours of the Phyrexian Invasion, dragons have filled Dominaria. Few of their stories have been told—until now. Learn the secrets of the most powerful dragons in the multiverse!

August 2001

The Myths of Magic
ED. JESS LEBOW

Stories and legends, folktales and tall tales. These are the myths of Dominaria, stories captured on the cards of the original trading card game. Stories from J. Robert King, Francis Lebaron, and others.

The Colors of Magic
ED. JESS LEBOW

Argoth is decimated. Tidal waves have turned canyons into rivers. Earthquakes have leveled the cities. Dominaria is in ruins. Now the struggle is to survive. Tales from such authors as Jeff Grubb, J. Robert King, Paul Thompson, and Francis Lebaron.

Rath and Storm
ED. PETER ARCHER

The flying ship Weatherlight enters the dark, sinister plane of Rath to rescue its kidnapped captain. But, as the stories in this anthology show, more is at stake than Sisay's freedom.

Legends Cycle Clayton Emery

Book I: Johan

Hazezon Tamar, merchant-mayor of the city of Bryce, had plenty of problems before he encountered Jaeger, a mysterious stranger that is half-man and half-tiger. Now Hazezon is caught up in a race against time to decipher the mysterious prophecy of None, One, and Two, while considering the significance of Jaeger's appearance. Only by understanding these elements can he save his people from the tyranny and enslavement of the evil wizard Johan, ruler of the dying city of Tirras.

April 2001

Book II: Jedit

Jedit Ojanen, the son of the legendary cat man Jaeger, sets out on a journey to find his father. Like his father, he collapses in the desert and is left for dead until he is rescued. But rescued by whom? And why? Only the prophecy of None, One, and Two holds the answers.

December 2001

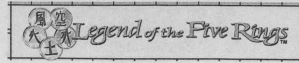

Legend of the Five Rings™

The Phoenix
Stephen D. Sullivan

The five Elemental Masters—
the greatest magic-wielders of
Rokugan—seek to turn back the
demons of the Shadowlands. To do
so, they must harness the power of
the Black Scrolls, and perhaps
become demons themselves.

March 2001

The Dragon
Ree Soesbee

The most mysterious of all the clans
of Rokugan, the Dragon had long
stayed elusive in their mountain
stronghold. When at last they
emerge into the Clan War, they
unleash a power that could well save
the empire . . . or doom it.

September 2001

The Crab
Stan Brown

For a thousand years, the Crab have
guarded the Emerald Empire against
demon hordes—but when the greatest
threat comes from within, the Crab
must ally with their fiendish foes and
march to take the capital city.

June 2001

The Lion
Stephen D. Sullivan

Since the Scorpion Coup, the Clans
of Rokugan have made war upon
each other. Now, in the face of Fu
Leng and his endless armies of
demons, the Seven Thunders must
band together to battle their
immortal foe . . . or die!

November 2001